FINDING EDITH PINSENT

HAZEL WARD

Hope St Press

www.hazelwardauthor.com

1

I AM HOPEFUL

EDIE – 2017

'It's almost time. I am ready. Let it come quickly and decisively.'

She'd felt it for some time but today it was strongest. She wouldn't fight it. The will to do that had petered out long ago. Still, the thought of no longer seeing those she cared for made her a little melancholic.

Giving up on the last ounce of hope also pained her. There had been a time when it was the one reason to soldier on. When faith turned out to be no more than an empty bag of air, hope kept her functioning. Hope and duty. There was always duty. Of course, she did eventually find other reasons but lately, hope had had something of a resurrection in her life. Resurrection? Edie raised an inward eyebrow. That was an interesting word to choose, all things considered.

In a way, it was a shame she'd lost her faith. If only she did still believe in some sort of god. It might help to know her people were waiting on the other side, along with her dearest friends. If not them, then perhaps… Was that too fanciful? One could always hope. Good old hope. Always there to help you put one foot in front of the other. One could say cautious optimism was her faith now. There. She hadn't lost her faith at all. Just found a new one.

She looked at the words that had taken her all morning to write. Possibly her shortest ever diary entry, but her eyesight was poor these days and inspiration was sadly lacking. Hard to be stimulated when one's world had become so small and faded. All the same, the fact that these could be her last written words stopped her from closing the book. Should she add something else? Yes. She wrote:

'I am hopeful.'

Last night, she'd left a note in the hall for Frank. Poor, dear Frank. Such a good neighbour. One of life's natural carers despite the troubles that had befallen him. The note asked him to leave everything as it was and contact James. Just as important, it left him instructions on how to care for Maud until the chosen person came along. She'd finished it off by apologising for the rather cheeky presumption that he would and wishing him future happiness.

Darling Maud could sense it too. In the last few days, she'd hardly left Edie's side. Edie had given her extra treats that morning and left out bowls of dried food around the kitchen in case it was a while before anyone came. There was a letter for James too, reminding him of the conditions; her plan. He was a good boy. She had complete trust in him.

She'd stayed up all night, quite an easy thing to do these days, to see the foxes one more time. Despite her failing sight, she always managed to see them clearly enough. They hadn't disappointed. Neither had the sunrise, bursting into the breakfast room and warming her bones. It made death seem almost out of touch – if she ignored the waves of exhaustion crashing in her head like an angry sea.

She pulled herself up and leaned against the table until

she felt steady. With her diary in one hand, she took slow, measured steps through the kitchen and hall, into the study. Even more care was needed in there because the room was such a mess. She liked it that way and resisted all attempts from well-meaning family members to tidy it up. For a long time, it had been the dining room, until they realised they didn't need one anymore and Daddy installed the bookcases and his old office desk. He'd be appalled at the clutter now. He had been a very orderly man. He'd have seen the funny side though.

Edie chose one of the more upright piles of books rising from the floor to place the journal on and breathed in the musty air of stale paper. The cleaner complained but Edie couldn't see what the fuss was about. She smiled. Losing one's sense of smell wasn't such a bad thing. Perhaps the only benefit of getting old.

Maud waited patiently in the doorway. Clearly, she had a more sensitive nose than her human companion. She gazed up at Edie with that look of optimistic expectation that always managed to melt Edie's heart. 'Maud, my sweet, shall we have another treat?' The little dog let out a short whine as if to confirm that was a good idea. Edie closed the study door and went into the kitchen to make tea with Maud trotting alongside her. There was one cake left from the box that Frank had brought in her weekly shop. That would do for her but for Maud? Hmm. There were two cookies left in a pack. They were the luxury sort – the type the supermarket promised to be their finest and most specially selected – far too fancy to be called biscuits.

'Well, I did say treat, didn't I?' Maud whined again. Edie put the tea, cake and biscuits on a tray and they returned to the breakfast room. With the tray safely placed on the little table, she eased herself into the chair and relaxed. This was her favourite spot in the house. She never tired of it.

Maud polished off the first biscuit almost immediately and sat up waiting for the second. Edie patted the dog's square head. 'You, my dear, are a greedy little mongrel. Here, you may as well have the last one.' She watched Maud eat it in two bites then turned to an open book on the table – *Wuthering Heights*, Heathcliff visiting Cathy on her deathbed. She returned to this particular passage quite a lot these days. It still had the capacity to move her. A lump formed in her throat: would this be the last time she'd ever read it? If so, then let it count. Let it hurt as much as it did in those lost days. Let her feel something one final time. She reached out for her reading glasses even though she didn't really need them: she knew the words off by heart.

Disappointingly, she could only manage ten minutes before the throbbing in her temples forced her to stop. She finished her tea and cake and let her eyes rest on the overgrown garden. It had been lovely out there once. So sad to see it in such a state. For a moment, she thought she saw someone out there but that was silly, it was the tiredness and her wonky eyes. She checked the time. The meals on wheels would be here in an hour. The waves in her head swooshed around again as she hauled herself up to standing. This time they carried with them a mild but discomforting ache. She went into the kitchen to set the table, making for the usual drawer for the cutlery, then deciding against it. If this was to be her last day, she would only surround herself with the things she loved. Instead, she took out the best tableware from the dresser, her mother's silver, and arranged it very precisely on the table around a good china plate. There. Such a pity her lunch would not be quite as inspiring. Oh well. These days everything tasted like cardboard anyway.

The memories of happier times kept her there for longer than was necessary. It was older than her, this table. It had seen her come into the world, and now… She took a deep breath and let her mind wander back to another life. The sturdy oak table had always been Hannah's domain back then. Vignettes from the past played before her eyes. Helping Hannah bake at this very table; making jam and chutney with produce from the garden; Hannah's pies. Now they never tasted of cardboard, even when the war was on. Sitting here for lunch with Hannah, Mummy, Jimmy and Vic. Occasionally, Daddy too. Mealtimes were such fun in those days. So much happiness. So much laughter.

A blurry image on the edge of her vision caught her attention and she turned towards the window to get a better view. At the same time, Maud sensed something and stiffened. She shot back to the French windows in the breakfast room and let out a low growl. Edie saw it then, the fox emerging from the trees at the side of garden. Strange. It was an odd time for it to be out. There was something next to it, shimmering, almost translucent and yet very bright. She shook her head. It was this dizziness. These blasted eyes. Silly old hope playing tricks. She shut her eyes and opened them again. She was sure now that there was something out there. A figure, holding its palm high and open in greeting. All at once, she understood. Her lips parted into a smile. 'Oh, it's you.'

Suddenly, a blinding pain ripped through her head and she heard a howl. At first, she thought it was Maud. Then she realised it was her. There was no more garden; no more window. Only darkness. She seemed to be falling.

So, this was it then?

2

TODAY WAS THE DAY

NETTA – 2019

Today was the day. Edie's day.

Netta pushed the door open with her foot and immediately regretted it when the room's musty, mouldy air caught the back of her throat. Today was also the day she had to admit what her family had been telling her for weeks was true. The smell in the study was quite unpleasant, like an old bookshop that no one had visited in years, or maybe a slightly dodgy vintage store. Definitely not like something had crawled in there and died as her daughter, Liza, had suggested. Definitely not that, but not far off. In the last few months she'd only been in there to add to the mess, preferring not to linger, but the new year was just a few days old and she couldn't think of a better time to make a start on finding Edith Pinsent.

Not that Edith was lost. Not as such. She was, in fact, dead but this had once been her home and she'd left it full of her memories. When Netta had first come to view this ramshackle old house, the study had been the most intriguing and the most daunting room. The bookcases lining its walls had been heaving with books and dust.

Hazardous mounds of tattered old notebooks, Edie's journals, were leaning against them, teetering on the brink of collapse. Some had already succumbed to gravity and had tumbled across the floor or over the bundles of papers scattered about it. Miss Havisham's library would probably have resembled this, although she was pretty sure Edie was no Miss Havisham. Netta had never actually met the late Edith Pinsent but all those who had known her gave the impression that she was popular, outgoing and a tiny bit eccentric. After her death, the extent of that eccentricity was clear in the things she left behind. The house was bequeathed to her great-nephew, James who lived in Australia, under very strict instruction as to the sort of person he'd be allowed to sell it to. That person had turned out to be Netta and last spring she was able to buy the house at a price that was well below its market value, as long as she agreed to Edie's conditions.

The first condition had been an unexpected joy – Netta had to take on Edie's dog, Maud. Since then, Maud had given birth to four puppies, three of which had been adopted by Netta's family and friends. The fourth, Betty, stayed with Maud.

The second condition had been a little more problematic. Netta had to clear the house of Edie's things personally and that included reading Edie's many journals. Netta had every intention of honouring that commitment, it was just that things had got in the way since she'd moved in. But those things were sorted now. She was sorted now. She'd changed her name back from sensible, dull Annette Grey to Netta Wilde and she was more like the person she used to be before she married Colin. There was nothing holding her back. It was time to keep her word to James Pinsent and make a start on piecing together his great-aunt's life.

The rest of the family were out so, in respect of human company, she was alone in the house. Maud and Betty were curled up in the breakfast room making the most of the thin winter sun streaming through the French windows. Netta had the place to herself. Still in the doorway, she assessed the chaos in front of her. There had been several attempts to tidy up since last spring but each time some semblance of order had been reached, more junk was dumped in from the other rooms as they'd been cleared. Now, with barely any visible floor space, it looked worse than it had when Netta moved in. Back then, she'd been sad and broken Annette and there had been something about those journals that called to her. She'd been dipping in and out of them ever since, gradually getting closer to Edie as her own journey unfolded. Time now to follow Edie's path.

She put one foot in front of the other along a narrow aisle that cut through the disorder. With a mug of coffee in one hand and a slice of Christmas cake in the other she realised she resembled a tightrope walker, using her sustenance to keep her balanced. On reaching the ancient desk in the middle of the room, she cleared a space for her mug and plate and flopped down into the chair, satisfied with her progress so far. After a sip of coffee, she scanned the room for a place to start. Another sip helped her to decide on the papers, guessing that most of them were low hanging fruit in the 'not worth keeping' department. She emptied the contents of two boxes onto a tiny space by her feet and scribbled an R, for recycling, on one box then a K, for keeping, on the other.

It didn't take long to draw the conclusion that Edith had been a hoarder: there were bills going back years, some even pre-dating Netta. The Pinsents had been quite meticulous in the storing, filing and checking of invoices. There were folders for each utility bill and every quarter was checked off against the same one in preceding years with comments on why consumption had gone up or down. There was even a summary of that period's weather.

In the winter of 1990, the handwriting changed. Presumably, the earlier writing had been Edie's father or mother. The later writing was definitely Edie's – Netta recognised it from her diaries. Edie, it seemed, had carried on watching the pennies. Or perhaps there was more to it than that. Netta remembered all too well how easy it was to get caught up in minutiae when there was nothing else to fill your day. She shivered, as if the ghost of her old self had just passed through her and a single tear formed in her eye. She wiped it away and told herself not to be so stupid. These days, any little thing was enough to make her well up. She put it down to years of suppressed emotions coming to the fore, although, she was fifty-one now and well aware that the menopause was just around the corner. She made a mental note to read up on the symptoms, just in case.

After a couple of hours, stiffness was setting in. There was no room in the study to stretch out so she went back along the little pathway into the wide hall where she reached her arms up to the ceiling; bent down to touch the floor, then rose back up again to bring her hands to her chest in prayer position. Over Christmas, Liza had taught her some basic yoga stretches and she'd been trying to do them every day. Not just because it pleased Liza but also because it was something they could share an interest in. It was a way of making up for the mother-daughter time they should have had in the past – time that had, for one reason or another, been denied to them. The church hall where Netta was a foodbank volunteer was starting Pilates classes on Wednesday evenings and, in a moment of new-year

madness, she'd agreed to go to with her friends, Paula and
Corrine. The difference between her new year's resolutions
last year and this year made her smile. In 2018 they'd been
the determinations of a woman on the cusp of a reawak-
ening to connect with herself and her children. This year?
Some half-hearted commitments to find more time to get fit
and do 'stuff'. Maybe that showed just how much she'd
come on. It wasn't a bad thing.

In the kitchen, she ran on the spot while the kettle
boiled, glad when it finally clicked off. This getting fit business was going to take time. The noise of her making tea
roused Betty and Maud and within seconds they were at her
feet with hopeful looks on their faces. Netta took down a tub
from the top of the dresser. 'One doggie treat, that's all.'
They snaffled the meagre offerings immediately and
followed her along the hall, perhaps hoping for more. Back
in the study, Netta cast her eyes around the jumbled mess of
boxes, books and papers. 'Which one to try next, girls?'

Maud sniffed the air and plonked herself down in the
doorway, sensibly deciding against going any further. Betty
showed no such restraint. Weaving in and out of obstacles
she stuck her nose in any gaps she could find. Netta kept a
close eye on her: Betty was still a baby and full of that
lolloping puppy clumsiness that often got her into scrapes. If
she knocked down a book pile, the ensuing landslide could
do her some serious damage. Eventually, she stopped at a
large flattish box at the bottom of a stack of five that had
been cleared from the small bedroom so that Liza would
have her own room now that she was living half the week at
Netta's. The box was sagging in the middle from the weight
of the others and its corners were torn and fraying. Betty
caught hold of a loose edge and tugged at it. It was too

heavy for her to move but the upper layers were beginning to show signs of toppling.

'Betty, leave it. Come away before you hurt yourself,' said Netta.

Undeterred, Betty dug her teeth and paws in. Maud's attention was caught and she ventured in to examine the box herself. As soon as she got close to it she began pawing at the cardboard, her tail wagging furiously which was enough to pique Netta's curiosity. Afraid to pick it up in case the whole thing collapsed, she took the upper tiers away and dragged the box around various obstructions until she reached the desk. On closer inspection, she could see faint lettering on the lid. It looked like Lewis's, one of her gran's favourite department stores. It was gone now, closed last century. Last century, that was a depressing thought. She ignored worries about how ancient that made her feel and returned her attention to the box. Inside, she found an assortment of plastic bags that were full of tissue-wrapped packages; papers tied together with string, and old photographs.

Maud's nose was glued to one of the packages. Netta prised it away from her. Underneath the tissue wrapping was a slim, hinged box. It had lost its lustre but the pale grey wood with its single inscription in faded gold font was still classy: *'Gloves'*. Inside the box, in between the silver-grey silk lining was a pair of powder blue gloves made of soft, buttery leather that were decorated with tiny embroidered flowers. They were exquisite. Maud sprang up and landed her front paws on Netta's lap. 'I'm sorry Maudie, you can't have these. They're too delicate. Let's see if there's anything else.' She found an old school scarf in there and Maud sniffed at it, her tail resuming its frantic round and round motion. Netta stroked the dog's rough fur. 'You haven't forgotten her then?'

One by one, Netta emptied the plastic bags. She found a pretty silver butterfly pendant, its body made of green glass with a delicate chain attached to each of its wings. There were cards, letters, and pictures of the Pinsent family that seemed to go back to the early days of photography. If Edie's journals were the longer version, this was her life in a box. Her most precious things. These were the things to take time over. If she really wanted to know Edie, she should start with these and move on to the journals.

It was getting darker outside. Snow was forecast and the clouds looked heavy enough for it. She turned on the light, and laid out the contents of the box on the desk. Right at the bottom she came across a large portrait photo of a pretty young woman in a forties-style dress. She was looking away from the camera with a dreamy half-smile. Underneath it was a second one. The same young woman. This time she was in uniform and looking directly at the camera, her expression more serious. Both photos had the photographers' addresses stamped on the back of them. The one in uniform was taken in Birmingham, Colmore Row and was dated 26th December 1942. The other one had a London address in Knightsbridge, no date. Written on both photos were the words:

'Dearest Bill
My love always
Edie x'

'So that's what you looked like?' It had never before occurred to Netta that she hadn't actually seen a picture of Edie, and now that she had, she realised she didn't need to. Absurd as it may seem, she had already known what she would look like. From the moment she moved into the house, it seemed as if she and Edie had always known each other. But who was Bill? A wartime sweetheart perhaps? Edie had never married so whoever he was, he hadn't stuck around. She'd have to ask James. She didn't know him that well but they mailed each other occasionally – mostly about Maud and how Netta was getting on with fulfilling her commitments.

A tap at the window gave her a start and made the dogs bark. Frank waved from the other side of the glass. She let him in through the front door and noticed snowflakes had settled on his hair and shoulders. He only lived next door so hadn't bothered with a coat but his jumper was already damp. He had Fred with him, the youngest of Maud's puppies. Snowy particles were sprinkled all over Fred's dark, shaggy coat and it occurred to her that there was more than a passing resemblance between the owner and his dog. Frank swept her up into a big bear hug. 'Hello you. Did I give you a fright?'

'Just a little. I was a bit engrossed. Can you believe it? I've met Edie at last.'

'You've what now?'

'Come and see.'

They sat at the kitchen table with the contents of the box. Frank took in the photos of the young Edie. 'Hard to imagine her like this. Especially in this photograph.' He pointed to the photo of Edie in the dress. 'She's so young and pretty, and glamorous. The Edie I knew was quite a stout little old lady. Very stoic and sensible looking. Young Edie looks like she's much more of a romantic.'

'Perhaps it was the war,' said Netta. 'Perhaps there was nothing to be romantic about by the time it finished.'

'Or age. Mind you, she might have been old but she still had the loveliest eyes. You can't tell in this black and white photo but they were bright blue, even towards the end of her life. They were quite striking.' He picked out a smaller photo from the pile. 'This one looks like it's from the same period. There she is again.' Edie was sitting on a picnic rug with two men and another woman. They were all grinning at the camera, as if they were about to burst into laughter. 'I wonder if one of these guys is Bill.'

Netta took a closer look. The men were kneeling either side of the women, except the one closest to Edie looked as if he was losing his balance. She pointed to him. 'Maybe this one?'

'God, they all look so good don't they?' He gestured towards the other woman. 'I mean, she's a real looker. Like a Hollywood movie star. What else have we got?'

'Let me see. We've got Edie's call-up papers from the war, telling her to report for training. Looks like she was in the WAAF. There are some letters addressed to her at a place called RAF Rudloe Manor. That could be where she met Bill.'

'Looks like you've made a good start today.'

'Thanks to Betty.' Betty was too busy play-fighting with Fred to notice Netta's gratitude. Netta nodded to Maud who had got herself tangled up in the scarf. 'I think that must have been Edie's: she won't let it go.'

'Not sure which school it is,' said Frank. 'I don't recognise the colours from any around here but I don't suppose that means anything. The school could have closed a long time ago.'

'Well it must have something to do with Edie, judging by the way Maud's attached herself to it, and it must have been important for her to have kept it in that box.' Her eyes flitted across the old photos and settled on the one of Edie in her uniform, staring straight back at her. There was a youthful confidence about her. Netta had it herself once, a long time ago. 'How old do you think she would have been?'

'Eighteen or nineteen I should think.'

'Same age as Will then. Only a couple of years older than Liza. I wonder what it was like to be sent off to war at that age.' Will was a sensible boy but Netta couldn't imagine her son as a soldier, fighting to the death for his country. Nor did she want to. Frank's daughter, Robyn, was in her early twenties and always seemed really capable, but all the same… 'Imagine how hard it must have been for her parents. If it had been Will or Robyn going off to fight we'd have been out of our minds with worry.'

3

LIMBO AND THE LOFT OF DOOM

NETTA – 2019

A week had passed since she'd gone through Edie's papers and filled two recycling bins – her own and Frank's. Having a partner who lived next door was an added bonus when it came to waste disposal. The plus side of her purge was that she had a bit more space in the study. The downside was that she'd have to start reading Edie's journals properly now. In Netta's head, she knew Edith Pinsent very well. She'd lived in the house less than a year but she'd already gone through some of the more recent diaries with their odd, sometimes touching, little notes alongside numerous recipes. She'd spent many a sleepless night in the breakfast room watching the foxes that frequented the garden, sensing that Edie was there with her. But, after finding that box and seeing the photos of young Edie, Netta realised that her version of Edie was an idealised one that she'd created. She didn't really know her at all, and that was the problem. What if the real Edie was nothing like the one she'd conjured up? She wasn't sure how she'd cope with that.

She'd just received an email from James Pinsent telling her no one in the family was aware of anyone in Edie's life called Bill and asking how she was getting on with her search. She blew air loudly out of her lips. Like it or not, she was going to have to get stuck in and stop fannying around. It wasn't even as if she had her work to distract her: the fledgling business that she shared with two of her friends had recently ground to a temporary halt. After half a year of making jam in her kitchen, she and her friends had finally gone professional and found a proper commercial premises, but they had to wait for the authorities to okay everything before they could start using it. Just before Christmas they'd had a big push to make as many jars as they could in her kitchen so that they'd have stocks to fall back on for their one regular order during the transition period, but they were in the process of agreeing two more suppliers and had applications underway for some of the more established local markets. Edie's Jams was about to become a real business. They'd given it that name because they'd found the jam recipes in Edie's journals, although they apparently came from the family's housekeeper originally.

All in all, the future was looking promising but, for the moment, they were in limbo. Or rather, Netta was in limbo. The other two didn't seem to be finding it quite so tough. Neil was filling his time experimenting with chutneys and pickles, something he was keen for them to move into. There were recipes for some of these in the journals too but also Neil's husband, Chris, suggested trying out something a little more Caribbean. His mum and aunties had several recipes that went back, probably as far as Edie's did and they were happy to share them. While Neil was beavering away at his research, Kelly was also keeping herself busy doing casual work at a fruit and veg stall in the market in town. She'd been doing it since early December and, so far,

hadn't come to blows with anyone which was unusual for
Kelly. She'd done well to stick it out, especially in this
weather. The snow yesterday had petered out but it was still
cold for standing outside all day.

   Kelly was only twenty and reminded Netta of her
younger self although, in truth, she'd had a much harder life
than Netta had by that age. Kelly's mum died when she was
twelve and she'd become the default family carer after her
dad had difficulty coping. If that wasn't bad enough, her
nose was put out of joint when her dad met someone new
and she left home far too young and fell in with a no-good
waster called Craig who was ten years her senior. When she
split up with him, last year, she moved in with Netta and
had been here ever since. She'd been the first. Shortly after,
Will fell out with Colin and asked if he could live with her.
Eventually, Liza came round too. So now the house was
filled with family and dogs which was a far cry from the dog-
free and largely people-free flat she'd existed in before. That
made Netta very happy.

   Kelly had offered Netta some of her market earnings for
rent but she didn't want it. It wasn't like Kelly was earning
much and Netta was managing to get by without dipping
too much into the money she'd received from Colin after
he'd bought her out of their old house, and she was hopeful
that the new business would soon be paying them something
close to a wage. Besides, Will was working part-time in her
friend Sean's record shop during his gap year and she didn't
ask him for rent money. She wasn't actually related to Kelly
but it felt like she was. As Kelly had once put it, she was
Netta's daughter from another mother. Thankfully, Netta's
actual kids seemed to be okay with that.

   On Tuesdays and Fridays all three business partners
volunteered at the foodbank, so Neil and Kelly appeared to

be fully occupied. It was only Netta that seemed to be at a loose end. Last year, the making and selling of jam had taken up nearly all of her spare time. Now, the gaps between foodbank days seemed strangely empty, just as they had done in the bad old days before her life changed for the better. Of course, they didn't need to be empty and her hesitancy to fill them usefully was beginning to annoy her.

A message from Frank pulled her out of her personal irritation. He was back from the college where he taught part-time. Normally, the rest of his time was filled with his other occupation – he was an artist – but after a morning of teaching English to a bunch of students who still hadn't settled back after the Christmas break, he needed some fresh air. She grabbed her coat and a dog lead. In a shot, Betty was careering through the hall with Maud ambling along behind her. Netta clipped the lead onto Betty's collar. 'Let's get going. We've got a date with your brother. Are you joining us Maud? The rain's stopped and the sun's coming out. Well, sort of.' Maud trotted back into the kitchen, clearly unimpressed by the offer. Netta rolled her eyes. If anyone had told her a year ago that she'd be standing here, in this lovely old house, talking to a dog as if she were trying to cajole a belligerent old dear into taking the air, she'd have dismissed it as madness. Yet here she was, and it was all thanks to Edie. Edie who'd died alone and yet seemed to have been loved by so many. Edie who she was letting down by not doing as she promised.

'What did James say in his mail?' said Frank. 'Could he throw any light on who Bill was?'

'No, not really. He thinks there was someone but he's not sure what happened to him, and he doesn't know his name. Edie rarely spoke about her time in the war, apparently, and neither did his grandfather.'

They were walking hand in hand through the park. It was a new development, this hand-holding thing. They'd only really been doing it for a few weeks. It was quite nice. There was something comforting about it, something solid, but she could only do it for so long before she was overtaken by the need to slyly slip her hand away. It still felt a bit awkward: she'd never been a touchy-feely person, particularly with Colin, but she and Frank had only been together for five months and her feelings were still evolving, as was her ability to express those feelings.

'I think it affected a lot of people like that. My grandad only talked about it when he was really pushed, and even then, he was very sparing with the detail. I think he saw a lot of things back then that he preferred to forget.' He let go of her hand to throw a ball and the two puppies gambolled over the grass in pursuit of it. Fred beat Betty to the ball but she caught up with him and tried to tear it off him making Fred growl in response. 'Come on you two, play nicely. It's like having kids all over again, isn't it?' Frank held out his hand but Netta had already stuck hers in her coat pocket. There'd been enough hand-holding for one walk. Not seeming to mind, he kissed her. 'Have I told you lately that I love you?'

She screwed up her nose. 'Jesus, Frank, was that one of the cheesiest songs in the history of cheesy songs, or what?'

'How can you say that about Van Morrison?'

'Oh well, why didn't you say it was Van the Man? That makes all the difference.'

He laughed. 'Come on dogs, time to go home. Looks like a hard rain's a gonna fall.'

She put her hand over her eyes. 'Stop it. I can't bear it.'

. . .

Back in the house, they looked at Edie's online war records but they only told them what they'd already found out. Aside from clearing the Pinsents' old invoices Netta had also read through the letters in the box. She'd hoped to find something that mentioned Bill, maybe even a letter from him but there was nothing at all. Most of them were from Edie's parents although there were a few from her brothers. James told her that Vic was the oldest and was his grandfather. Jimmy had been two years older than Edie and was killed in action. He said the family never really got over his death. Netta could see how that would be. Even though the letters from Edie's parents were more formal than she was used to, there was a real warmth in them. They must have been a very happy family before the war.

Netta picked up what she guessed was a Pinsent family photo. By the look of the fashions, it had been taken in the eighties. Next to the elderly Mr and Mrs Pinsent sat a softly rounded woman with a confident smile and shoulder length fair hair that was somewhere between blonde and grey. On her lap sat a dark-haired little boy. 'That's Edie, isn't it?'

Frank took a closer look. 'Yes. That's how I remember her when we first moved here. I think that's James on her lap. He was in his teens when we came but it certainly looks like the same boy. The couple behind her are his parents, Jimmy and Margaret.'

'What happened to them?'

'They're still alive. They moved out of Birmingham after Jimmy retired.'

'Strange. If he's still around, you'd have thought Edie would have left the house to him, wouldn't you?'

'There's no intrigue there. Edie doted on James and the

feeling was mutual. I think Jimmy was happy with the outcome. He ran the family business quite successfully and, since James wasn't interested in carrying it on, he sold it when he retired. So he didn't need the money. How's it going with the diaries?'

'Not great. There are so many of them that I've only really skimmed the surface. I think I probably need to go back as far as I can and start there.'

'Come on, I'll help you look through them.'

They checked through the piles of assorted notebooks. The ones that had already been in the study when Netta moved into the house were mostly this century. The ones that had been moved down from the Liza's bedroom were older but not the era she was looking for. There would be time to read them later but for now, it was the young Edie's words that she wanted to read and the era that interested her most was the time around those photos. More than anything, she wanted to know that young woman.

'It's possible she didn't keep a diary in those years, I suppose,' said Frank.

'Yes, it is, but I get the impression Edie wrote come what may from a young age. I don't know, I just have this feeling they're in this house somewhere.'

She didn't say because she knew it sounded crackers but she was sure Edie left them for her to find. Edie had been so specific about the person she wanted the house to go to that she'd given James detailed instructions. All those stipulations about her going through Edie's possessions herself had to be for a reason. James once told her he thought Edie had hoped that by reading the journals and going through her things, a bit of her would become part of Netta. She could see that was already happening. How else would she have known what Edie looked like when she found the photographs? It's not like there were any photos of her dotted around the house. She was a woman who seemed to eschew the limelight. James hadn't removed anything but there was little trace in the house of that enchanting young woman in the beautiful dress, just practical things. Edie seemed to be a very practical woman and yet, she came up with this fantastic idea to pass something of herself on to a complete stranger. Was all that just the desire of a childless spinster not to be forgotten? Netta didn't think so. Edie had chosen her for some kind of task, even if it was James Pinsent that had done the choosing. She just had to work out what it was.

'Well, if you've cleared all of the other rooms there's only one place left,' said Frank.

Netta chewed on her lip. 'The loft of doom.'

'The what?'

'Oh, it's just the name the kids have given it because it's so dark and spooky.'

'Have you been up there then?'

'Yes, I put a couple of boxes just inside the hatch in December. I couldn't get any further in, it's so rammed.'

'Shall we take a look?'

She sighed. 'I think we have to.'

Netta waited at the bottom while Frank climbed the ladder into the loft of doom. He stopped at the top so that only his lower legs were visible. The rest of him was hidden in the darkness above the ceiling until he switched on his torch and the square hatch lit up. After a few minutes, he was back on the ground. 'Yeah, pretty full. I think we'll need help.'

4

A LIFETIME OF POSSESSIONS

NETTA – 2019

Sunday mornings were usually reserved for a park walk with all four of Maud's offspring and their respective families. Netta's parents brought their puppy, Minnie. Neil and Chris brought Buster. Frank came with Fred, and Netta with Betty. Occasionally they were joined by Maud or the younger people in Netta's household but only occasionally: they weren't big on early starts, although they always managed to drag themselves out of bed for the post-walk brunch in the kitchen. Today, the racket in the house had forced them up early. Instead of the usual park walk, the humans had come to clear the loft of doom and the dogs were making do with a noisy run around the back garden.

Chris clomped down the stairs with an armful of dusty notebooks – presumably more of Edie's journals. 'Where do you want these?'

His dreads were crowned with cobwebs and Netta pulled a money spider off one of them before replying. 'Put everything in the study please. Just try to leave me a path to the desk.'

'You're not going to fit everything in there,' he said.

'How about if we put the furniture and obvious rubbish aside for now and have a look at it when we're finished up there?'

By the time they'd emptied the loft, its contents were spread around the lower half of the house. Netta climbed the ladder and hauled herself up through the hatch. Now that it was empty she could see that the loft ran the length and breadth of the house and it was massive. Much bigger than she'd assumed, although, judging by the amount of junk coming out of it, she should have guessed. James had told her the Pinsents' housekeeper had lived-in. Perhaps she'd slept in this room. If so, she'd have needed more than this ladder to get up here. There was no sign of a staircase though. At one end of the room, there was a small dormer window. Otherwise it was fairly gloomy. There were some light switches but they were ancient round black things that no one wanted to touch, so they'd run a lamp on an extension lead from the landing but the gloom persisted.

'Get a few more windows in here and it would make a great artist's studio,' said Frank, stepping off the ladder.

'Hmm, any particular artist in mind?' It was a rhetorical question, she wasn't expecting an answer and didn't get one. 'You must have one like this too.'

'Yes. Not quite as bad but it is full of junk. I'll get round to clearing it one of these days.'

'What's that smell? It's just as bad downstairs and it's fucking disgusting.' Kelly hung onto the top of the ladder with one hand and covered her nose with the other.

'It's age, my dear,' said Frank. 'It comes to us all.'

'Not my nan. She smells of Yardley English Rose Eau de Toilette. She's like a walking rose bush.'

'I'm sure your nan smells very nice, but this is the unperfumed smell of a lifetime of possessions,' said Frank.

'Well it stinks. Bacon sandwiches downstairs by the way. Neil says you need feeding up, Net. He reckons you're looking a bit peaky. Not you though, Frank. Quite the opposite with you, mate.' She gave him a sly grin. She did love winding Frank up but this time he refused to take the bait and they went downstairs to join Netta's dad, Liza, Will and Chris at the kitchen table. Neil and Netta's mum were sorting out the bacon sandwiches. Her mum was in her element. She was particularly fond of Neil and was always singing his praises. On Sunday mornings they'd often walk together sharing stories about what their dogs had been up to that week or talking about cookery programmes – something they both loved. She'd even asked Netta's dad to set up an email account for her so that she could swap recipes with him. Netta's dad had been astounded. He'd sent Netta a message immediately after to tell her the amazing news. Netta had been pretty shocked too: her mother, the IT refusenik, not only asking for an email account but also using it! When Neil suggested Facebook, she asked for Facebook. Next came a mobile phone and WhatsApp which was great, but Netta now found she had streams of messages several times a day from her which could be a little taxing. Her dad though, had been so pleased she thought he might actually embrace Neil when he next saw him.

Chris had once pointed out to her that Neil collected family in place of his own estranged one. In Netta's mum, he'd found his surrogate mother and she, her surrogate son and both seemed happy with the arrangement. Last year, when Netta confessed that she'd once had an affair that had resulted in a miscarriage, her mum hinted that she'd had miscarriages too and that they'd planted a rose bush for each child. Netta actually counted the rose bushes in their garden, after that. There were eight. Surely, her mother hadn't lost that many babies? Surely some of them had to be because her dad liked roses? Either way, she found herself wondering whether any of them had been boys. Perhaps Neil had replaced at least one of them. She couldn't begrudge her mum that. Besides, she loved Neil like a brother. A brother who happened to be an extremely good cook and who was now handing her a big, fat bacon sandwich dripping with brown sauce. She wiped sauce away from her mouth and looked around the table, feeling the same gush of warmth she always did when surrounded by her friends and family.

When they finished eating, they started on the junk piles and quickly decided that most of the furniture wasn't worth keeping, but there was one wooden chest that looked interesting. The only problem was that it was locked. There was a key but it had rusted and had somehow become stuck inside the lock. Netta's dad knelt down to examine it. 'I think the only way in would be to break the lock. It's too far gone to do anything else. I can jemmy it open. I'll be as careful as I can but it'll probably make a mess of the box.'

Everyone stopped what they were doing and crowded around the box. 'There's probably nothing in there,' said Netta. They all nodded in agreement. 'But I suppose we won't know, unless…?' They nodded again and she suddenly felt pressured into making a decision that they'd all agree with. 'Do it.'

In the end it was quite easy to force the chest open without too much damage. They flipped back the lid and found some old clothes. A collective sigh of disappointment filled the room. Netta wasn't the only one hoping for more. At least Liza was pleased with the find.

'Cool, more vintage.' She sighed in pleasure. A few months back, she and her friend Jade had spent a happy couple of hours going through Edie's wardrobes with Frank's daughter Robyn, and Kelly. Clearly she was excited at the prospect of finding more old clothes to try on.

Netta examined the top layer of garments. 'I think these might be past that, darling. The damp and moths may have got to them.'

They took the top layer of moth-eaten cardigans out one by one and laid them out carefully on the floor. Liza held up a blue silk dress. It was stained with mould and threadbare in places but, in its day, it must have been beautiful. 'I think I've seen this dress before,' said Netta. She found the photo of Edie that had been taken in Knightsbridge and held it against the dress. 'I'm sure it's the same one.'

They lay it down on the table and placed the photo next to it. 'She must have been quite small,' said Liza. 'The waist is tiny.'

'They all were back then,' said Netta's mum. 'Especially during the war. Rationing.'

Back in the chest they found a few more clothes and then something else, wrapped inside a blanket. Four journals, the first of which began in 1942. These were what Netta had been looking for. She touched the faded silk dress lightly. In her head she saw young Edie. She could have been standing in this very spot wearing this dress and those elegant powder blue gloves, waiting to go out somewhere special. Edie was getting closer. She could feel it.

5

HOW TO TOUCH AND TASTE THE SKY

EDIE – 1942

'I'm ashamed to say, I'm rather excited by it all.'

It was wrong, she knew that. She wasn't stupid. Quite the opposite in fact, but she was eighteen and the thought of being away from home, unchaperoned, was exciting. An adventure.

Perhaps if she had gone to boarding school like Jimmy and Vic, she'd have been more used to it but Mummy wouldn't hear of it. Edie was always rather annoyed at that. She hated being treated differently just because she was a girl. When she'd finished school, she'd hoped to be the first woman in her family to go to university but this blasted war had put paid to that. Instead, she'd done her duty and mucked in at Daddy's engineering firm, in the offices. Vital war work he'd called it. Vital but boring, she soon came to understand. Now, she was bound for RAF Rudloe Manor, near Bath, to do proper war work, at last. Gosh!

Naturally, her parents had been unhappy about it. They would have preferred the land army. Less chance of her being killed. They didn't say it in so many words but the intimation was there. You couldn't blame them for that. They'd already lost Jimmy, and with Vic fighting in Europe they lived in daily fear of that knock on the door. Now it was her turn, their little Edie, and they were worried to death that she wouldn't come back. So yes, she knew it was wrong but there was no getting around it, she was excited.

The train seemed to be full of servicemen. It reminded her of her journey from Birmingham to the initial training base just a few months ago. Mummy and Daddy had insisted on driving her to the station to make sure she got on the right train. At the time, she'd felt a tad insulted that they didn't credit her with the sense to find her way around but she realised there was more to it than that. They had been afraid for her, even though they would never have said it. They'd maintained an air of cheerful fortitude but the fleeting look of horror on her mother's face as Edie boarded the train, full of soldiers laughing and shouting, had said it all. They'd been as much afraid for her moral welfare as her physical safety.

She'd found a carriage with a spare seat and one of the soldiers had moved over so that she could sit by the window and wave goodbye to her parents. She'd thought that was very decent of him, but when he joined in with his pals singing bawdy songs – the sort they probably sang in pubs – she'd considered reassessing that assumption. He'd offered her an open pack of Park Drive. 'Cigarette, love?'

'No thank you,' she'd replied and had immediately worried that her response had been haughty. She'd thought of Jimmy and with that came all kinds of personal admonishments. These boys were just like him really. They could be dead in a few weeks. She could be the last girl that this soldier spoke to and she'd been rude. It was her duty to be kind and polite. 'I don't smoke.' She'd softened her voice and said it with a warm smile. Not too warm though. She hadn't wanted him to think she was a tart. He'd accepted this gracefully and carried on singing. During that journey, one or two of the other soldiers had caught her eye and winked, making her colour up immediately. Not really knowing how to behave in these situations, she'd looked away and done her best to stare out of the window all the way to the training base. All the same, she'd been thrilled.

Edie smiled to herself. That journey seemed like it was eons ago and yet, in reality it was hardly any time at all. She was a completely different person now. Where was that shy little girl who'd pressed herself up against the train window in fear of a cheeky grin from a soldier? The WAAF had soon sent her packing. The new Edie journeyed towards her posting feeling every bit the confident young woman. In just a few months, she'd learned so much from her more worldly-wise comrades, especially the working class girls. They certainly knew how to put a chap in his place. By the end of her training, she'd felt that she wasn't only fully prepared for her new job but also for life.

As the train approached Bath, she shoved her diary into her gas mask case and pulled her bag down from the overhead rack. Once off the train, a corporal directed her to a transport lorry. At the back end of the lorry, she wrapped her hands around a rope and scrambled over the tailboard rather ungracefully. She'd done this numerous times now but she still hadn't mastered it. Edie was relieved to see that the two men already in the truck had no interest in her ungainly climb. They were too busy laughing at the person that came after her – a petite, delicate-featured brunette who was looking even more amateurish than her.

'Use the rope, darlin,' said one of the men.

The girl glared at them. 'I am using the bloody rope.' From her accent, Edie guessed she was from Yorkshire. She stood up to help her but the men pushed her aside, grabbed the girl's arms and hauled her up. She huffed and puffed then sat down next to Edie to examine the burn marks on her hand. 'Don't know if I'll ever get the hang of it.'

'I didn't fare much better,' said Edie quietly.

The girl turned to look at her. 'Are you new as well?'

'Yes. I'm Edie. Edie Pinsent.'

'Hello Edie. I'm Lily Turner. Where are you going to be working?'

'In the Operations Room. I'm a plotter.'

'Snap! Me too.'

Edie and Lily were billeted a few miles from the base in a cottage belonging to an elderly couple called Mr and Mrs Jackson, along with two other WAAFs who were already there. It was quite a squeeze but the girls' changing shift patterns meant that all six people were rarely in the house together. All four WAAFs worked in 10 Group's Operations Room but only Lily was on the same watch as Edie, so she saw more of her than the others. Still, when they did have time off, living off base had its advantages. The local pub in particular was a new and pleasurable experience which, after some initial coaxing from Lily, Edie took to like a duck to water. If her mother had known, she'd have been appalled. Fortunately, Edie had no intention of telling her.

Edie's first few weeks in the Ops Room were both terrifying and thrilling. She had been fully trained up but she still went to work every day fearful that she would get something wrong. Being in there was like taking part in a huge and very noisy board game, with the highest of stakes. To the side of the room, and on a balcony above it were the higher ranking airmen and women – officers who kept an eye on everything and relayed instructions to and from the outside. In the middle was a large map table surrounded by the plotters, mostly airwomen, who assimilated the information fed through their headsets and moved wooden blocks and arrows around with long poles. One of the girls said they were like croupiers in a casino. Edie had never been to one so she couldn't say whether that was an apt description or not.

At first, the descent to the underground Ops Room gave Edie a queasy feeling. She thought it was the lift and the stale air but, without her noticing it, the feeling gradually disappeared. After a month, she realised it was completely gone. She saw then that the queasiness had been nothing more than nerves which was understandable. From day one she, not long out of school and not much more than a child, was responsible for her own section of that operations table. The fate of men's lives lay in the hands of her and others like her. From the moment she entered the room she felt an intoxicating surge of adrenalin like nothing she'd ever experienced before. It was the most exhilarating place to work in, a world away from her father's offices in Birmingham, and there was nowhere else she'd rather be.

These days she took it more in her stride but there were still times when she finished her shift so tense it was nigh on impossible to come back down to earth. When that happened she borrowed the Jacksons' bicycle and took herself off to the peace and quiet of the surrounding fields, regardless of the time of day.

Edie and Lily sat on the bus taking them back to the village.

They'd just finished one of those difficult shifts. One plane hadn't come home yet which always made it hard to hand over to the next watch. Quite often they didn't want to leave the room but they had to. Even if they were allowed to stay, they would have only got in the way. 'I hope they're okay,' said Lily. 'I heard one of them is courting a WAAF.'

The bus stopped before Edie could reply. It was a chilly March evening and their breath spiralled from them into the air. They weren't supposed to discuss what happened at base but it was hard to think of other things to talk about in these situations, and they soon fell silent. In spite of the cold, Edie was hot and agitated and she knew she would never sleep. She was considering going for a walk around the village when saw the bicycle in the Jacksons' garden. 'You go in without me, Lils. I'm going for a ride.'

Lily looked at her as if she'd lost her marbles. 'Ede, it's late and it's freezing.'

'I know. I just need to wind down. I won't be long.'

'If you must, I suppose but I'm going in for a nice warm drink. Be careful.'

A few minutes later, Edie was on the road leading out of the village and was already beginning to feel better. She loved the open countryside and she wasn't at all afraid of the dark: her father was keen on astronomy and had often taken her and her brothers to the top of the Lickey Hills to watch the night sky. Unlike at home, the air here was so clean that it was easy to see a wonderful starry sweep on a clear night. Up ahead, a shooting star tumbled down to earth and took her breath away. She stopped cycling to watch. There was another. She let the bike fall against a hedgerow and climbed over a gate into a field. Just in front of her was a small hill. The crisp grass crunched under her feet as she trudged on and up to its summit where she stopped to look out at the vast expanse ahead. In the distance she could see flashes, like fireworks, lighting up the sky. She listened to the rumbling, faint and distant. Someone out there was being bombed. Probably Bristol.

She turned to face north, towards home and thought of her family, recalling a time, long before the war, when she was a child. Eight or nine? No more than ten. The whole family had gone to the Lickeys to stargaze. It was the end of the summer holidays and Edie had been in a sulk because her brothers were due to return to their school. She hated them leaving. Of course, Jimmy understood and, in an effort to cheer her up, he'd grabbed her hand and pulled her up to the top of a hill. 'Watch this, Ede.' He turned his face upwards, held his arms out wide and stuck out his tongue.

'What are you doing?' she'd asked.

'Try it. You can actually touch and taste the sky.'

She'd copied him and when the rest of the family caught them up, their father had asked: 'What on earth are you two doing?'

'We're touching and tasting the sky, Daddy,' she'd said.

'I see. Mind if we join you?'

It became something of a family tradition after that. A regular game. Edie smiled at the thought of that night but it was a memory tinged with sadness. Dearest, darling Jimmy. How could they go on without him? She opened her arms and stuck out her tongue, imagining she was back there touching and tasting the sky. If she concentrated really hard, she could almost feel him there with her now.

'Hello there. Are you all right?' Startled, she dropped her arms and turned to see a man in an RAF uniform standing at the other side of the gate. It was too dark to see his rank insignia. 'Is everything okay? I saw your bicycle and thought you may have had an accident.'

'I'm fine, thank you. I just stopped to take a look at the stars.'

'Right. I wasn't sure if something was up. Especially with the … uh … arms business.' He reached his arms up in the air to imitate her. In spite of her embarrassment she couldn't help but find his stance rather funny.

'Oh gosh. Yes, it must look a little strange. It's a silly little family thing.'

'Ah, I see. That explains it. Might one ask the reasoning behind that particular posture?'

'My brother maintained it helped you to touch and taste the sky.'

'Is that so? I'd like to put that to the test. Mind if I join you?' He hopped over the gate and within a few strides was standing next to her, arms outstretched.

'You have to stick out your tongue too,' she said. 'Like this.' They stood together for a few minutes, mouths wide open, tongues stuck out as far as they would go.

'You know, he's right. Clever fellow that brother of yours. Is he serving?'

'No. He was killed last May. Crete.' Her stomach clenched: she still found it difficult to say those words. She wondered if her difficulty was obvious and was glad that the visible signs, at least, were hidden in this dark.

He nodded. 'We took quite a battering there. Lost a lot of good men.'

'You were there?'

'No, I'm a pilot. I fly bombers. I'm sorry, how rude of me, I didn't introduce myself. Robert Goodwin.' He shook her hand.

A pilot? That meant he was an officer and she hadn't saluted him. Technically that could see her on report but he didn't seem to have noticed. She decided not to point it out. 'How do you do, Robert. I'm Edith Pinsent.'

'And you're serving at Rudloe?'

'Yes, and you?'

'Near enough. We come back to stay here every now and then for some respite. Fire up the batteries before heading out again.' He looked upwards. 'Wonderful night for stargazing. You could almost forget there's a war on.'

'Yes, almost.'

'Well, now that we've established you don't need my help, I'd better get back to base. I've an early start in the morning. Are you going my way?'

'No, I'm heading for Corsham.'

'Well goodbye then, Edith. A pleasure to have met you.' He went back down to the road and waved. 'Tasting the sky. That's a new one on me.'

6

A STEELY SMILE AND A BLUE SILK DRESS.

EDIE – 1942

'I'm on the move again. Not exactly to new territory but at least I know what I'm getting.'

She was being sent back to Rudloe Manor after a short posting at Newcastle and she was relieved. Not that there was anything wrong with Newcastle per se. It was a perfectly decent place. It was just that it was a bit too much like Birmingham: full of grimy houses, hardly bigger than a matchbox and certainly not fit for a family to live in. So much hardship, made worse by the bombings. Just like home. But early this morning she'd said a cheery goodbye to Newcastle and now she was on the train to Birmingham. It was Christmas Eve and she'd been lucky enough to get a few days leave in between postings. She'd been looking forward to going home to her family but the closer she got, the more her spirits dropped. Part of it was the destruction. The city had been badly damaged by the bombings and it was hard to look upon it, in its present state, without feeling a great sense of loss. It may not have been everyone's cup of tea, but she'd always loved her home city with its down to earth busy-ness. No airs and graces here, as Hannah liked to say. Edie always saw the best in Birmingham. She knew that was probably because she was luckier than most and that she'd always had a comfortable life. Her parents had told her often enough, and she'd seen it with her own eyes when she went with her mother to do her welfare work in the slums. When she was younger and more selfish, she'd once asked rather indignantly why they had to go there all the time and why they couldn't go somewhere nicer. Her mother responded quite flatly: 'Because we have so much and they have so little, Edith. Because it's our duty.' It had been the day after her ninth birthday and it was the first time she'd been made aware of two facts. The first was that they had wealth and others did not. The second was that their wealth was bound up in duty. These days, of course, duty was on everybody's mind. Jimmy had sacrificed his life for it, Vic was risking his every day. Now she was doing her duty and, for a change, it didn't seem like something to endure.

Really, the main reason for her melancholy was Jimmy. While she was away, she could pretend it hadn't happened; that he wasn't really dead, and that his body wasn't rotting away somewhere at the bottom of the sea. Now that she was home, she had to once again face the fact that he wouldn't be coming back.

Her father met her at the station. He looked worn out and thinner than she remembered him. When he saw her, he smiled and raised his arms to envelop her. 'Hello, my darling. Goodness you look so grown up in that uniform, I hardly recognised you. I mistook you for a young woman.'

She rolled her eyes. 'I am a young woman, Daddy.'

'Not my little girl?' he teased.

She huffed. 'I expect I'll always be your little girl. Even when I'm old and grey.'

He took her arm. 'Your mother has been so looking forward to seeing you, and guess what? Victor's home too. Isn't that wonderful? Back together again for Christmas.'

They both knew that wasn't true of course: they could never be back together again. She flashed him a broad smile. 'That's marvellous. What a lovely surprise. Do you mind if we stop off at Lewis's before going home? I'd like to get Vic a Christmas gift.'

They strolled along Corporation Street arm in arm. When she was a child, coming into town had been a real thrill. She'd loved the grand buildings, the shops and the hustle and bustle. Especially at this time of the year. Now, she could barely look at the places where she and Mummy had once shopped. Some had disappeared into piles of rubble. Others were just about hanging on; empty carcasses of buildings waiting for something to do them the service of demolishing them completely. When they reached Lewis's, she was gratified to see it still relatively intact and things appeared to be slightly more normal. She settled on a warm scarf for Vic which she thought would be both practical and make him look dashing. Before the war, as a treat, her parents would occasionally take her and her brothers to a little café in one of the side streets for afternoon tea. For nostalgia's sake she would have liked to go and look at it. Perhaps, they might have even ventured inside once more, but she didn't ask. If that was gone too, it would have broken her heart.

.   .   .

Her mother and Vic were in the sitting room, deep in conversation, when they arrived home. The house had been decorated for Christmas. The same as every other year. She felt like a child again. She wished she was. She would have given anything to turn back the clock to those happy times when the world was familiar and she and her brothers were the three musketeers, always together, always looking out for one another. Vic picked her up and hugged her. 'Hello Sis. It's so nice to see you. My goodness you've grown. Especially these.' He tweaked her cheeks playfully.

She pushed him away, giggling. 'Mean as ever, I see Victor. It's the forces food. It's so heavy I'm developing muscles just carrying it to the table.'

Her mother stood by the fireplace and held out her arms. 'Pay no attention to him, my darling, he's just teasing you.'

Edie went to her and they locked hands. Turning to kiss her mother's cheek, she saw the stockings hanging in their usual place on the mantelpiece. Her mother took Edie's hands to her lips and kissed them. 'I'm sorry, my dear, I couldn't bear not to put his stocking up again this year. I know it's silly but I hope you'll indulge me?'

'Of course, Mummy. I understand.' As long as the stocking was there, they could fool themselves that everything was the same. Jimmy had been gone for over a year and a half but it was still a bitter pill to swallow. Her mother insisted on placing little reminders of him around the house, as if they could bring him closer to them. How long would it go on? And when they'd finished mourning Jimmy, who would be next? She didn't dare think.

'Is that our Edie?' Hannah's voice called out from the

back of the house. Edie rushed into the kitchen to find her standing over the table, her big arms wobbling as she battered the contents of a mixing bowl. She put down her spoon and wiped her hands. 'Well, look at you in that uniform.'

Edie threw herself on Hannah and they held each other in a tight squeeze.

'Be careful not to get flour on your jacket,' said Hannah. 'Don't want you getting into trouble.'

She loosened her grip and Edie saw there was a tear in her eye. She gave Hannah a tender kiss. 'Merry Christmas.'

In spite of her heavy heart, the two days at home were good for her. As soon as she got changed into her civvies, she helped to put the final decorations on the tree. It was a family tradition to wait until they were all gathered together to put the star on the top of it. Afterwards, they toasted the tree with a small sherry. This was the first Christmas that Edie had been offered the sherry which pleased her: at last, her parents saw her as an adult.

In the evening, Edie's father left for his patrol. He'd been in the Home Guard from the very early days but she still found it difficult to think of him as the country's last line of defence. He was such a sweet man, if he ever caught an enemy, he'd be more likely to give the fellow a cup of tea and a jolly good talking to than raise his gun to him. She knew really that was nonsense. Like everyone, Daddy was prepared to do his duty if necessary. Still, it pleased her to think of him in that way. It enabled her to keep up the pretence that things were as they always were.

On Christmas morning they went to church. She'd been attending services near the base as often as her shifts allowed but it wasn't the same as her home church. There was a comfort in being back here, worshipping in the same place that she'd been coming to for as long as she could remember. She even saw Catherine, one of her old school friends who was home on leave from the ATS. They stopped for a quick chat after the service. It would have been nice to catch up properly and reminisce about the old days but, since their time back here was short, they agreed they should spend it with their families.

Hannah managed to cook an excellent Christmas lunch considering the shortages. Edie made sure to compliment her and tell her how much she missed her cooking which pleased Hannah immensely. As was the custom, Hannah joined the family at the table and they served her for a change. She'd been with them from the beginnings of Edie's parents' marriage and felt the loss of Jimmy as acutely as any of them. She had nephews fighting in Europe and Africa too and had already lost one that year. She understood grief but rarely gave into it, just like Edie's mother. The two women ran this house together and, although it was never obvious, Edie suspected they gave each other strength and comfort.

After lunch, they opened presents. Inside Edie's stocking was a new pen, a bottle of ink and some chocolate. 'I'm afraid oranges were nowhere to be had this year but we managed to bag the chocolate,' said her mother. 'This one is thanks to Daddy. They're not quite as nice as your usual, but everything is in such short supply.' She gave Edie a brown paper package which she'd made prettier with a ribbon tied in a bow. It contained three notebooks, rather utilitarian compared to her usual leather-bound journals but no less welcome since she was down to her last twenty pages on her current one. Vic gave her a darling silver butterfly pendant.

Before she had a chance to thank them, her father handed her a large flat box, from Lewis's. 'And now, la pièce de résistance.'

She opened it to find the most divine silk dress, the colour of cornflowers. 'Oh gosh, it's beautiful. It must have cost the earth, as well as your clothing rations for a year.'

Her mother gave a little shrug. 'We have plenty of clothes. You're a young lady now, Edith. You're allowed to dress like one occasionally, even if there is a war on.'

On the morning of Boxing Day, the family drove into town. Edie's parents had arranged for photographs to be taken of her and Vic. It occurred to Edie that they might have done this in case they never saw them again. Perhaps they regretted not having one taken of Jimmy before he went off to fight. If Vic thought the same thing, his face didn't show it and he gamely went along with their request. They were both due back at their bases later that day so they were wearing their uniforms. It gave the event a rather sombre, businesslike air and in spite of the photographer's cajoling, she only managed a steely smile. Afterwards, they had lunch at the Grand Hotel, then her parents saw them both off at the station.

As the train chuntered away from the platform, Edie sat back in the carriage she was sharing with another WAAF and three soldiers. The soldiers soon tried to chat them up but the two girls laughed them off. She and the other WAAF tutted at each other good-naturedly. Edie had learned how to handle these raucous young men over the last few months. She reminded herself how much she'd grown up since being called up. She was a WAAF and an independent young woman now.

7

A BUCKETFUL OF FUN

EDIE – 1943

'Here I am again, at Rudloe Manor. It feels like I've come home.'

This time she was billeted at a rather grand manor house, near Corsham. Gone was the intimacy of the Jacksons' little house. In its place were dormitories with row upon row of iron beds. Someone told her it housed as many as a hundred WAAFs. Quite a contrast to the last time she was here but she wasn't fazed: she'd got used to similar sleeping arrangements at Newcastle. Not in such a lofty setting though. This place reminded Edie of a hostel she'd once stayed in for a school trip. That had been such a lark. With any luck this would be too.

It was the day after her return. She was about to leave the manor house for her shift when she bumped into Lily who told her that the other two girls they'd shared with at the Jacksons' had been posted elsewhere and she'd been found a place in one of the dorms. She'd always liked the freedom of living off site but the waafery, as everyone called it, had its benefits too. 'There's always something going on here. It's a lot livelier than living in the village and you're never short of company. But I'm glad you're back, Ede. Come with me to the New Year's Eve dance. You look like you could do with a bit of fun.'

Edie didn't need any persuasion. She was working the day shift on New Year's Eve and Lily was spot on with her observation: Christmas at home had been nice, but not exactly exciting. She really could do with some fun. She'd hardly had time to go to the NAAFI dances when she'd previously been here but she had been to some in Newcastle and they were a completely new experience. Quite an eye opener, in fact. She absolutely loved the dancing, particularly the new American dances. Far more exciting than the stuffy ones she'd been taught at school. After the other WAAFs had shown her how to do the steps there'd been no stopping her. Until then, her idea of fun had been playing rough and tumble games with Jimmy and Vic but this was on a different level. It was the most joyous thing she'd ever done. However, there was one thing that she really hadn't been prepared for. The men. When the girls at Newcastle warned her that she might need to fend some of them off, she didn't really understand what they meant but she soon found out. The gall of some of them was absolutely astounding. The way they tried rummaging around her body was nothing short of indecent. At her first dance, she'd made the mistake of accepting one very charming fellow's offer of taking the air. It was a warm night, even warmer inside the dance hall, so a breath of fresh air sounded inviting but no sooner had they walked a few yards than he'd pushed her up against a wall and tried to force himself upon her. His hands were all over her. Eventually they settled on her breasts. 'You've got the most beautiful tits,' he said, squeezing them until they hurt.

She was horrified. 'Let me go, you disgusting animal.'

He pressed his lips against hers and forced his tongue inside her mouth. That was just about the limit. She closed her teeth and bit down. He let out a squeal, well, as best a man could whose tongue was clamped into place by his victim's incisors. When she let go, he fell back. 'I'm bleeding, I'm fucking bleeding. Look!'

'Serves you right,' she said, triumphant. 'Let that be a lesson to you.'

In her next diary entry, she wrote:

'The girls and I had quite a laugh about it afterwards but I have to confess, it shook me at the time. I have never before been subjected to such disgusting language or to such lewd behaviour. I felt so ill-equipped. Thank goodness I had the presence of mind to use the one weapon I had at my disposal. My healthy, sharp teeth! I have learned a valuable lesson the hard way. I shall take greater care, from now on, to steer clear of the sort of men who want a woman for only one thing.

I'm sure there are men who aren't like that but how does one tell? It's not something Mummy and I ever discussed. The girls seem to think such men are thin on the ground and they're very worldly-wise. However, I won't let this put me off. I will continue going to the dances if only because I love them so. They're so lively. A great distraction from the woes of the world. I will just have to make sure that I stay strictly within the bounds of the hall and the WC and be choosier with my dance partners.'

It was New Year's Eve. Edie gave her hair a final brush and went downstairs to meet Lily. For a change, they were allowed to wear civvies for the dance. Normally they had to stick to their uniforms so this was a rare outing for their nice clothes. She chose to wear her new dress and Vic's butterfly necklace.

Lily was waiting for her in the sitting room, looking very fetching with her hair up in the victory roll. 'Oh Edie, you look like Joan Fontaine in that dress. We'll have a job to tear the chaps away from you.'

'Oh gosh Lils, do you think it's too much? It's just that it's so pretty and everything else I have is so drab.'

'Of course not, you daft thing. You look lovely. A real English rose.'

The other girls were extremely good about the dress and paid her endless compliments but she did feel terribly self-conscious at first. Her other dresses were all so little girlish compared to theirs. She'd thought this one would make her fit in with them but now she saw that the opposite was true. It was far too splendid to be inconspicuous in her little crowd. Still, she would have to make the most of it. There was a real band on, they were playing 'Don't Sit Under the Apple Tree' and she already had an invitation to dance. Carried away in the excitement, she soon forgot her embarrassment and began to enjoy herself.

After more dances than she could remember, she stopped for a breather. She and Lily got themselves a drink and found their friends who were huddled together in a group, swapping stories about their dance partners. They were all giggling so loudly and having such a lark that she didn't notice someone come up behind her until they tapped on her shoulder. 'It's Edith isn't it?' She turned to look at the man smiling tentatively at her. He seemed familiar but she couldn't place him. 'Robert Goodwin,' he said and proceeded to open his arms wide, turn his head up to the ceiling and stick out his tongue. Then she recognised him.

'The man in the field. I'm so sorry. You look different in the full light.'

'So do you. It took me a while to work out where I'd seen you before. Care for a dance?'

They spent the rest of the night dancing and chatting. Robert was a good dancer and knew all the latest ones. As midnight approached he snatched her hand and pulled her into a great circle of people to sing 'Auld Lang Syne'. Then they joined the conga line snaking around the room, getting into all sorts of scrapes as the line got tighter. Edie laughed until her sides hurt. But the evening went too quickly and it was soon time for the final dance, a waltz. Robert led her back onto the floor and swirled her around the room. He was taller than her, but not so much that she had to crane her neck to gaze up at him. It was all rather dreamy and romantic. As if she really were Joan Fontaine, dancing with her leading man.

'I'll be sorry to see the end of this night. It's been tremendous fun,' he said. 'I wonder, Edith, if we could see each other again. I have a few days off next week. If you're free, perhaps we could go out for a drink?'

Edie already knew that she rather liked Robert Goodwin and with her limited experience, decided he was probably one of those few decent men her Newcastle friends had suggested were rare. Besides, he'd had plenty of opportunity to take advantage of her when they'd first met and had been the perfect gentleman. She couldn't envisage him doing any of those revolting things that other men did. 'Yes, Robert, I'd like that, but please, call me Edie. That's what my friends call me.'

As she walked back to the manor house with her friends, she and Lily linked arms. The talk was all of Edie's handsome pilot. Lily gave her arm a squeeze. 'I said you needed a bit of fun, didn't I?'

Edie was bristling with excitement. 'Yes you did, and I've

had a bucketful of it tonight. I don't know if I'll be able to sleep. What a pity I don't have the Jacksons' bicycle anymore.'

The following week, Edie was on the night shift so Robert suggested a countryside walk. She found him easy to talk to and ended up telling him about Jimmy and the sense of loss that left her unable to feel grounded. To her delight, Robert understood perfectly.

'It's not just losing your brother that does that,' he said. 'Though God knows that's hard enough. I have a brother. He's less than two years older than me and we've always been the best of pals. I even followed him into the RAF. I couldn't bear the thought of losing him. No, it's more than that. It's this damn war, Edie. I think we all feel it, although we may not be brave enough to admit it. It's changing everything and it's frightening. I can't imagine what the world will look like when it's finally over. Or even what any of us will be like.'

'Perhaps things will go back to normal when it's over,' she said.

'Perhaps you're right.' He flashed her a charming smile. 'I shall treat you to a slap-up tea when we get back to the village. How does that sound?'

'Perfectly marvellous.'

'Then onward and upward Miss Pinsent, and perhaps we'll have time for some sky tasting before your shift.'

The next time, Robert borrowed his brother's car. They went to the flicks in Bath and then on to a pub. When they got back to the manor house, he turned off the engine. 'I've had a super evening. I hope you have too?'

'Yes, it's been wonderful.'

'Edie, would you mind if I kissed you?'

She had visions of the last man who'd tried to kiss her. She'd already told Robert about him – not about him putting his hands on her breasts, that would be unseemly, but about his attempt to manhandle her tonsils – so he knew she wasn't going to stand for that kind of nonsense. On the other hand, she was keen on Robert and she was sure he wouldn't be so rough. 'No Robert, I don't think I would mind. In fact, I think it might be quite nice, if it were gentle.'

He laughed. 'You're very funny Edie, and very pretty.' He kissed her lips quite tenderly and she felt a tingle coursing through her body. Apart from those few rough, ham-fisted attempts at previous dances, she'd never been kissed by a man other than her father and brothers, if that was indeed kissing. It was more of a cheery peck really. But this? This was something quite different. She pulled away and stared at him in amazement. He looked concerned. 'Was that okay, Edie?'

She frowned. 'I don't know. Would you do that again?' He kissed her once more. Yes, there was definitely a sensation there. 'I'm fine thank you, Robert,' she said. 'I'm absolutely bloody lovely, thank you very much. Astonishing!'

They laughed together this time.

Sitting on her bed later, she wrote:

I have no idea if this feeling that he engenders in me is love, but that kiss! Oh, that kiss! It was electrifying. I'm having such adventures. Is it wrong of me to be enjoying this horrid war so much? Is it wrong of me to be so happy, with all the suffering happening around me? Robert feels we should grasp happiness whenever it comes. Especially

*because we don't know how long it might last. I think I agree. I must
take what comes in the knowledge that it may not last forever.'*

Winter turned into spring, and spring edged towards
summer. By now, Robert and Edie were quite an established
couple and he'd recently told her that he wanted her to
meet his brother, Tom, who was also stationed in the area.
They managed to get time off for Robert's twenty-second
birthday and he'd arranged afternoon tea in Bath. 'I've been
telling Tom so much about you that he's keen to meet you.
He's bringing his fiancée, Mina, along. Perhaps you know
her? She's billeted in the manor house too. Mina Jacobson.
She works in the Filter Room.'

Edie couldn't recall the name. Hardly surprising. There
were so many at the manor house and the shifts were so
varied that, unless you bunked with someone or worked with
them, it was unlikely that you'd know them.

'She's a great beauty,' Robert said, a little too wistfully, in
her opinion. 'Tom rather pipped me to the post with Mina.
Don't know if brotherly love stretches as far as forgiving him
for that.' He seemed amused at his joke. Edie gave a polite
laugh but underneath, she thought it rather unfeeling of
Robert to say such a thing. It was the first time he'd said
something hurtful to her and it cut to the quick. When she
saw Mina though, she understood his fascination with her.
She recognised her too. She'd seen her around the base.
Only a few times but she had a presence that was hard to
forget. As Robert pointed out, she was something of a
vision: tall and lean with an almost masculine athleticism
about her that defied the conventional ideas of beauty and
yet, she was so very beautiful. Her skin was fair, the sort that
tanned easily in summer, unlike Edie's which just went pink

and burned. Her hair was the colour of old gold and her features quite feline. A sort of Germanic sphinx. She reminded Edie of Marlene Dietrich.

Mina held out her arms dramatically and embraced Robert. The contrast between the two was startling. Robert was dark and exotic-looking with a wide, expressive face and big brown eyes. Tom was very similar, although not quite as handsome as his younger brother. Edie had never really considered Robert's looks but, now that she thought about it, he was a rather attractive man. Strange then that she'd never noticed it before. Honestly, she was so inexperienced about these things.

Tom took her hand in his and shook it vigorously. 'Edith, we meet at last.'

Mina held out her hand. She was so regal, Edie wasn't sure if she should shake it or kiss it. 'Hello, Edie. May we call you Edie? Robert, you dog, you underplayed Edie's prettiness. I feel quite threatened.' Edie was a tad embarrassed. It was obvious that she was no threat whatsoever to Mina but it was nice of her to say so. Perhaps she wasn't quite as haughty as she appeared.

Despite her initial apprehension, Edie enjoyed the afternoon immensely. The tea itself had been splendid and in one of the best restaurants in Bath. She'd eaten in restaurants before. Once with Robert and many times with her mother, but they'd been less ostentatious, particularly with Mummy who always thought it rather bad form to overindulge when there were so many hungry people living just a few miles away. Tom and Mina seemed to have no such constraints and the decadence of this spread was quite a thrill. To top it off, Mina turned out to be a real hoot. She and Tom were constantly ribbing each other. They were a proper double act. As funny as Flanagan and Allen.

After tea they found a park to walk in. Mina took her arm and shooed the men away. 'Off you go. Go and talk about planes and things. I want a few minutes alone with Edie so that I can find out what you're really like, Rob.'

'Okay my darling. We'll go and have a smoke over there while you girls have a little stroll and a gossip,' said Tom.

Edie wasn't really sure what she could tell Mina about Robert that she didn't already know. She needn't have worried. Discussing Robert had not been Mina's intention. 'Now that we've got rid of the boys, tell me all about yourself, Edie. I want to know everything about you.' It sounded more like an order than a request.

'There's not much to tell really,' said Edie, already fearing she was about to disappoint. 'I'm afraid I've led a rather boring life. I was hardly out of school before the WAAF.'

'Tell me about your childhood then. Your people.' Edie did as she was told. Mina seemed genuinely interested. 'So, you were a tomboy then? Like me. I was the only girl, with four brothers. Much to my poor dear mother's dismay, I'm afraid I turned out just like them. Always getting into scrapes and punch-ups. I'd much rather play in the fields than with dolls.'

'Same here. The boys always seemed to be having a much better time. I desperately wanted to be one too.'

'And yet here we are, doing our best to look feminine in these dreadful uniforms with two charming men in tow. Funny isn't it? Robert said you lost a brother at Crete?'

'Yes, I did. Jimmy's ship went down there.' It still hurt to say it.

'Are you heartbroken?'

The directness of Mina's question shook her and the answer came out unguarded. 'Yes, I suppose I am. I loved him terribly. He was my best friend and my protector. It's hard to know how to go on without him.'

Mina stopped walking and looked directly at her. 'You probably think me very glib, Edie but I assure you I'm really not. I've lost two brothers already to this damn war. The jokes and the silliness, they help to make the pain bearable. Look beyond this shallow exterior and you will see that I understand.' She took Edie's hand. 'I shall be your protector now, my darling. You and I will be great friends. I'm sure of it.'

8

OLD FRIENDS AND BEST FRIENDS

EDIE – 1943

'At last, I have a few days off. I could jolly well do with the respite. I'm feeling quite worn out.'

She was going home again for a few days. In a way, she would have preferred to stay at the waafery and spend the time with Robert, Mina and Tom but they weren't able to get leave. She knew that Robert and Tom were due to go on some kind of mission but they never discussed work. They had an unwritten rule about that sort of thing – 'careless talk costs lives'. Careless writing too. She never wrote anything in her journals about work. They'd all signed the Official Secrets Act and weren't really supposed to keep diaries but she wasn't the only one that did, and she could no more stop writing than she could stop eating. She reasoned that, as long as she kept them for her personal thoughts, social events and sketches, they were an acceptable minor indiscretion.

Before she left, she gave Robert a sketch that she'd drawn of him. She thought the likeness a bit off but he'd been very pleased with it and promised to keep it with him in his breast pocket, close to his heart. Terribly romantic. He asked her to sign it and she wrote:

'To Robert
With fondest wishes
Edie.'

'Fondest wishes' seemed rather formal but 'with love' was far too forward. Besides, she wasn't really sure what love was, love between a man and a woman that is. Dolly, the new girl who slept in the bed next to her was endlessly talking about love. She seemed to fall in and out of it almost every week. Sometimes twice a week. She was younger than Edie but that didn't seem to hold her back. Lily said she was flighty and a bit too full of herself. It was true that Dolly did seem to think rather a lot of herself. She was convinced she looked like Betty Grable. Many of the airmen seemed to think so too which was probably why she was so often in love.

Her father wasn't there to meet her this time. He was at work. Instead, she took the local train to Selly Oak. It was a long walk to the house from there but it was a pleasant enough afternoon for late summer. The route home seemed odd with all the street signs removed. How were strangers supposed to find their way? That was the point, she reminded herself. Strangers could just as easily be Nazis. Her parents had told her there hadn't been any bombings for quite a while now, which was a relief. Before she'd been called up, they'd been rather more frequent and she'd hated those nights spent in the Anderson shelter. Still, the scars they left were visible to her now as she walked through the battered streets. There was a barrage balloon in the middle of the recreation ground where, as a child, she'd played games with her brothers. How strange that was.

There was no one in the house but she found Hannah in the garden. Before the war, only the far end of the garden had been used to grow a little fruit and vegetables. Now it was one huge vegetable patch. 'You look more grown up every time you come home,' said Hannah. 'Here, take these would you, love?' She gave Edie a basket of vegetables to carry inside.

Back in the kitchen, Hannah poured them both a cup of stewed tea from the pot. They sat down at the kitchen table. 'I thought Mummy might be here,' said Edie.

'She'll be back soon. She's at the WVS. She's been doing quite a lot of it lately. I think it helps to take her mind off things.'

As if on cue, her mother came in through the front door. Unlike her usual elegant attire, she was wearing a rather severe dark green uniform. 'Hello, my darling,' she said, bustling through the hallway. 'So sorry I wasn't here to greet you, we had something of an emergency. Never mind, I'm here now.'

'Cup of tea, Mrs P?' said Hannah.

'Yes please. Can you believe it, I've been serving drinks all day and haven't had time for one myself? Hannah my dear, I stopped off at the butcher and managed to get some rabbit. Do you think you'll be able to do something with it for this evening?'

'I'll put it in the pie,' said Hannah. 'You go and put your feet up, Mrs P. I'll bring your tea in.'

Her mother did as she was instructed and sat down with Edie in the sitting room. Edie watched her perch nervously on the edge of her seat. She looked as if she might take off at any minute. 'I'm going to talk to your father about taking some of them in. We have plenty of spare room at the moment.'

'Hmm?' Edie realised she'd been so busy watching her mother, she hadn't been listening to what she was saying.

'The refugees, darling. They need somewhere to stay. I'm going to talk to Daddy about taking some of them in. You don't mind them using your room, do you? It's only a temporary thing.'

'Absolutely Mummy. I don't mind at all. That's a splendid idea.'

'Well, one has to do one's bit. Why don't you come with me tomorrow? We could do with an extra hand.'

Edie thought of those days in her childhood when her mother dragged her around the slums to hand out food and clothing to the poor. It had been months since she'd had some proper time off. She could really do without a day of duty. 'I rather thought I'd have a rest tomorrow. I'm really quite tired, Mummy.' If she didn't immediately regret those words, her mother's disapproving expression told her that she should have. She may have wanted a day off duty but duty clearly wasn't inclined to grant it.

'We're all tired, Edith. No doubt we will continue to be tired long after this awful war is over but we have a responsibility to each other and our country to fight it.'

Edie cringed. She'd been well and truly told off. 'Sorry Mummy. That was very selfish of me. Of course I'll come and help.'

Her mother patted Edie's knee. 'Good girl.'

She slept so well that night, she didn't even hear her father come in from his Home Guard watch. After months of hard 'biscuit' mattresses and itchy brown blankets, it was lovely to be back in her own soft bed, under her cosy eiderdown. She got up feeling refreshed and ready to face a day of duty. They spent the day in a church hall near the city centre. Edie was surprised by the number of people that came in for the meagre sandwiches and watery tea on offer. Many of them were homeless or were living in rooms, having been bombed out of their own homes. Mostly it was mothers and children, or the elderly. There were refugees there too, from Europe and the Channel Islands and a small number of serving men and women, spending a few hours in between trains. Some of the volunteers had made biscuits and cakes from their own rations which were popular with the children. Her mother took some of Hannah's. Edie realised that living at the base had rather shielded her from all of this. She could see now why Mummy had wanted her to come along and she was glad she'd relented. She only saw her mother a few times throughout the day but she could tell how much it absorbed her. She understood then what Hannah had meant about it taking her mind off things. Here, she didn't have time to think about the loss of Jimmy, or the safety of her remaining children.

Seeing her old friend, Catherine there had been another surprise. The last time they'd seen each other was Christmas and they'd hardly had time to speak but she remembered Catherine saying she was in the ATS. When they stopped for a quick break, Edie asked her if was on leave too. Catherine shook her head. 'Come and see me tomorrow. I'll explain then.' It was all very mysterious.

They took the train back to Selly Oak. On the walk back from the station, Edie asked if her mother would mind if she didn't go the next day. 'It's just that Catherine's at home too and we thought it would be nice to catch up.'

'I don't mind you not going, but do be careful.'

'I'm only going to her house. Nothing to worry about,' said Edie, confused. Surely, she was quite safe walking to Catherine's?

'What has Catherine told you?'

'About what?'

'About her … circumstances.' Her mother's expression hardly changed but there was a sharpness in her tone.

'Nothing. Mummy, has something happened?'

'I'm afraid it has. Catherine's been a very silly girl. No doubt she'll explain tomorrow but that may have to be the last time you visit her until the whole business has been concluded.'

The suspense was killing Edie so she visited Catherine as soon as she could the next morning. She was still absolutely clueless about the thing her mother had referred to as 'the whole business'. Mummy had refused to be drawn further on the subject. Whatever it was, it had to be bad.

She'd barely stepped into the house before Catherine grabbed her arm and bundled her back out of the door and down the path. 'Let's go for a stroll in the park.'

Edie didn't have to wait long for the story to come out. 'I've been rather foolish.' Even though they were sitting on a park bench with no one else around, Catherine was whispering. 'I've got myself in the family way.'

Edie gasped. 'You're having a–?'

'Baby. Yes. As you can imagine my parents are terribly upset. They're trying to keep it very hush-hush but I know it's got out. I'm virtually a social leper at the moment.'

So that was it. Catherine had committed the worst sin a young lady could possibly commit. Edie didn't have the heart to tell her about her own mother's reaction. 'What will you do?'

Catherine shrugged. 'I'm not sure yet. It rather depends

on the baby's father. If he offers to marry me and we do it quickly then we might just be able to save face. If not, then I'll be packed off to some godforsaken place to have the baby quietly and it'll be given up for adoption.' She took a handkerchief from her gas mask case and sniffed into it. 'Oh Edie, it's awful. Daddy's furious and Mummy can't look me in the eye.'

Edie grasped her hand. 'Oh you poor dear.' She couldn't think what else to say.

When her mother came home, she didn't ask about Catherine. That night, her father arranged a night off so that he could spend a few precious hours with his daughter before her return. They sat at the dining room table long after they'd finished eating, reminiscing about those trips to stargaze on the Lickey Hills. It was a shame they couldn't do that while the war was on. They discussed taking in some refugees and agreed they should do it. All in all, it was a lovely evening and she didn't give Catherine another thought.

The next day her parents came with her to the station. It was only as her train departed that she realised she'd forgotten to tell them about Robert.

Before returning to work, she had one more day off. She'd come back early because Robert, Mina and Tom had managed to get leave too. They agreed to spend the day in the Cotswolds together before the summer was gone. They took a picnic with them and even managed to acquire two bottles of wine, courtesy of Mina who seemed to have a knack for accessing things that most people would have found difficult. Robert had recently purchased a camera, a Box Brownie, and had been snapping away at them all day.

'Let's try a group shot.' He placed the camera on a tripod and arranged them all on the rug for the best position. 'Everyone stay quite still and look into the camera. I'm going to press the button and make a dash for it before it goes off. No, don't fidget, Edie. Mina, you're doing that on purpose. Everyone, smile.' They all sat rigid with stiff smiles on their faces. 'Right, here we go.' Robert suddenly sprinted over to the rug. As he reached them, he lost his footing and slid along the ground, scrambling up at the last minute into position behind Edie. It was so comical all four of them erupted into hysterics, just as the camera clicked. 'Oh blast,' he said. 'That was the last one on the film and I've ruined it.'

'Wait and see,' said Mina. 'It will probably be the best one. You must get copies for all of us so that we can remember what a lovely day it's been. The best of friends having the best of times.'

9

A WEDDING AND A PROPOSAL

EDIE – 1943

'I have been graced with more happiness than I thought possible. I must be the luckiest person in the world.'

That was the last thing she'd written before going on duty. The thought of it had sustained her through the night. Of all the shifts, nights were her least favourite and this one had been hectic. They'd all been hectic lately. All she wanted to do was have a cup of tea, something to eat and sleep, in that order. The lift rumbled up to the surface taking her and the other WAAFs from the damp, chill air of the underground rooms to the relative warmth of the autumn morning. The bright sunshine hit their faces and they instinctively pulled the peaks of their caps down slightly to protect their eyes, before setting off for the NAAFI canteen. Someone was moaning about having to sleep through all this glorious weather. Probably Dolly. She was always moaning about one thing or another. Edie wasn't really listening. She was too busy watching the person coming towards them. The sun was nearly blinding her but she could recognise that figure, that way of moving, anywhere. Mina didn't so much walk as flow, like liquid. Her back was to the sun and it had the effect of appearing to bounce off her, giving her hair a glowing sheen. She was in uniform but it could just as easily have been Haute Couture. No one could fill a uniform like Mina. She was perfect.

'Edie, come quick, I have news!' She grabbed Edie's arm and pulled her away from the other girls. 'Oh my darling, I know you're probably exhausted but I simply had to tell you first. I'm bursting with excitement. Let me give you my news then I promise, you can go to bed. Tom and I are getting married.'

Edie set aside her tiredness. She was happy for her friend and for herself too; happy that Mina had chosen to give her the news first, above all others. It was a confirmation that they cared for each other. Mina was the glamorous older sister she'd never had. Some of the other girls weren't so keen on her, Dolly in particular was always saying spiteful things about her, but Edie adored her. She was both honoured and proud to have found a best friend in Mina, and now her best friend was marrying the wonderful Tom. They were already engaged though, so it wasn't exactly news, but the timing was. 'I thought you'd already planned a wedding next year?'

'Oh yes we had but Tom's lost another of his pals and was so down last night, we decided that we'd rather not wait. So we're going to get a quickie at the registry office. The folks will be livid but we're set on it. I'm sure Pa will be able to pull some strings and find us an available spot, and you, my delightful dear, will be my bridesmaid, maid of honour, witness thingy.'

. . .

If Mina's parents had been livid, it didn't last long but then, who could be angry for any length of time with Mina? A registry office in London with a suitable slot was found thanks to Mina's father who did, as she'd predicted, pull some strings. Time off was granted. There would be a small reception at Mina's parents' house afterwards but no honeymoon to speak of. Just two days in Brighton. They had no marital home, no threshold for Tom to carry her over. After two days of wedded bliss, each would go back to their stations and carry on with their wartime duties in the knowledge that they'd pledged themselves to each other until death parted them. There would be time to do the normal things that married couples did after the war, if they were both lucky enough to get through it.

It was the morning before the wedding. Tom and Robert picked up Edie and Mina from the waafery and they journeyed to London together. As they drove through the city, it was impossible not to notice the devastation wreaked on it by the Blitz. They passed vast spaces of ruin and rubble, spaces that had once been thriving streets. Edie felt the tragedy of London's demise. She'd come here a few times before the war and had found it such a wondrous place. It was sad to see it in its current state. That said, there were some establishments that had managed to withstand the bombing and come out of it relatively unscathed. The Strand Palace hotel was one such place. Mina had booked rooms for them there. She strode into the lobby with Tom at her side, and Robert and Edie following, a little sheepishly, behind. The first thing Edie observed about the hotel was that it was rather grand. The second was that it was full of American soldiers. The Yanks were all eyes for Mina with her angular beauty and her liquid walk. Those eyes openly looked her up and down and followed her as she passed them by, even though she was quite clearly with Tom. Edie thought them rather rude and uncouth.

Before they had time to settle in properly, Mina announced that she was taking Edie shopping. She'd asked Edie to wear her blue silk dress for the wedding but she, apparently, needed to be finished off. 'You need some accessories. My treat,' she said. They went to some exclusive little shops where the lack of clothing rations didn't appear to be an issue. Mina chose for her a jaunty hat with a peacock feather, and a pair of powder blue kidskin gloves, embroidered with tiny red and blue flowers. 'I've asked Ma to send over a little fur cape for you to borrow to keep the chill off,' she said. 'She'll do it but she's furious with me because I've refused to spend tonight at home. She thinks it's bad luck and bad form to see one's future hubby the night before the wedding. In my opinion that's silly old claptrap. Besides, we're in London. We have to make the most of it.'

With the shopping complete, they returned to the hotel, once more having to walk past the Americans with their lecherous looks. As the lift doors closed, one of them let out a long, drawn out whistle. Edie tutted but Mina seemed to be oblivious to it. 'We're meeting the boys in the bar at six, E. I'll call for you just before.'

They dined in the hotel and afterwards went to a nightclub. Edie had never been to one before. It was so much flashier than the NAAFI dances and again, she had that feeling of being in a film. With Mina, Tom and Robert, it was quite possible to believe she was in the presence of film stars. She could hardly believe her luck.

They fell naturally into couples as they walked back to the hotel. Mina and Tom were ahead of them, talking. It was too far to hear what they were saying but Mina's laughter found its way back to them. They were obviously having great fun. Robert took Edie's arm. 'Did you notice? No air raids tonight. Jerry must be on our side.' He winked. 'Perhaps Mina's father's managed to pull strings with Adolf too.'

Edie giggled. 'Robert, that's an awful thing to say.'

'Only joking. It's been quite the loveliest night though, hasn't it?'

'Yes, it has.' It was true, the evening had been wonderful. But now that it was coming to a close, her earlier excitement had been replaced by apprehension. She couldn't understand why she wasn't happier. Tonight had been one of the most thrilling nights of her life. Without a doubt, this last year had been a complete change for her. A change for the better. Especially since meeting Robert. What's more, Mina had helped her come to terms with Jimmy's death and had given her a new optimism. Life seemed to be opening out before her, and yet something was not quite right. Up ahead, Tom and Mina stopped to kiss. The sheer passion of it made her blush. Was that it? Did she want what they had?

Robert glanced over to them, then took her hand. 'Edie, this wedding has got me thinking. Fact is, I've been considering it for a while now but, I suppose this whole business with Tom rushing it through with Mina, well…' He looked at his feet. For once his self-assurance appeared to have deserted him. He seemed shy and embarrassed.

'Well what, Robert? What is it?'

'Dammit, I'm so bad at this sort of thing. What I'm trying to say is, why don't we get hitched too?'

'Are you asking me to marry you?'

'Yes, of course. What did you think I was asking? Well, Edie? Shall we? Will you? Will you marry me, Edith Pinsent?'

So many thoughts were rushing through her head right then. Too many to grasp and take account of. All she knew was, it seemed like this *was* the thing she wanted. Robert stood over her, his hands clasping hers, waiting for an answer. 'Yes of course I will, you idiot. Although I must say, that was a terribly shoddy proposal.' His furrowed brow softened, replaced by an ear to ear grin. He swept her up and kissed her so amorously she blushed for the second time that night. The heat of the blush filled her completely and she was happy again.

Mina's wedding outfit was a mid-length, off-white chiffon and silk halter neck dress with a matching fur jacket. The jacket was another of her mother's and the dress was made from a ball gown Mina already had. Edie had helped take Mina's measurements and urgent instructions had been sent to a seamstress to get it ready for the big day. There hadn't been time to buy anything new, or even for fittings so it was all a bit hit and miss but Mina didn't seem to mind at all. Perhaps it was because she knew that whatever she wore, she would be stunning. If that was so, she was right. Although, in fairness, the seamstress had done a remarkably good job.

The marriage ceremony seemed to be over in a flash. A photographer took a few pictures of the couple outside the registry office and then they were all whisked away to Mina's parents' home for the wedding reception.

During the reception, Robert introduced Edie to his parents. They were not at all what she expected. Robert and Tom were so full of energy, so warm, that she'd assumed their parents would be the same but they were, in fact, quite the opposite. They were rather cold and foreboding and for the first time in her life, Edie felt looked down upon. As if she were some cheap floozy Robert had just picked up on the streets. She imagined how they would react to the news that she and him were unofficially engaged and concluded they might need more time to warm to her. She took Robert to one side and whispered, 'Let's not say anything yet about our engagement. This is Tom and Mina's special day. It wouldn't be fair.'

He seemed to read her thoughts. 'You're concerned about my parents. Don't worry darling, they're not always quite this bad. They're just not happy about the speed of the wedding. They think it's unseemly. It doesn't seem to matter to them that lots of people are getting married quickly these days. I'm afraid they're rather old fashioned, but you're right. We'll let my brother and his new wife enjoy their day and give Mother and Father time to get over it before announcing anything publicly. I have a confession though. I've already told Tom. I couldn't help myself.'

'I have one too. I've told Mina.' They laughed at each other's foolishness.

'We're two peas in a pod you and I,' he said. 'We were made for one another.'

Tom came up beside them. 'Sorry to interrupt but Edie's presence is required by my wife. My wife? Hmm, haven't quite got my head around that one yet. Right! To the drawing room, Edie. The photographer awaits.'

Mina was posing for the photographer in the drawing room. 'Nearly done, E. Then it's your turn.' She leant back on the chair and turned towards the camera, her lips slightly parted into a seductive pout.

Next to the photographer was Mina's mother, immaculately turned out and doing her best to look stern. 'For goodness sake Mina, this is your wedding day not one of those vulgar American films you insist on watching. Do try to look more respectable.'

'Ma, you're such a bore.' Mina flung her head back and let out a loud raucous laugh. Sometimes she laughed like a man. These were the times Edie saw the tomboy in her.

'Enough,' said her mother. 'Edith my dear, please take a seat and show my daughter how to behave like a young lady.'

'Yes E, do show me,' mocked Mina. 'Imagine you're being cast for one of those vulgar American films. Look up towards me, darling. Imagine you're a star.'

Edie did as she was told and imagined she was Joan Fontaine, fair, wholesome and beautiful.

That night Robert came to her room. She was unschooled in the intimacies of men and women. Her mother had never spoken of them, except to say that there were things that a woman was expected to do as part of her wifely duties and she must bear them with dignity. She had no idea what those things were but she guessed Mina was doing them right now. By rights, the time had not yet come for her to find out but she let him in anyway. It wouldn't be that long before they were married and she was too curious to wait. As he removed her nightdress, she shivered and covered her breasts and private parts with her hands and arms. A wisp of hair fell across her face. He brushed it away with his index finger. 'Don't be afraid, my love.'

She grimaced. 'I can't help it. I don't know what to expect. You're the first, of course.'

'And the last too, I hope. Don't worry. I'll guide you. I'll take great care to be gentle.'

10

UNBEARABLE WIFELY DUTIES

EDIE – 1943

'What were these unbearable wifely duties Mummy hinted at? I have no idea but I'm sure it can't have been intercourse. Intercourse is absolutely splendid.'

That night, at the Strand Palace was a revelation. As he'd promised, Robert had been gentle with her. When she'd bled a little afterwards, he told her that it was quite normal for a woman on her first time. She didn't ask but she gathered, from his knowledge, that it wasn't his first time. That irked her a little. Not because he was more experienced than her, but because he was allowed to be so. It was almost expected of him. It brought back her childhood indignation about being treated differently from her brothers. Not for long though: she was too busy making up for lost time.

They stayed up all night, talking about their future life, when all of this was over. Just before dawn, she asked him if they might try intercourse again. This time he was a little more forceful but she didn't mind that. In fact, she rather enjoyed the physical reaction it created in her body when he thrust himself back and forth inside her. She was overtaken by something she could only describe as primeval. It erupted, from nowhere and made her thrash and squirm with pleasure. She gripped his arms and pulled herself up to his mouth, mad for his lips on hers. It was as if it wasn't her doing it but another version of herself. A version she had absolutely no control over.

Afterwards, he folded himself around her and they lay in bed, quietly intertwined. A while later, he sat up and lit a cigarette. He took a long inhale and gave her a quizzical look. 'You're a rum girl, Edith Pinsent.'

She sat up too, not sure whether to be offended or pleased at his observation. 'Whatever do you mean?'

He ran his fingers through her loose hair so lightly it felt like a caress. 'I mean I've never met another girl like you. You know, you're quite wild.'

'Am I?'

He laughed. 'Yes, I rather think you are.' He put out his cigarette. 'I'd better go while it's still early. We don't want to be giving you a bad reputation, do we?'

'That would never do. Your parents already think I'm some kind of jezebel as it is.'

He laughed again. 'They'll come round. If it makes you feel any better, they think the same of Mina. It's only money and connections that save her. Her mother's related to aristocracy and her father's family made a fortune in banking.'

'Shame on you, Robert. That's a dreadful thing to say about your parents.'

He pulled on his clothes. 'I know but I'm sorry to say it's true. Mina probably wouldn't have been their choice for a daughter-in-law but, like so many in our class, my parents revere the upper classes, so she just about gets away with it.'

She prodded him playfully. 'My goodness, I hadn't realised I was going to be marrying a communist.'

'Not a communist but maybe a socialist. I think I might like to get into politics when this war is done. If you could bear it, that is. Mr Attlee makes a lot of sense and I'd like to do something to make sure we haven't fought this war for nothing.' He kissed her. 'Goodbye, my sweet. See you at breakfast.'

The next two months passed quickly. Since that night at the Strand Palace, she and Robert had been intimate whenever the opportunity presented itself. Last month, they'd even had intercourse in a field, in the middle of the afternoon. The fear of being caught was an added titillation. The cold, soggy ground less so. It was now December. They hadn't seen any snow yet but it was chilly and wet. Too wet for such capers. They reluctantly agreed to curtail their field trips until spring. Good news came quick on the heels of disappointment though. Tom and Mina managed to rent a cottage on the outskirts of the village. It was reasonably remote so they were able to use it too, without drawing attention to themselves. Mina told her that lots of girls at the base were doing the same thing and most people were turning a blind eye. Society was being forced into a new outlook by this war. People were having to compromise on their old values and beliefs. All the same, for the sake of propriety, she and Tom told the locals that Edie and Robert were already married. In many ways it was true. A marriage certificate was only rubber stamping their already unshakeable commitment to each other.

She hadn't been lucky enough to get leave over Christmas this year. Neither had her brother, Vic, but her mother wrote quite positively about it. Her parents had given Hannah the time off over Christmas and she was going to spend it with her sister for a change. Mummy and Daddy were going to pass their Christmas Day at a welfare centre, helping to provide dinner for the remaining homeless and the refugees. Edie sighed. It seemed there was never a day when her parents weren't doing good. They were quite relentless in it.

She was trying to write a reply. She didn't normally have a problem with her letters home but this one was proving tricky. What to say? She wasn't allowed to write about work and she couldn't tell them what she'd really been up to in her spare time. They'd be horrified. At last it came to her. She would tell them about Robert. Not about their unofficial engagement. She'd give it time for them to get used to the idea of their little girl with a beau first. Maybe the next time they both had leave, Robert could come with her to Birmingham to meet them and officially ask Daddy for her hand in marriage. She filled her pen and wrote:

'Dear Mummy and Daddy,
I have to tell you, I've met the most splendid man.'

11

THE MAN HIMSELF

NETTA – 2019

Netta closed the diary. 'Robert then, not Bill?'

'Looks that way, doesn't it?' said Frank.

'So where, or when, does Bill come into it?'

'I suppose we'll have to read on but, since this is the last one for the forties, we may never know. I can't see any more until they pick up again in the fifties.'

'Bugger. That's frustrating.' She examined the photo of the four young people. So, now she knew who they were. Edie had even told them why they all looked as if someone had told them the funniest joke. 'They seem to be having the most marvellous time. It's intoxicating isn't it? The happiness just shines out of them.' She pointed to the young man kneeling lopsidedly behind Edie, his hand on her shoulder. 'That has to be Robert.'

'I guess so, and that must be Tom behind Mina.'

She nodded, still transfixed. 'They look so in love.'

'Robert and Edie, or Tom and Mina?'

'All of them. I wonder what happened to them.' She picked up the photo of Edie in the dress. 'This must have been the one taken at Tom and Mina's wedding. She does look as if she's imagining she's a movie star, doesn't she? It has to be the one.'

There was something quite disturbing about reading young Edie's words. Although Netta had been getting used to the idea that she didn't really know who Edith Pinsent was, she still imagined that she had a grasp of what Edie might think or feel. Now, she realised that all her impressions had come from the musings of someone whose life was behind her. They were thoughtful, measured and, in many ways, rather poignant. This new insight forced her to rethink. In contrast to the more recent journals, the earlier ones had been full of wonder and excitement, in spite of the terrible things that were happening at the time. Edie was on the verge of womanhood. Her future uncertain and desperately grieving, she was still eager for adventure. She realised that the person she'd conjured up was just one side of her. Edie was much more complex than that. She'd had a life once that was full of joy and hope and love. What happened to that sweet, funny young woman, and what happened to her friends and the man she agreed to marry? With no diaries to tell them, how would they ever find out?

She was awake in the middle of the night. After a great deal of tossing and turning she gave up and went downstairs. Her footsteps disturbed Maud and Betty and before she could reach the bottom of the stairs, they were there waiting for her. They followed her into the kitchen and watched her with earnestly optimistic expressions while she made a drink of hot chocolate. Their optimism was rewarded with a doggy treat each and they followed her into the breakfast room, presumably hoping for more.

Netta sat down in her usual seat. Her head and body

ached. Perhaps she was coming down with something, or perhaps she was just tired. She looked over to the empty chair on the other side of the table. 'It's all your fault Edith Pinsent. You've set me off again.' At the mention of Edith's name, Maud cocked her head to one side and let out a little whine and Netta immediately felt guilty. She scratched the underside of Maud's chin. 'Sorry Maud, I didn't mean to upset you.' The little dog pushed down on her fingers, seeming to want more and Netta took that as a sign that she was forgiven. All the same, she decided to keep her thoughts to herself. It was pointless saying them out loud anyway since only the dogs could hear her and besides, it wasn't really Edie's fault that her diaries had triggered something; something she'd been repressing for a long while. It was the way Edie wrote about her friends, especially Mina. It took her back to her university days and even before then. More precisely, it took her back to Claire, her best friend from her first day in senior school and right through university in Manchester. Claire, who she thought she'd be friends with forever, until Colin Grey came along.

She went into the study and retrieved one of the boxes that had come down from the loft a few days earlier. It was one of two that Colin had brought over last December. The result of a clear-out, he'd said but she knew what it was really. A peace offering. His way of saying sorry for putting her through all those years of misery; sorry for plundering all the things that made her Netta Wilde and turning her into dull, dreary Annette Grey; sorry for sucking the life out of her and leeching off her for much of their marriage and nearly all of their divorce, until she'd put a stop to it. She'd received it politely, had a quick look at the photos and swiftly put them away when she saw who was in them. After gifting her old Clash T-shirt and beret to Liza she'd hidden the boxes away in the loft, not expecting to have to see them for a long time but they'd come back down in the clear-out and now she was faced with them again. She might have been able to ignore them had it not been for Edie and the things she'd written about Mina. They reminded her of the bond she'd had with Claire, before they'd had a blazing row that blasted their friendship to smithereens. That wasn't just it, of course. The way Edie wrote about Robert; the feelings she had for him and the sex – yes, the sex – that reminded her of someone else. It reminded her of Doogie, the boy she'd loved in university who became the man she later had an affair with, who became the father of her miscarried child and was the reason Colin broke her into a thousand pieces.

She took out the photos one by one and saw the images of her younger self, full of that youthful confidence that Edie had. There were pictures of her and Claire, and Sasha who'd joined their little clique in Manchester. She went through them all until she found the one she was looking for – a group photo of her with her friends, 1986 if she wasn't mistaken. Her in the middle, Claire and Sasha on one side, Doogie on the other with his arm around her and his mate, Mac, next to him. They looked like they were having a ball, just like Edie's photo. Netta closed her eyes and tried to imagine herself back then. In spite of everything – her children, her new friends, her new life – in spite of all of those things, what she wouldn't give to be able to dive back into that photo right now and relive that moment, that life, again.

She shivered. It was too cold to be sitting up at this hour. She got up and peered out into the garden, only half-lit by the moon, hoping to see the vixen that had been a regular visitor last year but there was no sign. After giving the dogs a goodnight pat she returned the photos to their box, carried it into the study and went back to bed.

When he finished work the next day, Frank came over to give her a hand looking through the books and boxes from the loft, the smell of which now filling the study. As Kelly had pointed out in her own inimitable style, it was quite overwhelming and, after a while it was beginning to get to their throats. 'Coffee?' said Netta.

Frank rolled his eyes. 'Is that what you call that instant muck? Go on then. Anything to get this taste out of my mouth.'

'I've still got some of Neil's Christmas cake, if you're interested?'

'Now you're talking. I'll open the window a little to get rid of this stale air.'

When she got back into the study, she found him sitting in an armchair by the window, next to an open box. He had some photos in his hand. She recognised them at once. They weren't Edie's, they were the ones she'd been looking at in the middle of the night. She knew before she reached him which photo he'd be looking at. It was the one she really would have preferred him not to see. She cursed herself: she should have put them somewhere else. He was concentrating so much on that picture that he didn't even hear her come in. It wasn't until she was right on top of him that he noticed her. He looked up, a trace of guilt on his face. 'Sorry, I didn't realise it wasn't one of Edie's until I'd started looking through it. I should have known when I saw the records. I don't think Edie was ever a punk fan.' He gave a little laugh but he still looked flustered and he still had the photo in his hand. 'You look amazing. I love that hairstyle.' His Belfast accent was stronger than usual. Perhaps that was what discomfort did to him. She held out her hand to take the photo back but he wasn't ready to relinquish it yet. 'Who are the others?'

'That's Claire, that's Sasha, Mac and Doogie.' She speeded the names up towards the end only realising after that she'd drawn more attention to them.

'Oh, so that's the man himself,' he said, his finger aimed at Doogie. 'He's a good-looking fella. I almost fancy him myself. No wonder Colin hated him. You were a great-looking couple. You smoulder.'

She laughed but it came out false. She'd never been embarrassed about anything with Frank, until now. Of course he knew all about Doogie. He'd been the first of her closest friends and family to hear her confession. All of that was out in the open now. No more secrets, and Doogie was in the past but, as she found out last night, there was something about that photo that still stirred her.

She was saved from replying by Will and Kelly returning from work. Kelly must have called in at the shop for him on her way home. They took off their warm coats and stood at the open doorway. 'All right?' said Kelly.

Will stepped into the room. 'It's looking a bit tidier in here now. Smells slightly better as well.'

'That'll be the open window,' said Frank. He handed the photo to Netta but before she could put it away Kelly was on top of her. 'Is that you? Oh, he's hot. Oh my god, is that Doogie?'

'Yes, it is me,' said Netta, trying to deflect the conversation away from Doogie.

'Yeah, but is that Doogie though? Is that him?'

'Er, yes, that's him.'

'Fucking hell, Net. He's like a male model or something.'

'Let's see,' said Will. He examined the photo. 'You looked a lot like Liza, Mum.' A wave of relief washed over her. They were on safe ground now. Good old Will. Then he went and spoiled it. 'Who's that?'

'That's Claire. We were best friends at school and we went to the same uni.'

He frowned. 'You never talk about her. What happened to her?'

'We lost touch.' Netta snatched back the photo. 'A long time ago.'

A glance at the clock told her it was two-forty. Not that she'd needed to check because she'd woken at the same time every night for the past week. For a while, she lay in bed willing herself to go back to sleep and not think about the dream. It didn't work. She was still awake, and she was still thinking about it. She tried to focus on something else instead and then Claire popped into her consciousness. Shit! That was almost as bad. As if it couldn't get any worse, the thought that was stuck inside her head was the last time they'd seen each other. The moment she knew their friendship was over. 'Fucking Stepford wife now, are you? What the fuck has he done to you, Netta?' Those were the words that broke their unbreakable bond. They'd been inseparable. Nothing came between them, not even Doogie. Then Colin came along and everything went to pot. She hadn't seen Claire since before the affair with Doogie. God knows what she would have made of her after that. But in the last week she'd begun to realise that she missed her. Or maybe, it was just that she missed what they were?

She pulled on her dressing gown, grabbed her phone and a journal from the bedside table and tiptoed downstairs. Maud was waiting in the hall for her. They seemed to have got themselves into a little routine, the two of them. Sometimes Betty would be there too but not tonight. When Liza was staying over, she slept in her room. Netta made herself a cup of herbal tea. The tea was a desperate measure, suggested by Neil after she told him she wasn't sleeping. He and Chris guzzled the stuff in vast quantities, and they were the most serene people she knew. She'd also bought some herbal tablets that promised to calm you down before bedtime. Neither seemed to be having the desired effect. Well, not quite true. She was dropping off just fine. Her problem was staying asleep. She corrected herself. Her problem was the dream.

Maud settled down by her feet when she sat at the breakfast room table. Netta took a mouthful of tea. The taste of it made her wince. It was going to take some time to get used to this stuff. She opened the journal. With only the light from the kitchen on, it was too dim for reading but that wasn't really her intention. Instead, she gazed at the photo she'd hidden in there, the one Frank had been so interested in. What was it he'd said about her and Doogie? They smouldered. She could understand why he might think that but all she could see now was Doogie looking at her accusingly, just as he had been doing every night in her dream.

It was the baby – Doogie's baby, except he didn't know anything about her because she never told him. Last year, fifteen years after the miscarriage, when Netta finally gave the child a name - Ada, after her beloved Granny Wilde – she allowed herself to imagine what Ada might have looked like and she thought she'd found peace, but lately she'd come to realise it wasn't quite that easy and those bloody photos had only made it worse. She could have blamed Colin for bringing them over but the truth was she didn't need them to bring Doogie Chambers back to the forefront of her mind. He was never far away and never would be, until she told him the truth about why she walked away from him all those years ago.

The quiet stillness was broken by a sharp shriek of a bark coming from beyond the garden. There was a fox out there somewhere but it was too dark to see. Netta hoped it was the vixen. She hadn't seen her or her cubs for months. It was silly but she was worried about them. She guessed the young foxes had left home by now but where was the mother? She'd been fearing the worst for a while and had even taken to scouting the area on her walks with Betty, looking for a carcass on the roads and verges but so far, she'd found nothing.

Maud looked out into the garden then dropped her head down on to her paws. In spite of the nuisance of getting up in the night, Netta loved this time. Just her, Maud and the spirit of Edie. She didn't believe in ghosts but sometimes it was as if she could feel Edie guiding her, particularly in this room. Using the torch on her phone for extra light, she flicked through the pages of the diary until she came to the one she was looking for. An entry in March 2017. In amongst the mundane day to day thoughts, Edie had written:

'Lately, I have come to realise that the fear of being found out is worse than the finding out.'

Netta came across it last year, shortly after Colin's partner Arianne had told her that she'd known for years about the affair and miscarriage. The shock news caused some sort of physical trauma in her and it was while she was recovering that she stumbled across this random but appropriate entry. After reading it, she decided to tell her family and friends everything. Edie had been right too. It hadn't been easy to speak about it but the overwhelming response was caring and sympathetic. Even her parents. Even her children. No one blamed her for it and no one made her feel dirty. It was one of the best pieces of advice she'd ever received but one thing puzzled her. Why did Edie write it? Netta had searched this journal several times and couldn't find any clues as to a possible explanation. Of course, it could be absolutely nothing. She'd read enough of Edie's diaries to see their entries were chaotic. Lengthy ramblings were interspersed with the occasional profound remark, a beautiful drawing or a recipe. At first glance, you might think they were the unconstructed cogitations of an eccentric old lady but Netta knew there was more to Edie than that.

Suddenly, Maud sprang up and walked to the French windows. Standing rigid, she began to growl. Netta looked out and saw a fox in the garden. Her excitement flattened when she realised it wasn't their vixen. This one was bigger, more weather-beaten and anyway, Maud never growled at their vixen: they seemed to have a mutual respect for each other. The fox stopped for a moment and then went off through the gate that led into Frank's garden. 'It's not our friend, is it Maud?'

Maud raised her whiskery eyebrows. Netta gave the little dog a consoling pat and got up to go back to bed. As she switched off the kitchen light another sound carried itself through the darkness outside. It was one of the most eerie, mournful things she'd ever heard. She squinted out of the kitchen window but the moon was too cloud-covered to be of any use. The noise stopped, then out of the silence, it came again before resolving into a bark. She knew then it was a fox, perhaps her vixen. Maud's wiry fur brushed against Netta's leg and she let out a whimper. Netta bent down to comfort her. 'It's only foxes, Maudie. Nothing to be worried about. Come up and keep me company.'

They crept upstairs. Before she could climb into bed, Maud was already curled up on top of the quilt. She snuggled down under it to shut out the cold and as she stroked Maud's back, Netta was lulled into sleep.

12

IT DOESN'T ALWAYS DO TO DELVE

NETTA – 2019

Netta rubbed her eyes. Two hours earlier, she'd slipped out of bed and left Frank sleeping to join Maud in their nightly vigil. The sun would be up soon and the birds would be singing. It was one of the best times to experience the beauty of nature, yet here she was hunched over her laptop, looking for Doogie Chambers. The idea had come to her after deciding that the only way to get rid of these sleepless nights was to find Doogie and Claire. So, rather than go back to bed and warm her frozen toes on Frank she opened her laptop and set to work. Not that she had any idea what she would do if she found them. It just seemed really important to know where they were and if they were all right.

She started with Doogie thinking he'd be the easiest and quickly found some music press articles he'd written from years ago but that was it. There was nothing later than 2010. Undeterred, she tried all the usual social media outlets to no avail. As far as the worldwide web was concerned, Doogie Chambers no longer existed. She'd last seen him in 2003 when she slipped out of his apartment while he was still sleeping, leaving a goodbye note on top of her

Manchester clothes. She hadn't heard from him since. The memory of that moment and the heartache that led up to it made her ask herself whether she really should just let sleeping dogs lie. If she wanted to revisit her past, then maybe it was safer to stick with Claire.

Like Doogie, Claire had stayed on in Manchester after uni and Netta knew they'd been friends for a while. Claire had told her that, back when they were speaking. Funny really, considering the number of times she'd threatened to rip his head off when he'd upset Netta. God, she was fierce. She tapped in Claire Fogarty but that proved equally fruitless. The possibility that they might both be dead was briefly considered, then dismissed. Just because someone didn't use social media didn't mean they'd left this world, it just meant they didn't use social media. Or, in Claire's case, it could just be that she'd married, although, the thought of Claire marrying and taking a man's name seemed so inconceivable that Netta almost dismissed it. This was a waste of time. She closed down the laptop, watched the day break, then went to bed. Frank was still sound asleep. She snuggled up behind him, pushed her cold nose against his back and drifted off.

Six hours later, on the Sunday morning walk, she accidentally let it slip that she was looking for Claire, to her mother of all people. 'Are you sure it's a good idea? I mean, how long's it been since you last saw her?' said her mum.

'Late-nineties I think. Something like that.' Netta was lying: she knew the date exactly. It was 13th December 1998.

'Well, there you go then. That's a long time ago, love. You've both moved on a lot since then.' That was her mother's way of saying, you've finally got rid of that parasite, Colin. Actually no, that was her father's way of saying it.

Her mother was usually much more candid about it. She must be softening.

'What's that, someone moving?' said her dad, launching a damp stick into the air for the dogs to chase.

'No Arthur, Netta wants to find that old friend of hers, Claire. I was just telling her they've both moved on a bit since they last saw each other. She might not welcome it.'

'Well it has been a long time,' said her dad. 'How long's it been?'

'Late-nineties, Dad.'

'Late-nineties eh? Bit of a while then.' He tossed another stick. 'What's brought this on? I thought you'd had enough of the past.'

'Well, I have, mostly but I've often wondered about Claire. I just thought it would be nice to get in touch with her and see how her life turned out.'

Neil joined in. 'Have you tried Facebook, LinkedIn, that sort of stuff?'

'Yes. I can't find her on anything. I think she might have married, or changed her name, at any rate.'

'I thought it was Edie you were looking for?' said Neil.

'I was. I am. It's just made me think about Claire. I thought she'd be easy to find but it looks like I was wrong.'

'Why don't you try her old house?' said her dad. 'Her mum and dad might still be there.'

'Dad, that's a brilliant idea. Why didn't I think of that?'

'I have my uses.'

Netta smiled. Her father might just have come up with the answer to her problem. 'I'll pop over there tomorrow, see if they're still there.'

'Just promise me you won't press on if it gets too painful for you,' said her mum. 'It doesn't always do to delve into the past.'

'I promise but it's only Claire, nothing to worry about.' She linked arms with her mum. Nothing to worry about? She could only hope that was true.

On Monday morning, she waited for a respectable time to go over to Claire's old house. She'd actually been ready quite early but didn't think the Fogartys would appreciate her banging on their door before they had a chance to wake up. Thankfully, she'd had a night of unbroken sleep. That had to be good, a sign that she was doing the right thing. She passed a couple of hours by reading another of Edie's diaries. This one was from 1999 and, aside from her thoughts on the millennium bug, yielded nothing of consequence. By eleven o'clock she couldn't hold back any longer. Thirty minutes later she pulled up outside Claire's old front garden.

The house looked the same. It must have had a coat of paint in the years since she was last there but it was the same colour. That it was unchanged felt quite poignant: she had a lot of happy memories tied up in that house. It was in there that they first listened to Claire's big sister's old records and discovered The Sex Pistols, X-Ray Spex and The Clash and, despite punk rock having already moved on, they became wannabe punks. They still liked some of the music that was around at that time but their love of punk set them slightly apart from the rest of their friends. It made them different and they liked that. Netta recalled the hours spent pogoing in Claire's bedroom, Claire's dad shouting up to *turn that bloody shite down.* She shook her head. Such joy. Such promise. Pity it didn't last.

There was no answer when she rang the bell. After a few minutes she tried again. Still no answer. Maybe she should try another time? Maybe she should leave a note? Yes, she would do that; she'd put a note through the door and tell them that she would return on Wednesday. She went back to the car and scratched around for some paper and a pen, finally finding an old shopping list written on the back of an envelope and a pink felt pen down the side of the passenger door. Where on earth had that come from? She tore at the envelope to open it up and scribbled something down on the inside. It wasn't the best but it would have to do. She got back out of the car and opened the gate. From the corner of her eye, she saw someone coming towards her with a bag full of shopping. She was much older; her face was more lined and her hair, almost white but she was unmistakably Claire's mum.

'Hello Mrs Fogarty. You probably don't remember me. I'm an old friend of Claire's.'

Mrs Fogarty stopped in front of the gate and screwed up her eyes. 'It's Netta isn't it? Don't be daft, of course I remember you.'

'You still with that fella?' Claire's mum was putting her shopping away while Netta made the tea. They finished their tasks simultaneously and sat down at the kitchen table over a tin of biscuits.

'Colin? No. We split up a few years ago. You've upgraded the biscuit tin.'

'I should bloody well hope so, it's been years.' Mrs Fogarty laughed. It was less throaty than it used to be. Perhaps she'd finally given up cigarettes. It used to be a rare moment not to see her with one close by.

'You still smoking, Mrs F?'

'Nah, gave it up years ago, when I divorced Pete. Two

bad habits got rid of in one go.' She laughed again. 'Tell you what, it was a lot harder to give up the fags than the husband.'

News of the divorce didn't come as a surprise. Netta remembered Pete Fogarty. He was a small, tough-looking man, full of life, just like his wife. She recalled them laughing a lot but also arguing a lot. It was the complete opposite of her peaceful home where there was never a cross word said. Her mum could be short-tempered and waspish but her dad was the gentlest person on the planet. He was always there to smooth things down; always there to keep them on an even keel. In contrast, the Fogarty household was a rickety old boat, constantly sailing on choppy waters with Claire, her sister and brothers bailing out as often as they could. No wonder Claire preferred the sanctuary of Netta's house or, better still, Granny Wilde's where the two of them were free to play their music as loud as they wanted to.

'I was hoping to get in touch with Claire, Mrs F. I wonder, if I leave you my contact details, would you mind passing them on to her?'

'No, I don't mind. She phones me a couple of times a week. She lives in Brighton now. Married with kids. Her bloke's a lovely fella. She'll be pleased to hear he's out of the picture.' Netta must have looked confused. 'Yer husband, I mean. Whatshisname, Colin. She always hated him.'

13

THE JOY AND SORROW OF REUNION

NETTA – 2019

Netta stroked the butterfly pendant around her neck. It was so delicate she was afraid she would break it but when she left home that morning she felt compelled to wear it. It was as if she were carrying part of Edie with her; as if Edie might protect her from the storm to come, if there could be any protection. She was heading to Brighton, with a certain amount of trepidation. Not without cause. The last time she saw Claire she'd been made to feel ashamed of what she'd become. That was a long time before Colin set to work in earnest on her. It didn't bear thinking about what Claire would have said if she'd seen her at her worst. She imagined them meeting in the bad years; the awful years. Her – or rather Annette – repressed, oppressed, humbled. Claire, with that look of hers, the one that could slice you into pieces with a single sneer. She shuddered. At least she'd been spared that. She was more like Netta than Annette now but that gave her no comfort. What if she'd been fooling herself for the last year? What if Annette was still lurking there in the shadows, waiting for a chance to resurface? She felt her there sometimes when she was alone in the house and her confidence was at its lowest. She needed people around her these days to make her feel wanted and loved.

She'd been going through Edie's journals, trying to put them into order, when the email came from Claire. She was almost too afraid to open it, but open it she did. It was short but friendly enough, in a guarded sort of way:

'Hi Netta,

Mum passed your contact details on to me. She said you wanted to get in touch. Drop me a line back.

Claire.'

She chose the words for her reply carefully:

'Hello Claire,

Really pleased you got in touch. Don't know how much your mum told you but I'm divorced now. It's taken me a while to get myself back together but I'm feeling more like my old self these days. It would be great to see you and catch up.

Netta.'

She deliberately made no mention of Doogie. She would ask about him only if it felt right: this was about her and Claire. She had other female friends now but none were as close to her as Claire had once been. Reading about Edie and Mina brought it all back and made her realise just how much she wanted that closeness in her life again. Whether she'd get it was another matter and she tried to stay grounded in reality: even if Claire did agree to see her, it was unlikely they'd ever recapture what they once had.

Claire didn't reply straight away. She was obviously taking her time to decide if it was worth the effort. She must have decided it was, because a mail dropped into Netta's inbox a few days later:

'Hi,

A catch up would be good. Did mum tell you I was in Brighton now? I don't get to Birmingham much these days – three kids and a business to run. Can you come here? You can stay over, if that's easier.

Claire.'

The place they'd agreed to meet was a beachside cafe just outside Brighton. Claire was already there, waiting for her. She still had her dad's small, wiry frame but she looked more like her mum now. It was an awkward hello, neither being the sort to kiss or hug. It wasn't a thing when they were growing up. Kissing was mostly reserved for encounters related to sex not something between friends, or even family. Others who grew up in the place and time they did seemed to have learned to embrace embraces as a greeting. They were the sort who were able to shout, 'Love you,' to their kids in a crowded street without a hint of embarrassment. Not Netta. Clearly, not Claire either but then Claire had always been hard core.

'You recognised me then?' she said.

'You've hardly changed,' said Netta. 'Except the hair. It's longer, and I like the colour.'

She smiled but it didn't go all the way up to her eyes. 'Yeah well, black's very ageing. You have to be Siouxsie Sioux to get away with it once your face starts to crinkle up. I went natural for a couple of years, then went red when I moved here. It seemed to suit the area. You're looking good. Different to how I imagined you'd be. Divorce agrees with you.'

'Thanks. A few more wrinkles these days but I don't mind them. The hair's gone a bit mad too: I can't be bothered faffing about with it. Although, I have started moisturising in the last year and I'm rediscovering make-up, thanks to my daughter.'

'Fuck, you've only just started moisturising? You must have naturally good skin. If that were me, I'd look about a hundred. I've been laying it on with a trowel for years. Mind you, I seem to remember your mum having good skin. You look a lot like her, you know.'

'I was thinking the same about you. You look more like your mum now.'

Claire pulled a face, 'I know. Thing is, when I said you looked like your mum, I meant it as a compliment. She was really lovely-looking. My mum's always looked like a wizened old troll, even when she was young.'

Netta snorted. 'That's not true. Your mum has a really nice face.'

Claire laughed. 'Come on Netta, truth time. My mum's not exactly a looker and neither am I. It's not the end of the world, I can live with it. Anyway, you've got kids? I thought you were dead against them?'

'I was, but I got … persuaded. I have two. Will and Liza, and you've got three? Now that was a shocker.'

'I know. Bit of a shock to me too. My oldest, Meredith, she has a different dad to my youngest two. Someone I cared for a lot but it didn't work out. Buddy and Cara, they're Dom's kids. Dom and me, we've been together for eleven years now, married nine. You'll meet him later, if you're staying.'

'I'll stay if you want me to.'

She smiled again. This time it reached her eyes. 'That's sorted then, you're staying.'

As soon as they opened the door to Claire's house, they were hit by the sound of family noises – TV, music, children talking louder than they needed to – everyday things that Netta had forgotten about. When she lived with her own family these were the noises she walked into every evening after work. They'd been alien to her then; another barrier to cross, but now they were comforting and she found herself longing for times she'd never really experienced. The source of the loudest noises came from three boys, about nine or ten, playing video games in front of the TV. One of them had to be Buddy.

A tall slim man with black-brown skin and close-cropped afro-textured hair emerged from the kitchen, wiping his hands on a towel. He looked younger than Claire, maybe in his early forties. 'Hello beautiful.' He bent down and kissed Claire. Obviously, he didn't think she looked like a wizened old troll. 'Hi Netta, I'm Dom. Claire's told me a lot about the two of you when you were younger. It's nice to meet you.'

'Hello Dom, good to meet you too.' So Claire had talked about their friendship then? The neediness in her was pleased about that until she wondered what else she'd said about her.

'Where are the girls?' asked Claire.

'Merrie's gone to pick Cara up from dance class. They'll be back soon. Charlie and Asif are staying for dinner.' He turned to Netta. 'Sorry, it's a bit chaotic but you two can escape to the pub after we've eaten if you want to. I'll hold the fort here.'

Claire gave him a loud kiss. 'Such a good soldier.'

He grinned at her. 'That's me. Come into the kitchen and open a bottle of wine. Dinner's nearly done.' He returned to the kitchen to stir a large pan of something and gave Claire a spoonful to taste. She nodded approval. 'I hope you don't mind vegetarian, Netta,' he said. 'We're a meat free household.'

'I don't mind at all. My kids went through a vegetarian

phase but the lure of bacon was too much for them. They tell me they're flexitarians now,' said Netta.

The slamming of the front door and the sound of girls' voices interrupted the conversation. 'In the kitchen. Come and say hello,' called Claire. Two girls walked in, one around seven and one about fifteen or sixteen. 'Netta, this is Merrie and Cara,' said Claire.

The sight of them took Netta's breath away. Both girls had light brown skin and long, curly ringlets. They were just as she'd imagined her miscarried baby would be at different stages in her life. Her throat dried up and she couldn't speak so she raised a hand and gave a limp wave.

'Hello,' said Cara. She pirouetted over to Claire and jumped up and down excitedly. 'I've got a solo spot.'

Claire clapped her hands. 'Yay, I told you, didn't I? Well done baby.' She turned to Netta. 'Dance class show.'

Merrie tutted. 'She's going to be unbearable now until that show.'

Cara pushed out her bottom lip. 'Don't be mean.'

'I'm not being mean, I'm being honest. You've been a pain practising for the audition and you'll be an even bigger one practising for the show.'

'I wasn't. Tell her Mum.'

'Come on now girls,' said Claire. 'Netta hasn't come all the way from Birmingham to hear you two squabble. Put your stuff away Cara and come back down for dinner. Merrie, can you get the boys in please?'

Merrie gave her mother one of those 'I have to do everything in this house' sighs and stomped off to bark orders at the boys to finish their game. Liza was probably a year older than Merrie and Netta imagined she'd have been exactly the same if she'd had younger siblings.

. . .

'Your kids are great,' she said to Claire over a bottle of wine in the pub, 'and you're a great mum.'

'Yeah I am, aren't I?' said Claire. 'Surprised?'

'A bit, but only because I couldn't have imagined you having kids, and only because I thought you were more like me and I was a terrible mother. But you're not. You're a natural.'

'Not really a natural. It took me a few years alone with Merrie to really get into it. Those were difficult years.'

'You didn't get any help from her dad?'

'Nah, not really. He tried I suppose but he just wasn't any good at it. In the end it was easier when he stopped seeing us. I went over to Dublin for a bit to stay with my dad. He moved back there after mum divorced him. That helped: my aunties were brilliant. They showed me how it was supposed to be done. My mum, god love her, was not the best example of motherhood, but then she had a lot to contend with – the old man being a bit of an arsehole and all that. Do you remember those arguments they used to have? There were always bits of crockery flying around. We didn't have one matching plate in the house. I used to love going to yours for the peace and quiet, and your gran's. She was lovely. I was sorry to hear she died by the way. I nearly sent a card but I thought you wouldn't have wanted to hear from me.'

'Why would you think that?'

'Well, we didn't exactly part as best mates, did we? I seem to remember you insulting me and storming off.'

'I insulted you? I don't remember that.'

'Seriously? You don't remember what you said?'

Netta shook her head.

'You don't remember telling me I was jealous of you?'

Netta cringed. All she'd remembered was Claire having

a go at her but, now that she put her mind to it, she knew she'd been selective with her memory yet again. 'Did I accuse you of being jealous of me and Colin?'

'Yep.'

Shamed, she put her hand over her eyes and recalled that scene, not as she usually visualised it but in its entirety. Claire, telling her there was something wrong with Colin; that he was no good for her; pleading with her to leave him. Her, regurgitating the lines Colin had been feeding her on a loop since they'd become a couple. 'You're just jealous. You like having me around to bolster your ego and Colin takes me away from you. You don't like him because he's a threat to you.' She remembered the hurt on Claire's face as she spat out those cruel, horrible words. How could she have pretended that never happened? More to the point, how could she have said them in the first place? 'I should have listened to you. I'd have saved myself years of misery. I'm sorry, Claire. Really I am.'

Claire took a sip of wine. 'That part was pretty laughable really but you were actually spot on with the thing you said about me being jealous of your family. I was a bit. That's probably why it stung.'

Netta took a deep breath. That was another thing she'd conveniently forgotten. What a complete dickhead she was. 'I don't know why I said that but I shouldn't have. Again, I'm really sorry.'

Claire shrugged. 'You were angry with me and we all do stupid things that we regret, me included.'

'Mine ruined my life though. I lost everything that was important to me. Myself, friends, even my kids for a while.' She told her about the divorce, being made redundant two years later and how becoming a foodbank volunteer had saved her and given her the chance to make a new life in a new home, Edie's home, with its strange conditions. She told her about how Colin had changed his job from accountant to artist and sponged off her for years until she put a stop to it. When all that was done, she felt ready to tell her about Doogie and the baby and the loneliness and emptiness inside after she lost it.

Claire sat in silence for some time after. Netta watched her running her finger along the rim of her glass. She didn't want to push her into words, best to give her the space to find them. 'Shit,' she said at last. 'I hadn't realised it had been so bad. But you're happy now, with this Frank?'

'Yes, I think so. It's hard to know sometimes if it's real happiness or just relief.'

Claire scrunched up her nose. 'Sometimes that's all happiness is. As long as you're in a better place, that's all that matters. So, you haven't seen Doogie recently?'

'No, I haven't seen him since 2003. I've tried to trace him but it's like he's disappeared off the face of the earth.'

Claire raised an eyebrow. 'That's why you got in touch with me. Be honest with me, no bullshit. Is that why you came to me?'

'Not exactly.'

Claire's eyes met hers and then came the look that she'd been dreading. It was a look that made her feel dishonest and sly. Most of all, it made her feel small. 'So, you weren't really interested in a big reunion then? That figures.'

'No, you're wrong. I said not exactly because I'm not sure how I feel about seeing Doogie again but I did want to see you. Reading Edie's diaries has made me realise that there's been something missing since we fell out. I can't explain it but it's like there's been a part of me that doesn't connect properly.'

Claire took a swig of wine and eyed Netta. She looked

as if she was weighing her up; assessing how much of what she'd said was truth or just more bullshit. Eventually, she put down her glass and squeezed Netta's hand. 'Me too.' They began to laugh at the stupid tears welling up in their eyes. Claire shook her head. 'Fucking wine.'

'Yeah, I'm never gonna drink again,' sniffed Netta. 'Another bottle?'

'Hell yeah.'

'I came here after Ireland,' she said, halfway through the second bottle. 'Much as I loved it there, I was ready to come back home. Not Brum though: it doesn't really feel like home to me anymore, and I'd had enough of Manchester. So, I got a job as an editor on the local paper here. I stayed there until last year when I opened up my shop. Anyway, Dom was the paper's sports writer. We just hit it off straight away which, as you know, is unusual for me. He had no problem with me having a kid so we started to see each other. Before long, me and Merrie were spending all of our time with him. We're good together and as far as he's concerned, he's got three kids which is great for Merrie because she doesn't see her own dad. With Dom I feel settled, like I don't have to fight anymore. Everything gets easier when that happens. Know what I mean?'

'I can imagine,' said Netta. 'I haven't got there yet.'

'Do you think if you found Doogie it would happen?'

'I don't know. Finding you again already feels like I'm heading in the right direction.'

'Let's finish the bottle and go home. We'll get my old records out and pretend we're sixteen again at your gran's place. She had a bit of a soft spot for Joe Strummer, if I remember rightly.'

'Yeah, she did but Blondie was her favourite. She loved Debbie Harry.'

The next morning, Netta woke up in Cara's bed. Merrie was fast asleep in the opposite bed. She thought again of baby Ada who would have been a little younger than Merrie but not much. She didn't look too much like Claire. In fact, she looked more like Dom. Both were tall with angled features and high cheekbones. Merrie's dad and Dom must have been a bit alike. Perhaps that's what drew Claire to Dom in the first place. Still asleep, Merrie rolled over. A shaft of sunlight sneaked in through a gap in the curtains and settled on her hair showing up red high-lights that hadn't really been noticeable before. Netta wanted so much to reach over and stroke it. She was just about close enough, but she resisted. She'd dreamed of baby Ada last night. Not on the beach at Aberdovey with Granny Wilde, Liza and Will, as she often did. This time she was watching her in a dance class, until she changed into an older girl sitting sulkily at the dinner table, but neither of these were her baby. They were Cara and Merrie.

There was a knock on the door and Claire walked in with two mugs of tea. 'Morning Ladies. Thought you might need this.' She put one of the mugs down beside Netta's bed and sat next to Merrie, idly twiddling with Merrie's hair. Netta felt a pang of envy.

After a few minutes, Merrie sat up and took the mug from her mother. 'I suppose you got drunk last night?'

'Oh yes, horribly,' said Claire. 'Then Netta and me got out all my old records and we pogoed till dawn.'

'You did what?'

'Pogoed. It's an ancient dance consisting mainly of jumping up and down.'

'Huh, sounds infantile.'

'Yes, ever so, and we enjoyed every minute of it. Didn't we, Net?'

'Loved it,' said Netta.

'Come on. Breakfast. Then we'll go for a nice bracing walk,' said Claire, tugging at her daughter's arm.

Merrie resisted. 'Aren't you going to work today?'

'What, with my best friend of all time here? Patti's looking after the shop for me today so you've got me all day. Lucky you.'

They took a walk along the beach. It was a cloudy morning but the sun was finding its way through. Dom and the two younger children were trying to fly a kite but the wind wasn't really strong enough. Merrie was with Claire and Netta. Netta breathed in the salty air, she'd always loved the sea. 'My dogs would like it here.'

'You've got dogs?' Merrie was suddenly interested. Netta told her the story of how she came to live with Maud and how Maud became a mother. She showed them some photos of Maud and her puppies on her phone. 'Oh Mum, look,' said Merrie.

'The kids keep going on about having a dog,' said Claire. 'It wasn't really possible when we were both working full-time at the paper but now I have the shop, they think I can take it to work with me and won't stop nagging. I've told them we'll see.'

'I'll bear you in mind next time Maud and her gentleman friend, Colonel, get frisky then,' said Netta. 'Merrie, you can come over and see them whenever you're in Birmingham.'

. . .

They said goodbye after lunch, standing together on the drizzly street outside Claire's house. Dom and the children were still inside. 'I'm glad I came,' said Netta. 'It's been so good seeing you again. I feel like a missing piece of me has been returned.'

Claire have her an awkward hug. 'Me too.'

'Will we keep in touch now?' asked Netta, hopeful.

'Of course we will, you prat.'

'About Doogie.'

Claire folded her arms. 'I haven't seen him in ages but he does mail me every now and then. I'll see if I can dig out his last one.'

Despite their inbred discomfort with such practices, they kissed. Dom brought the kids out to wave her off. She waved back and drove away, wondering if she'd pushed it too far by asking about Doogie in their final minutes together. Claire hadn't mentioned it last night but Netta had remembered something else about the last time the two of them had seen each other. Another venomous missive she'd thrown out in the heat of the moment. Something she'd known would really hurt. She'd accused Claire of breaking her and Doogie up. It was rubbish of course and they both knew it: when she finished with Doogie that first time, it was because she saw him with another girl, one that no way on this earth was just the friend he said she was. But that wasn't the point. The accusation cut deep because Doogie was the only other person beside Claire that Netta had a connection with that was beyond the physical. Splitting up with him had killed her. If she'd have cut out her heart and eaten it, she'd have felt less pain, and Claire knew it. Blaming her for that was the worst thing Netta could have done. It was like telling your best friend who was closer than a sister that she'd ruined your life. Which was why she'd said it. She was absolutely sure Claire hadn't forgotten it. Maybe she'd decided it was best to act like she had.

When she got far enough away, she turned towards the beach again. The clouds had knitted together to form a soggy grey mass and it was already too wet to get out, so she sat in the car watching the sea. Claire hadn't been the nemesis she'd expected. Quite the opposite. They'd been the same people they were when they were kids and after a bit of discomfort at the beginning, they'd clicked back together again. Everything had gone well, even though she'd been prepared for the opposite, so why was her heart so heavy? Why was she sitting here in the rain with tears trickling down her face? It was Merrie and Cara. It was their closeness to the image she had of the child she nearly bore. All this time she'd been thinking she was fine about losing Ada but she wasn't. She was far from fine.

14

HOME COMFORTS

NETTA – 2019

The traffic hadn't been too bad on the way back from Brighton so she'd made good time. When she got home, the sight of her parents' car outside the house induced a wave of minor panic. It was just sliding into Sunday evening. Normally they left not long after the big walk. In her head, that meant only one thing, something bad must have happened but when she stepped inside the door, she was pleasantly surprised and mildly bewildered to find everything appeared to be okay. There was a smell of cooking in the air and music playing in the background. Ray Charles, one of her dad's old favourites. They hadn't noticed her arrival: they were too busy doing something industrious. She waited quietly in the hall, listening to Liza's laughter, her mother fondly chiding the dogs and the low murmur of men's voices – her dad and Frank. She'd spent the whole journey turning things over in her head and wondering if she'd done the right thing. Hadn't her mum warned her about the dangers of delving too deep? As she'd predicted, it had unsettled Netta. From the moment she pulled up at the beach, she'd been taken captive by a deep sadness. It stayed with her right up to this moment but now, the familiar sounds and smells of home and family enveloped her. She stroked the silver butterfly hanging between her collarbones and the distress slid away.

'All right Net? Didn't hear you come in.' Kelly emerged from the study with an armful of Edie's diaries.

Will followed her, with more books. 'Hey, how was the trip?'

'Good. It was good. What's going on?'

'Come and have a look,' said Will.

She followed them into the kitchen. Spread in lines on the floor, like some kind of large scale Solitaire, were Edie's journals. Her parents, Frank and Liza were shuffling them around, adding books as they went. Her mum looked up. 'Hello love, you're early. We were hoping to get this finished before you got back. The kids started it yesterday. We thought we'd stay and help out. I've got steak and mushroom pie in the oven for dinner. We'll drop Liza off at Colin's when we leave, so everything's sorted.'

Netta surveyed the rows and rows of diaries before her. That was a lot of books.

'They're in decades,' said her dad. 'They go back to the 1930s when Edie was a girl but, other than those four you've already read, there's nothing for the forties or the early fifties. Bit odd that. Perhaps they got lost or destroyed.'

When all of the books were sorted into date order, they moved them into some plastic crates that Frank had bought that day. Each crate was labelled by decade and stacked in the study. They were unsightly but they did allow more floor space in there. Afterwards, they all sat around the table for dinner.

Liza swallowed down a mouthful of pie. 'I bloody love your steak and mushroom pie, Nan.'

'Given up on being a vegetarian, have you?' said Netta's dad.

'I'm more of a flexitarian now, Grandad.'

'What does that mean?' said her grandad.

'It means she's a vegetarian when it suits her,' said Kelly.

'I'm a veggie at my other home,' said Liza. 'Since Arianne moved in, we're not allowed to have meat or fish in the house so I've got no choice.'

Kelly snorted. 'Like I said–'

Liza slapped Kelly's arm. 'Shut up, Kelly. I do try to eat mostly veggie when I'm not there. It's better for the planet, something you should think about when you're eating all those takeaway burgers and crisps.'

Will laughed. 'I think she got you there, Kel. Point to Liza.'

Kelly grinned. 'Yeah, right. Thanks, eco warrior. I'll give it some thought. Not.'

Netta's mum held up her hand. 'Behave, you three. Anyone would think you were little kids, and Kelly, Liza's right: all that junk food is bad for you and bad for the environment.'

Liza raised her hands. 'Yay, go Nan. I've been telling Nan how saving the planet is my thing,' she explained to her open-mouthed audience. The inflection at the end of the sentence gave the impression that her eco credentials were well known.

'Quite right too,' said Frank, looking for all the world as if he'd known this fact for ages.

Later that evening, when her parents and Liza were gone, she and Frank went over to his house. Alone at last, Frank embraced her as if she'd been away for weeks and yet they'd only said goodbye yesterday morning. 'You look done in,' he said. 'Make yourself comfortable. I'll get the music on and pour you a drink.'

They cuddled up on the couch listening to Otis Redding with Fred stretched out on the rug in front of them. 'This is nice,' she said.

Frank kissed the top of her head. 'I missed you last night. Had to sit here all on my own like a sad old git. I'd forgotten what that was like.'

'At least you had Fred.'

'Yes, but he's not great on the conversation.'

She kissed him. 'Poor you. Never mind, I'm back now.'

'Phew, thank God for that. So, was it worth going then?'

'Yes, it was. It really was, but I had a few wobbles. It was Claire's kids. They're beautiful, sweet, darling children but they reminded me of the baby, especially the girls. Everything about them was just as I imagined she would be. After I left them, I had to find a quiet spot to take it all in and, like the stupid idiot I am these days, I'm afraid I just blubbed.'

He held her hand. 'It's all right, my darling girl. You're still grieving, that's all. You locked it up for so long, it's bound to come out more easily now.'

'I know. It's still hard when it happens though.'

'But you'll see Claire again?'

'Yes, she's already sent me a message saying so.' She decided not to say anything about Claire looking for Doogie's email address. If she found it and Netta decided to do something with it, she'd tell Frank then but for now, she didn't want to drag him out of his blissful ignorance.

'Are you staying over tonight?'

She yawned. 'As long as you don't mind me falling asleep as soon as my head hits the pillow.'

He squeezed her closer. 'I don't mind at all.'

. . .

The next morning, they sat in his breakfast room, huddled over a small café style table in front of the French windows. Behind them were two half-finished canvasses on easels. There were several finished paintings leaning against the back wall. The room was really his studio but he'd recently installed this table and a couple of chairs because he knew how much she loved to sit in her own equivalent room next door. He was thoughtful like that, always doing things to please her. The pastries too. He'd gone out earlier to get some just because he knew how much she liked them. She smiled at the sight of his burly figure wrapped around the tiny table. He had a few days' stubble on him. Flakes of falling pastry had got caught on it and settled themselves there. She grinned and brushed it off. He grinned too and wiped a speck off her cheek. 'We're a couple of messy sods,' she said.

He laughed. 'Who cares? It's just you, me and Fred, and he's quite happy about it.'

Fred licked the stray flakes off the floor. He looked up at them for more, his dark eyes almost hidden in the scruffy black fur. On the tip of his nose was a large sliver of croissant. Netta giggled. 'Fred, you're such a mess. You look more like your dad every day.'

'I take it you mean Colonel, not me?' said Frank.

She put her hand to her chin. 'Well, now that you mention it, it is the most bizarre coincidence that you managed to pick the scruffiest, clumsiest one of the litter, don't you think?'

'It was no coincidence. We warmed to each other straight away. Kindred spirits, me and Fred.'

The spring sun poked its head around a cloud and shot

its rays through the glass doors, lighting up thc room. 'Your dad said he'd come over on Saturday to get the garden prepped for this year's fruit crops. Neil and Chris said they'd help,' he said.

'Okay. Oh, I meant to say, I think we have a new fox. I think it might be male. He looks bigger than the vixen. I've seen him a couple of times. I haven't seen the vixen though; I hope she's all right. I'm really worried that she might have died.'

'It happens I'm afraid, but she might just be having another litter. I think they stay with the cubs for a while when they do and tend to rely on the male to bring in the food.'

'I hope that's all it is. I have a terrible sense of foreboding. I know it's silly and it's all part of nature, but still...'

Frank wasn't due at his college that day. By rights he should have been painting for his next exhibition but he offered to help her go through Edie's things. Fred followed them over to her house, much to Betty's delight. The two rolled around together as Netta and Frank assessed the remaining piles to be sorted in the study. Netta pointed to some boxes of papers that had been left in one corner of the room. 'I'm expecting those to be mostly bills and things like that. Edie and her family seemed to have kept everything. I wonder what makes people do that. I can understand keeping things that belonged to someone they loved but bills, everyday things like that, it makes no sense to me.'

'Maybe it's a way of clinging to normality when you have nothing else. I mean, they went through the war, that must have been terrible and they lost a son. Later on, Edie lost her parents and her other brother and maybe her sweetheart too. It's not as if the world stopped being a scary place after the war either, was it? There was the Korean war, the cold war, worries about the nuclear bomb. I can understand why people focus on little things when everything else is crumbling around them. It gives them a sense of order, as if something matters, I suppose.'

'When you put it like that, it makes perfect sense,' said Netta. The things Frank came out with surprised her sometimes. He had an ability to put himself in other people's shoes. She always felt she was stumbling around in the dark and envied him for it. She was still thinking about this when something occurred to her. 'Frank, do you think Edie was lonely?'

He'd been fiddling with one of the boxes and the question made him stop. 'I'm not sure. I'm ashamed to say, I never really gave it much thought when she was alive. She always seemed so active and lively, even when she was well into her eighties. She had a great sense of humour too, not in the least bit stuffy, and she loved kids. I suppose you could say that in many ways she was quite childlike and I guess I always put that down to living at home with her parents all her life. Although I now realise that she did leave home at least once, in the war. So, part of me wants to say that she wasn't lonely but then, I look around at all of this, I see those photos and read between the lines of her journals and I wonder if I'm just kidding myself. I wonder if she was a dear, sweet, lonely lady who was making the best of what she had left.' He took a huge breath. 'Jesus, I wish you hadn't asked me that. I'm now thinking I should have done more for her.' He surveyed the boxes and crates of books. 'I should have done more for her.'

She hugged him. 'I'm sorry, I didn't mean to upset you.'

He looked away and wiped his eyes. 'It's okay, Net. It's just me being a daft eejit, that's all. How about a cup of coffee?'

While she made the drinks, Frank carried the container with the oldest diaries into the lounge. 'Shall we start with the 1930s?' he said as she joined him on the couch. He took a sip of coffee and she could have sworn she saw him wince. He really did like his proper filter coffee. She resolved to get a coffee maker for the kitchen. He deserved that much at least.

Edie's diaries began when she was seven. She'd had her first one as a Christmas present and appeared to have a new one every year until her entries became too long for a regular diary to hold. After that, they were leather bound journals, except for those four from the war years which were much more functional paper notebooks. They spent most of the day reading those early books but as they finished them Netta couldn't help feeling frustrated: they were charming reads but they weren't going to tell them what happened to either Robert or Bill. Only the missing diaries were likely to do that. Edie was such a prolific writer that it was hard to believe she would have stopped in those years. Perhaps Netta's dad was right. They must have been destroyed or lost.

'Hey, how's it going?' Will popped his head around the door. He was back from the centre where he spent his Mondays helping people whose first language wasn't English.

'Hi darling. Good day?' said Netta.

'Yeah, really good. I've brought a friend with me. She volunteers at the centre too. Okay if she stays for dinner?' He opened the door fully. Smiling coyly behind him was a pretty, fair girl with long blonde hair. She was about the same age as him. Netta couldn't help thinking that would be around the same age that Edie would have been when she met Robert. 'This is Belle.' He gulped and looked at his feet. He did that when he was embarrassed.

Belle gave them a timid little wave. 'Hi.'

Netta put further thoughts of Edie to one side. Her son was bringing a girl home for the first time ever. She did her best not to appear too delighted. 'Hello, Belle. I'm Netta and this is Frank. Yes, dinner's fine.'

'Are you sure?' said Belle. 'Sorry, it's a bit of a cheek just turning up like this, but Will said you wouldn't mind.'

'Not at all. I always make too much,' said Netta while mentally searching through her kitchen cupboards for something that might stretch the casserole out to feed five.

'I can go home and sort myself out for dinner,' whispered Frank when they'd gone upstairs. He'd obviously been thinking the same thing.

'Oh no you don't. I need you here for moral support and to make sure I don't put my foot in it. I'll throw in a can of exotic looking beans and make some dumplings. It'll be fine.'

Kelly came in just as she was putting the dumplings in. The frosty air outside had given some colour to her normally translucent skin and she had an unusually healthy glow. 'All right? Dinner smells nice.' The sound of Belle and Will found its way downstairs and caught her attention. 'Liza back, is she?'

'No, Will's brought a friend back,' said Frank.

'A friend?'

'Yes, her name's Belle. She volunteers at the same centre as him,' said Netta.

Kelly's eyes narrowed. Netta had seen that look before, back in the days before she and Kelly became proper friends. 'Belle?' It came out as a sneer. She turned on her heels. 'Give us a shout when dinner's ready, yeah?'

Netta and Frank looked across the kitchen at each other. He raised his eyebrows as if to say, what was that all about? Netta shrugged, meaning she hadn't got a clue.

Dinner was made only slightly awkward by Kelly's insistence on giving Belle the third degree. Judging by the amount of gulping and shoe gazing, it was making Will uncomfortable but it didn't seem to bother Belle. On the plus side, it allowed Netta to find out much more than she would have done with her polite questioning. Belle was, apparently, doing an extra year at college before university and was filling her spare time volunteering at the centre. She and Will had been seeing each other since December.

'Since December?' said Kelly. She shot Will a piercing look. 'Kept that quiet, didn't yer?' Will met her eye and frowned. Within seconds, Kelly's mouth broke into a wide grin. 'I'm just messing with yer, you twat.'

Will tutted and smiled but the look in his eyes suggested he still wasn't sure.

15

THE SKELETON IN THE CUPBOARD

NETTA – 2019

In the morning she went, as usual, with Kelly and Will to the foodbank. She was glad to see that whatever had been going on last night had fizzled out and things were back to normal with them. When Will first came to live with them, there were signs that he was attracted to Kelly. The feeling didn't seem to be mutual and, as they got to know each other better, they became more like brother and sister. Netta guessed that Kelly was probably just being over protective last night, but there was another potential explanation. Kelly was more vulnerable than you might think. She didn't cope well with change and Belle was change – a new dynamic that threatened to disrupt the happy family group they'd made between them. The fear of it may have put Kelly on heightened alert and made her edgy. That was one possible theory anyway. Netta didn't want to contemplate any others.

Netta and Paula were manning the job club. It was something they'd started last year to help people who had job interviews. They taught them basic interview skills and loaned out clothes for them to wear for the big day, if needed. It was popular with the foodbank clients and some days were busier than others. Today was a quiet day, giving Netta time to help out in the foodbank which was always busy. After reading Edie's journals, she found herself looking at the clients differently, particularly the elderly ones. She tried to imagine younger versions of them and wondered if they'd been like Edie when they were that age. Many of them liked a chat but somehow, asking about their innermost feelings as young men and women didn't feel right. Besides, they were so rushed there wasn't really time for in-depth conversation.

By the time they closed up for the day, they were glad to pull up their chairs in the foodbank's café. Neil sat down next to her. 'I've chased up the new business registration with the council. Sounds as if they've been short-staffed but the approval should be coming through soon, then we can get back to work. I was thinking we could move the equipment over to the new kitchen, unless you want us to buy some new ones?'

He meant Edie's pots and pans. They'd come with the house and were pretty old but they were still in good condition and were perfect for jam making. She didn't think Edie would mind if they moved them. Better that than leave them there, untouched and, anyway, new equipment cost money. 'There's no point in paying out for new pans when we have perfectly good ones already. We'll move them. If we get to the point when we're making much bigger quantities, we can get some more but let's stick with Edie's for now.'

'I was hoping you'd say that,' he said. 'It wouldn't be Edie's jams without Edie's pots, would it? I'll take them with me on Saturday.'

· · ·

On Saturday, Neil, Chris and Netta's dad came over to get the garden ready for that year's fruit crops. Last year's bounty had been more by luck than anything but they'd managed to make a good amount of jam with it before having to do a deal with the local allotment holders. This year, her dad wanted to give the garden a head start. Frank came over to lend a hand and Kelly had said she wasn't needed at the market so stuck around.

When they finished in the garden, Frank said he had a theory about the loft that he wanted to test out so he and Chris went up there. After ten minutes of listening to knocking and tapping noises, Netta and Kelly's curiosity got the better of them and they climbed the ladder to find them in consultation by the chimney breast. Frank turned to Netta. 'I knew there was something that was different to my loft but I couldn't put my finger on it, so I took a look in mine. Once I'd climbed over the junk, it was obvious. My loft has a walk-in cupboard to the side of the chimney breast. You have a wall that's flush with it, a wall that sounds hollow.'

'They must have blocked it up. I can ask my dad to have a look at it, as a favour,' said Chris.

'You don't think he'd mind?' said Netta.

'Nah. He's supposed to be retired but he still does little building jobs for family and friends. Any excuse to knock things down. He'll be happy to: he likes this old house, keeps telling me he'd love to get his hands on it.'

Netta laughed. 'That sounds ominous. Well, if you really don't think he'd mind.'

Kelly rapped her knuckles on the wall. 'Wonder why they sealed it up.'

'Probably just dodgy brickwork,' said Chris.

She tutted. 'Boring. I was hoping for a dead body.'

.   .   .

'What do you think of Belle, then?' Kelly dipped a chip into a pool of curry sauce and dropped it into her mouth. It was just the two of them tonight and they'd treated themselves to fish and chips.

'She seems nice,' said Netta.

'Yeah.'

'Will seems to like her.'

'Yeah.'

'What do you think of her?' Netta thought she'd better ask.

Kelly jabbed at her fish. 'Seems all right I suppose. How's it going with Edie? Found out any more?'

'Nothing I haven't already told you. The main mystery is who Bill is and what happened to Robert. There's no mention of either of them in the later diaries. I'm going to read more tonight to see if there's anything I've missed.'

A message beeped on her phone. 'It's from Chris. His dad's coming over on Saturday morning.'

'Yeah? Shame, I'll be working. If there are any skeletons in there, send me photos.'

She left Kelly to watch TV and went into the study, guessing the questions about Belle meant that she still hadn't fully processed her arrival on the scene. Will was out with her tonight and Kelly seemed a bit lost without him. It was a pity she didn't have any friends of her own apart from Robyn who lived far away in Edinburgh. Netta had been so preoccupied with thoughts about Edie's loneliness lately that she'd neglected to be concerned about Kelly's. She had visions of Kelly in ten or twenty years' time and they worried her, but there was nothing she could do about it tonight. Tonight, she'd spend a bit more time on Edie.

She was rereading Edie's diaries from the 1940s. It was the third time now that she'd read them: there was something about them that kept drawing her back. When she got to the end, she realised what it was. This Edie reminded her of her younger self, when she'd left Birmingham for university. Edie was much braver than her, she went off to war on her own. All Netta did was go to Manchester with her best friend to study English. Aside from those differences there were as many similarities. They both revelled in the newness and the freedom of being away from home and they both met men who celebrated the fact that they were 'rum girls', although that wasn't a phrase Doogie would use in a million years. The way Edie described sex with Robert, it could have been her and Doogie. That primeval energy that Edie wrote about was not what she was expecting at all, given the era and Edie's background. It made her think about all those times she and Doogie couldn't keep their hands off each other, back in university, and in 2003 when she lost her senses over him again. Like Edie and Robert, they'd had sex in fields. They also did it in restaurant toilets, on a beach, very nearly in a lift and even in the side entry of a derelict house. It was their thing and they couldn't get enough of it.

Side by side on the desk were two photos. The one of her and her friends, Doogie and his friend Mac and the one of Edie with her friends. They were forty-odd years apart but both groups were young and in the prime of their lives. Both looked like they were having one hell of a great time.

Her thoughts turned to Claire. Apart from a couple of initial messages, there'd been no contact since her visit. She thought about calling her but it was late so she tapped out a message:

'Hi. How are things with you? Drop me a line or give me a call.'

She pressed send, then reeled herself in, away from

Doogie and Claire and back to Robert and Edie. She remembered the online military records that had told her where Edie was stationed. It might tell her something about Robert and Tom Goodwin, maybe Mina too. The only other information she had was that the two men served in the RAF, somewhere near Edie's base and that Robert was a pilot. Frustratingly, Edie had written very little else about what they did. She logged on to the site. Although Goodwin wasn't a really common name, it wasn't exactly unusual, so her search brought up several possibilities for both men. There were three potential Robert Goodwins in the RAF at that time, one of whom had been killed in action, but she had no way of telling if that was Edie's Robert. She scribbled down the details and checked her phone for a reply from Claire but there was none. Next, she tried Mina Jacobson but she reached another dead end. She heard Kelly letting the dogs out, then back in again. Two minutes later she came in and said goodnight. Netta was tired, she should go up too. With any luck, she'd sleep tonight.

Chris's dad, Lanvil, turned up bright and early on Saturday morning. 'Christopher not here yet? Probably still in bed. He do like his beauty sleep. Got a lot a catching up to do.'

Netta chuckled. 'He's on his way, Lanvil, he just messaged me. He got up late.'

'Hah, what did I tell you? That boy needs to face it, he's never gonna get any prettier. Might as well just get up at a sensible hour, like the rest of us.'

By the time Chris arrived, Lanvil had already been over to Frank's to check the whereabouts of his cupboard and had made a start locating Netta's. Chris rubbed his eyes, still looking half asleep. 'I suppose Dad's been here ages?'

'Afraid so.'

'I'd better get up there then, or I'll never hear the last of it.'

The house was soon filled with banging and crashing. Netta waited for it to subside before popping her head up over the ladder. 'Fancy a cuppa?'

Chris was levering plasterboard from the wall by the chimney breast. The clouds of dust and his large frame made it difficult to see past him but Netta could tell that his face, hair and clothes were covered in grey powder. Lanvil was a few feet away in a neatly pressed, but still lightly dusted, pair of overalls. 'Tea would be good but you'd better take a look at this first.'

Chris stepped away and through the haze of dust particles, a door became visible. He wiped sweat from his brow. 'The cupboard, I presume. There's no handle but it seems to be locked. Do you want us to force it open?'

Netta climbed into the room. There was an uncomfortable feeling in the pit of her stomach: what if Kelly was right and there was an actual skeleton in there? Why else would it be locked? 'I suppose. I mean, what do you think? Should we?'

'It's probably empty but we might as well take a look,' said Lanvil.

'Okay then,' said Netta, even though she wasn't sure that was what she really wanted to do. Chris manoeuvred a crowbar between the door and its frame until he came to the lock. It wasn't quite as easy or elegant a job as the one her dad had done on the wooden chest but, after a couple of attempts, he broke through. The door swung slowly open. To Netta's relief there were no bodies, no bones, just two large grey plastic boxes. Still, bodies can be chopped up small enough to fit into a box.

'Shall I check inside?' said Chris. She nodded and held her breath. He lifted the lid of the top box. 'Just papers.' He carried it out of the cupboard and opened up the bottom box. 'More notebooks. Kelly will be disappointed.'

She let her breath out. So, there were more boxes to sort through but unlike the others, these were airtight. Whoever put them in there, may have wanted them hidden but they also wanted them to stay clean, dry and mould free.

Frank came over, as Lanvil and Chris were leaving. She showed him the boxes they'd brought downstairs. They opened up the one filled with note books. Netta picked a book up and leafed through it. 'The missing journals?' he said.

'Looks like it. What could be so bad in there that they had to be sealed away?'

'Whatever it was, it wasn't bad enough to destroy them.' He pulled back the lid from the other box. 'Papers and letters. Hang on, something else.' He reached in and took out a shoebox. The feeling in Netta's stomach returned. She opened the box tremulously and peered in, still expecting to find the remains of something, but it wasn't. Well, not exactly. More the personal effects of something, or someone. She thought she'd already found Edie's most precious memories but she was wrong.

'It's like a time capsule,' said Frank, his voice lowered almost to a whisper.

Netta carefully unwrapped a tissue parcel of tiny garments. She picked up a blue velvet box held shut with a metal clasp. The box was a worn at the edges and the clasp was a little rusty but it was still in reasonable shape. Nevertheless, she took great care in prising it open. Inside was a silver object, one end a rattle and the other a teething ring. Her dad had one just like it, it had been a christening present from his grandparents. Underneath the blue box was a piece of paper, a document. She read it and passed it to Frank. 'Actually, I think it's a memories box. A mother's memories box.'

16

DUTY BEFORE SELF

EDIE – 1944

'This must be how it is with love.'

'Edie, we'll be late.' Dolly called out to her across the dorm. They were on the morning shift. Edie put her diary away, she'd been scribbling her last few thoughts down and lost track of time. There was a letter for Catherine to be posted. She'd written to Edie to let her know she was married. The baby's father had done the decent thing, after all. It had been a quick registry office wedding before the groom went back to his regiment. She'd been found a house near his base. She would have preferred to stay at home but her parents thought it best to stay away until the gossip died down:

'In short, I'm not allowed back until the baby is old enough for its birth date to be ambiguous. They can then pretend it was conceived after the wedding and decorum is maintained.'

Edie slipped the letter into her pocket and followed Dolly out. She'd post it after her shift. The other girls on their watch were waiting downstairs for them. They ribbed her about being a slowcoach but it was all good humoured: there was plenty of time really.

As soon as they left the manor house, the frost hit them. It was exceptionally cold, even for February. In spite of her heavy woollen greatcoat, Edie was already chilled to the bone. They quickened their pace and tried not to slip on the icy path, glad to reach the relative warmth of the Operations building. Unfortunately, the relief wouldn't last long: they were all fully aware that once they got down below, it would be every bit as cold as the outside. That was one of the drawbacks of working underground.

It had been over a week since she'd seen Robert. Although they never discussed it, she knew he was involved in a new offensive on the German aviation factories so it would be a while before they'd be able to see each other again. The last time they'd been together, they'd been able to spend a few hours at the cottage. It was such a delight, pretending to be Mrs Robert Goodwin. A while before, he'd asked if she would sketch a self-portrait that he could keep it with the one she'd drawn of him. It was a little embarrassing to draw oneself. She imagined Lily saying it made her look a bit full of herself but she did it anyway: it was her gift to him. She used the photograph that had been taken of her at the wedding as a template. Mina had given it to her as a thank you for being her bridesmaid. She gave him the sketch during that visit to the cottage. He said it was perfectly delightful and folded it up with the one she'd made of him, which was a little worn by now. She made a mental note to draw a new one. When he put them in his breast pocket, she noticed he had that photo of the four of them in there too, the one from their day in the Cotswolds. He told her they were his talismans, keeping him safe and giving him the courage to do what he had to do. It was the closest they'd come to discussing his feelings about work and it sealed an intimacy between them that was stronger than anything she'd known before. After he'd gone, she thought about it for a long time, writing page after page about it in her diary and finally concluding that morning, this must be what love was all about. This must be how it was when your love for someone knew no bounds.

The Operations Room was a hive of activity. At least that would keep her warm. She hated the quiet shifts most times but especially when it was as cold as this. Not only was it boring when you had nothing to do but sit around, it also made you colder. The nervous energy of a hectic shift was like an internal boiler and, if that wasn't enough, you were too busy concentrating on the job to think about your freezing fingers and toes. Edie's watch made for the briefing room in readiness for the handover update. She was about to follow them when she saw Lily making a dash for her. She grabbed Edie's arm. 'Ede, we're missing two bombers. One of them is Robert's. I'm sorry, I have to go but I thought you should know.'

As soon as she said it, Lily rushed back to her station but Edie was rooted to the spot. Lily's words were rolling over and over in her head, *one of them is Robert's.* Then, Dolly was shaking her. 'Ede, pull yourself together. You've got stay in control. You're at work.'

She nodded. 'Yes. Yes, of course. Thank you, Dolly.'

She joined her team for the handover and went on to work. What else could she do? There were other lives at stake beside Robert's, men who depended on her accuracy and focus. She could not allow herself the luxury of panic or worry, she could only put him out of her mind and do her job. In spite of it, or possibly because of it, she concentrated more than she'd ever done before. She had this strange sensation that she was watching herself; directing herself through each instruction that came through her headset. Each move on the board was made with an absolute purpose. Even so, every minute seemed to take an age to tick over to the next and the shift appeared to be endless.

When the first missing bomber limped home, she allowed herself a flicker of optimism. It was only when her shift ended that she gave in to hope, fear and, when the confirmation came, despair. Robert's plane had been shot down before it had a chance to expel its load. It burst into flames and exploded while still in the air, before any of the crew could bail out. He was gone, just like Jimmy. The future they'd planned was no more and yet the war raged on. The horror of it was endless. How foolish she'd been to ever think it exciting and fun. She wanted to dig herself a hole and crawl in like a wounded animal to wait for death, but, of course, that wasn't possible. Her country needed her and she had to do what was expected of her. Duty before self.

She kept her emotions buttoned up inside her during her shifts. When she wasn't working, she went to the field where they'd first met and waited for something to release this great weight that was dragging her down. She waited in vain. Nothing made her feel better. Just as he'd said, they were two peas in a pod, she and Robert. Now that he was dead, she might as well be.

She avoided Mina and Tom. Not because of any ill feeling towards them but because the sight of them brought back too many memories and Tom bore too close a resemblance to Robert to make his presence a comfort. Any offer of help or friendship from Mina was met with polite distance. The only two people she allowed near her were Lily and Dolly. They seemed to have made it their mission to keep her going. It was they who made sure she ate and got to work on time, they who made sure she was presentable enough to avoid being put on report. She became an automaton, working; sleeping; eating to order rather than for anything remotely pleasurable.

Six weeks had passed and she still hadn't told her parents. Her mother had written twice since Robert's death but she'd been unable to bring herself to write the words. Mummy joked that they were looking forward to meeting this most splendid man. When was Edie going to bring him home? If only because she couldn't bear to read those words again, she summoned up the courage and wrote:

'Dear Mummy,

I'm sorry to tell you that Robert's plane went down over Leipzig. He and his crew were all killed.

Yours,

Edie.'

She sealed the envelope before she could look at it, as if not looking at it might make it go away.

Her mother's reply was swift:

'My dearest child,

I am so sorry to hear about Robert's death. You must be feeling dreadful at this moment. I wish I could be there to comfort you. I can only say that, when we lost Jimmy, I found solace in God and duty.

I know you're doing your duty but, my darling, are you going to church? Have you spoken to your local vicar? If not, why don't you try it? It may help.

Daddy and I are praying for you.

With deepest affection,
Mummy.'

No, she had not been to church, well, not of her own accord. There was the compulsory church parade but that didn't count as far as Edie was concerned. She attended those in body but not in spirit. She'd stopped bringing her spirit with her after she started having intercourse with Robert. They were unmarried, it was a sin but it was a sin she enjoyed. To go to church and pretend she was sorry seemed hypocritical, so she stopped going there – spiritually, at least. She thought about the possibility of returning. She thought of Robert with his talismans that did him no good whatsoever. She imagined the drawings she'd made for him, and that photo burning in his breast pocket. She wondered if he'd clutched them in his last few minutes, if he'd thought of her, or Tom, or maybe Mina. He'd always been a little too fond of her for Edie's liking. She thought of Jimmy, and she decided against going to church ever again.

Turning away from the church, gave room for a new emotion to take hold of Edie – anger. She directed it at God Himself for being so cruel as to take so much from her and for allowing the deaths of Robert, Jimmy and others like them. What purpose did it serve other than the infliction of suffering on good people? She was beginning to wonder about God. She was beginning to wonder if there was actually such a thing because, if a benign divinity did exist, why did he allow so much evil in the world? She decided then that there was no God. That left her with a problem. She was not yet done with anger, she needed something else to fix it on. So she turned it on Hitler and the Nazis, then on Churchill and anybody in high office for sacrificing the lives of so many. None of those sated her. She turned her fury on Robert, for making him love her and for giving her hope of a future. She placed it on Mina and Tom for still having each other. She told herself it was Tom's fault: if Robert hadn't followed him into the RAF, he might still be alive. The anger kept her going, it gave her the will to get up each day and go into work but it was also exhausting. She was sleeping badly. She felt nauseous all the time and her monthlies had stopped. Before long, she was too worn out for anger and settled on a feeling of isolation that carried her through from one day to the next.

17

MOTHER NATURE INTERVENES

EDIE – 1944

'We have something new to fix our hope on. Something that might yet save us from our despair.'

Edie was in the NAAFI canteen with the other girls on her watch, eating lunch before their shift. Except for Dolly who was making a show of not being able to eat because she was too upset. She'd worked herself up into a panic because her time of the month hadn't arrived. Edie was only half-listening but she couldn't see why it mattered. Surely Dolly was better off without them? She couldn't remember when she last had hers. She couldn't even remember how long she'd been without Robert. Everything was a blur. Dolly continued to prattle on. She was saying something about the chap she was courting, one of the ground crew from Robert's base. 'It was only the once we didn't use a johnny. Just my luck if I've caught for it. Thing is, he's already married so it's not like we can get hitched or anything.' She said it so loudly that the WAAFs at the next table looked over and shook their heads. It was typical of Dolly: she couldn't do anything quietly. Everyone had to know her business. The other girls on Edie's table rolled their eyes at each other, some looked cross and some were visibly cringing, realising that the onlookers would assume they were as loose as her. They got up and left for their shift ten minutes earlier than they needed to. Edie followed them, leaving Dolly to relay her woes to the next table.

The next day, Dolly was back to her usual self, all smiles. 'False alarm, Ede. I was just late, not pregnant. I won't make that mistake again though, it's a johnny or nothing in future. He can like it or lump it.'

Outwardly, Edie hardly appeared to register Dolly's relief, but something lodged in her consciousness. It occurred to her that while Dolly's canteen outburst had been somewhat uncomfortable, it had also been informative. Since joining up, she'd come to realise that she was quite ignorant about many things to do with the workings of her body. It seemed rather ridiculous now that she thought about it, but she'd never before realised that her monthly visitor had anything to do with having children. No one had ever explained it to her. Her mother rarely mentioned it and Hannah only ever referred to it as the curse. Even now that Dolly had suggested the two were related, she still didn't know how. She simply did not know enough about how these things worked. On her solitary walk that evening she tried to decide what to do. She'd been assuming that the lack of her own monthlies had something to do with Robert's death but now she considered that there might be another reason, not entirely unrelated to him. She needed to talk to someone who was more worldly-wise than her. Dolly was the first person that sprang to mind but she was far too much of a gossip. Lily might think the worst of her. There was only one person she could trust. Mina.

Mina greeted her like the proverbial prodigal sister. 'I'm glad you came: I've been so worried about you. Both you and Tom have been so remote, I haven't known which way to turn, and you look so peaky, my darling little Edie. So very tired and sad.'

The warmth of Mina's strong arms around her was a comfort. It made Edie think of the last time she saw Robert. They'd talked about going back to Birmingham to meet her parents. They'd even made plans for their wedding and their future together. He'd kissed her and they held each other for a long time before parting, longer than usual and it made her wonder now if he'd had a feeling that he might not come back. At last, the release she'd been waiting for came and she broke down.

'So, when did you last have your monthlies?'

Edie shook her head. 'I'm not sure. I think, maybe about a month before ... Robert...' They had walked around and around the grounds and were now sitting in a quiet spot, as far away from the waafery as possible.

'Did you always use a johnny?' That word johnny again. She'd heard the term before Dolly had used it but she wasn't actually sure what it meant. Mina frowned. 'A sheath, darling. A condom. Did you use them when you and Robert had intercourse?'

So that's what a johnny was. 'Oh, I see. Yes, most of the time. Well, maybe half of the time. If we ran out, then he would withdraw before ... you know. If he could.'

'So, is it fair to say then that it's possible you and Robert had full intercourse, at least once, without protection.'

'Um yes, I suppose so, if you put it like that.'

'Stand up for a minute would you, E?' Mina ran her

eyes up and down the length of Edie's body. 'Have you been
feeling sick at all, particularly in the mornings?'

Edie nodded. 'Yes, a little.'

Mina rested her hand on Edie's tummy. There was a
sudden flutter, as if she had butterflies. Mina took her hand
away and sighed. 'Sweetie, you do understand what this
means, don't you?'

Edie wasn't fully sure she did but she had an inkling.

'I think we may have to get you to a doctor. I think I'm
about to become an aunt.'

The news at least gave the three of them something to focus
on beside their grief. Mina got the message to Tom and he
came over as soon as she could. Edie was shocked by the
change in him. He looked much older. It seemed as though
he'd lost part of himself which of course he had: he and
Robert had been best pals as well as brothers. She understood this: she'd been that way about Jimmy. With Robert it
was different for her, but no less painful. At least though,
he'd left something of himself with her.

'What will you do?' asked Tom. 'Will you go back to
Birmingham?'

'I don't think I can, at least, not yet. I'm not sure they'd
be able to live with it. It would be different if Robert and I
had married but we didn't, so that's that.' From the moment
Mina had pointed out her pregnancy she'd been thinking
about this. Her mother's reaction to Catherine was stuck in
her mind. Luckily for Catherine, she'd been able to marry
the baby's father but socially, she and her family were still set
apart. She couldn't do that to her parents. She knew too
that while they were good, decent people, they had a strict
moral code. She was certain they would insist she went away

somewhere quietly until the baby was born and then give it up for adoption. She wasn't sure she wanted to do that: the baby was her only link to Robert and she couldn't bear the thought of giving it away. She had a little money saved. When her dismissal came through, she would find some rooms and stay there until she was ready to tell them.

Mina's head moved a fraction, a tiny gesture that seemed to act as a signal to Tom to take Edie's hand. 'Well then, let us look after you. When your discharge comes through, move into the cottage. We'll hire a nurse to take care of you and the baby until you're back on your feet. Mina and I will stay as often as we can.'

She gasped. 'Oh Tom, would you do that for me? I don't know what to say.'

'For you and for Robert,' he said. 'Please say yes, Edie. I know it's what Robert would want.'

She turned to Mina. 'Are you sure I wouldn't be in the way?'

Mina tutted. 'Don't be a fool, E. We're a family.'

'Then yes please. I'll do it.'

18

ROBERT JAMES GOODWIN ENTERS THE WORLD

EDIE – 1944

'From death comes life.'

Mina opened the door to the cottage. They walked into the little sitting room and Edie cast her eyes about the place remembering the last time she was here with Robert. No, she mustn't think about that now. She must only think of the baby. She touched her belly and the baby gave a little kick. It had been an eventful morning so far, her last at Rudloe Manor. Her friends had lined up to say goodbye to her in the dormitory and promised to visit as often as they could. Before then, she'd handed in her uniform and it had taken all of her resolve to keep a stiff upper lip. She was no longer a WAAF or an independent woman. Her life was changing again and she didn't know what to. It made her feel both sad and afraid.

Mina had carried her suitcase on the long walk to the cottage. Now that they were here, she took it upstairs to the bedroom that would be Edie's and the child's. Edie sat on the couch and listened to her footsteps coming back down-stairs and into the room.

'I have to get back, E. Will you be all right?'

'Yes, I'll be fine.' Edie wasn't sure she would be but it seemed the right thing to say.

'I'll knock on Amy's door on the way back through the village. She'll come right over so you won't be on your own for long.'

'Amy?'

'The nurse. You remember, don't you? She's very pleas-ant, she has four children of her own, so she's quite expe-rienced.'

'Of course. And, does she understand my … situation?'

'She thinks you're a widow. They all do.'

'Right. Yes. Good.'

Mina stood in the doorway, fumbling with the keys. 'Are you sure you'll be all right?'

Edie summoned up the will to smile. 'Yes, off you go. If you leave it any longer, you'll be on report.'

Mina swooped her up into a tight hug. She looked a little teary-eyed. 'I'll be back as soon as I can.' She disap-peared into the hallway. Edie heard the front door open but within a few seconds, Mina was back. 'I forgot to leave the keys for you.' She dropped them on the sideboard. 'Take care of yourself, my darling.' Then she left.

Amy was a robust looking woman with a curvaceous body and dark hair tied up in neat bun. Edie guessed that she was in her mid-thirties. She wore a skirt and blouse with short sleeves that revealed firm, strong arms. Perched on one of those arms was a small boy who buried his face in her large chest and clung to her neck. 'Don't worry, Mrs Goodwin, I won't bring him every time. He's a bit under the weather at the moment and made such a racket when I tried to leave him with my mum. They can be very clingy when they're ill. You'll find that out, I suppose.'

'Bring him whenever you like, I don't mind, and please, call me Edie.'

'That's very nice of you, Edie.' Amy gave her a smile that made her think of Hannah. Hannah – more like a second mother than a housekeeper – she would have liked her to be here now but that not being possible, Amy would be a good substitute. They agreed that she would pop by morning and afternoon until Edie's time grew close but Edie was to call on her any other time that she needed or wanted to. The important thing was that she should not feel she was on her own in this. 'I don't like to think of you all alone here. I won't lie to you, having a child is hard, even when you've got a husband and family around you. So anytime, Edie, anytime.' She fussed around, preparing some food for Edie to eat later and then took herself and the little boy home.

When she was gone, Edie took her place back on the couch and listened to the sounds of the cottage. Aside from the odd creak, there were none. After about an hour she heard voices through the open window – two men greeting each other as they passed. Just a few words, then silence again. It was all so desolate. She wiped away a stray tear, got up and took a seat at a little writing table under the window. There was some notepaper and envelopes in one of the drawers. She took a deep breath in and inhaled the scent of roses from the front garden. This would be a nice spot to write her journal entries. For now though, she had to write to her parents to tell them her billet had moved back into the village and ask them to send letters here. She couldn't risk them writing to her at the base and having their post returned. She hoped they would be too preoccupied to question why they weren't going through the usual official routes.

When the letter was finished she went out the post office, in the heart of the village, to purchase a stamp. The postmistress was a friendly woman who addressed her as Mrs Goodwin. She would have to get used to that. She wondered what the postmistress would make of her parents' letters addressed to someone called Pinsent. She'd have to think of a feasible explanation. With nothing else to do, she had plenty of time to work on that one. There were children playing on the village green. She recognised the little chap who'd been with Amy earlier, this time clinging on to what must have been his big sister. For a while, she stopped to watch them. One or two women walked past and said hello. Perhaps the place wasn't as bleak as she'd first thought. Perhaps she could make a go of things here until the child was born.

It was 3rd September. Amy had been with her for the last two days. Nothing had happened on the first day but she was convinced the baby was too close to leave Edie alone. She knew the signs, she said. Amy's mother had popped in with the children. It had been a pleasant distraction from the boredom of waiting on the couch. Edie was so big now that she'd been camped there for weeks. Half the time, she couldn't even be bothered to go to bed at night. It felt like this baby was going to remain inside her forever, growing and growing until her stomach was stretched to bursting point, but today, something had changed. This afternoon she'd woken up from a nap to find a damp patch on the

mattress and soon after, the pains began. It was early
evening now. The midwife had been sent for via the postmistress who possessed the only telephone in the village and
now she was here, directing them as if it were a military
operation and she the commanding officer. She loomed over
Edie on one side of the bed, looking as if she had better
things to do than wait for this rather tardy infant to make an
appearance. Amy was on the other side, mopping Edie's
brow with a cold flannel and generally providing the
warmth sadly missing in the midwife.

Amy had warned Edie what would happen. She'd been
quite candid but at this very moment, Edie was certain she
hadn't been candid enough. Nothing had prepared her for
the pains that were so intense they made her lightheaded. At
first they'd been spaced well apart but now there were
hardly any gaps at all, just one interminable wave of agony.
From somewhere amidst this torture, an animalistic urge to
bear down at all costs overtook her and she began to scream
and push at the same time.

'Come now, Mrs Goodwin, there's no need for that sort
of racket,' said the midwife.

Amy grabbed Edie's hand. 'Leave her alone.'

The midwife huffed. 'It's unseemly. Absolutely no need.'

Amy tutted. 'There speaks a woman who's never had a
baby. Come on, Edie. You scream and shout all you like, my
lovely.'

The two continued to bicker but Edie was no longer
listening to either of them. Her attention was caught by
something in the far corner of the room that in the half-
light looked like a figure. Common sense told her it was the
shadows in the dull evening light but in this addled state of
frenzy she thought it was him. Another surge of pain
washed through her; another compulsion to expel this devil

child, all the time without taking her eyes off the figure. She opened her mouth and roared until the words formed. 'Help me, Robert.'

'It's all right, my lovely. The baby's coming. Here's the head. Another push, Edie. One more push,' said Amy from what seemed like miles away.

Another wave, another roar. Edie gritted her teeth and bore down. For a moment she looked at her hand gripping Amy's as if her life depended on it. When she turned back to the corner, the figure was gone. Where was he? How could he leave her? How could he go? As the baby slid into the midwife's hands, Edie wept uncontrollably.

'It's a boy!' said the midwife. Edie's son welcomed the world with a loud cry. A thick mass of black hair with bright blue eyes, he was placed in his mother's arms and all at once, she saw where Robert had gone. The midwife smiled: the sight of this newborn must have softened her. 'He seems quite healthy. Lovely eyes. Mind you, they all start off blue. They may change later.'

Edie kissed the top of his head. 'I'm sure they'll stay like that. He has the Pinsent eyes.'

'What will you call him?' said Amy.

'Robert James Goodwin.' Edie cradled her son in her arms. Her son, she liked the sound of that. There would be no adoption. Whatever happened she would not let him go.

19

LOOSE MORALS AND DASHED HOPES

EDIE – 1945

'I heard on the radio that the Allies have all but taken the Rhine. The end may yet be in sight.'

Dare she hope that this horror might be over soon and that good would triumph over evil? So much had happened in the last six years, it was hard to be optimistic. Every time she felt a glimmer of hope; every time she thought of the future, something happened to drag her back down, and here it was again, just when victory was beginning to look tangible – her mother's letter:

'Dear Edie,

I'm afraid I have bad news. We've been informed that Victor was badly injured in one of the earlier advances in the Rhine. We don't have any further details about the extent of his injuries but we do know that he's alive and is on his way back to an English hospital. Pray for him, darling.'

Pray for him? She would if she thought it meant some-thing. Robbie stirred in his cradle and let out a little mewling cry. That was what they called him now. His name had been shortened by Amy and Edie had liked it from the start: it gave him his own identity, separate from his father. His eyes opened and he let out another cry. She shook the silver rattle Mina and Tom had given him as a christening gift. They doted on him as much as she did and were over-joyed when she asked them to be his godparents. Initially, she'd resisted having him christened but they persuaded her that she should do it for his sake, so she gave in, reasoning that it might be something in her favour when she plucked up the courage to tell her parents.

Robbie's cries became louder and more persistent. She picked him up and he snuffled at her breast. 'You're hungry, is that it? My, you're a greedy little fellow.' She unbuttoned her blouse and let him suckle. He was such a bonny boy, such a sweetheart. She sang a lullaby to him, one that her mother sang to her as a child, and thought about how lucky she'd been to have had such a happy childhood. Her parents and Hannah had done everything possible to make it the best. Now she was a mother, she wanted the same for Robbie.

Her thoughts turned to God. Perhaps Robbie was her gift from Him. A consolation prize to make up for the loss of Robert and Jimmy, and now with Vic... Could it be that He was testing her? Perhaps she should give Him another chance, if only for poor Vic. She rocked Robbie in her arms and closed her eyes. 'Hello God. It's me, Edith Pinsent, sinner and lapsed Christian. Please, don't let Victor die.'

Edie alighted the train at Selly Oak, just as she'd done on her last visit. It was a chilly, grey March afternoon and, this time, the walk home was less pleasant. Not least because her mood matched the weather. She'd only come because her parents were going to see Vic. It was the first time that she and Robbie had been apart and the separation was agonising. He was in good hands with Amy, and in enthusiastic but less good hands with Mina but it didn't make it any easier. Amy didn't ask why she hadn't been able to take Robbie with her. Possibly that was because with four children to feed and a husband serving abroad, she'd been glad of the extra work but Edie was beginning to suspect that Amy had guessed the real reason. Ordinarily, that would have made her uneasy but Amy was a kindly, live and let live sort of person who had no time for gossip. She felt safe in her hands.

The sound of children's laughter hit her as soon as she stepped into the hall. A small girl ran in from the kitchen and stopped dead at the sight of her. Following up from the rear and crashing into her was another girl and a boy, both older than the first child. 'Hello,' said Edie, slightly taken aback by their presence.

The children continued to stare at her in silence. A young woman appeared in the kitchen doorway and said something to them that made them retreat to the kitchen and then out into the garden. Edie didn't quite catch what she said but the language sounded German. When she looked more closely, Edie realised that the young woman was not much more than a girl herself. She was wearing an apron wrapped around her thin frame. She gave Edie a polite but unsure smile. 'Pardon my brother and sisters. They have a little difficulty with strangers. You are Edith, I think? I am Birgitt.'

'Birgitt?' said Edith.

'Yes. Mrs Pinsent has not yet told you, perhaps? We are staying here until we can go back home.'

'Back home?'

'To Germany.'

Of course. Edie had forgotten that her parents were now taking in refugees. All at once, everything clicked into place. Birgitt and her family were German Jews who had fled the Nazis. 'I'm so sorry. You must think me very rude. Yes, I'm Edith, but everyone calls me Edie. Is my mother here, or perhaps, Hannah?'

'They are shopping. The queues are so long. They try to share the task.' She said it as if she were reciting it. Edie guessed she'd learned it from her mother.

'And your parents? Your mother and father, are they here?'

Birgitt lowered her eyes and gave a short shake of the head. 'I am preparing the vegetables for dinner. Will you come into the kitchen?'

The front door opened behind Edie and there was a look of relief on Birgitt's face as Edie's mother and Hannah appeared. Edie's mother embraced her. 'Edie, darling we were hoping to get home before you. You're looking well. You've met Birgitt and the children, I see? We have quite a houseful but we're all mucking in together, aren't we Hannah?'

'We are,' said Hannah. She gave Edie a hug. 'Get the tea on, Birgitt, there's a good girl.'

The children came in from the garden full of excitement, hugging and kissing her mother and Hannah. After a few minutes, Birgitt ushered them back outside.

'They're like that every time we go out,' said her mother. 'They've been like it since they realised that they didn't have to fear us. I think they're just so overjoyed that we've come back. It's their parents, you see. They have no idea whether they're alive or dead. It's quite tragic.'

· · ·

Birgitt had taken the children to the park and her mother had gone to check on an elderly neighbour. Edie was helping Hannah in the kitchen. 'They have a good effect on this house, those kids,' said Hannah. 'Brought us all back to life again.'

'I'm glad,' said Edie. She hoped they would feel the same about Robbie when they met him.

'Everything all right is it? You getting on with things?' It was Hannah's way of asking if she'd come to terms with Robert's death.

'Yes, I think so.'

'How come you weren't wearing your uniform? I thought it was compulsory when you were travelling.'

Edie had to think quick. How stupid of her not to realise that someone would notice she was in civvies. She'd got off quite lightly with some highly dubious story as to why her address had changed but her parents were more trusting than Hannah. Hannah was far more sharp when it came to noticing the little things. 'Special dispensation. There was an accident in the canteen. Someone knocked over a pan of stew and my uniform was covered in the stuff. My spare one was already being cleaned.'

They set out early the next morning. The hospital was several hours drive away, in Sussex. It was Edie's only time alone with her parents; her only chance to broach the subject of Robbie. The day before, she'd spent the entire journey home trying to work out what to say but, short of blurting it all out, nothing sprang to mind. In the end she decided the best course of action was to start with Catherine. 'I meant to say, Catherine wrote to tell me she and David have a daughter.' No one said anything. It was as if they hadn't heard her. 'You know she married last year, don't you?'

'Yes Edith, we were aware of it,' said her mother. 'I had no idea you were corresponding with Catherine. I thought we had agreed that you would not.'

'I know but Mummy, she's married now.'

Her mother sighed and looked out of the window. 'My dear, I know this sounds harsh but Catherine has brought disgrace on her family. Sadly, she's not the only one. In my work, I've come across so many girls who, either through loose morals or simple foolishness, have found themselves in the same predicament. Many will end up abandoned with no other recourse but adoption, and their unfortunate offspring will always be branded with unmentionable names.'

'Have you no sympathy for those girls at all, Mummy? What if that were me?'

'Don't be ridiculous, Edith. You're far too sensible and decent to do something like that. Yes, of course I have some sympathy for them but that doesn't change the plain fact that an illegitimate child is a source of great shame.'

Edie stared at the back of her mother's head. How could someone who did so much good in the world be so brutal? These girls that she spoke of were no different to her own daughter, if only she knew. She had to make her understand that such things happened these days and one simply had to make the best of it. She made another valiant attempt. 'But surely, when this war is over, things will be different? Surely society will have no option but to change?'

Her father coughed. 'Not in that regard, no Edith.' The subject was closed. They drove the rest of the way in an uncomfortable silence.

It was a relief to reach the hospital. The rain had started

not long after their awkward conversation and the inside of the car was muggy and oppressive. It matched exactly the general feeling of claustrophobia creeping through Edie. As soon as they pulled up, she got out and breathed in the cold, drizzly air. The journey had been tortuous but they were here now. At least Vic would be a friendly face.

Just before they went into Vic's ward, her father said: 'Don't expect too much. Victor was badly burned. We're lucky he survived.'

Edie braced herself. As they approached his bed, she was relieved to see that his face wasn't horribly scarred. There were some burns on there but not nearly as much as she was expecting. However, most of his body seemed to be covered in dressings and his legs were suspended in the air. Not only had they been burned, both legs had also been broken when he leapt from the top floor of a building. He'd been taking shelter there when a rocket exploded next to it and sent the entire building up in flames.

'Hello Ede,' he said. 'Forgive me for not getting up, I'm a little indisposed.'

Edie giggled. The giggles turned into laughter and then to tears. To hell with a stiff upper lip: she was in despair.

The next day, she returned to the cottage, happy to see the back of Birmingham. When she got in, Mina was playing with Robbie on the floor. Edie scooped him up and showered him in kisses. He chuckled and pulled at her hair. 'Has he been good?' she asked.

'The perfect little gentleman. How did it go?'

She tickled Robbie's tummy. 'It could have been better. I have more work to do before I can introduce them to their grandson.'

20

CAST ADRIFT BY VICTORY

EDIE – 1945

'Against all odds, victory is ours. That gives me some comfort at least.'

Edie blotted the ink dry. Jimmy and Robert were dead, along with countless others and it would be a long time before Vic was fully recovered but at least the Allies had won. At least decency prevailed. It was hard to believe it was over at last, but it was. They'd celebrated VE day and, more recently, VJ day to prove it. It was definitely over.

In spite of the ups and downs, the last year had been a good one. She'd taken to motherhood surprisingly well. If her own mother had known, and if the circumstances had been different, she was sure she'd have been extremely proud of her. But her mother didn't know. Her parents were still unaware of Robbie's existence. She hadn't been back to Birmingham since that last trip in March, partly because she didn't want to be separated from Robbie again and partly because she still hadn't worked out how to tell them. She was sure though, that she would tell them in due course.

The other fly in the ointment was Robert's parents.

They knew about Robbie, Tom had told them, but it was only recently that they'd accepted him as their grandchild and they refused to acknowledge Edie. On this they seemed to be unmoveable, despite Tom's protests: she and Robert were not married and he had never mentioned that they were intending to marry. As far as they were concerned, she was a charlatan and a hussy and wanted nothing to do with her. On the writing desk was a letter from Robert's mother telling her just that.

Mrs Goodwin's words wounded Edie deeply. After putting Robbie to bed, she sat in the garden clutching the letter. How could people be so cruel? It was a silly question. She knew there were people in this world who were capable of being a great deal crueller than the Goodwins. A cuckoo called out from the nearby fields. How peaceful it was, now that there were no planes shooting across the skies. Just birds, the early evening sun and stillness.

She'd been sitting there for some time watching the night draw in when she heard a movement behind her. It was Mina, standing a few feet away, arms folded, gazing at her. Edie's glance broke Mina from her spell. 'You looked so far away, I didn't want to disturb you,' she said. 'Where were you?'

'Nowhere. I was just thinking about Robert and how much easier it would have been if we'd done the same as you and got married quickly.'

Mina sat down next to her. 'I suppose it would have been but you can't change the past, much as we'd like to. You've had a letter. From home? Is everyone all right?' Edie, shook her head. The lump in her throat made it hard to speak so she gave her the letter. Mina read it. It didn't take her long: it was very short and precise. She handed it back. 'Hateful bitch. The woman has no compassion.'

Compassion. Where was compassion in this world of today? It was nothing but death, destruction and spite. Edie heaved a great sigh and let the sadness flow out of her. Mina held her and kissed her head softly. 'It's all right, E. It's going to be all right.'

It was the end of November. Edie wrapped her cardigan around her to keep out the chill. The roses in the front garden were brown and shrivelled. The lawn was soggy from last night's rain and the clouds appeared to be threatening more. She felt as gloomy as the sky but was trying to put on a brave face for fear of upsetting Lily.

'You will write to me won't you, Ede?'

'Of course I will.'

'I shall miss you so much, and little Robbie too.'

'And I shall miss you too, my dear friend.' There, they were both crying now.

One by one, her friends' demob numbers had come up. First Mina, then Dolly, now Lily. Dolly had become quite tiresome of late and Edie was actually glad to see the back of her. She didn't say as much when Dolly came to say goodbye. That would have been unfair. Besides, Dolly had looked after her as much as Lily had in those dreadful days after Robert's death. But, after Mina, she was closest to Lily. She'd been a good friend, and never judged her harshly over Robbie. Saying goodbye to her was hard. The other girls who she hadn't been as close to had already drifted away. There was only Mina left now. Since her discharge, she'd moved into the cottage. When Tom wasn't there, she and Edie spent all their time together. They went for long country walks. Sometimes, they took a trip into Bath. When Tom had leave, they drove to the sea or further into the Wiltshire countryside. Everything felt so much freer.

The letter from Mrs Goodwin had brought Edie down but from it came some good. It strengthened her relationship with Mina. They became even closer and while Tom worked tirelessly to change his parents' minds, the fact that they remained resolute seemed to matter less and less to her. She'd even allowed Tom and Mina to take Robbie to see them for a few days, using the time to visit her own parents. Again, on that visit she'd resolved to tell them but the talk was all about Vic and the possibility of him coming home. The mention of illegitimate grandchildren seemed inappropriate. She'd returned to the cottage, disappointed and irritated with herself: her courage had failed her yet again. At least Mina had been there to console her.

'There's a letter for you, E,' said Mina as soon as Edie got in. She'd walked Lily back as far as the village and then went shopping. Even in that small village it took ages what with one queue or another. Mina, never one to volunteer on the food shopping front, stayed at home to keep Robbie amused. He was walking now, in a fashion, and it was a full-time occupation keeping up with him.

Edie glanced at the letter and, when she saw it was her mother's handwriting, her heart sank. Another barely disguised request for her to return home, no doubt. The first one was in September and they'd been coming every few weeks since then. She'd fobbed them off at first saying she was one of the last to be discharged but that pretence couldn't be kept up for too long. Mummy began reporting on the sons and daughters of friends as they returned home, almost as if she were testing Edie, or suggesting that she wasn't trying hard enough to extricate herself from the WAAF. Eventually, Edie changed her story and told them she was staying with friends for a while, to help with her friend's husband who'd been badly injured. All lies, of course. Completely disrespectful but what could she do? They accepted it at first but when Vic came home, there were hints that while his body was healing, his spirit was broken. There were suggestions that her presence would be beneficial to his recovery. After a while, the suggestions became more like subtle demands.

'I'll read it later,' she said. 'Did Tom come to see you?'

'Yes. He could only stay for an hour but he wanted to tell me his news in person. His discharge has come through. He'll be leaving the RAF at the beginning of January.'

'Oh! Gosh, that all seems a bit sudden.'

'Yes, doesn't it. He'll be able to spend more time here until then, now that his duties are being wound down.' Mina chewed on her lip. 'I suppose we'll have to start thinking about the future now.'

'I suppose so.' Edie took the shopping into the kitchen. She didn't know what else to say. She really wasn't sure how she felt about Tom being there all the time. The cottage was small and cosy. A little too cosy for three adults and a small child, and Tom was no longer the man that Robert had loved so dearly. He was much more serious and irritable. The war had changed him. Robert's death had changed him. Of course, there was another reason why she was so hesitant. One which she could hardly bring herself to admit. She was worried that Mina's attention would be pulled towards him and away from her and Robbie. It was irrational, she knew, but she was jealous.

. . .

They'd had a lovely Christmas together. Tom was able to take some leave and was in good form; almost back to his old self. Edie made sure to make him feel welcome. It was, after all, the season of goodwill to all men. Mina's parents sent them a food hamper, managing to circumvent the rationing restrictions, as always, and Edie managed to cook a passable Christmas lunch. Yesterday, they had been to Weston-Super-Mare. They took a walk on the beach, along with the other families making the most of the crisp Boxing Day weather, and had a picnic of Christmas Day leftovers for lunch. All in all, it had been a very pleasant time. This morning however, there was a change in the air. They had scarcely finished breakfast when Mina and Tom told her Tom had found a job in the city and they were moving closer to London after his discharge. 'Of course, you're welcome to come with us,' said Tom. 'We're very attached to you and Robbie. We'd be very happy to have you both but Edie, don't you think it's time to decide what you're going to do?'

'What do you mean, what I'm going to do?'

'About the future. Your future, Robbie's too.'

'I haven't given it any thought,' she said, taken aback. 'This has all come rather out of the blue.'

'I see. Well, as I said, you can stay with us for as long as you like. The new house is big enough to accommodate you both. Or, you may prefer to go back to Birmingham.'

New house? So, they'd already arranged everything, without consulting her. 'It's not that I prefer it, Tom. Rather, my parents seem to be insisting on it.' She was becoming cross now. How could he press her on this, and why wasn't Mina standing up for her?

'Well then, here we are,' he said. 'What to do next?'

They were face to face. Tom's eyes were set on hers.

From behind her Robbie began to cry: he'd fallen over. She continued to stare Tom out. Mina picked Robbie up and was trying to comfort him but he wouldn't stop crying. She brought him over to Edie. 'Darling, you must see that we have to move? We have no choice. I know you feel obligated to go back home but you still have to decide what to do about this little chap. I have a suggestion. Why don't you go back to Birmingham and we'll look after Robbie for you until you've told your parents? You can come and collect him when you're ready.'

Edie looked at her aghast. 'Do you really think I would abandon my son?'

'You're not abandoning him, E. You're leaving him with us until the time is right for you to take him home. We'll take great care of him and you can come to see him whenever you want to.'

Edie shook her head. 'No, I'm not listening to this. I won't have it.' She put on Robbie's outdoor clothes and sat him in his pram, then grabbed her own and clattered through the front door, down the path towards the village. She half-expected them to call after her but no call came, so she carried on through the village and out the other side. When it got too cold and Robbie was beginning to be miserable, she turned back and called in on Amy. The children made a fuss of him and he was soon happy again. She stayed for a while before returning home, noticing as she got closer to the cottage that Tom's car was gone. She hoped that was because he'd returned to the base but she found a note on the writing desk informing her they'd gone to see Mina's parents and wouldn't be back until tomorrow. So this was how it was going to be from now on?

When she put Robbie to bed, he refused to sleep. He thrashed around in the cot, desperately fighting tiredness. It was as if the tension in her had transferred over to him. She sang him a lullaby to settle him. Becalmed, he lay down and let her stroke his dark curly hair. He put his thumb in his mouth and said the word she never tired of hearing: 'Mama.'

'Hush my little man. Sleep now, sleep now,' she whispered.

His eyes closed and then he was asleep. She remained there watching the rise and fall of his chest, thinking about what to do. There was only one option. She would go to this new house and start a new life with her son and friends. She went back down to the writing desk, took out a sheet of notepaper and wrote:

'Dear Mummy and Daddy,

I'm afraid it's impossible for me to come home. I'm ashamed to say that I've been lying to you…'

When she was finished, she felt a sense of relief even though it was likely they may never speak to her again. Before sealing the envelope, she put in a photograph of Robbie that she'd had taken in Bath.

The next morning, she wrapped Robbie up warm in his pram and made for the village again. She was determined to post the letter, whatever the consequences. She tried not to think about her parents' reaction when they read it; tried not to imagine their disappointment in her. She refused to believe that on seeing the photograph of her dear, sweet little boy, they would not forgive her and welcome them both home. All thoughts of their heartache over Jimmy and their worries about Vic were pushed to the back of her mind. She had to do it, for Robbie's sake and for her own.

When she reached the postbox, she took the letter out of her pocket, lifted it to the slot and froze. In her mind's eye, she saw her mother opening the letter. She saw the look on her face when she realised that her daughter was no better than those other fallen women. No, this was not the way. She would have to tell them face to face, to explain that Robbie was an accident, a happy accident. She put the letter back in her pocket and turned around.

A week later, she packed her things and left the cottage. She cried nearly all the way to Birmingham. Her life was empty without Robbie and Mina. She was cast adrift.

21

NAN THINGS AND A SEX TALK

NETTA – 2019

Will had already left when Netta got up that morning. Kelly was still in bed but she could hear her stirring. Still half asleep, she put the kettle on. She could have done with another couple of hours really but it was already past her self-imposed morning watershed of nine o'clock. Anything after that felt too decadent to be acceptable at her age. She'd had a restless night. She'd taken Edie's diaries up to bed with her and fell asleep, somewhere around the time that Edie received that awful letter from Robert's parents. When she woke up an hour later, she was sobbing. She couldn't remember what she'd been dreaming about but it must have been quite powerful because she couldn't shake the feeling of absolute loss. Unable to get back off again, she'd read the diary to its conclusion – Edie leaving for Birmingham without Robbie. She understood how devastating that must have been for her: back in those dark times after the miscarriage when Colin found out about everything, the threat of losing her children hung over her daily, with crippling consequences.

She'd somehow managed to get back to sleep but it was

fitful and she'd woken up several times, fretting about what could have happened next with Edie and wishing she'd taken the next diary to bed with her. Now it was morning and she was still fretting. She filled the teapot that had once been Edie's. She'd only recently taken to using it after Liza pointed out that it was more environmentally friendly than a single bag for every mug. Since then, she'd been waiting for her to discover that some teabags contained plastic. It might have to be tea leaves or nothing then. She heard Kelly on the stairs and poured out another cup. The cups were Edie's too. Another new habit, this time thanks to her mother who'd persuaded her to use them instead of her own more modern stoneware ones: 'So much tastier in a china cup, Netta. Granny Wilde swore by it. She only ever drank tea in a good china cup.' Netta had to admit, it was a superior taste. Once she'd started, there was no going back.

Kelly shuffled into the kitchen, bleary-eyed and still in her pyjamas. 'It's fucking freezing in here. Has the heating packed up?'

'No, it's just a draughty old house. Put a jumper on.'

Kelly dropped down onto a chair. 'You sound like my nan.' She eyed the china tea cup that Netta pushed across the table. 'You're beginning to act like her too.'

'I can do you a mug.'

Kelly took a sip. 'Nah, you're all right. Tastes better in china.' Netta raised her eyebrows and Kelly grinned back at her. 'It's a nan thing. Toast?' She pulled on a jumper that was hanging over the back of a chair. It was Will's, far too big for her. She stood up and it fell to halfway down her thighs, reminding Netta of the first time she'd come across her at the foodbank, causing havoc because she had a menstrual emergency. It was Paula who'd rescued Kelly on that day by giving her tampons and her own cardigan to cover her blood-stained crotch. Like Will's jumper, it was far too big for Kelly's petite frame. It made her look tiny and vulnerable, in spite of the huge row she'd caused not long before. She still looked like that now.

Kelly chewed on her toast. 'You were up late.'

'I've been reading Edie's diaries when I should have been sleeping.'

'Yeah, me too. You don't mind, do you? I took one of the ones you'd already read. The one where her and Robert are getting jiggy.'

'No, I don't mind. What did you think?'

'I thought it was pretty amazing to be honest. I couldn't sleep until I finished it. It was like a proper book, only interesting.'

Netta suppressed a smile. 'Books can be interesting too. You just have to find the ones that strike a chord with you, but Edie does write well. She makes you feel as if you're there with her.'

'Yeah. The stuff she writes about the sex though. Like they couldn't get enough of each other. I mean, she was around twenty then, wasn't she? He was her first and she just loved it from the get-go. Did you ever have that?'

'Not with my first, no. That was very disappointing.'

'What about with the others?'

Netta put down her toast. This could turn out to be a tricky conversation. 'Er, well, yes. With Doogie. Definitely with him. With Colin, not so much. What about you?'

'Nah. Craig was about the best but I was never that arsed about it, to be fair. I thought sex was always like that but now, I'm beginning to wonder if there's something wrong with me.'

'I think it's just that you haven't met the right lover yet.'

Kelly smirked. 'A bit like books, you mean. I need to meet someone who strikes the right chord.'

'Exactly, you piss-taker. Seriously though, Craig and the others probably weren't very attentive lovers.'

Kelly frowned. 'What does attentive mean?'

'It means they spend as much time pleasuring you as they would like you to pleasure them.'

'Ugh. Now you've just made it sound gross.' They both laughed. Kelly poured more tea. 'Never thought I'd be talking to you about sex.'

'Neither did I.'

'We must be bored. When do you think we'll get the approval on the business?'

'Any day now, I should think.'

'Good.' Kelly pursed her lips into a tight little smile. 'So, is Frank an attentive lover then?'

Before Netta could tell her that was one conversation that was definitely off limits, somebody knocked the front door.

'Claire!' Netta stood on the doorstep, mouth wide open.

'You going to ask me in then?'

'Shit, yes, sorry. Come in.'

Claire looked hesitant. 'Have I come at a bad time?'

'No, it's great to see you. Sorry, I haven't woken up properly yet. We found another load of Edie's things stashed away in a secret cupboard last weekend and I was up half the night reading them.'

'Very mysterious. Anything shocking?'

'Well it was in its day. While she was in the WAAF, she fell in love with an airman and got pregnant. He was killed before either of them knew and before they could marry.

His parents didn't want anything to do with her and she was too frightened to tell her own parents in case she brought shame on the family.'

'Poor cow. What happened?'

'She had the baby, a boy. I've just got to the end of the war. She's left him with her friends while she goes back to Birmingham to tell her parents. I need to read the next diary to find out how it turns out. Anyway, this is a surprise.'

'Yeah, Mum's not been well so I'm staying with her for a bit. Merrie's got some time off for study days so she's come with me. I've left her revising history.'

'That must be a bit boring for her.'

'Not really: she likes a bit of time on her own. She's nearly sixteen. Remember what we were like at that age? She can just about tolerate me sometimes, never mind the rest of the family. Strangely though, she loves being with her nan.' Claire bent down to stroke Maud and Betty. 'Oh you are gorgeous, aren't you? My Merrie's going to love you.'

They went into the kitchen where Kelly was hovering. She gave Claire a wary nod. 'All right?'

'Kelly, this is Claire. Claire, this is Kelly,' said Netta.

'You're Net's friend from school?' said Kelly.

'Yeah, that's right. You're …' Netta was willing Claire not to say, Netta's lodger: that would have broken Kelly's heart.

'I'm her mate,' said Kelly. She gave Claire a look that dared her to dispute it.

Claire's expression softened. 'Of course. Netta's told me lots about you. I think you're more than just mates though, aren't you? That's what I understood from Net, anyway.'

Kelly's face lit up. 'Yeah? Well we are pretty tight. I better go and get dressed. Nice to meet you, Claire.'

'Likewise,' said Claire.

When she was sure Kelly was in her room, Netta whispered, 'Thank you.'

They'd been sitting in the breakfast room for a while, talking about nothing in particular. Claire was stroking Betty's back idly. 'By the way, I've heard from Doogie. I emailed him after you came to see me but it took him ages to reply. I think he's pretty much off grid these days.'

'What do you mean, off grid?'

'Don't worry, he hasn't turned into a hermit or a tree hugger, or anything. I think he just prefers a quieter life.'

'Doogie?'

'Yeah, I know. Mad isn't it? He said he's okay with you contacting him, if you still want to.'

22

THE T-SHIRT MAKES AN APPEARANCE

NETTA – 2019

Since Claire turned up on her doorstep four days ago, they'd spent a lot of time together. After the first visit, she brought Merrie with her to see the dogs. Merrie seemed to have grown since Netta saw her last. She looked taller. Her long limbs seemed to dangle awkwardly. She folded her arms and rounded her shoulders inward, as if trying to make herself seem smaller and less loosely defined. When Netta spoke to her, she muttered one-word responses and it was left to Claire to do that thing that mothers so often do to try to make up for their child's lack of interest – pretend she was an active member of the conversation: 'Merrie would like a dog, wouldn't you, love?'

'Yeah.'

'Merrie's loving being in Brum, aren't you, Mer?

'Yeah.'

She'll be sorry to go home, won't you?'

'Mmm.'

Thank god for Liza and her friend Jade who'd walked in just when this exhilarating exchange was drying up. They'd greeted Merrie as if they'd known her forever and took her off to be with her own kind, away from these awful adults with their prying questions. Since then, Merrie had been a regular visitor which was great because it gave Claire an excuse to be here too, if one were needed.

Tomorrow was Saturday and Claire's mum had arranged a family get-together before they went back to Brighton on Sunday. It was a good enough reason for Netta and Claire to make the most of their last night together. Liza and Jade were having a little farewell sleepover party for Merrie. Kelly was in Edinburgh, spending the weekend with Frank's daughter Robyn. Will had sensibly made a break for it before the party got going and went to stay at his friend's, leaving the three girls to take over his room for the night. Netta ordered in takeaway pizzas and left them to it. She and Frank took Claire out for a curry. They went to the Rajdoot, the place where Colin had once told her, over a family meal that he wanted a divorce. It had taken her two years to summon up the courage to set foot in that place again and, even then, she'd only managed it with the support of her friends. The second visit had been easier. The third, easier still. Now, she went quite often. Unfortunately, so did Colin, so there was always the chance their visits might coincide. That didn't bother her anymore. They were quite civil now, almost to the point of friendliness. Almost.

Mr Shah, the Rajdoot's owner, was talking to some customers when they walked in. He gave Netta a little wave, said a few more words to the other customers and excused himself. 'Mrs Grey. How nice to see you again.'

'Hello, Mr Shah. Good to see you too.' Netta gave him a warm smile. She'd told him several times that she'd changed her name back to Wilde but he still insisted on calling her

Mrs Grey. She'd even tried suggesting he called her Netta but Mr Shah liked to keep things friendly but formal.

He took her hand and led them to a table in the window. 'Best seat in the house for my favourite customer and her friends. By the way, you might be interested to know that we have a booking this evening for Mr Grey.'

'I see. Thanks for preparing me.'

He nodded and left them with the menus.

They were still on their starters when Colin and Arianne walked past the window, arm in arm. Arianne was wearing the usual Clash T-shirt stretched across her ample bosom. The way Netta's table was situated made it impossible for both parties not to see each other. When he noticed Claire was with them, Colin did a classic comedy double take. To make matters worse, he then pretended he hadn't seen them at all and carried on walking, dragging Arianne along with him. Arianne clearly hadn't cottoned on because she was still giving Netta the side eye, all the way past the door. He stopped just before they got to the shop next door and she very nearly bumped into him. He muttered something to her and she jerked her head in the opposite direction, away from Netta. They stood on the pavement, refusing to look back into the restaurant and at the same time trying to appear as if they were casually making up their minds where to go next, as if they hadn't booked a table at all. Netta had some sympathy for him: she could see his predicament. There were only two people from her past that Colin really loathed, or was afraid of – the two were often interchangeable for him – Doogie and Claire. Liza must have not told him Claire was back on the scene. He wouldn't have come to the Rajdoot if he'd known, in case there was any chance of bumping into her.

'They have seen us, haven't they? I'm not imagining it?'

said Frank.

Claire took a sip of wine and kept her eyes on Colin. 'Oh yes, they've seen us.'

'Maybe we should stop staring at them,' said Netta.

Claire's mouth contorted into a wicked side-grin. 'Give it a bit longer.'

Colin had his back to them. He'd let go of Arianne by now and his hands were rammed firmly in his trouser pockets. Arianne glanced slyly over his shoulder and must have realised they were being watched. She said something to him and his whole body appeared to sigh. They turned, walked in, and had to wait, right next to Netta's table, for someone to attend to them. He had no choice, he had to acknowledge them. 'Oh hi!' he said, feigning complete surprise.

They said hello in a manner that suggested they'd only just seen them too. 'You remember Claire, don't you?' said Netta.

'Claire?' He looked as if he was trying to dredge up some long distant memory. 'Oh yes, of course. Hello Claire. Nice to see you, after all these years.'

'Yeah, likewise,' said Claire.

Neither of them meant it.

'It's nice here. Peaceful,' said Claire.

Netta topped up Claire's glass. 'It's my favourite place in the house. Day or night, rain or shine, it doesn't matter. I love being here. It's comforting.'

'Do you sit here a lot at night then?'

'When I can't sleep.'

'Or when you're getting pissed with old mates?'

Netta laughed. 'That doesn't happen too often. Usually

I'm on my own. Just me and the nocturnal animals.'

They were sitting, just the two of them, in the breakfast room. Frank had left them to enjoy their last night together hours ago. The old photos that Colin had given back to her were scattered on the table but it was too dark to see them. The only source of light shone through the open door from the kitchen. It was late – two, maybe three in the morning. Neither of them had checked the time for hours. Everyone else in the house was asleep. The girls had partied until sometime after midnight before finally crashing. Betty was with them, no doubt tucked up in someone's bed.

Claire shook her head. 'I can't believe we bumped into Colin the Creep. Honestly, his face when he saw us. And that woman! What was she thinking of, wearing that T-shirt? Do you think she knows?'

'Oh yes. I told her. I think she's just wearing it as an act of defiance now. I'm sure he bought it for her. Is that weird? I think it's weird.'

'It's weird. She really hates you, doesn't she? The looks she was giving you.'

'Yeah. She seems to think I destroyed Colin. Complete shit, obviously, but there you go. Then again, it could be because I told her that T-shirt she insists on wearing at every opportunity is an exact copy of the one I had on when Colin first met me. Or it might be because I told her the T-shirt was way too small for her. Take your pick.' Netta sighed. She regretted that last comment now: she didn't normally go in for criticising other women on their appearance but she'd been angry and a bit pumped up at the time. Anyway, it didn't seem to have stopped Arianne wearing it and yes, it was still too small. 'You know what else is weird? When he came over with those photos, he told me he wasn't ready to move on yet.'

'He hasn't changed. Still a manipulative bastard. Don't you worry about Liza living with him?'

'I did but since everything came out, he's lost his influence over her. I mean he's still her dad and she loves him but she's no fool. She knows what he's like and she'll tell him when she thinks he's out of order. Besides, she spends half of her time here now.'

'At least he's around for her. I suppose that counts for something. She's a nice kid.'

'She is, isn't she? Mind you, she's had her moments, but she's come through that. There was a time when I thought I'd lost her but we're closer now than we've ever been.'

Claire suddenly jumped up. 'Shit, what was that? There's something out there.'

Netta leaned forward to get a better view. Maud, who until now had been sleeping quietly at her feet, got up and moved to the French windows. There was some movement by the bushes, stillness, then another movement towards the house. The movement became a shape and as the light from the kitchen window gave it more form, Netta recognised it. 'It's a fox, my fox. She's alive.' She sniffed back a happy tear. 'Sorry. Bit pathetic. I just really love that fox and I thought she was dead.'

Maud pressed her nose against the glass. The vixen came closer and stared at them. Netta felt a pang of guilt: she'd stopped leaving food out for her a few weeks back. 'I'm sorry, I gave up on you. I'll put something out tomorrow, I promise.'

Claire laughed. 'You haven't changed either, have you? Still a nutter.'

They talked until a faint glimmer of light heralded a new

day and until there was nothing left to talk about, except the one thing they'd avoided talking about since that short conversation four days ago – Doogie. 'Is he with anyone now?' asked Netta.

'I don't think so. As far as I know, he didn't marry or live with anyone long-term after you last saw him.'

'Is he happy?'

'Who knows? He wouldn't tell me if he wasn't. It's not his style, is it? Net, why exactly do you want to get in touch with him?'

'I feel like I have to; like I need to know he's okay.'

'Really? You do know you only asked me if he was happy after you found out he wasn't with anyone? Doogie's never gonna be good for you. You must see that? You've come through a lot and you've got a nice life now; a great family, a lovely bloke and some good friends. Don't let this obsession with him fuck things up for you, Net. I promise you, he's not what you remember.'

Netta shrugged. 'To be honest, I really don't trust any of my memories. There are so many I've distorted over time; so many I've misremembered that I approach everything with an open mind these days. For years I convinced myself that Doogie was a selfish bastard who was only interested in one thing but lately, I've been wondering if that was true. Lately, things keep popping into my head that make me think he did actually care. Am I wrong?'

Claire pulled a piece of folded paper from her pocket. 'He cared, but it was a long time ago. A lot's happened since then, and you know what he was like. Nothing was ever straightforward with Doogie.' She passed the note over. 'Think it over properly before you get in touch. Use your head, not just your heart. Your heart's always been a bit dodgy.'

23

TWO PROMISES AND ONE DISCLOSURE

NETTA – 2019

With the conversation exhausted, they stopped talking and sat in a comfortable silence. They'd got to the point of not being able to face another drop of wine ages ago. They should have gone to bed really, but neither of them seemed to want the night to end. Once or twice, Claire looked as if she was about to say something, then changed her mind. Probably didn't want to spoil the moment with more warnings about Doogie. Finally, she stood up. 'I'm going to bed, I need sleep.' She put her hand on Netta's shoulder. 'It really is good to be back together again, Net. Let's not let anything or anyone pull us apart again.'

Netta placed her hand on top of Claire's. 'Friends for a lifetime. Cross my heart.'

'Yeah.' Claire bent down and kissed her cheek. 'Goodnight, mate.'

Netta listened to Claire trying to tiptoe unsteadily upstairs to sleep in Kelly's room. The kiss surprised her. If she put her mind to it, she could probably count on one hand the number of times Claire had kissed her and one of those was when they last said goodbye in Brighton. Must be the drink, unless Claire was getting sentimental in her old age. Young Claire would have been horrified at the thought. For some reason, that made Netta smile.

She shone the light from her phone on to the group photo with her and Doogie in the middle. It had been so intense back then that there were times when she felt sick with love for him. Was that youth, or just the way she was made? It was true, she'd always thought she was different; not quite the same as everyone else. Colin had led her to believe that was a bad thing but not Doogie. Quite the opposite with him, but then, he was different too. Not quite black, not quite white. Never really at home being one or the other. She'd once given him a copy of *Wuthering Heights.* Inside the cover she wrote:

'With love from one outsider to another.'

In her childish, romantic brain she saw him as Heathcliff. He made out he was offended by that and asked if she was going to haunt him, like Cathy. Even so, he kept the book. She came across it once, tucked away in a drawer in his student room. It was hidden between his underpants – the closest place to his heart, you could say, given that his heart was so often in his dick. When they split up, she'd assumed that would be one of the first things to go but when they got back together all those years later, she found it in his bookcase. Surely that counted for something? Of course, her being her, she made some stupid, crass comment about it that she regretted straight away because she saw, as soon as it fell casually from her lips, she'd made him feel small. She could be such a cow back then. Still, he had the last laugh since he was the one that had haunted her for years. Claire was right, Doogie was her obsession. A very unhealthy one. Ridiculous really: if you added up the number of years they'd actually known each other, it was less than four. He'd probably forgotten all about her, until now. She really should leave well alone.

A small, shadowy figure moved across the garden towards Frank's. It was too dark to see but she guessed it was the vixen back from her night-time sortie. It brought her back to a phrase that the older Edie had written in one of her later diaries. It had been one the first entries she'd read after she moved here:

'*This is life.*'

Yes, it was. This was the real stuff. She thought about Edie's group photo. Had Edie loved Robert as passionately as she'd loved Doogie? His death had certainly struck her down but she'd had the baby to keep her going. Netta hadn't lost Doogie in that way, but she had lost their baby. That made them kindred souls, her and Edie. She'd sensed it the first time she'd come to view the house. As per Edie's instructions, everything had been left exactly as it had been on the day she collapsed – the day she left this house for good. Netta had walked into this room and found an open book, next to a tea-stained china cup and plate. The remains of a few cake crumbs were still on there. The book was *Wuthering Heights*. Kindred souls.

She rubbed her eyes and yawned. 'I promise you Edie, I will find Robbie. I understand now, that's what you want.'

The next morning, Netta dragged herself out of bed. Her head felt like a lead weight and she badly needed a wee. Naturally, the bathroom was busy – full of giggling girls. She tapped on the door and Liza called out: 'Just coming.' The door opened and all three filed out, their faces aglow with freshly applied make-up. 'Sorry Mum. We're just getting ready to go out.' Netta nodded and grunted: her voice box hadn't been sufficiently oiled to be fully working yet. She needed tea, and lots of it.

Claire came down just as the kettle was coming to a boil. 'I'll have a gallon of that,' she said, pointing to the teapot. Netta squeaked something incomprehensible, even to herself, and made the tea. They took a few sips in silence both letting out gasps of relief as the hot liquid went down. 'How are you feeling?' said Claire.

'Crap.'

'Me too. When did the morning after get so hard?'

'Difficult to say. It creeps up on you.'

'That explains it. Growing old's a bit of a bastard, isn't it?' They caught each other's eye and laughed, croaky, achy laughs. 'Do you think I'll be able to commandeer the bathroom long enough to get a shower?'

'I think the girls are going up town in a bit, so we'll have the place to ourselves. More tea?'

Claire pushed her cup over to Netta. 'Yes please.'

The girls came down as they were finishing their second cups. 'Colonel's here. I'll let him in.' said Liza. She opened the front door and they could hear the girls in the hall cooing over Maud's four-legged gentleman friend. The massive dog romped into the kitchen and glanced at the two women dismissively.

'That's never the puppy's father?' said Claire.

'It is.'

'But Maud's so little.'

'I know what you're thinking and the answer is we have no idea.'

When Colonel first turned up on the doorstep with his owner, Clyde, the puppies were quite newly born and everyone doubted that he could be the father, just because he was so much bigger than Maud but now that their offspring were older, the truth was indisputable. Betty had already outgrown her mother and was beginning to resemble Colonel in the looks department too – a big Brillo pad on legs. After greeting his beloved Maud, Colonel allowed Betty to gnaw at his massive paws. He didn't seem to mind, or maybe he didn't notice through all that hair. After a while he put a paw on Betty's head and pushed her away with his nose. He and Maud took themselves off for a stroll, leaving a disconsolate Betty to watch them through the French windows. Behind Netta's garden was the Rec, a green space that was flanked by houses on each side. Clyde and Colonel lived in one of those houses. Netta guessed it was the place where Maud and Colonel had conducted their illicit romance. Both being rather free spirits, they often met there.

The girls joined Betty and cooed a bit more, then decided it was time to hit the town. 'What time do I need to be back at Nan's?' said Merrie.

'Four, and no later,' said Claire.

'I'm staying at Jade's tonight, Mum. I'll see you in the morning,' said Liza. They went off in a perfumed haze, still chattering and giggling.

'You can have first dibs on the bathroom,' said Netta.

'Cheers.'

An hour later, they were showered, dressed and revived and had regrouped in the kitchen. 'Want coffee this time?' said Netta.

'Yeah. Net, I didn't say when you told me about what happened to you, I suppose it was the shock of what you said, but I was around in Manchester at that time. Me and Doogie, we were still seeing each other. We used to have a regular Sunday lunch date. After I went to bed last night, I remembered he told me once that he thought he saw you.

He must have been trying to tell me you were back together again but I didn't want to know. I bit his head off and he never mentioned you again. If I hadn't shot him down, maybe things would have been different.'

'For me and Doogie?'

'For all of us.'

The boiled kettle interrupted them. Netta made the coffee and handed a mug to Claire. 'He asked me about you too and I did the same thing. Maybe it was just the wrong time.'

'Yeah, maybe. It's a shame though. We could have been there to help each other through the crap we were going through at the time.'

'I suppose so. You would have been expecting Merrie around then, wouldn't you?'

'Yes. Net, I need to show you something.' She reached for her bag, took out an envelope and dropped it on the table. Netta gave her a puzzled look. Claire pushed the envelope towards her. 'Take a look.'

Netta opened the envelope. Inside was a photo of Doogie, somewhere in his mid-thirties. He was holding a baby. 'What is this?' she said, even though she already knew.

Claire sat upright, her eyes fixed on Netta. 'Doogie is Merrie's dad.'

'Are you going to say something?' Claire was still sitting opposite, waiting for her to respond to the bombshell she'd handed to her in an innocent looking envelope a while ago – she wasn't sure how long ago: her sense of time had gone askew.

Netta looked at her hands. They were trembling. How had she not realised before that Merrie was Doogie's child?

She was the image of him. It was obvious to anyone but her. What an idiot she was. What a stupid, blind fool.

'Talk to me, Net. Please.'

Her attention switched to Claire who was pleading with her to say something that might make her feel better but all she wanted to ask was, how could she? With Doogie, of all people. How could she? 'Can you leave?'

Claire sat back. 'Is that it? Is that all you've got to say to me after we promised last night to stay friends whatever?'

Netta clenched her fists. Yes, it was all she had to say, because if she said anything more she'd be breaking that promise right now; a promise which, by the way, she made not realising that her supposed best friend of all time had betrayed her. 'Yes. I need you to leave. Now.' She sounded calm but she really wasn't.

Claire stood up. 'Okay. I can explain, I promise you. I'll be leaving Mum's by one o'clock tomorrow. I really hope you come and talk to me before then.'

She held her breath and waited for Claire to go. When the front door closed she let the air out of her lungs and screamed. Her chest tightened and she stood up to get more oxygen in but that only caused a pain to tear across her stomach. She fell to her knees. Bent double on the floor, she began to howl. The pain was ripping through her now, as if she was losing her baby all over again. She lay on her side on the cold, tiled floor with the draught from underneath the back door on her face, waiting for it to ease. She noticed a scratching sound coming from the other side of the door. She ignored it at first until she heard a yelp. Betty who'd been cowering in the breakfast room ran to the door and began to whimper. Netta reached up to open it and Maud stepped in. Still seeming unnerved, Betty greeted Maud timidly. Netta sat up on the floor and pulled her knees into her chest. Maud watched her for a few seconds, then nudged her way in through the tangle of legs and arms to press her warm body against Netta's chest and lick her face. Netta pulled the little dog closer. 'Oh Maud, whatever would I do without you?'

24

LET NO MAN PUT ASUNDER

NETTA – 2019

So, Claire and Doogie had been together before and after she'd had the affair with him and they'd made a baby between them. A baby that went full term and grew into a beautiful young girl who looked just like him. When she and Doogie had their brief affair in 2003, Claire was pregnant. If Netta had gone full term, her own baby and Merrie would have been born within months of each other.

There were so many things to unpick in those mental ramblings that she didn't know where to start. She criss-crossed from one thought to another until eventually it dawned on her. There was only one reason why this was bothering her so much. Envy. She envied what Claire had with him and what she'd made with him. The realisation sickened her. Of course, she was angry with herself too because deep down she'd known from the first moment she set eyes on Merrie. Nobody really needed to tell her. She might have refused to acknowledge it but she'd sensed it from the start.

She opened the note with Doogie's contact details then folded it again. Edie's glowing words about Robert had fooled her into recasting Doogie in a different light but he was no Robert. She'd built him up to be some kind of Prince Charming, forgetting the reality. He'd always been more in love with himself than her, or Claire for that matter. He'd strung them both along. Well, fuck him. He wasn't worth it.

Netta made an excuse not to see Frank that night: she needed time to think it all through without distractions and she couldn't bring herself yet to tell him that Doogie was Merrie's father. Not without breaking down anyway and that could have consequences. But there was another reason that she didn't want to see him. All these thoughts about Doogie and Claire; all this envy, it felt unfaithful and the guilt was coming off her like a bad smell – she could sense it. Instead she spent the night alone trying to work out what to do next; trying to decide what to do about Claire.

Claire's car was outside Mrs Fogarty's house. Netta parked up behind it. She'd spent another night hardly sleeping and it was only this morning that she decided she had to come because, if she didn't, she'd never know what happened and she'd probably never see Claire again. She rang the bell and in a few minutes Claire opened the door. She looked as tired as Netta felt. Netta suddenly felt uncomfortable. She searched her head for something to say but could only manage: 'I'm here.'

Claire's lips twitched, like she was trying to suppress a smile. 'So I see.'

Netta jabbed her finger in the air. 'Don't fucking laugh, okay? It's not funny.'

'Sorry, you're right but that was a stupid thing to stay.

Come in. Mum and Merrie are out. I stayed in to wait for you.'

Netta followed her along the hall and they sat facing each other across Mrs Fogarty's kitchen table, both with their arms folded tight across their chest. Claire heaved a sigh and leaned forward. 'I wanted to tell you earlier. Before we met up in Brighton, I was all geared up to tell you. I thought Doogie would be in your past so it wouldn't matter but then you told me about losing the baby. How could I say anything after that?'

'It's all right, I get it but what I don't understand is how you ended up having Doogie's baby. I mean, I didn't even think you were attracted to him.'

Claire raised her eyebrows. 'Come on. Who was it that accused me of splitting the pair of you up? Who was it that accused me of wanting to take him off you? I suppose you remember that do you.'

'Yes but I didn't actually mean it. I never for one minute thought you actually fancied him.'

'Of course I fancied him. Everybody fancied him. He was fucking gorgeous. But, and this is the god's honest truth, I never did anything about it while the two of you were together, or for a long time after, because Doogie and me were mates. We just grew on each other and it developed into something more than friendship.'

'When I got back with him in 2003, he told me he'd just split up with his partner because she wanted children and he didn't. That was you, wasn't it?'

Claire nodded. 'We had five good years together but it had run its course. I was at the point where I wanted a family and he didn't. We decided to go our separate ways but stay friends. It was all fine, and then one night we were out on a bender and ended up having a drunken fuck for old times' sake. I'd been off my pill for a while because I hadn't got round to renewing the prescription. Stupidly, I forgot to mention that a condom might be a good idea and hey presto – a child is born!'

From the dark recesses of Netta's mind came a memory of another girl Doogie had been stringing along at the same time as her when they'd been students. A girl he used to visit in Bristol; the one who finally made her realise she'd had enough of him. Doogie had done it again. This time with Claire. 'I can't believe he was seeing me when you were pregnant. What a bastard.'

Claire grabbed Netta's hand. 'He wouldn't have known. The night we got together must have been just before you got back with him. I didn't tell him at first because I was considering an abortion, but then I realised this might be my only chance to have a baby with a man that I truly loved. And I do love him. Not the same way I love Dom, but Doogie means a lot to me. I don't want him hurt.'

Netta pulled her hand away. 'What's that supposed to mean?'

'Don't be angry, Net. He's not as strong as you think he is. You know he had his problems. With his dad, with fitting in, and with you.' She left it there for a minute or two; let it sink in. 'You do something to him. I didn't know about the two of you at the time but I remember him being really strange and distant. I put it down to the pregnancy but now I can see, it was losing you. When Merrie was born, he was good with her. He asked if we could give it another go and for a while it seemed like it was going to work out, even though he wasn't really himself. Then, out of the blue, he said he was off to St Kitts to see his git of a dad. I knew then things weren't working. I mean, it's not like that waster ever had any time for him and he knew it. So, it was obviously just an excuse. We argued. He went. He never came back. He keeps in touch now and then; still sends money every month for Merrie, but that's it. Looking back, I don't think his heart was ever really in it.'

Claire looked as if she was about to break down. Netta felt for her, she really did, but Claire was misguided. 'You've got it wrong. I didn't hurt Doogie. I don't have that power.'

'You sure about that? You two. You're as bad as each other. Like Cathy and Heathcliff. Don't look so surprised. I saw that book on his shelf, I read the inscription. Just about sums you two up, I reckon.'

That bloody book again. Netta was beginning to regret writing that stupid inscription. There should be a portal of some kind specially made for young people to see into the future so that they could see what a crappy mess one silly little action can cause. She'd pay good money for that.

Claire checked the time. 'Mum will be back with Merrie soon.'

Netta got up. 'I'll go.'

'What will you do about Doogie now that you know?'

She shrugged. 'I don't know. I haven't decided yet.'

Claire nodded. 'Listen, if you do speak to him, would you try to persuade him to do something with Merrie? A mail, a call, anything. It's really killing her, not knowing him. I've tried but he won't budge. He might listen to you.'

'I doubt that but yes I will, if I do. I'm not sure I will now: there doesn't seem to be any point.'

Claire followed her out to the door. 'Are we still good, you and me? Am I forgiven?'

'I don't know, are we? I forgive you. Do you forgive me for being such a shite friend?'

'I think I can manage that.'

Netta chewed on her lip. The reality was, she wasn't

absolutely sure they were good but she'd already let one man come between her and Claire in the past and she wasn't going to let another one do the same, even if he probably was the love of her life. 'Should we do the hugging thing to seal it then?'

Claire grimaced. 'Go on then. Just this once.'

25

WELL, HELLO DOLLY

NETTA – 2019

It was sunny but it was cold. Netta was sitting in the garden, wrapped in a winter coat with her sunglasses on. There'd been a downpour overnight and the seat was damp, so there was one bag for life stuck between the bench and her rear end and another keeping her back dry. She'd been out there for a while. Long enough for Maud to decide it was too cold and leave her and Betty to it. Betty didn't seem to notice or care and was sniffing around the empty dish that Netta had put out for the vixen last night. Netta was thinking about Doogie, Claire and Merrie. She was thinking about something her mother had said weeks ago: 'It doesn't always do to delve into the past.' Well, she'd delved and now she had to agree with her mum, it doesn't do.

'Everything okay?' Frank was walking through the gate between their gardens carrying two steaming mugs. He sat down on the bench next to her and jumped up again when he realised how wet it was.

She whipped the carrier bag out from behind her back and put it down on the seat for him. 'Yes, I think so. Just being a bit of an idiot.'

He grinned. 'Hmm, that's new.'

'I know, incredible isn't it?'

'Want to talk about it?'

She wrinkled her nose. She had to tell him: it would come out anyway, soon enough and it was better for her to manage the way it came out. 'Merrie is Doogie's daughter.'

His mouth opened and closed, then opened again. 'That is a surprise. How do you feel about it?'

That was a question she wasn't expecting. She took a mouthful of coffee to give herself time to think: she didn't want to give him the wrong impression with a badly formed answer. 'I'm not sure. Shocked, I suppose. I hadn't realised Claire and Doogie had that kind of relationship.'

'But you haven't fallen out with Claire over it?'

'God no. I let her down once with Colin, I'm not about to do that again. Sorry, I just need a bit of time to process it, and I'm more interested in following Edie's trail at the moment. Do you mind if we leave it there?'

He kissed her. 'No, but I do have something to talk to you about. Something to do with Edie. I have news. I've found someone who was in the WAAF with her.'

Dorothy Maidstone was a tiny woman with wispy white hair and the peachiest skin Netta had ever seen on a person of her age which was, she told them, ninety-five. Her grand-daughter, a middle-aged woman with the same complexion, sat next to her. It was she who'd been posting Dorothy's wartime memories online; she who'd arranged the visit. But it was Dolly who was in full flow right now. 'Yes, I remember Edie very well. We were friends. She was such a pretty girl and so pleasant. Not very worldly-wise though. We girls were always having to take care of her. She was older than me. I was one of the youngest you know, but I was much more grown up than Edie. She was like a child in some ways. Far too trusting. I was forever telling her to watch the company she kept but she wouldn't listen. Thought I was jealous. Silly girl. Learned the hard way.'

That word jealousy again. Always popping up unexpectedly. Netta exchanged glances with Frank. 'Mrs Maidstone—'

'Netta was it? Call me Dolly. Everyone else does. Like the song. Well hello, Dolly.' She broke into a song and waved her hands, jazz-style for the last bit. 'Even Edie used to call me Dolly. I was Dolly Baxter when she knew me though.'

'Dolly, I've been reading Edie's journals.'

'Journals? Those diaries, you mean? She was always scribbling away at them. Not proper diaries with locks, mind. Any exercise book would do. You had to settle for whatever you could get your hands on back then. Goodness those diaries. I bet they make good reading, don't they? I had a sneaky look at them myself sometimes when no one was around. The things she got up to. Not that she realised it was racy. Poor Edie.'

'With Robert, you mean?'

'Robert? He was the pilot, wasn't he? He was a good-looking chap. We all thought he looked like Tyrone Power. Do you remember him? A bit before your time, I suppose. From a good family too. She was all set but then he was killed, like so many of them. Such a shame. Edie was beside herself. There was no consoling her.'

Netta showed her the photo from the day at the Cotswolds. She pointed to the man behind Edie. 'Is that Robert?'

Dolly had a pair of glasses on a chain around her neck. She put them on and studied the photo. Her face creased into a smile. 'Yes, that's him. I told you he was good looking. Such a lovely fella he was too. Very polite. Not like some of them back then. That's his brother with Mina.'

'So, that other woman is definitely Mina?' said Netta.

'Yes, that's definitely Mina. You couldn't mistake her. No one else like her. I suppose you know about the baby, do you? Lovely little thing. So sweet. Poor Edie.'

'Do you know what happened to the baby?' asked Frank.

She shook her head. 'I know she left him with Mina and went home without him. She was going to tell her family first. The last time I saw her was a couple of years after the war. We used to have a big reunion on the anniversary of VE day, until we all got too old or too dead. He was still with Mina then. Edie didn't come to any more reunions after that. Neither did Mina. Didn't she keep him then?'

'We don't think so,' said Netta. 'We're still reading through the journals.'

Dolly screwed her mouth up. She gazed at the photograph and let out a raspy sigh. 'Poor thing.'

'Dolly, do you know if Edie met someone else? Only we found this photo of her from the same time. It looked like she meant to give it to someone called Bill.' Netta passed her the photo of Edie in her dress.

'Bill?' Dolly's laugh was more of a throaty cackle. It took her a few minutes to recover from it. She took the photo in her shaky hand. 'I've seen this before. It was taken at Mina's wedding. That dress was beautiful. Cornflower blue silk it was. Gorgeous. She looked like Joan Fontaine in it. Joan Fontaine and Tyrone Power. They were such a handsome couple.'

'She kept the dress,' said Netta. 'I found it in the loft. It's a bit worse for wear now though, I'm sorry to say.'

Dolly sighed again. 'Did you? Lovely it was. Lovely she was too. Bill, you say?'

'Yes.' Netta pointed to the photo's inscription. 'You can see she's written there, dearest Bill, love always, Edie. He must have meant a lot to her.'

This time Dolly laughed out loud. Her granddaughter looked alarmed. 'Steady Gran, you'll do yourself an injury.'

The old woman waved her away. 'Stop fussing Lucy.' She smirked at Netta and Frank. 'Dearest Bill, love always. Poor, silly Edie. Bill wasn't a man! Bill was a woman! It was Mina. Her real name was Wilhemina but everyone called her Mina for short, except for Edie. They gave each other nicknames. They were always going on about being tomboys, so Mina became Bill and Edie was Eddie. I think they used them when they were alone together but they slipped out in public every now and then. Edie sometimes called her B in her diaries. After she moved into that cottage, the pair of them lived in their own little fantasy world. I was always surprised Mina's husband didn't get wind of it but he seemed to be oblivious. He worshipped her too, of course. Most people thought the sun shone out of her backside and she loved it. Queen B, I used to call her. B as in Bill, not the little buzzing things.'

Netta and Frank exchanged glances again, then looked at Lucy. Lucy raised her eyebrows at them. 'Gran, are you saying what I think you're saying?'

'I don't know. What do you think I'm saying?'

Lucy swallowed. 'Are you saying that Edie and this Mina were in a relationship.'

'Relationship? Is that what you call it these days? I'm saying that Edie worshipped the ground Mina walked on. She idolised her. She was Mina's little lapdog, and Mina took advantage of it. Especially after Edie's fiancé died.' She held up her fist and opened it out. 'Mina had her in the palm of her hand. Didn't give the rest of us a look in. I tried to warn Edie to keep away from her but it was useless. We fell out over it.'

'Okay,' said Lucy. 'I thought for a minute you were saying they were–'

'What, lesbians? I have heard of the word you know, Lucy. I'm not sure if that was Edie's natural inclination. I think she was just lost after Robert died and Mina made the most of it. Mina was though. Or maybe she was, what d'you call it? Bisexual, because she slept with men and women.'

'How can you know that, Gran?' said Lucy

'About Mina? Well, she was married so she must have slept with at least one man and the way she and Edie behaved around each other in that cottage, you could tell they were more than good friends. And I'll tell you how else I know. That thing Edie fell out with me for? Mina tried it on with me. I mean I didn't have a problem with it, if that was the way you were made but I wasn't, and that's what I said to Mina. I thought it was in Edie's best interests to know what she was up to behind her back, but Edie was furious. She said I was just trying to spoil things because I was jealous. Practically threw me out of the house. As I said, she could be quite childish at times. Don't look so shocked, Lucy. I'm ninety-five, I've seen life.'

Dolly sat back in her chair with an air of defiance. Then, as if suddenly remembering something else, she jabbed at the photo with her bony finger. 'And that doesn't say Edie. Look closer. It's Eddie.'

Netta and Frank sat in the car outside the nursing home where Dolly lived, trying to make sense of what they'd just heard. Frank had his glasses off and was holding Edie's photos up close to get a better look. 'She's right, it does say Eddie. How can we have missed that?'

'I don't know. It looks like we missed a few things,' said Netta. 'We have to get home and get back on with those diaries.'

26

THE REAL BILL AND EDDIE

EDIE – 1946

'Tom has spoiled everything.'

Edie put down her pen and left the diary open to give the ink time to dry. The rest of the family were in the sitting room listening to the after dinner shows on the radio and, having finished her duties for the evening, Hannah was in her room. It was the end of March. Almost three months had passed since she'd left the cottage, plenty of time to think about her departure and the events leading up to it. One of the few benefits of being back home was that she could, at last, write truthfully about her and Mina. In the cottage there had always been the worry that Tom might come across her diaries. She'd had that same concern about her family when she first returned to Birmingham but she'd recently found a remedy. She'd bought a chest to keep them in. A chest with a lock. Now, she could write whatever she liked and every evening for the last week she'd come up to her room to do just that. She was surprised how easily it all came spilling out onto the page. She was equally surprised at the relief that writing the words down gave her. Yes, it was a benefit but it was still one she could have happily done without.

Everything had changed, and it was all Tom's fault. If only he'd been killed too. Things would have been so much better. They could have stayed at the cottage and lived happily ever after. Just her and her little family. It would have been perfect. A few months ago, she'd been in complete heaven. Now, thanks to him, she'd been pushed away from the two people who meant the most to her, Robbie and Bill.

Bill and Eddie. They were the pet names they gave each other. It was Mina's idea because they always said they were more like boys than girls. It was their own little private joke that they tried to keep between them. Edie liked that: it made it all the more special. At some point, she couldn't remember when exactly, Bill and Eddie became B and E. She liked that too. The initials could mean anything, and no one would know. Often when she used B, she was thinking of other names, like Beauty, or Beloved. Occasionally, one of them would accidentally call the other by their secret name in public but no one seemed to notice, except Dolly who made a point of mentioning it and thought it extremely amusing and clever to call Bill, Queen B. It wasn't clever at all and it certainly wasn't in the least bit amusing. Ridiculous that she, of all people, should call Bill by that name, since she was the one who loved being the centre of attention. Dolly was such a cat. Especially when her nose was put out of joint.

She hadn't expected things to escalate the way they did. She and Mina had been close from their first meeting and it was true they'd held hands and even embraced sometimes, but only as friends. Now that Edie looked back on that time, she felt she could pinpoint the moment when it changed but it was so subtle, you would hardly have noticed. It was the evening before Mina and Tom's wedding, when they stopped on the bridge. As Edie watched them kissing so passionately, Mina tilted her head slightly and caught her eye. Her lips were still on Tom's but her eyes were locked on her. Something inside Edie stirred at that moment. She thought at the time it was because she wanted what they had but she knew now, that wasn't it at all. She wanted what Tom had.

Later that night, when they'd all gone to bed, there was a knock on her door. She opened it to find Mina, in silk pyjamas and dressing gown. 'Can't sleep. Can I come in?' Edie let her in and she threw herself down on the bed. 'Oh Eddie, I'm in such a dither about all of this. I'm absolutely dreading tomorrow.'

Edie sat down beside her. 'I expect it's nerves. You'll be tip top in the morning. You'll see.'

'Do you think so? I can't help feeling I'm making a mistake.'

'I thought this was what you wanted?'

'It was but I'm such an impulsive fool, and so fickle. I change my mind from one minute to the next. I mean, I do love Tom. It's just… Oh there I go again. Honestly, I'm a danger to myself, I really am. Would you mind if I stayed with you tonight? You exude a permanent calmness. I'm sure it will help me to sleep.'

They snuggled up in bed together like a couple of spoons. Mina rested her arm on Edie's waist, her firm breasts pushing against Edie's back. 'You know I'll always love you, don't you, Ed? No matter what happens,' she said, before falling asleep.

The next evening, when the knock came at the door, she'd expected it to be Mina again and was almost disappointed when it turned out to be Robert, but then he'd made love to her, and she'd experienced pleasure she didn't know was possible. She told herself then that she'd been wrong about her feelings for Mina. It was just a silly girlish crush on someone more glamorous and dazzling than her. She knew girls at school who'd experienced something similar. Not her though. Until now. She was a late developer in that regard. Everything had been super again after that first night with Robert. She was overwhelmed with love and desire for him and Mina went back to being no more than her friend and future sister-in-law. When Robert died, she assumed she'd never feel such passion again, but she was wrong.

That day Mina found her in the garden with the letter from Robert's parents, Edie had been at her lowest. Mina held her and told her everything was going to be all right; that she would look after her. As the night grew darker and cooler, they went inside and Mina poured her a glass of whisky. 'Drink this. It will help. For tonight, at least.' Edie drank it too quickly and it burnt her throat as it went down but she welcomed the numbness that came afterwards. She held out the glass and Mina poured another, then another. She wasn't really a drinker and was feeling quite drunk. What would her parents think of her now? She realised she no longer cared. She wanted Robert. She wanted Mina. She reached out for Mina's hand and before she knew it, they were kissing and touching and loving each other in the way she thought only men and women could love. When Mina brought her to that point of ecstasy that she'd missed so much, she cried. Not in sadness but for all the joy in the world.

And so began their new life. They were closer than friends. Closer than a married couple even. They loved each other. Not as a man and woman did, that was nothing. Theirs was beyond the physical. They had a sixth sense, a telepathy almost. They knew each other's thoughts and feelings without the need for words. The merest touch from one to the other was a soothing balm that washed away any concerns, any irritations, any anger. So, when Dolly told her that horrendous lie and she exploded, Bill had been able to calm her down almost instantly. Afterwards they'd laughed at the absurdity of it. Did she really believe that Bill would be interested in that common little slut? How could she have so little trust? Hadn't Bill loved her from their first meeting?

When Tom came home on leave, Bill became Mina and Edie moved from their bed to her own. She would hardly sleep on those nights so intent was she on listening out for Mina having to perform her wifely duties. Perhaps that's what her mother meant. Perhaps Mummy would have preferred to be loved by someone like Mina, even though it was against the rules of decency. Sometimes she'd hear Mina groaning or giggling through the bedroom walls which was infuriating. She'd be consumed with rage and refuse to share a bed when Tom had gone back to base, regardless of Mina's protestations that she had to do it to keep up the pretence. When that happened Mina would do anything to get back in her good books; waiting on her hand and foot or showering her with gifts. Once, after Edie had been particularly upset, Mina gave her a card. Inside was a photograph of her in a ball gown. She looked stunning. On the card she'd written:

To Eddie, my greatest love.
Keep me close to your heart.

Bill x

At the sight of it, Edie immediately melted. To show that she'd forgiven Mina, she found the only two photographs of her that she had. The one taken at the wedding and a copy of the one taken in Birmingham of her in her WAAF uniform. She wrote on both of them

'*Dearest Bill,*
My love always.
Eddie x'

She changed the sheets on Mina's bed, to get rid of the smell of Tom, and left the photographs on the pillow along with a rose she'd cut from the garden. She was putting Robbie to bed when Mina returned from work. She heard her go into the bedroom to get changed. A minute later she ran into the nursery, flung herself at Edie and wept for joy. It was impossible to explain how powerful Edie felt at that moment. She could have asked for almost anything and Mina would have done her bidding. It was so thrilling that she began to laugh. The noise startled Robbie. Confused and anxious, he burst into tears. She picked him up. 'Oh poor darling, don't cry. Mummy and Auntie Mina are just being silly billies. It's all over now. We're pals again. See how we're smiling?'

The ink was dry. Edie turned the page and started afresh to document her thoughts about her last weeks at the cottage and the abruptness of Tom's announcement. Everything was fixed by the time he'd deigned to tell her. He had a new job, with Mina's father's company as it turned out, and they had a house to go to in Surrey. They must have been planning it long before his discharge. It had to be Tom's doing:

Mina would never have betrayed her like that unless she'd been forced to. And yet, Tom adored Mina. He'd have done anything she asked. So why did she go along with it? It didn't make sense.

When they broke the news to her, Edie had been so angry with them that she'd left for Birmingham far too quickly. She could have stayed on for several more weeks. Instead she left poor, bewildered little Robbie there, just to spite them. Obviously, she regretted it within days, within hours, but it was too late. The die was cast. What a silly, selfish fool she'd been.

Since returning home, her time was spent helping her mother with the post war effort, or keeping Victor company. Not that he wasn't recovering physically. He walked with a limp and his burned skin was terribly damaged but, on the surface, he appeared to be on the mend. The trouble was the invisible scars that hadn't yet healed. They weren't obvious to the naked eye but they manifested themselves in other ways; in his permanent restlessness, his sense of hope-lessness and his nightmares. She still hadn't got used to hearing his screams at night. When they took hold of him, no one was able to pacify him except Birgitt, the Jewish German refugee. She seemed to know exactly what to do to soothe his terrors away. Edie assumed she'd learned it from her years in hiding from the Nazis and having to keep her younger sisters and brother quiet.

Birgitt's parents were still unaccounted for and as the reports of the atrocities inflicted on the Jewish people were coming to light, it seemed increasingly unlikely they would be found. Not alive, at least. After the war, Edie's parents had been happy for the children to remain with them but Vic's return home posed difficulties. To aid his recovery, he needed peace and quiet, something in short supply with three children in the house. They came to the reluctant conclusion that they needed to find them a new home and were put in touch with a kindly childless Jewish couple who lived locally. At first the whole family moved there but Birgitt visited every day. She became friends with Vic and, eventually, key to his recovery. She had already moved back in before Edie came home. Not that Edie minded: she liked Birgitt and having her around made it easier for her to visit Robbie.

Three times she'd tried to tell her parents about Robbie but each time she'd held back. Something always seemed to get in the way. There was always some new disaster to be averted or some new scandal involving yet another unmarried mother. Each time, Edie recalled that conversation in the car when they'd made their feelings quite plain. Each time she bit her lip and resolved to try again when the opportunity arose.

Edie counted the pages she'd completed that evening. Twenty-one, another mammoth session. She closed the book and placed it in the chest, next to Mina's letters. They wrote to each other every week. Mina kept her up to date with Robbie's developments. She missed them both so much. She hated being parted from them. On the very rare occasion that she was alone in the house, she telephoned Mina. Not only to talk to her but also just to hear Robbie's cooing and babbling down the line. Once a month she travelled to their new home to spend a week with them. She told her parents it was to support her friend and they didn't question it now that they had Birgitt to take up the slack.

She heard laughter coming from downstairs. Must be one of those comedy broadcasts. She considered joining them but she wasn't in the mood for laughs. Instead she curled up on the bed with a book, *Wuthering Heights.* It had been a favourite when she was at school and she'd recently returned to it. She rubbed her eyes. All that writing had tired her out. Just one chapter before turning in. She opened the book and began to read but after a few pages she was already asleep and dreaming of happier times.

THE ROAD TO INDEPENDENCE

EDIE – 1946

'At last, I have a goal. I am no longer drifting and dependent on the whims of others.'

Edie got off the train at Walton-on-Thames. The May sunshine added to her already good humour. It was an easy walk to Mina's house and it was still afternoon, plenty of time to enjoy being outdoors with Robbie. She was so looking forward to seeing him.

The first few visits to the new house had been difficult. She'd been so worried that Robbie wouldn't remember her that she'd whipped herself up into a state of ridiculously heightened emotions, causing her to break down as soon as she saw him. This only served to make him teary too which didn't get the visits off to a good start. Leaving him was just as hard. It put her in a dark mood that lasted days, sometimes weeks, after she'd said goodbye but by April, their monthly routine was established and things became more settled. She had begun to manage the visits without too much obvious distress.

Before long, Edie had the new house in her sight. It was quite grand, at least four times as big as the cottage, and she disliked it. She missed the cosiness of their old home and the privacy too. Tom and Mina had staff. A cook, a maid and a gardener. It was almost impossible to get time alone in the house with Mina. All of their private talks had to be taken outdoors. Any opportunity for intimacy was lost.

The maid answered the door to Edie and informed her that Mina and Robbie were in the garden. She left her things in the hall and went straight out to see them. They were sitting on the lawn with their backs to the house and didn't see her at first. Robbie was lying against Mina's leg, his head in her lap. She had a book in one hand which she was reading aloud to him. The other hand was rhythmically stroking his hair. They looked so natural together it made Edie's stomach lurch. She took a step closer and Mina noticed her. 'Look Robbie, Mummy's here.'

Robbie sat up and held out his arms to Edie. She swept him up and hugged him. 'Hello, my darling. How lovely to see you. You look so sleepy. Are you tired?'

'It's just a little cold, E. He's over the worst of it now. We thought the sunshine would do him good. Come and sit down. You can finish the story. It's his new favourite. I've read it to him so many times we could both probably recite it without the book. I'll organise some tea.'

Edie sat on the rug and picked up the book. 'Thomas the Tank Engine? I haven't heard of this one before. Now let me see, shall we start here?'

Robbie yawned and said something that sounded like: 'Mummy's here.' Sitting in her lap, he edged himself closer and snuggled his head against her breast. Everything was fine again: her little boy still loved her. When Mina came back he was already sound asleep.

'I had a feeling that might happen,' she said. 'We tried to get him to take a nap after lunch but he's been fighting it. Two minutes in your arms and he's off. He was clearly waiting for Mummy before giving in. I'll get Alice.' She went off again and returned with a matronly looking woman who was probably younger than her appearance suggested.

Alice stood over Edie, a saintly smile on her face. 'Oh bless him he's worn out, poor little mite. Shall I have him for you, madam?'

'Perhaps if you could take him so that I can get up? I'll carry him up to bed then,' said Edie.

Alice nodded, still smiling. 'Certainly. If you prefer, I can take him up?'

'No, that's quite all right, thank you. I can do it.'

'Yes, of course.'

Alice picked Robbie up. He hardly stirred. Edie stood up and took him off her then carried him up to his room. As she laid him down in his cot, he opened his eyes. She sang the lullaby she sang to him as a baby and he went back to sleep. For a while she stayed there, drinking in every inch of him. God, she'd missed him. Her need for him sated, she opened the door to his bedroom and was startled by the presence of Alice hovering outside. She regathered herself. 'Is something wrong, Alice?'

Alice smiled again, less saintly and more businesslike this time. 'Oh no, I just thought I'd give you some time on your own with your little boy. I'll sit with him now. I like to keep an eye on them when they're unwell.' She winked. 'Don't worry, I haven't lost one yet.' This seemed to amuse her and she chuckled to herself as she bustled past. 'I'll bring him down to you when he wakes from his nap, shall I?'

Before Edie had a chance to respond, Alice went into

Robbie's room and closed the door behind her. There was nothing left to do but go back downstairs to find Mina.

Mina was still in the garden. She'd moved to a table further away from the house. The tea things had been brought out for them and she poured Edie a cup when she saw her approaching. Edie was dry and could have done with something to take the thirst away but she was too agitated to sit down. 'Who is that woman?'

Mina placed a cup in front of an empty chair. 'Alice? She's the nanny.'

'The nanny!'

'Yes. Do sit down, E. I know what you're going to say. I know I should have consulted you first but she'd already had other offers when I found out about her so I had to snap her up sharpish.'

Edie remained on her feet. 'Yes, you should have consulted me. That aside, Robbie doesn't need a nanny.'

'E, please. You're making me uncomfortable with all that pacing. Sit down and let's talk about this sensibly.' Edie dropped down on the chair and folded her arms, waiting for Mina to say something that couldn't be said while she was pacing. 'The fact is, I'm just not as adept as you at the practical mothering stuff. I tried but poor Robbie was as good as being neglected through my own stupidity. Alice is marvellous. She makes sure he has everything he needs and Robbie is mad for her. Tom and I still do all the lovely things with him. He has the best of both worlds.'

'Not quite. He doesn't have his mother.'

'Obviously not, but we're making do until you take him back with you which, I'm sure, won't be too long and it's so hard to find a good nanny these days. Think of it as a way of keeping Alice's motor running until Tom and I have children.'

For the second time that afternoon, Edie was startled. She had never considered that Mina and Tom might have children of their own. Just the thought of it made her sick. 'Are you expecting?'

'No. You'd be the first to know if I was. We've had a couple of close shaves but they came to nothing in the end.' Her voice lowered and she let the sentence tail off so that it sounded quite wistful.

'But you'd like to have children? With him?'

'It's not a case of like, E. I'm his wife. Children come with the job. You know how these things work.'

She could have said that yes, she did know how they worked. She had a child of her own to prove it, but Robbie had been conceived out of love and desire, not out of duty. So no, she didn't know how they worked. She didn't understand how Mina could love her and have intercourse with Tom. It confused and troubled her so much that she came straight out with it and asked her. Mina glanced around, presumably checking there was no one within earshot. 'Eddie, you know I love you. When I'm not with you, I'm empty. I wish we could be together all the time, you, me and Robbie, but we can't. Even if I wasn't married to Tom, we couldn't.'

'Why ever not?'

'Because we're not allowed to. Don't you see? It's unnatural. If we lived together as a man and wife does, we'd be social outcasts.'

'No one need know. No one knew at the cottage. We were fine then.'

'That's because I have a husband and everyone thought you were a widow. We got away with it, but things are different now the war's over. There's so much more scrutiny. So many expectations.'

Edie stamped her fist down on the table. 'And I suppose these expectations include you allowing Tom to bed you. They include you having his children.'

Mina's eyes shot around the garden again. 'Eddie, stop it. You're a grown woman, not a child. Tom and I have normal marital relations. One day, that might result in children. You have to accept that. Our time in the cottage was wonderful but it was only ever going to be temporary. You have to accept that too.'

Edie gasped. 'Is that your way of telling me that you don't love me anymore? That you love Tom?'

Mina took her hand. 'I wish it were that simple, my sweet darling. I love you both and there's nothing I can do about it.'

As always, the days flew by. Robbie soon recovered under Alice's care. Edie was still furious about her appointment but she had to give the woman her due, she knew how to look after a child and Robbie did seem keen on her. On the train home she did the thing that she so often did these days, she spent the journey poring over every minute of the last week.

The revelation that Mina cared for both her and Tom hurt her deeply. Wrongly, she'd been assuming that Mina had married him out of some passing infatuation, or even an impetuous sympathy after his friend had been killed. Now it turned out she loved him. She remembered that time on the bridge in London again. The way Mina had kissed him so passionately while looking straight at her. It was the look of a woman who had both her loves right where she wanted them. She knew she should be angry with her, but she couldn't be. In spite of everything, she still ached for her.

As Edie processed all of this, something else dawned on her. She and Mina would never be together in this life. A love like theirs was beyond social boundaries that were too strong to break. In many ways, it was the same with Robbie. Although she hadn't yet been able to bring herself to tell her parents, she was certain she would do so soon. She expected then that they would insist she gave him up and, when she refused, they would disown her. If that happened, she was sure Tom and Mina would take her in, but for how long? Especially if they did have children of their own. How long before they tired of her and Robbie? She had to be able to stand on her own two feet. She had very little savings of her own and relied solely on a monthly allowance from her parents. She needed a job, but with very few skills other than a bit of filing for her father and her WAAF work, there was little chance of that. Unless? An idea began to form. She would ask Daddy if she could join him in the family business, on the proviso that she should be paid a proper salary and allowed time off for her monthly visits to Surrey. She wasn't sure how welcome her request would be but she had two things in her favour. Firstly, the war had clearly exhausted him and secondly, Victor was still too delicate to work. She might not be Jimmy or Vic, but she was alive, healthy and sharp witted and she might be the only one in the family capable of sharing his burden.

As soon as she got home she asked to speak to her father in the dining room and laid out her proposal. Now, she was standing in front of him, her hands behind her back. She wasn't quite standing to attention but it did feel rather formal. She'd been waiting for ten minutes while he filled his pipe and deliberated. Finally, he spoke: 'I can't say I'm not surprised, Edith. You never seemed to take to it before the war.'

'Things are different now, Daddy. I was rather young and silly then but the WAAF has taught me the meaning of proper work. I can't while away my days doing nothing.'

'And yet you're still demanding one week off a month.'

'Just to help my friend. It's so difficult for her and she has no one else to turn to.' She averted her eyes from his gaze. She hated this lying.

'So you say.' He lit his pipe and gave it a few puffs. 'Very well. I'm willing to give it a try but you must promise to take it seriously. You'll have to learn everything about the business, starting with the office work. If I am to rely on you Edith, I need to be confident that you can deal with anything that's thrown at you. That means you can't be shielded from the difficult things. Even if you fail at something, you will learn from it. It also means, my dear, that you must do even the most mundane things so that you understand exactly how the place ticks. No matter how boring you might find it.' He peered over his glasses at her and his mouth twitched into a little smile. He was still her dear old daddy, even when he was being stern.

She threw her arms around him. 'Thank you, Daddy. I promise.'

So, for the first time since the WAAF, she would be undertaking proper paid work. The road to independence was opening up to her. Such a shame it was for all the wrong reasons.

28

MOVING ON, AT LAST

EDIE – 1946

'There are so many things to be positive about.'

The kettle's whistle sang, breaking Edie's concentration. She'd been watching over it, waiting for it to boil, her thoughts drifting aimlessly over the last six months that she'd been employed in the family business. She poured the boiled water into a large pot, stirred the tea leaves and left it to brew. She was employed. She liked the idea of that. It was rather nice being back at work. She'd forgotten how much she enjoyed the sense of purpose it gave. It might not have been important war work but it was going to secure her future and when the time came, she would have the experience to find a job elsewhere.

For several months, she'd borne the tedium of lowly tasks with a quiet dignity, telling herself it was a means to an end. It even gave her something to talk about when she visited Surrey. Tom, especially, was impressed that she was working. She told them she'd joined the business because she wanted to be an independent woman. She didn't say why exactly she wanted that independence.

By autumn, she was beginning to take on extra duties. When Janet, her father's secretary, told her she thought she was ready to take a step up to the next level, she realised the mundane work had been something of a test to make sure she really was serious. She'd proved herself. She felt a sense of achievement. At last, she was getting somewhere.

A place was found for her at a secretarial school in town. Every Friday, she spent the day learning shorthand and typing. Shorthand was fascinating. It was like another language. One which only communicated through the written word. It was mostly girls in her classes. Just like the WAAF, they were from a mix of backgrounds and some were nicer than others. She'd made friends with a couple, occasionally going out with them to a coffee bar or to see a film. It made her quite nostalgic for her old life.

Things were looking up at home too. The old Victor was slowly emerging from the haunted individual Edie found when she first returned home. She'd played a small part in his recovery but it was mainly thanks to Birgitt and a psychiatrist her parents had engaged. There was even talk of him eventually being well enough to join the business too. With a degree of optimism, she imagined the two of them working side by side, shouldering the family burden.

It was obvious to anyone who saw them that Vic and Birgitt's friendship had blossomed into something deeper, so it was no surprise when they announced their engagement. Although they'd made a commitment to each other, they were in no rush to marry. Their preference was to wait for him to be closer to full recovery and there was still a faint hope that Birgitt's parents might yet turn up. The news lifted the household above the doldrums of post war rationing and as the end of the year approached, there was a sense of hope in the Pinsent household. Edie felt it too. That year had seen her taking the first steps towards being able to support herself and her son. Robbie was two now. They'd spent a glorious birthday week together and she'd taken him out on her own a few times. She was getting on better with Tom too, now that she'd accepted she must share Mina with him. Perhaps it was just that she was so busy these days, she had less time for resentment.

Oddly, it was Mina who seemed to be the unsettled one. Lately, whenever Edie visited, it was as if she couldn't wait to whisk her away somewhere private and make a fuss of her. Sometimes, she had to remind Mina that she was there to be with Robbie, first and foremost. If Edie didn't know better, she'd think Mina was missing her.

Janet popped her head around the door. 'How's that tea coming on, Edie?'

Edie pulled herself out of her daydream. 'Just pouring it out now.'

Janet gave her a curt nod. 'All right. Thought I'd better check. You know Mr Pinsent doesn't like it stewed.'

'Sorry, Janet. I was miles away.'

Janet's brow wrinkled. 'Not while you're here, Edie. Concentration is key while you're at work.'

'Yes, I know. I do apologise. It won't happen again.' Well and truly chided, Edie picked up the tea tray and followed Janet into the office, reminding herself not to be offended by the telling off: Janet was only carrying out Daddy's instructions, that she should have no special treatment and actually, she was right. Work was no place for daydreams. Edie would never have entertained the idea of daydreaming in her old job and she shouldn't do it now.

She knocked the door into her father's office and placed

the tea on his desk. He looked up from his books and gave her a warm smile. 'Is it afternoon tea already?' His eyes fell on the cup of dark brown sludge and the smile weakened somewhat. 'Did you make this, my dear?'

'Yes,' she said, trying to bluff it out but she'd been on tea-making duties since her first day and had yet to make one that didn't look like brown boot polish. No matter how much she experimented, she couldn't seem to get the hang of the extremely large pot in relation to the amount of leaves required.

'Jolly good. We must get you moved on to something more stimulating. Janet keeps telling me, you're rather wasted on the junior jobs.' She watched him trying not to shudder as he took a sip of tea. He put the cup down, defeated. 'Yes, I'll talk to Janet about that today.'

An hour later, Janet called her over to her desk. 'I think you'll be happy to hear that Mr Pinsent wants you to pick up more responsibilities, Edie. I've told him that your typing and shorthand are coming along a treat so we'll start you in accounting. They need someone to do basic secretarial and clerical work. Also, Mr Pinsent wants you to take some time understanding how the department works. He tells me you're very good with numbers so we should be able to make the most of your skills.'

Moving on, at last. Edie was elated. 'Thank you so much, Janet.'

Janet gave her a wry smile. 'Don't thank me, thank your tea making. I think we've all realised that it's best to move you on, for the sake of your father's health. I'll make the arrangements and you can start after the Christmas break. In the meantime, stay away from the teapot.'

. . .

The papers called it one of the worst winters on record. The temperatures had plummeted in the middle of December, causing a frightful snowstorm that blanketed the whole country in heavy snow. For a while, it looked like she would have to stay in Birmingham but God answered her prayers. Three days before Christmas, a thaw set in and she'd managed to get to Surrey. She'd gone back to God after Vic pulled through. She felt she owed it to Him. She continued to pray for Vic, and for Robbie and Mina, even though God probably wouldn't approve of Robbie being illegitimate and definitely wouldn't approve of her love for Mina. She reasoned that since she had rediscovered her belief, things had improved for her, so He couldn't be that upset with her, could He?

Her parents were unhappy about her going to Surrey. Probably not just because of the dreadful weather, but she was determined not to miss Christmas morning with Robbie. She wanted to be there to watch him open his presents. She wanted to do motherly things with him.

The journey to Tom and Mina's was rather harrowing. Especially when the train drove through the countryside. At times, it felt like they were Arctic explorers ploughing through a snow tunnel. She half expected not to make it but, against all odds, she finally reached Walton-on-Thames. Tom met her at the station in the car. She was frozen stiff and welcomed the warmth of his arms, wrapped around her in an unusually exuberant hug. It immediately brought Robert to mind and, for a moment, she was transported back a few years and was almost overcome. The ground was slippery and he held onto her to keep her steady all the way to the car. 'You poor dear. You look absolutely freezing. Let's get you inside.' He opened the door for her and threw a rug over her knees. What a considerate man he was. Edie thought of all those times when she'd wished him dead and was ashamed of herself. She muttered a silent prayer to God, asking for forgiveness.

As soon as they got to the house, she was whisked over to a seat next to the roaring fire and a hot toddy was placed in her hand. Mina knelt down in front of her and rubbed her feet until the life came back to them. Robbie climbed on her lap and squeezed his arms around her. She had the two people she loved most within arm's reach. The arduous journey had been worth it for this. It could have snowed for the next ten years and she wouldn't have cared less.

29

WELCOME HOME, PECULIAR GIRL

EDIE – 1947

'We're going home.'

It was early April and, for the first time since the festivities, she was back at the station in Walton-on-Thames. What a dreadful start to the year it had been, especially after such a wonderful Christmas break. She'd stayed to see the new year in and, when the time came to leave, it had been hard to say goodbye. More so because Robbie was upset at her going and could only be consoled with a promise that she would be back before he knew it. But it wasn't to be. January brought with it yet more snow, so much that it held the country in its grip until late March. Travel was impossible. It broke Edie's heart not to keep her promise but she had no choice.

On the rare occasions that she was alone in the house and the lines were working, she managed a telephone call. Mostly, she'd been writing twice weekly, hoping against all hope that her letters were getting through. She enclosed stories in them for Mina to read to Robbie and funny little sketches to cheer him up. But three months is a long time in a child's mind and the minute she saw him, Edie could tell something had changed.

Despite it still being a little chilly, she'd walked from the station to the house. The area was semi-rural and after months of being stuck in a stuffy office, it was good to get out in the fresh air. Mina opened the front door before she got to it. She must have been looking out for her. At her side, holding her hand, was Robbie. At Mina's instruction, he waved to Edie but his face was unsure. As she got closer, Edie could see Alice in the background, her hands clasped together in front of her, the usual beatific smile resting on her face. She shifted her sight away from Alice onto her son and stepped into the hall. 'Hello, my darling. What a joy it is to see you again. Mummy's missed you so much. Come here.' She knelt down and held out her arms for him to run into but he refused to move.

Mina pulled him closer to Edie. 'Robbie, say hello to Mummy. She's come all this way to see you.' Robbie said nothing, his only communication a shake of the head.

'Won't you at least say hello to me?' Edie held out her hand to take his free one. It was enough to send him fleeing into the safety of Alice's skirt. He buried his face in it and clung to her leg.

Alice picked him up. 'Well now, who's being a silly sausage? Don't you recognise your own mummy? She's been trying so hard to come and see you but the nasty old snow's stopped her and even though she couldn't get here, she's been with you all the time, hasn't she? All those lovely pictures and stories she sent to you. You really liked them, didn't you? Especially the ones about the adventures of Robbie.'

Robbie lifted his head away from Alice's bosom and said in his childish little voice: 'In the train.'

'Yes, that was your favourite, wasn't it? How about giving Mummy a nice big thank you kiss?' Robbie thought for a minute, then nodded. Alice put him down and guided him over to Edie who put her arms around him and gave him a kiss. Fearful of overwhelming him, she reined in her enthusiasm which had, in any case, been severely dampened. It was all she could do not to break down and sob. Alice caught her eye and gave her another of those smiles. Perhaps she was a saint, after all.

Mina shared none of Robbie's reticence. The minute they were alone, she practically threw herself on Edie. 'Oh E, I've missed you so. It's been desolate here without you. So very bleak. Robbie's the only thing that's kept me sane, but I have the most wonderful surprise. I've managed to convince Tom to rent a cottage in the summer. He'll have to work, of course so I'll be mostly there on my own with Robbie but I'm so fed up of this dreary place. I need to get out into the country for a while. You must come too.'

'What about Alice?'

Mina waved her hand. 'Don't worry about Alice. I'll send her away when you're there so we can have the place to ourselves. Eddie, say you'll come. If only for a week or two.'

Edie pictured the three of them together, their little family, just as it had been when Robbie was a baby. The excitement was already beginning to build. 'That sounds lovely. I'll have to ask Daddy first. Now that I'm employed, I can't just go off whenever I like, you know.'

'I know, but you haven't heard the best of it yet. It's our old cottage. Won't it be splendid? Just like old times. You have to come.'

. . .

Daddy was not pleased at her request to take a month off. 'Edith, you said you were going to take this seriously. You can't just swan off for four weeks when the fancy takes you.'

She thought that a little unfair, given that she'd worked every week during the winter months. Obviously, that was because it had been too treacherous to travel but that wasn't the point. She was owed some time off. In the end they settled on two weeks in July – her birthday month. Two whole weeks of just her, Mina and Robbie. She couldn't wait.

The time between April and July was endless and it seemed like it was never going to come. She occupied the long days getting to grips with the accounting department and improving her shorthand and typing. She was becoming quite the star pupil in that regard which pleased her father. One of the accounts clerks left to get married and rather than replace her immediately, Janet suggested Edie should pick up her work for a while. Janet had become something of a champion for Edie. A spinster, she'd been Edie's father's secretary for as long as anyone could remember and had always seemed rather stern. In fact, although she kept order in the office, she was very kindhearted and encouraging. She also had Daddy's ear, so when she said Edie would soon be ready to learn bookkeeping, Edie knew, it was only a matter of time. This was good. Like her, the friends she'd made at the secretarial school were still living at home. Having tasted the freedom of living elsewhere in the war, they were keen to regain their independence. They often discussed the cost of rent, in a city short on housing, relative to their wages. Those conversations made her realise that being a short-hand typist alone was not enough.

. . .

At last, the day was here. She closed the front door and walked down the path with a lightness inside that nearly made her giddy. It was a fine morning which always lifted one's spirits but that wasn't the reason for it. She was thrilled. More than thrilled, if that were possible. She virtually skipped along the pavement swinging her suitcase at her side. She felt she could break into a dance at any time, just like Ginger Rogers. She was going so fast that she caught up with a young woman, patiently walking hand in hand with a small girl, about Robbie's age. The child was chattering in that funny, unintelligible way that small children do. It sounded so like Robbie. The anticipation of seeing him in a few hours made her smile.

The woman glanced at Edie and tutted. 'It takes ages to get anywhere these days but she won't let me push her. She loves to walk.'

'She's lovely. Very sweet,' said Edie. There was plenty of time for her train so she slowed down her pace a little. 'I have one about the same age. A boy.' The words spilled out naturally. It was only when she'd said them that Edie was surprised how easily they'd come.

'You're lucky to get a bit of time to yourself then. Good, is he?'

Before she could answer, a group of children on the other side of the street called over to them: 'Bastard, bastard. Bastard baby.'

The woman carried on walking but the words brought Edie to a standstill. 'Go away, you nasty, horrible children.' The children laughed and ran off to play on one of the bomb sites.

'Ignore them, love. They don't understand what it is they're saying,' said the woman. 'They just pick it up from their mums and dads.'

'But it's so unfair.'

The woman shrugged. 'Yes, it is but that's the way it is. There's nothing we can do about it.' They reached a corner and she picked the little girl up. 'Come on, bab. Let's go and see Nanny. Maybe she'll have a biscuit for you. You want a bic-bic?' She turned to Edie. 'Thanks, love. It's nice of you to speak up for me.' She took a few steps along the pavement.

Edie felt a sudden sense of urgency. Before the woman disappeared, she had to ask: 'Your parents, do they support you?'

The woman gave her a quizzical look, then smiled. 'It's just me mum left now. She's got no choice. Neither of us have anywhere else to go. It's hard for her but she ignores the gossip and gets on with it.'

'But how do you cope with that kind of thing?'

'Worse things happen at sea, eh? Take care of yourself, love, and that little boy of yours.'

Edie watched her go. For the first time, she understood what her parents had tried to explain to her. They had endured a tortuous war; lost countless loved ones and were living in the ruins of their former lives and yet, still, old standards prevailed. The lightness in her deflated. She walked on to the station in a low mood.

She'd been upset by that encounter on the way to the station but when she got to Corsham and saw her two darlings waiting for her, she pushed it to the back of her mind. Mina was driving now and she had a little car of her own to run about in. They were all set for a delightful holiday.

The cottage was just as Edie remembered it: nothing had changed. While Mina made tea, she wandered around touching the furniture, its familiarity distant yet comforting. This place held so many memories for her, not all of them good. Even so, it was a part of her that she had no desire to be separated from again. In the main bedroom, her eyes settled on the bed. It was the same one she had, at different times, shared with Robert and Mina. Happy, happy times. The second bedroom differed only in the addition of a small bed in the place where Robbie's cot used to be. Her little boy was growing up. She smiled and went back downstairs.

'Tom will be here at the weekends but we have the weekdays to ourselves,' said Mina. She planted her lips on Edie's. A surge of exhilaration shot through Edie, all the way to her groin. It made her blush. Mina giggled. 'Did you feel that too? Welcome home, Eddie.'

Edie put her hand on Mina's cheek. 'Welcome home, Bill.'

Robbie ran over to a box of toys, picked out a train and held it in the air. 'Mummy.'

Both women instinctively turned their heads and simultaneously said: 'Yes?' There was a moment of awkwardness and then they laughed it off.

Robbie fell asleep in her arms as she read to him in the early evening. She carried him upstairs and laid him down in bed. He didn't stir once. They'd spent the afternoon in the cottage and its garden, as if going elsewhere would break the spell. They'd played games the entire time and it was only now, she realised, he'd missed his afternoon nap. He must have been worn out. She tiptoed downstairs to Mina, who was pouring them both a whisky. Mina moved over to the couch with that liquid walk of hers and sat down elegantly. She patted the seat next to her. 'Come and join me.' Edie sat down and Mina reached over to the side table for a glass and handed it to her. 'Here's to Bill and Eddie, back together again.' She clinked her glass against Edie's.

'To us,' said Edie. She took a large gulp that burned her throat as it slid down. She still wasn't much of a whisky drinker but the feel of it reminded her of that night, two years ago, when they'd affirmed their desire for each other and for that reason alone, it was a nice feeling. She put the glass down and pulled Mina to her, their mouths locking in a kiss.

The kiss over, Mina took her hand and led her upstairs where she sat on the bed and watched Edie undress. When she was finished, Edie lay down and watched her do the same. Mina's body was still perfect. Everything about her was still perfect. She stretched out and let Mina caress her. 'I've missed this so much,' said Mina. 'Sometimes, when I'm lying awake at night with Tom next to me, all I can think about is you. I don't think there will ever be a time that I don't love you, E. I do believe that my love for you transcends life itself. If there is such a thing as an afterlife, I choose to spend it with you.'

Edie woke up the next morning to find Robbie standing next to her, looking a little puzzled. Presumably the sight of her in the same bed as Mina was confusing for him. He was probably too young to express his confusion to anyone but there was always the chance that something might slip out. For a minute, she considered whether this would actually be a good, rather than a bad, thing. Then she told herself not to be so ridiculous. She swung her legs out of the bed and grabbed a nearby dressing gown to cover her naked body. 'Shall we go and get some breakfast?'

Half an hour later Mina emerged in her silk pyjamas.

Edie realised the dressing gown she was wearing matched them exactly: they were a set. 'Did Robbie come into our room this morning?' she whispered. Edie nodded. 'Oh gosh, I hadn't thought of that. We'll need to make sure we're more careful. We'll have to get up earlier.'

Edie raised an eyebrow. The only time Mina had been able to get up early was when she'd been required to in the WAAF. Mornings were not her strong suit. 'We?'

'Okay, yes, obviously not me.' Mina smirked.

''B, you really are quite hopeless.'

'My point exactly, darling. You see now why I employ Alice.'

Edie shook her head in dismay. Mina was impossible. Quite impossible. She looked out through the kitchen window. The sun was bright and it was going to be a glorious day. 'Let's go for a picnic today.'

A few hours later, they were driving along the country roads in the direction of Rudloe Manor. They drove past a field with a small hill just beyond the gate. Edie didn't notice it until they'd almost gone past. 'Stop!'

Mina slammed her foot on the brake and they nearly went through the windscreen. 'What is it? What's the matter?'

Robbie was sitting on Edie's knee looking startled. She smiled reassuringly at him. She hadn't meant for the stop to be that abrupt. She lifted him up and got out of the car. 'This is where your daddy and I first met. We used to come here often and play a little game. Shall I show you?'

They walked up to the top of the hill, Robbie in the middle holding each of their hands. When they got there, Edie told them to stretch out their arms and tongues so that they could touch and taste the sky. The sun was brilliant but she closed her eyes and pretended the stars were out. She imagined Robert and Jimmy were with them and perhaps Mina's dead brothers too, even though she didn't know them. Her mouth widened into a broad grin. Robbie began to chortle. She and Mina joined in and all three collapsed to the ground in hysterics. She tickled Robbie. He squealed with joy and they all laughed until they could laugh no more.

Not wanting to lose the moment, they set up their picnic there and stayed on top of the small hill looking out across the fields. She recalled the times she came here to watch the night skies and saw the bombs falling on Bristol. She remembered Robert calling to her in the dark, asking if she was all right. 'I was standing right here in the pitch-black night, playing that little game by myself when Robert came strolling along that lane and saw me,' she said. 'He must have thought it strange but, nonetheless, he came up and joined me. I wonder what he would have made of me now.'

Mina squeezed her hand. 'He would have loved you just as much as I do. He always said you were a peculiar girl.'

She smiled. 'Maybe I am.'

Mina looked out towards Bristol. 'Maybe we both are.'

30

SUSPICION AND LOSS

EDIE – 1947

'I suppose loss is the price we pay for love.'

Mina loved her again. The thrill of it. The titillation. It was electrifying. Almost to the point of being unbearable. They spent so much time together during that holiday that they were back as they used to be, anticipating each other's thoughts and feelings. Mad for each other.

After the holiday, they took every chance they could to get out and be away from the scrutiny of others. Sometimes, even the scrutiny of Robbie. Although she felt guilty about it, they occasionally left him with Alice and went off on their own. The lines between her love for Robbie and her love for Mina were beginning to blur. There was no doubting the strength of the bond with her son but she craved Mina more than anything. She was drunk on Mina. She was desperate for her. She'd been wrong to doubt that Mina would ever tire of her. She knew now that they would love each other for a lifetime. Maybe even more.

Since July, she was finding returning to Birmingham

increasingly difficult. It was a wrench to leave them both behind each month. When she wasn't with them, her thoughts constantly darted between Robbie and Mina. It was getting harder to concentrate on her work and she was making silly mistakes which set back her training. On top of that, her family's inquisitiveness was becoming more intrusive. Several times, her mother had asked what it was that kept her returning to Surrey. Edie fobbed her off by saying that Mina was her best friend and she needed her. But now, it had come to a head. Her mother had just asked her, in her most exasperated voice: 'I understand that you're very close to this Mina but don't you think it's time to get on with your own life? You're twenty-three. Don't you want to get married and have children?'

If ever there had been a perfect opportunity to tell her that she already had a child, this was it. Whilst her mother was sitting there, wringing her hands and waiting for an answer, Edie could say that very thing. As she carefully considered her words, she thought of the woman in the street with the illegitimate child and the things she'd said about how her mother had to grin and bear the gossip. Could she do that to Mummy? Then she thought of Mina. Supposing her parents did accept Robbie? There would be no excuse to see her every month. 'I haven't really met anyone I'm interested in. I'm afraid I still miss Robert. Mina helps me in that respect. So, you see, it's a two-way thing really: we help each other.'

'I see. Have you considered the possibility that visiting her every month is having the opposite effect?'

'No, I don't believe it does.'

'Very well. Then we must hope that you pull through this soon. By the way, we've invited the Clarksons to dinner next week. Their son, Edward, will be coming too.'

Edie opened her mouth to protest but the look her mother gave her told her, in no uncertain terms, not to bother. She knew exactly what Mummy was up to and there was nothing she could do to stop it. She nodded and left the room to seek out Vic in the hope of finding a sympathetic ear.

Vic was not in the least bit sympathetic. In fact, he was finding it very amusing. 'Come on Sis, don't be such a shrew. Ma's only trying to help. You don't want to end up an old maid, do you?'

'There's nothing wrong with being single.' She stormed out of Vic's room in time to hear her mother leaving the house. Still outraged, she decided to find Hannah. If anyone could understand, it would be Hannah who had never married.

Hannah was making Christmas chutney in the kitchen and was equally unimpressed by Edie's grievances. 'Ask yourself why she's so concerned about you.'

'She just wants to see me married off. That's all there is to it,' said Edie.

'Is it? Don't you wonder why she's worried about you visiting that friend of yours every month? She thinks you've got something to hide but you know your mother, it's not in her nature to just come out and say it. She's far too much of a lady for that.'

A blast of heat broke out across Edie's chest and rose to her face. 'That's ridiculous. What could I possibly have to hide?'

Hannah put her hands on her hips and stared at Edie. 'You tell me, Edith. Is something going on with that friend of yours?'

'No!'

'You're sure? You're not courting someone you shouldn't be? Someone married, maybe?'

All at once, it dawned on Edie that Hannah and her mother had got the wrong idea. She began to laugh. 'You think I'm having an illicit affair with a married man? How absurd. Oh Hannah, what must you both think of me?'

Hannah spooned the cooled chutney into jars. 'I don't know what I think of you, Edith. All I know is, you're not the same little Edie I used to know. You might not be courting a married man but you're up to something. I know it and so does your mother.'

Edie stood on the other side of the saucepan. She began to fill an empty jar and, rather than look at Hannah, kept her attention firmly fixed on it. 'You have my word, I'm not up to anything.'

Hannah glanced over; her face expressionless. She took a short, deep breath and turned away. 'We need more jars.' Edie watched her go to the larder and come back with the jars but when Hannah returned her gaze with a cold, hard stare, she looked away. Hannah knew she was lying. Hannah always knew.

The next morning, she made an excuse not to go to church and instead sat in the breakfast room watching the grey winter morning unfold. The trees had shed their leaves and most of the plants had gone over. The garden was a bleak sight and it matched her mood perfectly. Hannah's accusations compelled her to consider her behaviour, and the lies she'd been forced to tell yesterday didn't sit well with her. Something needed to be done to allay their suspicions. She recognised that the little she normally said about her visits to Mina's were probably fuelling their concerns. From now on she would go out of her way to give them more information, albeit sanitised versions of events. She would even have to bend the truth a little. It was wrong but if it kept them happy then perhaps it wasn't too wrong. Besides, it wouldn't be for long. If she doubled down on her training she'd soon be a decent bookkeeper, as well as a shorthand typist. Then she'd be able to reveal the truth to them and if they didn't like it she'd have the skills to find work to support her and Robbie.

With that resolution determined, she turned to the next thing that was bringing her down. Earlier, she'd managed a telephone call to Mina about the upcoming Christmas arrangements. Mina had informed her that, unfortunately, Tom's parents were coming to stay. That meant only one thing, Edie was not invited. It was yet another blow. The colder months had brought less opportunity for outdoor privacy and things had already calmed down between them but just to be in the same room as Mina was enough. Now she would have to wait until January to be with her again. She consoled herself with the knowledge that being at home would, at least, please her parents. This was a special Christmas for the Pinsents. Vic was fully recovered now and had already started working at the family firm. He and Birgitt were getting married next year and would be moving into their own home a few streets away. Edie decided to do her best to savour the last Christmas that they would all be living under the same roof.

A knock on the front door brought a close to her reflections and she went to answer it. It was Birgitt, her eyes red and swollen. 'My parents are dead.'

Without saying a word, Edie brought her into the hall and wrapped her arms around her. The first thing she noticed was how cold Birgitt was. She wasn't wearing a coat.

She must have rushed out of the house. Edie tried to coax her into the sitting room where the fire might warm her up but Birgitt stood motionless, stiff and straight as a soldier. Edie held on and pulled her closer. The action seemed to trigger something in Birgitt and she instantly fell into Edie as the grief poured out of her. Edie waited until her weeping quietened down and guided her to a chair in the sitting room, near the fire. She wrapped her in a blanket and made some hot, sweet tea. These were the things her friends Lily and Dolly had done for her when Robert was killed. At the time she hadn't really registered it but she could see now, it was part of the process one needed to grieve. Being here with Birgitt brought it all back and she was suddenly weighed down with the memory of it. The realisation that her grief for him was still with her almost crushed her but she pulled herself back from it: Birgitt needed her. She sat on the floor next to Birgitt's chair and held her hand. It was still cold, the shock, probably. Birgitt took a letter from her skirt pocket and gave it to Edie. It confirmed that her parents had been killed in the Auschwitz concentration camp.

Birgitt stared into the fire. 'I think I knew, in my heart, but to have it written on paper… I will have to tell my brother and sisters.'

'Would you like me to come with you?'

'No. It's something I must do alone, or perhaps with Victor.' She turned to Edie. 'Thank you. You are so kind. I think you understand more than anyone, don't you?'

Edie rubbed Birgitt's hands. 'Yes.'

31

DAMN DOLLY BAXTER

EDIE – 1948

'Oh but it was horrible. Just horrible.'

It was April and once again, the first visit of the year. As had been the case last year, the rough winter weather had made it difficult to travel before then. Rather than try to fight her way through it, Edie had concentrated her efforts on providing Birgitt with some comfort. They'd become quite attached to each other in the last few months. Sisters in loss, soon to be sisters-in-law. Despite missing Robbie and Mina terribly she had written to them in January to explain that she couldn't visit until the spring because Birgitt needed her. Mina had been very understanding and as they had done last year, they wrote to each other once or twice a week. Once again she sent stories and funny little pictures for Robbie. All of this in the hope that he would be happy to see her when she returned but her hopes had been quickly dashed on her arrival yesterday when she tried to embrace him and he ran off to Alice. This time, even Alice hadn't been able to persuade him. Edie sank down on the couch, defeated. Mina put her arm on her shoulder. 'Don't be upset, E. He'll be fine in a few hours. It's just because he hasn't seen you for a while, that's all.'

Yesterday had been difficult but this morning, things had begun to look up. While she was still in bed, Alice had knocked on the door with some papers in one hand and Robbie in the other. 'Sorry for the intrusion. We've been reading your stories and the thing is, I'm not very good at reading them out. I keep getting the words mixed up, don't I Robbie?' Robbie gave a shy nod. 'So, I had a thought. Wouldn't it be so much better if the person that wrote them read them out and we thought that was a very good idea, didn't we Robbie?' Again a little nod. 'You don't mind do you, madam?'

'No, not at all.' Edie sat up quickly before he changed his mind. Alice lifted Robbie up onto the bed and handed her the stories. She spread them out across the eiderdown. 'Which one would you like me to read, darling?' He picked one with a picture of a train on it and she began to read it out, taking care to use as many funny voices as she good because she knew they made him laugh. Minutes later she looked up and noticed Alice had quietly left the room.

When they got down to breakfast, Mina had another surprise. She offered to drop them off in the little town centre for a couple of hours so that Edie could take Robbie to look at the trains in the station, one of his favourite pastimes. Now, they were sitting on the platform with little notepads, each drawing sketches of the trains coming in and out of the station. Robbie was putting all of his concentration into drawing oddly shaped lozenges. 'That's very good,' said Edie. 'Well done. May I have it?'

He smiled up at her proudly. 'Yes. It's for you.'

'Thank you, darling. I'll take it home with me and keep it with my special treasures.' She checked her watch. 'We must go. We're meeting Auntie Mina for afternoon tea. Won't that be nice?'

'Will there be cakes?'

'I expect so, if Auntie Mina has anything to do with it.'

They walked hand in hand towards the tea room she'd arranged to meet Mina in. As they passed the shops she noticed a wooden train set in one of the windows. She stopped and lifted him up to see it. His eyes nearly popped out at the sight of it. She put him down and took his hand. 'Shall we go in and take a closer look at it?'

Mina waved to them when they entered the tea room. She looked so polished and stylish that she stood out like a beacon amongst the sea of browns and greys surrounding her. Her outfit was in the new style from France, the 'New Look'. Edie's friends from secretarial school often discussed it but none of them could afford it and clothing was still rationed, although you wouldn't know it to look at Mina. She was above such things. Edie both loved and loathed that about her. Robbie's eyes lit up when he saw Mina. He ran over to the table to show her his new train set. So, she and her son had at least one thing in common. They both adored Mina.

Edie put some sandwiches on his plate. His attention, of course, was all for the cakes. 'Eat the sandwiches first and then you can pick whichever cake you want.'

'Promise?'

'Promise.'

Satisfied he began to tuck into his sandwiches. Edie was about to take a bite into one of hers when Mina put her hand out to stop her. 'I've had an idea, E. Do you think you can reshuffle your week here next month? If you can come the week before or the week after the reunion, we could travel together from here and stay overnight in London. What do you think?'

'I think I should be able to change it.' A night together. Just her and Bill. A whole night. They'd have to be careful of course, book separate rooms but gosh, yes, it could work. 'That would be marvellous, B. Tremendous fun.'

A few weeks later, Edie was pulling in again at Walton-on-Thames. She'd managed to change her week to the one before the WAAF reunion. Mina had arranged everything and insisted on paying for it. Instead of ploughing all of her wages into her savings account that month, as she normally did, Edie had treated herself to a new dress to wear in London. The 'New Look' it definitely was not but it was stylish enough to make her feel less drab when standing next to Mina.

She stepped off the train and was surprised to see Robbie waiting on the platform, seemingly alone. He ran over and threw his arms around her. What a difference to last month. She picked him up and squeezed him tight. It was only then that she saw Mina, a few feet away, leaning against the waiting room. She was wearing mannish trousers, à la Katherine Hepburn. Edie wanted her, there and then. She winked at Edie as she pushed herself off the wall. 'He wanted to meet you himself, E. Quite the little man, don't you think?'

Edie gave Robbie a kiss. 'Yes indeed. Such a big boy.'

Robbie beamed at her, quite pleased with himself. He put his hand into his coat pocket and took out the little wooden train she'd bought him last month. 'Look, Mummy. It's the same as that one.' He pointed to the train engine.

'Yes it is. What a clever fellow you are. Big and brave and clever. Just like your daddy.' Edie smiled inwardly. Everything with Robbie was as it should be and the week was going to be a pleasant one. Because she'd brought her visit forward, it would be longer between this and the next one so she must savour every minute of it, even though part of her couldn't wait for the week to end so that she and Mina could be alone together.

At last the big day was here. She'd felt only a little guilty as she kissed a teary Robbie goodbye and left him with Alice that morning. They travelled first class. Naturally. This was Mina. Second class was not in her nature. They had adjoining rooms with an interconnecting door, in a delightful hotel on the Strand. A little further on was the Strand Palace Hotel, where they had stayed for Mina and Tom's wedding. Edie had stipulated only one condition about their accommodation, it must not be the Strand Palace Hotel. She would always associate it with Robert and for that reason alone, she couldn't set foot in there again.

They were taking lunch with Mina's mother at a restaurant on Mayfair. Mina blamed Tom for this. He'd told them that they were staying over and her mother had insisted on meeting them both. Edie didn't mind at all: she'd always rather liked Mrs Jacobson and the feeling seemed to be mutual. The Jacobsons knew she was Robbie's mother and, in the few times she'd seen them since the wedding, hadn't shunned her because of it. It made them all the more endearing.

'Edith, my dear, you're looking a little peaky,' said Mrs Jacobson. 'Are you sure you're well?'

'I'm tip top, thank you, Mrs Jacobson.'

She put her hand on Edie's arm. 'My dear, we've been through this before. Call me Audrey. Mrs Jacobson makes me sound positively elderly.' She was an older, smaller, neater version of Mina. Edie could imagine Mina in thirty years' time looking just like her. 'Tell me Edith, how are things with you? Are we to expect news of any engagements from you soon?'

'Ma, for goodness sake,' said Mina. 'What a thing to ask.'

Audrey Jacobson was undeterred. 'Nonsense. Edie is such a lovely little thing, I'm sure there are plenty of young men in the world who'd give their right arm to be her beau. Regardless of her … complications.'

Edie shook her head. 'No news on that front, Audrey. There hasn't really been another man for me since Robert.'

Mrs Jacobson squeezed her arm. 'I understand, my dear. Give it time. You'll find someone, I'm sure. Just remember that it doesn't have to be love. As long as you like them and they're kind, kind enough to take Robbie on. You can be perfectly happy settling for that, you know.'

Mina caught Edie's eye and the corner of her mouth twitched upwards. 'Shall we order? Edie and I have an afternoon's shopping planned so we can't take all day.'

Mrs Jacobson sighed. 'You young girls and your shopping. There is more to life, you know.'

When they'd frittered away the rest of the afternoon at the shops they went back to the hotel and spent some time in Mina's bed before getting dressed for dinner. Edie wore her blue silk dress. It was a little old fashioned now but it was still her favourite and Mina loved her in it.

They ate in the hotel and took a cab to Chelsea. When the cab drove away, they walked on for a while until they reached a building at the end of a street. Edie had no idea where they were but Mina seemed to know. She knocked on the door and said something to the man who opened it. Edie was too distracted by the music coming from inside to hear what it was. The man pointed them in the direction of a steep staircase that led down to a smoky cellar. Edie recognised the music to be jazz. It was louder now and drowned out the low hum of voices and laughter from the many people packing the small room out. A waitress wove them through the crowd, past lovers leaning into each other across tables to their own table at the back of the room. Mina ordered cocktails and they sat quietly watching the couples dancing closely together; closer than was actually decent. 'Shall we dance, Eddie?' said Mina.

'With whom?' For once, all eyes were not on Mina and there were no men clamouring to be their dance partners.

Mina laughed in that full throated mannish way that she sometimes did and pulled Edie up. Edie laughed too. What did it matter if they didn't have partners? They could dance together as she and her friends had done at the NAAFI dances. They were just having fun. But Mina had other ideas. She pulled Edie in so that their bodies were touching and moved herself harmoniously in time to the seductive rhythms. It was so erotic that Edie was both flabbergasted and aroused, and just a little afraid. 'Bill, we'll be reported to the police.'

Mina laughed again. 'I doubt that very much. Take a look around you, Eddie. No one cares.'

Edie hardly dared to look in case she was met with disgusted stares but she forced herself, and then she saw what Mina said was true. No one cared because they were the same as them. The lovers leaning into each other across tables and the couples dancing so obscenely were women. 'My god, they're…'

'Just like us,' said Mina. She kissed Edie so passionately that when she finished they were both gasping for air. They giggled, giddy with excitement.

'Kiss me again and don't stop,' said Edie. 'I never want you to stop.'

She woke up the next morning still buzzing with excitement. It had been a most astounding night. There were other women like them. Who'd have thought it? She looked at Mina – exquisite, even in sleep – and picked up a strand of her hair to tickle her face with. It did the trick. She stirred and opened her eyes. 'I've been awake all the time.'

'Liar!' Edie blew a loud raspberry on Mina's bare stomach sending Mina into giggling convulsions. She would have liked to have stayed there all morning but time was pressing on. 'We have to get up if we don't want to miss breakfast.'

Mina screwed up her nose. 'I don't want to leave this room, ever.'

'Well you'll have to, my darling. We have a reunion to go to and I'm absolutely starving.'

Mina rolled over to the telephone on the bedside table. 'We'll have breakfast up here. I want to keep you all to myself for as long as possible.'

Edie retreated to her room to have a wash and brush up while they waited for the breakfast to be brought up. Before long, she heard tapping on Mina's door. Mina made a show of knocking the interconnecting door and asking if she was up. 'On my way,' she called and went to open it but caught sight of her own bed, still made up. She turned back and ruffled it up enough to make it look as if she'd spent the night there. When she opened the door, the waiter had gone and Mina was already tucking in to a large breakfast.

'Wasn't last night wonderful, E?'

'Absolutely. I can't believe no one batted an eyelid at us kissing like that.'

'Simply marvellous, wasn't it?'

'That place, how do you know it?'

Mina spread a slick of butter across some toast. 'My dressmaker.'

'Is she…?'

'No, I don't think so. Her studio's just around the corner from the club. She mentioned it as a place to avoid more than anything. I think she has some clients that go there. Did you love it?'

'I did. Did you?'

'Yes. I thought it was an absolute blast. Such a shame we probably won't be able to go again. Too risky.'

'Yes, I suppose so.' Edie sighed. She'd rather hoped that wouldn't be the case.

The reunion was in the same room, in the same modest hotel as the previous year and the one before that. It was a little tatty but Edie didn't mind that. Everyone chipped in to pay for it equally and for some of them, it was a stretch. Mina took a less benevolent view and all the way there, she complained about how awful the catering was likely to be. Thankfully, when they arrived, she turned on her charm and nothing more was said about wilting sandwiches and watery tea.

She left Mina surrounded by an adoring crowd and

went to find Lily. She preferred to see her on her own. It wasn't that they didn't get on but Mina and Lily weren't the best of friends. They tolerated each other, probably for Edie's sake. She found her quite quickly and Lily immediately pulled her over to two chairs in the corner and began unloading her news. She flashed her left hand under Edie's nose to show an engagement ring with a tiny stone. 'I'm getting married next month, Ede. Can you believe it? I'm so sorry I can't invite you to the wedding. Of all my friends, you'd be the one I'd want there, if I could. It's just that we're trying to keep it small. Family only. Things are a bit tight at the moment. But we'll be all right. Harry's got a new job in a village school in the Yorkshire Dales. It comes with a house so we'll be set. You can come and visit us there if you like. I'd love you to meet Harry. He's such a sweetheart.'

She was practically exploding with happiness and it was rubbing off on Edie. 'What wonderful news, Lils. Of course I'll come and visit and don't worry about the wedding, I understand completely. I'm so pleased for you.'

'Now, tell me what you've been up to. How are you? How is Robbie? He must be nearly starting school now.'

'Not a lot of news really. You know me. I just keep soldiering on.'

'And Robbie?'

'Robbie's still with Mina and Tom. I don't seem to have been able to find the right moment to tell my parents but I'm hoping I'll soon be able to support myself and then it won't matter how they react to the news.'

'Oh Ede, I'm so sorry. It must be absolutely awful for you.'

Edie nodded. 'I make the most of it. I spend a week with him every month, at Mina's. She and Tom have been absolute bricks.'

'Oh, I bet they have,' said a sharp voice from behind. Edie turned around but she needn't have: she'd know that voice, that gloating tone, anywhere. It was Dolly Baxter. Her face painted like some spiv's tart.

Lily glared at Dolly. 'Don't be nasty, Dolly and what's more, don't be so nosy. That was a private conversation.'

Dolly tossed back her blonde curls. 'Come off it, Lily. You know as well as I do Queen B would never do anything that didn't suit her and as for a private conversation, she's telling anyone that listens how she's as good as Robbie's mum. Edie's so in love with her, she can't see the wood for the trees. Someone's got to do the decent thing and tell her. Wake up, Edie. She's just using you.'

Edie jumped up from the chair to face Dolly. She wanted to slap her stupid, cheap face hard. That's how much she hated Dolly Baxter. Dolly must have seen that because she took a step backwards and let out a loud gasp. One or two people in close proximity stopped what they were doing and stared at them. Lily got up and stood between them. She spoke quietly but firmly: 'Dolly, I think you should go and talk to someone else now.'

Dolly huffed. Now that she had a crowd watching, she was in no hurry to move away. She did love to be the centre of attention. 'Look, Ede. I know what you think of me and I'm sure you believe that I'm being spiteful but I'm not. I'm trying to make you open your eyes to the truth.'

'Dolly, please,' said Lily.

Edie put her hand up. 'It's quite all right, Lily. I'm afraid Dolly is just being her usual self. You've always been a nasty cat, Dolly. I put up with it when we were in the WAAF because I had to see you every day. I don't have to put up with it now.' She pushed past her and walked towards the doors. Her heart was pounding, her hands shook and her legs wanted to give way but she kept on going. Lily was calling her name, Mina was nowhere to be seen, but she didn't stop. She collected her things from the cloakroom and left the hotel before Lily could catch up with her. It had been awful. Horrible. Damn Dolly Baxter. Damn her to hell. She would never see her again. Never.

32

SEEING THE LIGHT IN A DINGY BEDSIT

EDIE – 1948

'Everyone else is moving on. In the meantime, I travel back and forth, always ending up in the same place.'

It was July, Birgitt and Vic had been married for two hours. Edie was the maid of honour and Birgitt's sisters were bridesmaids. Clothes rationing was still in force so Edie was wearing her cornflower blue silk dress with the little hat and gloves that Mina had bought her. Everyone said she looked a picture. There was a band at the reception party and they were dancing to all the latest tunes. Aside from last month at that strange nightclub, Edie hadn't danced since the NAAFI dances. She'd forgotten how much fun it was just letting oneself go like that. She stopped for a breather and went to talk to Birgitt. Vic came over and introduced her to one of his friends from the army, a rather tall, pleasant looking chap called Ken who was now training to be a doctor.

'You're a very good dancer,' said Ken. 'Mind taking me for a spin?'

He was nothing like Robert but he reminded her of him. Perhaps it was because he clearly enjoyed dancing and, like Robert, was good at it. Perhaps it was because he was funny and made her laugh. It didn't matter what it was, she was having a good time. As they took the last dance together she spotted her parents looking on approvingly. No need to guess what they were thinking. Ken cleared his throat. 'It's strange, Vic talked about you so often when we were serving that I feel I already know you quite well but in fact we don't know each other at all. That said, I'd like to get to know you better, Edie. There's a dance I was thinking of going to next week. Would you like to come with me?'

Edie looked over at her parents again. They were still watching her. She wasn't looking for a husband but Ken was fun and after the reunion, she needed something to lift her spirits. When she'd seen Mina in June, neither of them mentioned what had happened. She wasn't sure why Mina chose to keep quiet about it but for her part, she didn't want Dolly Baxter sullying their time together. All the same, Dolly's words weighed heavily on her mind and would continue to do so unless she had something to distract her. She smiled up at Ken. 'I would love to.'

As she'd hoped, Ken proved to be a pleasant distraction. Over the summer, he'd given her something new to focus on when she wasn't in Surrey and, for once, the oncoming winter didn't look quite so bad. It was October now. Robbie had started school a month ago and she'd coincided her visit with his first week so that she could take him herself. It felt like a momentous occasion to watch him walk through the school gates for the first time. He took a few steps and glanced back anxiously to make sure she was still there. He looked like he was about to cry. She waved to him and gave him a reassuring smile. He gave her a sad little one back and went into the building. He hadn't settled too well in that first week but now it seemed he was doing just fine. Tom and Mina had been talking about how his favourite lesson was music, if you could call bashing on a tambourine music, when she'd let it slip out that she'd been to a dance with Ken. Despite seeing him every week when she was in Birmingham, she hadn't mentioned him until now. Tom wanted to know all about him. She gave him the details on his background and their weekly dates.

'Well, I think it's great news,' he said. 'It's about time.'

Edie glanced at Mina. She looked like she didn't think it was such great news which was a bit rich considering she had Tom. Still, Edie didn't want to give the wrong impression. 'Steady on, Tom. Ken's a nice chap but he's just a friend, nothing more.'

Mina's face brightened. 'Talking of which, did Robbie tell you he has some new little friends?'

'No,' said Edie.

'Oh yes. It's quite sweet. We've had a couple of them over to play with him. It's nice for him to have the company. Children should have friends of their own age, don't you think? I've asked their mothers over for a coffee morning tomorrow. I thought you'd like to meet them, now that Robbie's branching out. Nice to see what kind of people they are.' Mina smirked. 'It'll be fun, E. We can vet them. What do you think?'

'Why not.' She wouldn't admit it to Mina but the thought of meeting these other women made her uneasy. She was nervous about what they would make of her. That unmarried mother that she'd met on the way to the holiday last year popped into her head. She did that on occasions. Usually when Edie's mood was at a low ebb. Normally, it was the child she thought about, condemned to grow up labelled a bastard. She worried about what effect that could have on a child. Today though, she considered the appellation assigned to the mother. Slut, perhaps? Fallen woman? Whore? Is that how these other mothers would see her? She cast such noxious ideas from her head. She was a widow who worked. That was her story and she would stick to it.

The coffee morning wasn't going nearly as badly as she'd been expecting. The three women that came were perfectly nice, although they were oddly similar. Sort of indistinguishable. It was hard to remember which was Anne, which was Amelia and which was Daphne or, indeed, who was mother to which child. They sat together on the couch like the three wise monkeys, each dressed almost identically; each looking as pristine as newly packaged dolls. One of them, it could have been Amelia, inquired about Edie's work. They listened politely to her reply. No one asked why she had to work or why Robbie didn't live with her. She took this as a good sign.

They talked endlessly about how their children were doing at school. Edie wondered how there could be so much to say about it, given that the children had only started a month ago. At long last, even they realised they'd exhausted the subject and they went on to debate the best places to buy good cloth and where to find a decent dressmaker. They seemed to think Mina was an expert on these matters. She must be, they said, since she was always so well turned out and stylish. Mina was in her element, dispensing words of wisdom here and there, nodding sympathetically to their tales of shopping woe. As she quietly observed them, Edie suddenly heard Dolly's voice in her head saying: 'Queen B.' Disappointed in herself for giving room in her mind to that woman, she turned to the children in an effort to keep Dolly Baxter at bay. They were playing with Robbie's toys. He was being a perfect little gentleman about sharing them. Until school, he hadn't really had any friends, other than a nephew and niece on Mina's side. Perhaps Mina was right about the company being good for him. He was such an easy-going child that it hadn't occurred to her he might be missing out but then she only saw him once a month. Mina was with him every day so she could see it. She knew him better than her. Oh! She was suddenly shocked by her own thoughts. She reprimanded herself. Robbie was her son. She knew him better than anyone. Mina didn't even look after him, she had Alice to do that. How ludicrous to think her knowledge of him was superior to her own.

She drew back into the conversation. Anne, or perhaps Daphne, was saying what a delightful child Robbie was. 'Such a handsome little boy too,' she continued. 'He's the image of his father, isn't he?'

'Yes, he is rather,' said Edie.

They finally closed the door on Amelia, Anne and Daphne and their offspring and returned to the sitting room to flop down on the couches. Mina could hardly contain herself, such was her amusement. 'Well, I won't be repeating that experience in a hurry. What perfectly dull people.'

Edie giggled. 'Don't be so cruel, B. They had their good points.'

'Oh really? What were they? Do tell.'

'Well, they were all nice. Very pretty, in a sterile sort of way. You're right they were rather boring.'

Mina let out a hoot of laughter. 'You see! Even you can't think of a good thing to say about them. Pity me, Eddie. I have to mix with those women at the school gates. It's all so terribly unfair.'

The train clattered along the tracks. Edie looked up from her journal at the ploughed fields whizzing by. She had just finished writing about the coffee morning and was still grinning. She and Mina had been laughing about it all week. Hilarious as it was though, when those women had said what a beautiful boy Robbie was, she still felt a swell of pride. He *was* a handsome little chap with his dark wavy hair and blue eyes. Her blue eyes. But they were right: other than the eyes, he was the image of his father. Suddenly, something occurred to her. Those women couldn't have known what Robert looked like. They must have assumed Robbie was Tom's son. With that realisation came another new awareness. The remark about Robbie hadn't been made to her but to Mina. They'd assumed Mina was Robbie's mother.

For the rest of the week, Edie had been plagued by Dolly's heartless words about Mina telling everyone she was practically Robbie's mother. She tried to push them away but they kept coming back to haunt her. The only thing that had stopped her from being dragged down was the knowledge that work was going well and she was getting closer to the point of taking Robbie back. On top of this, she'd received some good news that had quite cheered her up this morning.

A letter from Lily. She was expecting a baby. When she had the time, Edie would write back to offer her congratulations and promise to visit her soon. In the meantime, she had a full weekend planned to occupy her. On Sunday she was having lunch with Vic and Birgitt and tomorrow she was going out with her friends from secretarial school, Pat and Helen. Now, it was Friday night and she was at another dance with Ken.

They'd been dancing practically all night and her feet were sore. Thank goodness he had a car to whisk her home in. She liked going out with him: he made her feel young and carefree again. As she said goodnight he leaned over and kissed her for the first time. He hadn't asked permission, as Robert had, but he was quite gentle so she didn't mind. She allowed him to kiss her again before saying a final goodnight and watched him drive around the corner. The kisses had been nice. Nothing like those with Mina, or with Robert, for that matter but they were nice. She wasn't attracted to Ken but she enjoyed his company and she needed someone to stem the loneliness. Lily was married with a child on the way; Vic and Birgitt were married; Robbie was at school and Tom and Mina were settled in their suburban lives. She was the one who seemed to be standing still, forever caught between two lives.

She was still mulling this over as she journeyed into town the next day. She'd arranged to meet Helen there. Pat had managed to move out of her parents' home and had invited them over for tea before going on to the flicks to see *The Red Shoes*. Edie got on very well with Pat and Helen. They were the friends she went out with occasionally but this visit was something new. Aside from Pat, she didn't know any other woman of her age who didn't either live with their parents or their spouse. Pat was terribly brave. Helen too wanted her own independence. Edie admired them both so much. Just being with them gave her more confidence to think about finding a home for her and Robbie.

The new flat was in the north of the city, in Handsworth Wood so they jumped on another bus to get them there. 'I have to admit, I'm quite excited to see Pat's new place,' said Helen.

'Me too,' said Edie and she meant it.

Pat was waiting for them at the bus stop. She looked frozen to the bone. 'It's a ten-minute walk. The fire's on in the flat. That should warm us up.' They followed her through streets with houses not dissimilar to the ones where Edie lived and stopped outside a large black and white house. Pat opened the front gate. 'Here we are.'

'Oh Pat it's lovely,' said Edie.

Pat gave her a funny look. 'Don't get your hopes up too much, I only live in the top bit.' She unlocked the front door. The hall was as cold as the outdoors but the trek to the top of the house warmed them up. There were three floors, each with several locked doors. The top floor had one door which Pat opened. Inside was one room with a bed, wardrobe and drawers on one side and a kitchenette, a small oven, a table and two chairs on the other. In between, two battered armchairs sat facing a small fire which was nearly out. It was like Hannah's room, but not as nice. One small window let in a little light. It wasn't enough to brighten the drab walls but Pat had made a decent job of trying to enliven the place with a colourful tablecloth and cushions. 'I'll put some more coal on the fire. Bathroom's on the middle floor if you need it,' said Pat. 'It's not much but it's my own place. That's all I care about.'

'Oh no, it's lovely and cosy,' said Helen. 'It's much nicer than my sister and her husband's place. I'm so envious, Pat.'

Pat looked relieved. 'I've got plans to make it nicer when I can save the money. I'd like to put some pictures up on the walls.'

'Edie, could do you some pictures. Couldn't you, Ede?' said Helen.

'Yes, if you want me to. I'm sure you'll be able to buy much better though.'

'Would you?' said Pat. 'That would be lovely. I like those little drawings of yours and it'll be ages before I can afford to buy any.'

'Yes, of course. What would you like?'

'I don't mind. Something bright. The brighter the better. Right, now the fire's burning again who's going to do the toasting?'

Helen set to toasting bread on the fire with a long fork. They spread butter and crab paste over it and wolfed it down. It wasn't something Edie normally ate but it was very tasty. She'd brought some of Hannah's cheese scones. They ate those next and finished off with a slice of fruit cake.

'I'm so full I don't think I can move,' said Helen. They were all three lying on their backs on the floor.

'Well, if we want to catch the film we've got to go,' said Pat rubbing her stomach. Edie and Helen groaned, rolled over and pulled themselves up. None of them wanted to miss the film.

It was a terribly sad film. Pat and Helen were sobbing. Edie was too, but it wasn't only the film she was crying for. Pat's dingy bedsit had been such a disappointment. Not because it was something to look down on. She'd had a super afternoon there and if she was on her own like Pat, she would have seen it as a great adventure. But she was not planning to be on her own. She'd been hoping to find a home for her and Robbie. Even if she earned more as a bookkeeper than a shorthand typist, even if she became a secretary, she would never be able earn enough to house them both in a decent home with money left over to pay for his care while she was at work. It was hopeless, and she knew it.

33

DOLLY'S WORDS RING TRUE

EDIE – 1949

'It's too late. I've lost him. All I can do now is try to hang on to her.'

Edie threw her cutlery down. It crashed against the plate and she thought it might have cracked. She hoped it would, that would teach them. 'So you're trying to steal my child?'

Tom leaned across the table, his hands clasped together, as if in prayer. 'That's not it at all, Edie. How can you think that? I was just saying that Mina and I haven't been lucky enough to be blessed with children and we've come to love Robbie as if he were our own son.'

'And what happens if you do have a child of your own? What will happen to the substitute then?'

'For goodness sake. He's not a substitute.' Tom was becoming increasingly irritated. As if he had any right to be. He had everything – her son, her lover, everything – while she had nothing.

Mina stretched out her hand across the table but Edie shifted away so it was left there, aimless and with nothing to hold on to. 'E, darling. It's not just that. It's for Robbie's sake. He's come to think of us as his parents. It can't have escaped your notice that he's begun to call us Mummy and Daddy. I know that's terribly hurtful and I'm so sorry to say it, but it's the truth. He doesn't understand.'

'You could correct him. You could make him under-stand,' said Edie.

'But that would be cruel. You can see that, can't you?' said Mina.

'And what about me? Can no one see the cruelty I'm having to endure?'

'He's just a child, E.'

'He's my child.'

'That's enough, Edith!' Tom slapped his napkin down on the table. 'We've been very patient with you but the time has come to take action.'

Edie glared at him. Was this how he'd spoken to his men in the RAF? Well he wasn't Squadron Leader Goodwin any longer, and she wasn't one of his men. They were trying to take Robbie away from her and she wasn't going to stand for it. 'What action do you intend to take, Tom?'

He took a sip of wine then put the glass down, slowly and deliberately. 'As we've been trying to tell you, we'd like to adopt Robbie. Whether you like it or not, it's a practical solution. You can still come and visit as often as you like. It'll be just the same as it is now. The alternative is that you take him back to Birmingham with you, although you should know that would be a devastating blow to him. He's very settled here. He knows only one home, one set of doting parents and, of course, he's very attached to Alice.'

One set of doting parents? How dare he? Edie fixed her eyes on her half-finished meal. She had no appetite for it now. The silence in the dining room was filled by the ticking of the clock. They were waiting for her to say something.

She would not. She would not give them the satisfaction. She dropped her napkin on the table and went to her room.

She slept fitfully that night. Every noise heard carried the hope that Mina might come to her room to shower her with kisses and apologies but, of course, she was fooling herself. There was little intimacy between them these days. There'd been a gradual cooling since the new year. She hadn't understood why but it all made sense now. Mina had been building herself up to this. Lately, last year's reunion had been on her mind again. Dolly's words had been dogging her for a while now. Of course, she still hated her but she was beginning to think that Dolly Baxter may not have been entirely wrong about Mina.

She woke early in the morning and went in to see Robbie. She sat for a while beside his bed. The only part of him that resembled her was his eyes and they were closed so she could see nothing of herself in him. He was so like his father in every other way. So like Tom too. No wonder everyone thought he was his son. He woke up and, on seeing Edie, he frowned. 'Where's Alice?'

She pulled back the bedclothes. 'It's her day off. I'll help you to get dressed.'

'I can dress myself now, silly.'

'Of course you can. Stupid Mummy. Let's take a holiday from school today. Just you and me.'

She got him out of the house before anyone else had stirred, promising him a trip to the seaside. Aware that Tom might be on the early morning train, they travelled by bus into London and then took a train to Brighton. As they walked along the front he chatted happily to her about his friends, his lessons and how he was hoping to get a proper train set for Christmas. He'd clearly outgrown the little wooden one he'd been so pleased with just a year ago. 'Daddy said, if I do get one, we can set it out in the playroom and I can be the station master and he'll be the guard. When I'm bigger, he's going to take me train spotting.'

'Perhaps you and I could go train spotting where I live.'

'Where's that?'

'In Birmingham. There are some big stations there. We'd be able to spot lots of trains.'

'Can Daddy come too?'

'Perhaps.'

By mid–afternoon he was growing tired and fractious. She'd done all she could to amuse him but the early start and the excitement had worn him out. She wasn't sure what to do with him now. She'd got out of the habit of being a mother and she hadn't really thought any further than getting away from Mina and Tom. Rest, she told herself. He needs rest. 'Shall we find somewhere to stay the night? Would you like that?' They were sitting on a bench on the pier. It was cold and windy and he was shivering.

He shrugged. 'Can we go home?'

She sighed. 'Yes, if that's what you want? *Is* that what you want to do, Robbie?'

'Yes please.'

He fell asleep on the trains back, his head resting in her lap. She stroked his hair and imagined what could have been if Robert hadn't died and if Mina hadn't taken her to her bed. There was nothing left now. Even her son didn't want her. She took a taxi back from the station to the house and carried him up the path. Tom reached out to take him from her but she turned away.

'We've been so worried,' said Mina. 'We didn't know what to think, what to do. You didn't leave a note.'

'I wanted to spend a day with my son. Just him and me,' she said. 'Before it was too late.' She carried Robbie upstairs and put him to bed, then she went to her own room and closed the door behind her.

She woke up late in the morning. Tom had already left for the city and Alice had taken Robbie to school. Mina was in the dining room waiting for her. Edie sat down for breakfast, expecting some kind of admonishment for yesterday but none came. 'I thought we'd go out for a long hike today like we used to in our WAAF days. What do you say, E?'

Edie studied Mina's face. It was expressionless. She was trying to give nothing away but Edie knew what she was up to. She was buttering her up, just as she used to in the cottage when Edie was angry with her for enjoying Tom's company. She was offering her a consolation prize. She wanted to throw it in her face, but she took it. In spite of everything, she still craved her.

Mina drove them to a place she said was good for hiking. They set off and for the next few hours they walked, rarely speaking. When they reached a wood, Mina pointed to a small clearing. 'That looks like a good place to stop for lunch.' Edie grunted her assent and they laid out their picnic on a rug. It wasn't the warmest of days but a shaft of light shone directly on them through the trees. It gave them some heat and began to mellow Edie's mood.

'Do you remember that day when the four of us had our picnic in the Cotswolds? Robert with that damn camera,' said Mina. 'It was the most perfect time. I didn't want that afternoon to end.'

Edie smiled at the memory. She'd been thinking about that day too. 'It was wonderful. Too wonderful. We should have known that nothing could remain that perfect forever. Do you miss our time in the cottage, B?'

Mina filled up their cups from a flask of hot coffee. Steamy wisps escaped into the air and dwindled to nothing. "Of course I do. I'll always love you, Eddie. There isn't a day that I don't think of you. I'm at my happiest when you're with me. You know that, don't you?'

'Then why don't you touch me anymore? You act as if there's nothing between us.'

Mina pulled her knees to her chest. 'I have no choice. I can't be the way I was at the cottage. All this sneaking around is getting too difficult. Things have changed.'

'I haven't changed. I can't.'

'You must.' She took Edie's hand and held it to her mouth. Edie moved it away and kissed her. Mina jerked back. 'No E, we can't.' Edie silenced her with another kiss. She put her hand around Mina's head and pulled it towards her, caressing her neck as she unbuttoned her coat and then the layers underneath until her beautifully carved breasts were visible. Mina lay back and let Edie move her hands down her long, slender legs to reclaim her.

Afterwards, they lay huddled together on the rug, listening for the sounds that would mean they'd have to let go of each other and appear respectable. Mina played with Edie's hair. Edie lay, content in her arms until Mina broke the idyll. 'It's getting late. We'd better get back.'

'Kiss me again before we do.'

Mina kissed her. 'Dearest Eddie. My true love. You mustn't be angry with us about Robbie. We're only doing this for him. Questions are being asked now that make it hard for him.'

'What questions?'

'His friends are asking why his real mummy and daddy

don't live with him. There are awkward questions coming from their parents too, well, the mothers really. I can deal with it but it upsets Robbie. It didn't really matter to him before school but now… Now he can see that he's different, it's confusing for him. He's begun to say that we're his parents. I'm sorry to say this, E but I think he really believes we are.'

Edie sat up. The back of her neck bristled. If this was true, her worst fears had been realised. 'What does he say about me and Robert?'

'It varies. Sometimes he says you're his aunt.'

'And other times?'

'And other times, he says his real parents are both dead.'

They were quiet again on the hike back to the car. Mina didn't seem to have anything left to say and Edie's mind was occupied. She was replaying the thoughts she'd been having since visiting Pat's bedsit; since she'd realised that the time had passed to take Robbie away from Mina and Tom. She'd been angry when Tom suggested it but, in truth, she was angry because she'd already been thinking about it for months. She loved Robbie with all her heart but it wasn't enough. He needed a steady, comfortable home where he could grow up without being seen as illegitimate. The thought of him being chased around the playground by other children calling him names like bastard made her shudder.

They reached the car. Mina was rummaging around in her rucksack for the keys. It was only early summer but already she had the beginnings of a golden tan. Even now, Edie hungered for her. At least this way, she would still be close to her.

'Aha!' Mina held up the keys in triumph. She unlocked the car doors and they got in.

'You can have Robbie.'

'What?'

'You can have Robbie. I'll sign the adoption papers. I have to face it, I'm not in a position to take him, and even if I was, he's happy here. It would break his heart to leave.'

Mina hugged her. 'Thank you. Thank you so much. You won't regret it. I promise you.'

Tom produced the papers for her to sign the next day. It made her think of the way they'd secretly planned their move to Surrey after the war. Much as she wanted to, she resisted the urge to tear the papers up. There were four more days before she had to return home and she wanted them to be happy. For the first two, with Tom at work and Robbie at school, she and Mina spent the daytime solely in each other's company, seeking out secluded places where they could talk freely, hold hands and make love. But now it was Saturday and everyone was at home. Last night, Tom had suggested a trip to Southend and here they all were, playing cricket on the beach. Edie couldn't help noticing how happy and relaxed Robbie was, in contrast to his miserable mood when she'd been with him in Brighton. Being with Mina and Tom was his natural environment now, however she felt about it. If she needed convincing that signing the papers was the right thing to do, this day had done the trick.

After lunch, she took Robbie for a ride on the funicular to the top of the cliffs. She wanted to tell him about the adoption herself and she'd refused to sign the papers until it was done. When they got to the top, she pointed upwards. 'Look how high we are, Robbie. We're almost in the sky.' He looked up and squinted. 'Let's play a game. Do you remember the one I taught you when you were smaller? The one I played with my brothers, and with your daddy too?'

'Daddy Tom?'

'No darling, your other daddy. Robert.'

'The one that died?'

'Yes. Hush now. Close your eyes and put your arms out as high and wide as you can. No, no, don't open them. That's it. We're touching the sky. Do you feel it?'

He began jumping up and down with excitement. 'Yes.'

'Now stick out your tongue, as far as you can. Can you taste the sky? Doesn't it taste wonderful?' Her eyes were closed but she could hear him chuckling. 'Always remember, darling that if ever you're missing me, you can do this and know that I'll be doing it too. It will be our way of being together, even if we're apart. Do you think you'll be able to remember that?'

'I think so. I'm good at remembering.'

She ruffled his hair. 'I know you are. You're a very clever boy. Robbie darling, you know how you sometimes call Uncle Tom and Auntie Mina, Mummy and Daddy? Well I've agreed that they can become your proper mummy and daddy. Would you like that?'

'But what about you and my dead daddy? Aren't you going to be my proper mummy and daddy anymore?'

'Yes, we'll always be that but I just thought you'd like to have a mummy and daddy to live with, all of the time. Your real daddy will still watch over you in heaven and I'll still come to visit you. When I'm here you'll have two mummies, you lucky boy.'

He frowned. 'You can't have two mummies. That's silly.'

'Yes, you can.'

'No, you can't. I already asked my friends and they said I

can't have two mummies.' So, Mina had been telling the truth. Robbie was discussing his situation with his friends and was already struggling.

'Well, if it makes it easier, you can call me Aunt Edie. Then you can tell your friends you only have one mummy.' Her throat caught on the words as she said them. She held her breath while waiting for his response, willing him to disregard it.

'Okay,' he said.

The carriage was empty on the train back to Birmingham. It gave her the privacy to weep. When she got home, she went to her room and prayed for strength and guidance but there was no bolt from the blue, no sudden epiphany. The next morning, she got up and went to work as usual. Everything was the same, except that she had signed a paper that made everything change.

34

A PERIOD OF UNEXPECTED ANNOUNCEMENTS

EDIE – 1950

'Everyone is cross with me and I have no one to turn to.'

Edie pressed her hands to her face. She was so tired, so weak. All she wanted to do was sleep but she knew, sleep on its own would not be enough to get her better. Medication and the will to do it would be the key factors. The doctor was supplying the medication, but the will? That was her own responsibility and at the moment, it was in short supply. She'd missed Christmas with Robbie again and it was her own fault. All through December she'd had the most awful cold that she hadn't been able to shift but she'd been determined to soldier on through it. Work had been terribly busy with the build up to the Christmas break. On top of that, there'd been two parties to organise – one for employees and one for their children. The employees' Christmas party had taken place the day before she was due to travel to Surrey. She'd spent the whole time feeling hot and sick and when she got home, just fell into bed and slept. The next morning she felt no better. She forced herself out of bed to get ready

for her journey but as soon as she stood up, she was overcome with dizziness and she blacked out. When she woke
up, she was back in bed in her nightdress, her mother and
the doctor at either side, like a couple of concerned book-
ends. It was pneumonia. Edie was going nowhere. Aside
from the odd venture downstairs, she'd remained bedridden
for the last three months. If it hadn't been for frequent visits
from Pat, Helen and Ken, she'd have gone mad.

She fell into a restless half-sleep. Her dreams were wild
and chaotic and when she awoke she was covered in a film
of sweat. On the bedside table sat a new letter from Mina.
Someone must have brought it in while she was sleeping.
She eyed it nervously, almost afraid to pick it up in case it
brought more misery that would sap her will further. Since
her last visit the letters had grown less frequent. What had
once been outpourings of emotion from Mina were now
nothing more than updates from one friend to another. It
seemed the separation had given Mina the time to recon-
sider their relationship. The last one had been almost a
month ago and the news had sent Edie's progress backwards. They'd bought a Labrador puppy that Robbie absolutely adored and when he had his train set for Christmas,
his delight knew no bounds.

The deterioration in her health had been on the cards
since the adoption which had been rushed through with
indecent haste. Private tears followed by prayers, became a
pattern in the subsequent months as Robbie drifted further
away from her and closer to Mina and Tom. He was thriving. For Edie, the opposite was true. The happier he was, the
further down she sank. Noticing the change in her, her
parents tried to persuade her to stop the visits but she
refused. 'Mina needs me,' she told them. 'Things are awful
for her at the moment.' Things weren't awful for Mina.

Things were bloody marvellous. She had everything she wanted. A doting husband, an adoring lover and now a legitimate child without even having to go through the pain of childbirth. Things were just great for Wilhemina Goodwin.

Eventually, the need to read Mina's words got the better of Edie and she snatched the letter up and opened it. Two photographs of Robbie fell out from between the pages, both taken at Christmas. One with his new train set and another with the new puppy. She kissed them both and opened the letter. The waft of Chanel invaded her nostrils. At least she was getting her sense of smell back. The letter contained the usual nonsense about things that were going on, the kind of things Edie had become accustomed to by now; the kind of things that were pretty much meaningless but then, right at the end, a chink of light:

'I do hope you're on the mend, E. I can't tell you how much I'm missing you and so is Robbie. Come back to us soon, dearest.'

Edie held the Chanel scented pages to her nose and breathed them in. She had found her will, in the least expected of places.

It was late spring and Edie was feeling much better. In the last month she'd returned to work and was picking up the threads of her life again. She spent the entire journey to Surrey looking out of the train windows and taking in the familiar sights as if they were new. It was good to be alive, and well, at last. Mina had written a week ago and asked if she would take a taxi from the station as she wasn't driving at the moment. Her case wasn't heavy so she walked instead. It was a warm day and it felt glorious being outside after so many months cooped up at home.

When she got there, Mina was waiting for her in the garden. She was all smiles, talking ten to the dozen. 'E, darling, it's so wonderful to see you and you're looking well. I was so afraid after your illness that you'd be worn out but you look simply marvellous.'

Edie's smile froze when she saw an obvious change in Mina's slender frame. 'You're—'

'Expecting? I know, it's a miracle isn't it? That's why I couldn't come to the station. Tom's so worried I might lose it, he's pretty much confined me to barracks.'

'You didn't tell me. In your letters. You didn't tell me.'

'I tried, but my courage failed me.' She grasped Edie's hand. 'I know this is hard for you but please be happy for me. I've wanted a baby for so long.'

Edie placed her free hand on Mina's. 'Of course I'm happy for you. Why wouldn't I be?' It was a lie. She was furious.

Mina patted her bulging belly. 'We'd given up all hope and then it happened! It's as if adopting Robbie has given us a new lease of life.'

Robbie. What did this mean for him? 'But what about Robbie, B? How will you feel about him with a child of your own?'

'What difference would another child make to the way we feel about Robbie? He's our little boy. Are you suggesting we'd discard him just because there was another child on the way? Oh Edith. You really don't understand us at all, do you?'

'I'm so sorry, B. I didn't mean to suggest that. It's just seeing you like this. It's such a shock. I don't know what I'm saying.' Edie moved to kiss her on the cheek. Mina flinched. Very slightly but enough for it to register. Damn that child. Edie hated it already.

. . .

There hadn't been much time for Edie to get used to the idea of the baby. Estelle was born in June. After her arrival, all of Mina's time was devoted to the children, even though Alice did all of the hard work. Trust her to make something as simple as keeping them entertained and taking Robbie to and from school sound like a full-time job. Whenever Edie visited she was in the way. Not just with Mina but with Robbie too. He was infatuated with his little sister and all his attention was given over to her or his new puppy. There was no room left for Edie. The Goodwins were a family unit now and she was the outsider. She could have taken that if Mina had shown her the slightest bit of affection but the intimacy that had waxed and waned between them in the last few years was well and truly gone. On the few occasions Edie tried to attempt any she was brushed off. At first, she accepted it, recalling how infatuated she'd been with Robbie when he was born but now she'd become irritated by it. It wasn't as though she was expecting much. An embrace or a touch would have been enough but Mina simply wasn't interested.

These days their walks were confined to public spaces where their behaviour was clearly visible to all and sundry. Their walk today had so far been an argumentative one despite Mina's attempts to make it appear otherwise to passers-by. Perhaps that was why Estelle who was generally a contented baby, was so fractious. On any other occasion Edie would have offered to help soothe her but she was in a high state of agitation herself. Two days ago, Estelle had been christened. It was an horrendous affair made worse by the fact that Mr and Mrs Goodwin senior were there and, as usual, refused to acknowledge her existence. How she despised them. At the moment, her feelings towards Mina and Tom were much the same. Since she had already given them the gift of a son, they might at least have done her the courtesy of asking her to be Estelle's godmother, but no: the child's godparents were pillars of the community and family friends. She, apparently, was neither. If they could have got away with it, they probably wouldn't have even invited her to the christening at all.

Edie and Mina sat on a park bench. Mina was rolling the pram in small movements back and forth. A little track had formed in the sodden leaves scattered on the ground by the autumn drop. They'd walked around and around the park until the baby had finally given up crying and settled. Now she was being eased into sleep by the steady movements of her mother's hand. It had been ten minutes since either of them had spoken and the silence was getting to Edie. At last she broke: 'You don't love me anymore.'

'Of course I do. Don't be silly. I'll always love you, E.' Mina paused, as if trying to weigh up her words. 'But my love for you has matured into something else now. I have to consider the children.'

'It didn't seem to bother you when it was just Robbie and me. You couldn't keep away from me then.'

'Those were different times.' Mina put her hand to her forehead and sighed. 'Can't we just keep those moments as happy but finished memories? We can still be close. We can still love each other as old friends.'

So that was that. They were friends now, nothing more. That's how they would exist from now on. Two old friends taking walks with the children, going shopping and laughing at Tom's gags and pretending to be interested in his stories. But they weren't really friends. They'd gone past that point long ago and it was too late to go back.

. . .

The sky was dull and dark when Edie's train reached Birmingham. Smoke billowed from the chimneys of the houses that lined the track and hung in the air like a huge black cloud. Edie's heart sank. She had begun to hate these journeys and this filthy city. The week in Surrey had not ended well. Not badly exactly, just not well. After the difficult park walk, Mina had been cool with her. For the rest of the week, she invited other friends to join them whenever they went out. They were other mothers who looked upon Edie with pity because, in their eyes, she was a childless spinster. Amelia, Anne and Daphne even made a reappearance. Mina was sending her a message and Edie knew exactly what that message was.

She was greeted by Ken on the platform. These days, he always picked her up at the station when she got back from Surrey on Sunday afternoons. Since her health problems he'd been a regular at the Pinsents' for Sunday evening tea, along with Vic and Birgitt. The sight of his friendly face was the one thing that cheered her returns up. He took her suitcase and they set off for his car. 'How was your trip?'

'Oh much the same. How was your week?'

'Great actually. I've been offered a job. It's a post in one of the new National Health Service medical practices. Quite out of the blue. I'd enquired ages ago and completely forgotten about it.'

'Oh Ken, that's wonderful news. How exciting.'

'Yes it is. Just one problem. It's in Liverpool.'

'Why is that a problem?'

'It means I won't be able to see you. Unless you come with me. Edie, I know this is a bit sudden but, will you marry me?' Edie's mouth hung open. Ken stood over her looking anxious. 'You don't have to say anything now, but will you think about it?'

'Well, this is a surprise. Would you mind terribly if I didn't answer right now? I need some time to think it over.'

'Absolutely. I know it's a big decision and I've just thrown it at you but I've been thinking about it all week. I know I haven't said this to you before, Edie but I really do love you.' He looked at her, as if waiting for her to profess the same feelings for him. When no announcement came, he jolted himself into action and opened the car door for her. 'If we don't press on, we'll be late.'

Vic and Birgitt were already there when they got in and the tea things were laid out on the table. Before they could start eating, Vic tapped the side of his teacup with a spoon. 'I have an announcement to make. Birgitt is expecting. We're going to have a baby in the spring.'

Edie's mother looked astonished and then with tears in her eyes said: 'That is wonderful news, my darlings. A new addition to the family. How very, very wonderful.'

'Hear, hear. Goodness, I'm going to be a grandfather,' said her father.

Edie swallowed down the cruelty of those words. 'Congratulations. I'm so very happy for you both.'

A week later Ken was back at the house again for tea. She had been thinking about his proposal since last Sunday. He was a good, kind man who never failed to make her smile but she didn't love him. Still, she seriously considered accepting. She remembered Audrey Jacobson's advice that loving someone was not necessary, as long as they were kind; as long as they were willing to take Robbie on. The problem was that she'd never told Ken about Robbie and even if she had, it was too late for him to take Robbie on now. She'd signed any chance of that away. Besides, her heart was already married to someone else, for better or worse. When the time came for him to leave that evening, she walked with him down the path. He bent down and gave her a peck on the cheek. 'Is there something you want to say to me, Edie.'

She cleared her throat. 'Yes. I'm sorry, Ken. I can't marry you.'

He gulped. 'I see. Well, thank you for considering it. Goodbye, Edie.'

Another week had passed. She hadn't heard from Ken and she assumed she would never hear from him again. Over tea, Vic informed them that Ken had taken the job in Liverpool. 'I have to say, Sis, he was terribly cut up by your turning him down. If you weren't interested in him in that way, you really could have told him earlier instead of leading him on like that. You've let a good chap down.'

'Victor, are you saying that Ken proposed to Edie?' said her mother.

'Yes, I am.'

She turned to Edie. 'And am I to believe that you've refused him?'

Edie sat up defiantly. 'That's correct. I'm very fond of Ken but not in that way.'

She shook her head and gave Edie her most exasperated expression. 'Oh Edith.'

35

DEFIANCE AND RETRIBUTION

EDIE – 1951

'How I got myself back here, I have no idea. And yet, here I am, alone in my room, waiting. For what, I do not know. I only know that there is a punishment coming that is mine to take.'

Edie had spent the first two months of the year in Italy. Her parents had had taken her there in January. Last Autumn her health had begun to fail once more and it got progressively worse over winter. She'd managed a visit to Surrey in November before illness took hold and it looked like she was destined to spend the next few months in bed again. This time, Mummy and Daddy had insisted on taking her abroad for the warmer weather and left Vic to look after the business. Italy was such a colourful place compared to Britain. Such an interesting place. The food so different; so rich and tasty. The weather so much warmer. She'd put on a little weight and her skin had taken on a healthy glow. She felt rejuvenated.

She'd been writing to Mina and Robbie every week but, nothing had come back. On her return home she wrote again to say she was coming to visit. A week later she'd had a brief reply that said Tom's parents were staying with them so it was not convenient that month. She wrote back immediately to ask when would be convenient. That was six weeks ago and she still hadn't had a reply. She'd been patient but enough was enough. Today, she was alone in the house. It was Saturday afternoon. Her father had gone into the office, her mother was shopping with Birgitt for baby things and Hannah was visiting her sister. She picked up the telephone and made the call.

'Goodwin residence.' Mina's unmistakeable voice trilled down the crackly line.

'Hello Bill.'

'Edie, is that you?'

'Yes. It's nice to hear your voice.'

'It's nice to hear you too but why are you calling?'

'You haven't replied to my letter. I want to know when I can come to visit.'

'Oh! I'm sorry, Edie. I've been so busy. I'm afraid it's still not convenient. I'll write to you when it is. I must go. Goodbye.'

The line went dead. Edie held the receiver in her hand waiting; willing Mina to come back and speak to her. She was still there when her mother and Birgitt came in. Her mother closed the door and came over to her without even removing her hat and coat. 'Edie, what is it? Has something happened? Was there a telephone call?'

Edie put the receiver down. 'It's nothing, Mummy. I just thought I'd telephone Mina. It seems everything's all right at her end. She's managed just fine without me. That's good, isn't it?'

'Yes, I suppose it is. Come and see what Birgitt and I have bought for the baby.'

.   .   .

Two months had gone by and Edie had still not received a single letter from Mina. She'd been calling the house at every opportunity and each time the maid answered with the same message: 'I'm sorry madam, Mrs Goodwin isn't here.' Today was Sunday and everyone was at church except her. She was in the hall, telephone in hand, calling Mina again. This time though, it wasn't the maid that picked up the receiver. It was Tom. 'Edie, you must stop calling.'

'I just want to speak to Mina.'

'She doesn't want to speak to you. You must give up this pursuit of yours.'

'Pursuit? Is that what she said this is? Did she mention that she was the one who pursued me? And now she's cast me aside. Did she mention that to you?'

'Come now, Edie. You're being hysterical. This is exactly the reason—'

'Has she told you about us, Tom? Has she told you about the things we've done together? About our feelings for each other?'

There was a long silence. She thought for a minute that he'd gone, but then he spoke: 'Yes Edie, she has. We have no secrets. That's what makes our marriage so strong. I've tolerated you because my brother loved you and because you're the mother of his child but my tolerance has reached an end. Do not call us again.'

She slammed the receiver down and ran up to her room, sinking onto the floor, screaming and tearing at the air with rage. He knew. She'd told him everything. Him of all people. How could she? She felt dirty. Sullied. Desperate for revenge.

She went to bed early that evening and got up before

anyone else. She planned her next steps on the way to Surrey but the train from London was delayed and the journey took longer than expected so she had to run all the way from the station to get there before it was too late.

The school secretary was a little stiff but pleasant enough. She accepted her explanation that Robbie's mother had forgotten to inform them of his dental appointment and said it would be acceptable to take him out of school early. Robbie was surprised to see her but was not unduly bothered. He put on his coat and cap, along with his school scarf and skipped along with her footsteps all the way to the station. He was overjoyed when she explained that they weren't really going to the dentist, they were going on a train. He loved trains. He was just as happy when she bought him an ice cream to pass the time because they'd missed the one she'd intended to catch and had to wait for the next one. They sat on the platform watching the other trains coming and going. He told her about the ones he and Daddy had seen when they went to London. The ice cream was dripping onto his scarf so she took it off him to wipe it with her handkerchief. Meanwhile, the clock ticked away. The minute hand clicked past three-thirty. Mina would be waiting at the gates with the other mothers. It was only a matter of time before she realised Robbie wasn't coming out. The question was, was it time enough for them to get away?

In the quiet of the afternoon, it was easy to hear brakes screeching to a halt outside the station. Edie seized Robbie and pulled him with her towards the exit but Mina was already there, her face full of anguish. She made a grab for Robbie but Edie pushed him behind her. 'You can't have him. You don't deserve him. I'm taking him back.'

Robbie began to cry. Mina clutched at Edie's coat. 'Let him go. You're frightening him. He doesn't want you.'

'Liar!' The anger welled up in Edie. Before she knew it, she'd swung her arm around and landed a hard slap across Mina's face. The force of it sent Mina reeling backwards onto the floor.

Robbie screamed. He wriggled free and ran to Mina. The fracas alerted the station staff. They helped Mina up onto her feet. 'I'm going to call the police,' said the station master.

Mina put up a hand to stop him. 'No. There's no need for that. It was just a misunderstanding. My friend is leaving on the next train and I'm going to take my son home.' She nodded slowly at Edie as she said it.

Robbie clung to Mina. She gripped his hand and led him out of the station. Edie wanted to run after them but her legs wouldn't move. She could hear Mina's soothing words: 'It's all right. Mummy's got you, Mummy's got you. It's all going to be all right.' The car doors slammed, the engine started and tyres rolled away.

Someone was speaking to her. It was the station master. 'Your train's coming in now, miss. I think you'd better get on it and get yourself home. Come on now, let's have no more trouble.'

'I can't … I can't…' She stopped herself and looked at the man. He was about her father's age. His face was hard, unfeeling. Nothing like her father at all. She so wanted it to be Daddy, guiding her; leading her gently but instead he pulled her roughly onto the platform. She looked over to the bench to where she'd been sitting with Robbie. His scarf had fallen to the floor underneath it. 'Wait.' She loosened herself from his grip and picked it up. Then she let him manoeuvre her onto the train. He kept guard over her carriage until it moved away, first slowly then picking up speed until houses, fields and trees flashed by. Edie gripped her son's scarf and buried her face in it, breathing in the scent of him.

It was a week later. A large brown envelope arrived for her, in Mina's handwriting. Inside were the photographs she'd given to her all those years ago in the cottage, along with a note:

'*Eddie*

We cannot see each other again. It's best this way. We're only causing each other intolerable suffering. Please stay away from us. If only for Robbie's sake.

Bill.'

She had been waiting for something. Now that it was here, she couldn't bear it. She took to her bed, and gave herself up to self-loathing and disgust.

36

THE BIG REVEAL

NETTA – 2019

It was after midnight. Netta was sitting in the breakfast room, her head resting on her arms, folded on the table. She was used up. She'd lived and breathed Edie today and for weeks before that. Edie had permeated into her consciousness, her very bones. Right now, it seemed as if she was more Edie than herself and she felt every word in those journals as keenly as if she'd been the one who'd written them.

In the earlier diaries, Edie wrote in big, round, flowing letters. Except for the time around Robert's death, the tone was warm and light. There were sketches of birds and other animals, baby Robbie and her friends at the base. There was even one of Dolly who was a little out with her assumption that it was all Mina. Or was she? It was hard to tell. One thing was sure, it wasn't as black and white as she'd painted it. Dolly hadn't been completely honest about that last reunion either. She didn't tell them she was the reason why Edie stopped going.

The change in Edie's writing was gradual so it took a while to pick up on it but she was able to trace it back to around the time of the move to Surrey. It became brooding, and at times resentful, hostile and even paranoiac. The handwriting style changed too. Little by little, the big, extravagant shapes of the first books morphed into small, tight letters in heavy ink that were crammed so closely together they were sometimes barely legible. Edie was like a person possessed. The last thing she wrote was:

'I disgust myself.'

Then, everything appeared to stop, but as Netta flicked through what she thought were empty pages, she found another entry further on. It wasn't dated but it looked like it had been written retrospectively. The handwriting was back to normal and it detailed her attempt to kidnap Robbie, a half-formed idea with no real plan of what to do with him after she'd stolen him away. Hardly surprising that she'd failed. The final page explained the consequences of her actions on that day – the letter that came a week later.

Frank brought in two mugs of hot chocolate and handed one to her. 'Get that down you, then we'll go to bed.' His eyes were as raw as hers. They'd both been crying like babies. At least it wasn't just her – bloody fool, getting so upset. She had to be peri-menopausal. She wasn't sure what Frank's excuse was though.

'There's something to cheer us up,' he whispered, pointing out into the darkness. It was the vixen with four new cubs. She stopped in the middle of the garden and looked straight at them.

Netta raised her hand. 'Hello again.' One of the cubs made a tentative move towards the French windows and sniffed the air. Netta allowed herself a little smile. 'New life. Isn't nature wonderful?' She felt marginally better. There was some hope left in the world after all.

. . .

The next morning, they took Fred and Betty for a walk in the park. It was a fresh morning, good weather for recharging their worn out batteries and discussing what they'd read about Edie. 'I think she regretted not telling her parents,' said Netta. 'Do you remember last year when Colin's partner, Arianne, told me she knew my secret about the baby? When I was in bed recovering from my break-down, I read something that Edie wrote in 2017, a few months before she died: 'I have come to realise that the fear of being found out is worse than the finding out'. I think she wished she'd told them and faced the consequences early on.'

Frank nodded in agreement. 'I don't think she ever told anyone in the family. I'm sure, if she had, James would know. Do you think it's time to tell him?'

'Everything?'

'Everything we know so far.'

'It's quite a lot to take in.'

'He's a grown man. He can take it.'

'Okay.' Netta considered the best way to tell James that his great-aunt was not the person he thought he knew. 'I'll email him first and give him the main facts. We can have a Skype call after, if he wants it.'

'Good plan. Do you want to see Edie's grave? It's not far from here.'

The Pinsent family graves were positioned in a square formation, in the far corner of the churchyard. They all looked pristine, even the oldest. Someone was probably being paid to look after them. Edie's parents shared a head-stone with Jimmy. Or rather, there was an inscription in his memory. To their right lay Victor and Birgitt. Netta noticed that Birgitt was only fifty-eight when she died. Just seven years older than her. It seemed so unfair, after all Birgitt had been through. Edie's grave was to the left of her parents. Netta read the words on the headstone:

'*Edith May Pinsent*
7th July 1923 – 8th July 2017
Beloved daughter of James and Ethel
Much loved aunt and great-aunt.'

'It should have mother to Robbie on there too,' said Netta.

'She died the day after her ninety-fourth birthday,' said Frank. 'I knew it was in July, but I don't think I knew when exactly. Look at the date though.'

Netta hadn't really looked at the dates closely: she'd been too busy focussing on the words but she saw it now. 'It's the same day as mine. That's bizarre.'

Back at home, they typed out a long email to James Pinsent. With her phone, she took a copy of the group photo and attached it to the mail before sending it off. They were eleven hours ahead in his home town of Melbourne. It was lunchtime here, so they weren't sure if he'd pick it up but he came back within an hour to ask for a Skype call in the morning, his morning. Nine o'clock, Melbourne time.

It was ten in the evening. Netta and Frank had been out to eat early to get back for the call. They'd spent the evening debating which possible reaction they could expect from James. Now they were here, hunched nervously over the laptop, waiting for him to join them. His face popped up on the screen. They did a round of greetings and waited for him to say something. He scratched his head. 'Well, Aunt Edie certainly was a dark horse, wasn't she?' The ice was broken. Netta and Frank relaxed. James asked lots of questions: he wanted to know more details before he broke the news to his dad. 'Mina, she was quite a stunner, wasn't she? No wonder Edie fell for her. Was that Robert behind Edie?'

'Yes, Dolly confirmed it was him,' said Frank. 'Sorry to ask but do you think anyone in the family had any idea about Robbie, or Edie and Mina?'

'No,' said James. 'They were quite old fashioned. It would probably never occur to them that Edie might be gay. I expect they knew she'd lost someone in the war. I think they probably assumed her heart was broken when he died. They definitely didn't know about Robbie. I can't understand why she didn't say something after my grandparents died. I guess she thought it was best left in the past.'

'Except that she obviously wanted someone to find it, otherwise why all those stipulations?' said Frank.

'True,' said James. 'My wife thinks the affair with Mina is very romantic. Doomed lovers, and all that. All very *Wuthering Heights*.'

That book again. Netta shifted in her seat. 'They certainly had a stormy relationship. James, there's one other thing, a strange coincidence we've discovered. Edie and I share a birthday.'

'I know. It was in your application details, remember? Actually, that was one of the reasons I said yes to you. My wife again. She thought it was a sign from Edie. I don't really believe all that stuff, neither did Edie, but almost everything else about you fitted so I went along with her.'

It was the middle of the night. Netta had been lying awake for hours. Frank was next to her but he was out for the count. She crept out, down to her usual station in the breakfast room with Maud. The house was full. Liza was here for the weekend and Belle was staying over with Will. Her son had reached a new stage in his life – his first serious girl-friend. Edie would have missed that milestone with Robbie. Countless others too, she suspected. It was possible that she carried on seeing him right up to her death, or maybe his if he died before her, but Netta thought it unlikely given her last entry about the letter.

It was the letter that was stopping her sleeping. It reminded her only too well of a note she'd left for Doogie the last time she saw him in 2003. She cast her mind back to that morning and saw herself sneaking out of bed and taking one last look at him. She saw herself scribbling that note:

'It's better this way x.'

Four simple words, sealed with a kiss. How many times had she regretted that morning? Her thoughts slipped back to Claire. Despite their friendship being tested again, she'd put things right with her but not with Doogie. Since discovering that he was Merrie's father she'd all but decided to abandon the idea of contacting him but Edie's diaries had left her gripped by a deep sense of déjà vu. Their stories were different but the themes were the same. Love, loss, grief and shame. Both she and Edie had been forced to sacrifice their own happiness for their children's sake. She didn't yet know how Edie would come out of it but in the last few weeks she'd begun to realise that her own journey was far from over and there was only one person that could help her find her way to the end.

She went into the study and took the package of university photos from the desk drawer. As she opened it, a piece of paper fell out. It was Doogie's contact details. She read them over a couple of times, then picked up her phone. Opening up her email app, she tapped out a single word:

'Hello.'

37

THE RETURN OF THE MAN HIMSELF

NETTA – 2019

North west Scotland. It was about as far away from a place she could ever imagine Doogie Chambers living. It had taken her two days to get here and would be another two to get back. Four days travelling, just to tell a man she hadn't seen in sixteen years that she nearly had his baby. She must be out of her mind.

After Claire had said he was practically off grid, she hadn't expected a response for weeks but something came back the next day:

'Netta Wilde

Fuck's sake. Never expected to hear from you again. You're like my own personal bad penny.

Come and see me xx

And what the fuck is 'Hello' supposed to mean anyway? Not like you to be short of words.'

So here she was, at the furthest end of the country, turning up again. His own personal bad penny coming to see *her* own personal bad penny. She'd been driving for what seemed like hours on a single-track road through breath-taking landscapes, shared only by sheep and red deer. Her body was stiff and her mind was overwhelmed by the vast beauty of the place. At last, she pulled up next to the remote cottage he'd suggested she rented, and it was very remote which was a little nerve racking for a city dweller like her. She touched the butterfly pendant around her neck, hoping it would bring the same good fortune she'd found in Brighton.

She'd been only slightly disappointed that he hadn't offered to put her up but she reasoned it was probably for the best. The cottage's owner had warned her that there wasn't much in the way of shops nearby so she'd brought enough provisions to last. That included several bottles of wine, in case she needed some Dutch courage. As she unpacked them, she realised she'd unthinkingly brought a bottle of Saint Emilion Grand Cru, one of Frank's favourites. She imagined him sitting at home, trying not to think about what she was up to. She imagined him painting, trying not to think about what she was up to. She imagined him thinking about nothing else, other than what she was up to. Yes, she must be out of her mind.

It was late afternoon and still very bright, although quite cold. Still time for a nice soak to ease her aches and pains before letting him know she was here. She took a hot bath but couldn't relax in it and it wasn't long before she got out and began to make herself look presentable. She put on some warm clothes – jeans, T-shirt and one of those thick fisherman's jumpers. Not exactly fetching but she'd gone for substance over style and was regretting it slightly. She sighed. It was too late to start worrying about it now. At least she wouldn't be cold. She put on some make-up: she didn't want him thinking she'd gone to the dogs completely.

With a glass of the Saint Emilion in one hand, she went into the garden at the front of the house. Wrapped up in a warm coat she sat at a table overlooking the sea. She could hear nothing but the sound of crashing waves and the cries of sea birds, two of her favourite sounds. A feeling of peace flooded over her. Was that why Doogie lived here now, was he seeking peace and quiet? If so, he'd certainly changed. She took out her phone and was pleased to see she had a signal. No point in putting it off any longer. Her fingers ran swiftly across the keys to tap out a simple message:

'I'm here.'

She put the phone on the table in anticipation of his reply and let her eyes fall on some sand dunes beyond the road directly in front of her. Unable to sit still, she picked up the phone and crossed the road for a quick peek at what lay beyond the dunes. There was a higgledy-piggledy path that snaked down to an endless white beach and an azure sea. The sight of it took her breath away. She hadn't expected it to be so heart-stoppingly gorgeous. She took some photos. Frank would love it here. The colours and the light would be just perfect for him. She stopped herself. It was no good thinking about Frank now: she was already feeling bad enough as it was. Still, she couldn't help recalling his reaction when she told him she was coming here. 'You're sure you want to do this? You're sure you're strong enough for what could happen?'

She hadn't been sure what he meant by that. Was he telling her it could break her again, or was it more to do with them? Was he saying that it could break them? 'I don't know Frank. Are we strong enough, do you think?' she'd said.

'Do you have to ask? You know I love you? It would be so easy for me to say don't do it. This guy meant a lot to you and I'd be lying if I didn't say it worries me that you want to see him again, but it wouldn't be right of me to ask you not

to go and I think I know you well enough now to understand that it's something you must do. Go and see him and
maybe then you'll be able to move on. Whatever happens,
I'll still be here. We were friends first and we'll always be
friends.'

Netta breathed in the smell of the sea. Frank was a good
man. Too good for her. She returned to her seat, afraid to
move too far from the house in case she lost the signal. She
checked for a reply. Nothing. She couldn't even tell if he'd
read it. Bloody shit Wi-Fi. To test it out, she checked her
emails and sent messages to the kids and her parents. It
seemed to be working. She thought about sending one to
Frank, maybe send him the photos – *'look what I found'* – but
the guilt was already ganging up on her, best not to add to
it. She glanced up and there he was, the man himself,
walking along the road towards her. The dazzling sunshine
and the distance made it hard to see his features but it was
definitely him. She'd recognise that long, loping gait
anywhere. His close-fitting jacket told her that he still took
care of himself.

The first time she saw him, back when they were
students, she hadn't been able to take her eyes off him.
There was something about his looks and the way he
carried himself that conveyed both strength and vulnerabil-
ity; a mixture of cocksureness and shyness. She thought he
was the most beautiful creature she'd ever seen. Unfortunately, she wasn't the only one who felt that way. He had a
string of girls gagging for him, all much better looking and
less weird than her, but he said he wasn't interested. She
believed him for a while, or rather, she kidded herself she
believed him. If it had just been his looks, she'd have soon
dropped him but with Doogie, it was always about more
than looks. Terrific sex for one thing. Always terrific sex.

When she bumped into him again in Manchester, back in 2003, he told her he didn't mess around anymore. He'd just come out of a long-term relationship and he'd been faithful to her. She didn't know then that the her in question was Claire. In true Doogie fashion, he'd played those particular cards very close to his chest. For the six glorious months they were back together, he swore there was no-one else. He told her he loved her. She believed him then. She wasn't so sure now.

He got near enough for her to see him properly. He looked older. His hair was receding slightly and was flecked with silver. It accentuated his high cheekbones. He smiled at her like she was his best friend in the whole wide world. He was still beautiful. Fuck.

He stood at the end of the garden path shaking his head, the grin still there. 'Netta Wilde.' He said it in that way of his – slowly and joyfully, as if the words themselves really gave him pleasure; as if he'd really missed saying them. 'Still fucking gorgeous, I see.' He held out his arms and she almost threw herself into them. He laughed. 'It's good to see you too.' He kissed her cheek. 'Really good.' He smelt of aftershave, fresh air and the sea. Something inside her shifted into place and she remembered, that's how it was with Doogie. Everything always fell into place.

38

DOOGIE CHAMBERS, MAN OF NATURE

NETTA – 2019

'I was expecting a car,' she said, when she regained her composure.

'No need. I only live up the road. So, what do you think of the place then?' They were sitting on the beach. The only other beings they shared it with were some seagulls, oyster-catchers and a small herd of ebony-coloured cattle grazing on washed up seaweed.

'It's amazing. Just incredible. I didn't know places like this existed in the UK. You could be in the Maldives.'

'Yeah, I know. It's like this all around here, not just this bit. First time I came here though, it felt like I was coming home.'

'To Nottingham?'

'No, you clown, St Kitts. And Scotland. My uncle has a place a bit further south of here. I used to go there a lot after uni. My grandad practically lived there the year before he died.'

She smirked. 'I was joking. St Kitts is where your dad's from, isn't it?

'Yeah. He's gone back there for good now. He's well settled.'

She knew that of course. Claire had already told her but she wasn't ready to talk about Claire yet. For the moment, she wanted to pretend there was just her and Doogie and there were no complications. 'What about your mum?'

'Same as ever. Actually no, she's doing all right now the old man's out of the picture. She lives in Birmingham now. Got herself a new fella. They're married. He's a bit straight but he's okay. He makes her happy, so it's cool.'

'Birmingham? Your mum moved to Birmingham?'

'Yeah, the north side. She's been there since 2003, a few weeks after… Don't know if you remember how she was always going on about my Scottish roots? She's still going on about them but now she thinks I've gone too far to find them. Mothers eh? You just can't please 'em.'

His mum lived in Birmingham? Netta tried not to think about all the times Doogie might have visited his mum since 2003. She tried to cast out of her mind the idea that he could have been in the same city, breathing the same air, countless times and she didn't know it. Instead she pushed her thoughts towards Julie Macrae, Doogie's mum. 'I can see her point. This is a bit of a departure from Manchester.'

He shrugged. 'Manchester was doing me in. Too many bad things all at once. I got to the point where I couldn't stand being there anymore. A mate was coming up this way with his band to record an album and I tagged along. While they were working, I did a bit of sightseeing, some walking and a lot of thinking. One day, I pulled up here and had this fantastic feeling of calm. Like I said, it felt like home and yes, I am aware that makes me sound like a dick because I'm actually from a shit town in the Midlands but anyways, I still sold up and moved here.'

'I have the same feeling about Aberdovey. I think it's because we used to go on holiday there when I was a kid, with my gran. She always used to say that coming from Birmingham made you appreciate the sea because it was a bit too far to get to without a good drive. I think it's probably true of anyone in the Midlands.'

'Maybe that's it. Although, I've only been to St Kitts two times and they were fairly recent and we never came here when I visited Scotland as a kid.'

'So, what are you doing workwise?'

'Still doing marketing and promo stuff now and then. More the thinking side of it though: it's a bit hard to do much else when you're this far away from the action. Mostly, I write. Had a few books published under a different name.'

'That explains why I couldn't find you online then. An author? Wow!'

He shrugged. 'It keeps me out of trouble. You eaten?'

'No. I brought lots of food with me though.'

He stood up and brushed the sand from his jeans. 'Let's take a look at what you've got then.'

An hour later they were back on the beach, cooking chicken and sausages on a barbecue he'd made with sticks, boulders and a grill rack. He cut open a piece of baguette, filled it with sausage and handed it to her. She laughed. She couldn't help it. 'What?' he said.

'Sorry, it's just that you've gone a bit Bear Grylls, haven't you?'

'Damn right. I'm a survivor me.' He grinned but there was something about the look he gave her that made her think he wasn't necessarily joking. Of course, she already knew he was a survivor. She'd banked on that in 2003 when she walked out of his life. And yet... Claire's words came back to her: 'He's not as strong as you think he is.'

'So, what do you do when you're not working or fashioning rudimentary cooking apparatus from nature?'

'Funny.' He passed her a plate of chicken and salad. 'In my spare time, I grow vegetables and I help Grace out.'

'Vegetables? You?'

'Yep.'

'You? Vegetables?'

'Again, yes'

She gaped at him, mouth deliberately wide open to make a point. His expression dared her to ask again and she was about to oblige him when something occurred to her, something she'd ignored at first what with the shock of imagining him growing vegetables – for Christ's sake. She cleared her throat. 'Grace?'

'Yeah. She's a local farmer. Although, she's scaled that down a bit now and turned some of the land into a campsite. Motorhomes and campervans mainly. She owns a few holiday cottages as well. The one you're in is hers.'

'Right, okay. I didn't realise. So you're not completely alone here then?'

'No, not completely.' He gave her a little sideways smile that told her all she needed to know about him and Grace. She resisted the urge to slap herself. How stupid was she? She hadn't considered that he might have moved on from her and Claire, especially after Claire said he wasn't with anyone. But why wouldn't he? It had been sixteen years, for god's sake.

'Claire didn't mention you were in a relationship,' she said, trying to sound casual about it.

'I don't think I told her. Anyway, it's not that kind of relationship. It's a bit more complicated than that.' Of course it was. Wasn't it always the case with Doogie? 'We're mates first and foremost.'

'So you don't…?'

'Fuck? Sometimes, if we feel like it but we're not exclusive.' Netta cast her eyes across the vast beach to the empty land behind it. It must be difficult to be anything but exclusive here. He guessed what she was thinking. 'It's not always this isolated. There is some life here, I promise you. She has other men that she sleeps with.'

'And you?'

'There's the occasional holidaymaker but generally, I don't. I like it that way.' Well, that was a change.

He filled her glass with wine. They were on the second bottle now. 'So you finally left the accountant, then?'

'He hasn't been an accountant for about fourteen years but actually no, I didn't leave him. He threw me out. Not physically, but as good as.'

'But you're with someone else now?'

She took a large gulp of wine. 'Yes. Sort of, I mean, yes I am but we don't live together. We live next door to each other. I mean I am with him but, you know, I'm not with him.'

He laughed. 'Same old Netta.'

'What's that supposed to mean?'

'You figure it out.' He looked upwards. It was dark now and the sky looked like it was encrusted with diamonds. 'I come out here a lot to look at the stars. Sometimes it makes me think about the very last time I saw you. I went to Crosby beach afterwards and sat out all night. It was a beautiful starry night like this and all I could think of was you.'

She didn't know how to respond to that so she looked up at the sky and said nothing. They sat there for a long time, wordlessly watching the stars and listening to the sound of the tide's movement. At last, he leaned over towards her and she thought for a minute he was going to take her in his arms but instead he picked up some sand and tossed it on the fire until it was out. 'Time to go.' He piled the dirty plates and glasses into a bowl and carried them up the snaking path and across the road. She brushed past him in the garden and opened the door for him but he stayed on the step, handed her the bowl and kissed her cheek. 'Goodnight, Netta Wilde. I'll come over in the morning.'

She clutched the bowl in her arms, her eyes following him down the road until he disappeared into the darkness, and wondered if he was going to see Grace.

39

HOME TRUTHS AND HARSH WORDS

NETTA – 2019

Surprisingly, she'd slept well. Doogie was due at ten and she woke with a couple of hours to spare, feeling refreshed. With nothing left to do after breakfast but wait, she found herself checking her appearance in the mirror; mussing her hair up in an attempt to look less like a middle-aged frump, and counting the number of greys and wrinkles. She wondered how many Grace had or if she had any at all. She was probably young. She could imagine a young woman being attracted to this mature version of Doogie. Yes, Grace was probably no more than thirty-five. She drifted around the cottage aimlessly, opening cupboards and drawers for no reason other than to have something to do. In the end, she made herself a drink and sat outside in the garden.

As soon as she got to the table and chairs, her phone pinged. She had messages from Liza, Will and Kelly. Just replies to ones she'd sent the day before. There were three from her mum as well. Netta sighed: three and it wasn't even ten o'clock. She searched her mails for the booking confirmation for the cottage. It had come from a company rather than an individual but there was a link that took her to a website. It told her that the Buchanans had lived on this land for generations and the current custodian was Grace Buchanan. There was a picture of her too. She was probably about the same age as Netta. Possibly a little older. She had a strong, handsome face; a no-nonsense look about her and a body that suggested she rode horses; big, sturdy horses. An image of Grace riding Doogie suddenly flashed before her eyes and she screwed them up in horror.

'Something wrong?'

The words startled her and made her drop the phone. Doogie bent down to pick it up but she just about managed to get there first. God forbid that he saw what she was looking at. 'Sorry, I didn't see you there. You made me jump. Coffee?'

'Nah, I'm good, ta. Fancy a beach walk?'

'Sounds great.' She searched his face for signs that he'd seen anything and concluded she'd got away with it.

'Mind if we get on further down the road? I've got to pick someone up from my place, if they're there.'

'No, not at all.' Shit. It had to be Grace.

They walked along the road until they came to a gravel track. At the end of it was his cottage. It was more substantial than hers with a bigger garden. She recognised some of the vegetables growing in it and tried not to grin at the idea of Doogie as a man of nature. Lying on the front doorstep was a large hound. When it got up to greet them, she could see it was like a shaggy greyhound. It trotted nimbly and gracefully down the path. Doogie raised his arms up and dropped them down again so that they slapped his thighs. 'Aw mate, where were yer? I shouted, I waited, but you'd fucked off again, hadn't yer?' He wagged his finger at the hound. 'You're lucky I came back for yer.'

The dog's ears fell and it looked as if it were about to

burst into tears. Netta wanted to hug and kiss it and make it feel better, and not just because it wasn't Grace. Instead, she ran her hand along its back. 'This is Spike,' Doogie said. 'I was going to bring him down with me but he'd gone off somewhere. He kind of follows his own path does Spike. He's a bit wayward.'

A bit like his owner then, thought Netta. Doogie turned back up the track and Spike caught up with him. Netta hung back and observed them both loping along, side by side. A lot like his owner in fact. She wondered if anyone thought the same about her and Maud. 'I have a dog who goes her own way too. Her name's Maud.'

'Yeah? You never used to be a dog lady.'

'I am now.'

The black cattle were on the beach again. This time they were on the move, seeming to have a destination in mind. Netta, Doogie and Spike followed in their path, on and on, along the never-ending pristine beach. When the cattle found some seaweed to graze on, they took this as their cue to stop for a rest but Spike had other ideas. He dragged a piece of driftwood over and Doogie threw it for him, sending him shooting off after it and returning within seconds to drop it back at Doogie's feet. Maybe there was some greyhound in him. He was certainly fast enough.

'You couldn't have picked a more similar dog to you if you tried,' she said. For a brief moment, Frank and Fred popped up in her head. What was it about men and their dogs?

'Cheers mate. Anyway, I didn't pick him, he picked me. He turned up one day, out of the blue. The door was open and he just walked in and sat down. He was only a pup then. Grace reckons he was with some travellers and they either left him behind or he'd had enough of travelling.

Either way, he's good company. Isn't that right, Spike?' At the sound of his name, the dog came over and rested his head on Doogie's shoulder. Doogie put his arm around him. 'See what I mean? Unconditional love, man. It's fucking brilliant.'

'Seems to me you get plenty of that,' she said, only half joking.

'Is that so? Wait, are you jealous?'

She huffed. 'Don't be so ridiculous. I just meant you've got everything you could want on tap here, no strings attached.'

He shook his head and grinned but it wasn't a happy grin. 'No, no, no. I know that look. I know that tone. You are jealous.'

'Look I'm not fucking jealous, all right? If you and Grace want to be friends with benefits, then I'm sure that suits you both. From what I remember, it certainly suits you.'

She turned away from him towards the sea, wishing she hadn't said anything in the first place but he was like a dog with a bone. 'That thing with Lila was a long time ago. I was a stupid kid who got sex and friendship mixed up and I paid the price for it, but this? I mean, come on, Net. You don't get the right to be jealous. You really don't. You dumped me, remember?'

'I didn't dump you. You knew it was only ever going to be temporary. You always knew that.'

'No. You always knew that. I was always hoping for something more permanent.'

'Why? I never gave you the impression it would be. We had our last night together–'

'And I thought I had the morning to convince you but when I woke up you'd gone and left that shitty note for me to find.' He got up. Spike dropped the driftwood on the ground and looked up at him expectantly but Doogie ignored him. 'This was a bad idea. We should've left this back in the past where it belongs. Just follow the beach that way to get to your cottage.'

'What, you're leaving me here, just like that?'

'Yeah. It's better this way.'

She took a sharp intake of breath. How dare he? How dare he quote her own words back to her? 'You're a bastard Doogie Chambers. A selfish bastard. It's no fucking wonder I dumped you.'

He walked away without looking back, Spike trotting after him. She wanted to scream his name at the top of her voice but all she could do was stand there and cry. After a while she looked around the empty beach. Doogie was far off in the distance and even the cows had moved on. She wiped her eyes and began her trek back to the cottage.

It had been easy enough to find her way back and she'd been sitting in the garden, nursing a glass of wine, for a while now. At first she'd considered packing up and leaving straight away but that wouldn't have solved anything. She had one more night here and she had to make it count. She thought about walking up the road, knocking on his door and letting it all come out, but what if he wasn't alone? What if he was with Grace? She told herself to stop it. She was not jealous. Absolutely not. She considered calling him but wasn't sure what to say. Instead, she sat, not drinking her wine and staring into space. There was a beep from her phone. She expected it to be the fifth or sixth message of the day from her mother but she still checked. It was from him – a photo of a bottle of Saint Emilion. The message read:

'Peace offering. Come over for dinner?'

She let out a relieved sigh and replied to say she was on her way.

He was waiting for her on the road outside his cottage, hands in his pockets and looking sheepish. 'Sorry.'

'Me too.'

'You got back okay then?'

She rolled her eyes. 'Obviously.'

'Friends?'

'Friends.'

He held her hand and took her inside. The cottage had thick stone walls, painted white with little else for decoration except a couple of bright prints. He must have refurbished it to his modern tastes but the original open fire and thick beams were still there. The fire was lit and Spike was laid out before it. Doogie poured her a glass of the Saint Emilion. 'We have similar tastes in wine.'

She thought about telling him he actually had the same tastes as Frank but decided against it: she didn't want to add Doogie to her guilt pile, it was already high enough with Frank.

'Dinner's nearly ready. It's just a chilli.'

She followed him into the kitchen. 'Do you remember that first time you made me dinner back in 2003? It was chilli.'

'Yeah, I remember. I also remember you taking the piss out of me for being able to cook.'

She screwed up her nose. 'Sorry. I could be a bit of a cow back then.'

'Yeah, you could.'

She slapped his arm. 'I thought we were supposed to be friends again.'

He laughed. 'I used to like cooking for you. Those were my favourite times.'

'Mine too. I loved it when it was just the two of us in your flat.' She smiled to herself at the memory. Then she realised the reason he probably liked it was because he was terrified of running into Claire when they were out and the smile faded away.

She excused herself and went upstairs to use the bathroom. There were three other doors up there and she couldn't resist poking her nose around them. His bedroom was much like downstairs. Plain, modern and comfortable. His office was behind one of the other doors. Her eyes were drawn to the flashing lights of the equipment next to his computer. It looked like a serious bit of kit. Presumably that's what you needed for half-decent Wi-Fi in these parts. He wasn't as off grid as Claire thought he was. On the wall above the computer, was a noticeboard and pinned onto it, plainly visible, was a photo of a toddler. Merrie, it had to be. So the man did have a heart, after all.

When she got downstairs, he was laying the table. 'Anything left for me to do?'

'Nah. Almost done. Why don't you put some music on?'

She leafed through his music collection. All his old records and CDs were there. Steel Pulse, lots of house music and the Bristol sound. She chose Portishead. 'This used to be our chill out music, remember?'

'Of course I do.'

She cast her eyes across to his bookcase, scanning the shelves, wondering if he might still have that book.

'It's not there,' he said.

'What isn't?'

He gave her a look that told her it was useless pretending she didn't know what he was talking about but she refused to acknowledge it. Her pride wouldn't let her.

'I burned it, after you left me. I burned everything you left behind. Even that book. Especially that book.'

They held each other's gaze until she broke it. 'Was it that bad?'

He smiled at her and said nothing.

'Claire said the accountant gave you a rough time. She said your head was in a bad way when you came out of it.'

Netta wasn't going to bother telling him again that Colin stopped being an accountant years ago: there was no point. 'Yeah, pretty much. Did she tell you why he gave me such a hard time?'

'Apart from him being a bastard, d'you mean?'

'Well yeah, apart from that, obviously.'

'No.'

'It was because he found out about you and me. He couldn't get over it.'

'Okay. She didn't tell me that. But you and him were never going to stay together. You were the worst matched couple in history. It was always doomed to failure.'

He was right of course. It had taken her a long time to realise what she'd always known really and what everyone else could see without too much effort. 'What about you and me, Doog? Were we always doomed to failure as well?'

'Who knows? I've always been useless at relationships, you know that, but when I told you I loved you, I meant it.'

'I know.'

'Did you? It wasn't enough for you though, was it? You still left me and went back to him.'

'I didn't go back to him, I went back to my kids. You said you didn't want kids. What could I do?'

'If you'd really loved me—'

'What? If I'd really loved you, I'd have walked away from my kids? Even I couldn't have done that.'

'I told you I was prepared to give it a go with them.'

'Colin wouldn't have let me take them and you can't just give it a go with kids. You need a bit more commitment than that. Anyway, there was another reason. I was pregnant.'

His eyes widened and he blew a soft whistle through his teeth. 'Was it mine?'

'Of course it was yours, you stupid fucker. I hadn't slept with Colin in months. I couldn't when I was with you. I was pregnant and I lost it. Lost her. It was a girl. I was so brought down by it that I let Colin walk all over me.'

'It was a girl, you said?'

She could see he was trying to take it all in. She reached across the table and took his hand. 'Yes.' Her tone was softer now. 'I'm sorry. I didn't mean it to come out like that. I didn't mean for us to argue again.'

'You could have told me. We could have worked something out.'

'You really think so? What about you and Claire? It didn't work out so well there, did it? What about Merrie?'

He took his hand away and leaned back in his chair. 'I send money for Merrie every month. She's got everything she needs.'

'So that's what you meant by we could have worked something out, was it? Pay me off? And incidentally, Merrie hasn't got everything she needs because she's missing her dad.'

'Is that why you came here, to lecture me about my responsibilities as a father? Did you and Claire cook this up between you?'

'No. I came here to tell you about our baby because I kept her secret for years. The only other person who knew about her was Colin and he used it to destroy me. Last year, I told everyone about her and it should have been a weight off my back. Except that I hadn't told you and I needed you to know. We made her and she could have been the best of us but I lost her and I've mourned that loss ever since. I can't explain what that does to you. I'm sorry. I'm so sorry.'

He stood up, pulled her up to him and held her. 'Don't be.' He kissed her cheek, then her neck. Every ounce of common sense she had left in her told her to break away and run for the hills but that wasn't the way things worked with Doogie.

40

THE BREAKTHROUGH

NETTA – 2019

She woke up in Doogie's spare bed. The radio was on downstairs and she could hear him pottering about in the kitchen. Last night, just when they were about to undress each other, he pulled back and asked: 'Do you really want to do this?'

She shook her head. 'I'm not sure. I don't think I do.'

He kissed her tenderly on the lips. 'I don't think I do either. So, what do we do now?'

'We could talk.'

'About what?'

'Us.'

They talked about the times they spent together – mostly the good bits but occasionally the bad. She gave him a blow by blow account of the disintegration of her life after their affair and the eventual restoration of herself as Netta Wilde. To a degree, he filled her in on what happened to him after-wards too. He spoke a little about being driven off the rails when she left but Netta knew he wasn't telling her the full story. That was another thing about Doogie. He had a habit of locking things up inside, as if it was a weakness to let them out. It was a way of protecting himself, she supposed; a shield she'd have to break through. She went down to find him.

The kitchen was spotless. He must have been up a while. 'Coffee?' He gave her a smile that told her he thought she was the most magnificent woman on the planet. It was one she'd seen many times, back in the day. It made her heart ache for the people they used to be, two outsiders who needed no one but each other.

'Please.'

'It's a nice morning, if you want to sit outside with it.' He poured her a cup from a coffee maker that she realised was the same as Frank's. These little coincidences were beginning to unsettle her.

'Why not. You can show me your vegetables.'

'Are you gonna take the piss out of my veg patch for the whole time you're here?'

'I expect so. It gives me the upper hand which, as you know, I'm all in favour of.'

He sniffed. 'Fair enough, but don't you be asking for any of my prize turnips to take home with you.'

They found a warmish spot in the garden. She waited until the fresh air cleared her head enough to restart last night's conversation. 'What we talked about last night, about you being driven off the rails after I'd gone. What did you mean?'

'I told you. Too much weed, too much drinking. I guess I spent too much time with Mac. You remember him, don't you?'

'How could I forget him? Lovely guy but no off switch. Is he still alive?'

'Yeah. He actually cleaned himself up. He's with someone. He even has kids.'

'Now that is a surprise. I would have put money on him drinking himself to death by forty. Or worse. Really though, it wasn't what you did, it was why you did it. What did you mean when you said were driven to it?'

He shrugged. 'Bad choice of words.'

'Come on, Doog, don't lock me out. I want to know. I need to know.'

He glanced at her, then looked down at his hands. 'The first time we split up for good, in uni, I didn't know it was possible to hurt that much. I thought I'd never be fixed but after a few years, it felt like maybe I was. But when we got together again in 2003, I realised I was never going to be fixed without you. So, when you left, that was me broken all over again. I came to find you a couple of times, you know. I went to your house and watched you from the other side of the street. I was pitiful, man. The last time I went to see you, I drove back to Manchester to pick up the things you'd left behind and burned them on Crosby Beach.'

'Did it help?'

'A bit. Sometimes you have to do drastic things to make you keep on going. I made a promise to myself that night that I'd get back on with my life but it wasn't that easy.'

'Is that why you went back to Claire?'

'I didn't mean to. I hadn't planned to stay but that's what I ended up doing. I was just going to help her get through the pregnancy. I know she always comes across as tough but she was really scared. When Merrie was born I just had this need to be with them. To prove there was something solid in my life, I guess and also maybe to spite you. I wanted to show that I could survive you but I just ended up hated myself for using them both. Claire's the best friend I've ever had and I love her, but I've never loved her in that way. One day I realised I was using her to soften the blow of losing you. I couldn't do it to her anymore: she deserved better.'

'So why didn't you face her and tell her? In fact, why didn't you tell either of us about each other?'

'Well, you could say it was because I loved you both and didn't want to hurt either of you. I mean, you were lifelong friends until you had that big bust up over the accountant. Or you could say it was because I was a stupid, selfish prick who thought he could get away with it. Take your pick.'

'And what about Merrie?'

'She deserved someone better as well.'

A few hours later, they were sitting on the beach opposite her cottage watching Spike chasing the waves. Netta tried to drink it all in before she had to leave. 'It's so incredibly beautiful here.'

Doogie nodded. 'Yep. It took me a while to appreciate it though. After the honeymoon period when it hit me that I wasn't actually on holiday, I thought I'd made a huge mistake. I really craved the bright lights, big city thing so I went to stay with Mac. I lasted a week and couldn't wait to get back. That's when I understood, surviving isn't enough. Life should be about more than that.'

She thought again of one of Edie's diary entries: *'This is life'*. The inspiration for it had been seeing a fox in the garden while watching the day break. She'd been right, of course, and so was Doogie. 'I agree, it should.' She gazed at the sea long enough the let the conversation settle. She didn't want to spoil the moment but she had to ask: 'If I *had* told you, at the time, about the baby. What do you think you would have done?'

'I can't know, can I? Seeing as you didn't trust me

enough to tell me. I'd like to think I'd have stuck around but I don't know for sure. Like I said before, I did offer to set up house with you and your kids but you turned me down. I guess I wasn't the only one who thought I'd be bad at it. Those times I went to your house and watched you through the window, I saw Colin with your kids; the way he was with them. He seemed like a good father and I knew I couldn't be that good. Also, I saw you for the first time. I mean, the whole of you. You weren't just Netta, you were Annette as well. I loved Netta but I didn't know if I could live up to Annette's standards.' He kissed her on the forehead. 'That isn't what you wanted to hear is it? I'm sorry. I could have lied and said I'd have stayed, come what may but I'm working on being more honest these days.'

'No, you're wrong. It's exactly what I needed to hear, even if I didn't know it until you just said it.'

She moved closer to him and he put his arm around her. 'This is nice. Why couldn't we have been like this all weekend?'

'Because that's not the way we work, is it?' she said. 'About Merrie. She wants to know you.'

He let out a heavy sigh. 'How do you know that? Is that what Claire told you?'

'No. Liza, my daughter, told me. She and Merrie have become friends. You know what girls are like.'

'It's been a long time since I had anything to do with teenage girls and I don't think I was particularly good at knowing what they were like even then.'

'They talk to each other about stuff. She told Liza that she wants to know her real dad. She's a lovely girl, Doog. She's just like you. That photo you've got on the wall upstairs is way out of date. She's so grown up now and she's really sweet but there's a sadness about her. Like she's missing something. You, of all people, should know how that feels.'

He sucked air through his teeth. 'She's better off without me.'

'Can't you let her be the judge of that?'

He scratched his head. 'You don't give up, do you? I saw Claire and Merrie every now and then till I moved here. Thing is, when I came up here, it was to sort myself out for Merrie but the more time goes by, the harder it is to reconnect with her. Does that make sense?'

'Yes, it does. I know how you feel, believe me. It happened with me and my kids but I found a way back to them. Merrie might end up hating you and that's a scary prospect but it's worth trying.' She pulled out her phone and swiped through to a photo she'd taken of Merrie with the dogs. 'This is what she looks like now.'

He studied it. 'She does look like me. And my mum, I can see my mum in her. Will you send it to me?'

It was time for her to go. They stood by her car in each other's arms. 'I'm glad you came,' he said.

'Me too. Doog, you're not your dad. You know that, don't you?'

He frowned at her. 'I know.'

'So, talk to your daughter. Let her decide whether or not you're a useless wanker.'

He groaned. 'Netta Wilde. Fuck off before I kidnap you.'

'Don't tempt me.'

She kissed him for the last time and climbed into the car. He leaned into the open window. 'So, that thing you said about girls talking to each other about stuff. Did you and Claire compare?'

'Compare what?'

He smirked. 'The sex.'

She let out a little laugh and shook her head. 'Fuck off, Doogie.'

She stopped for the night at a pub with rooms in Berwick. It was a nice place. At any other time, she'd have been out exploring but she was too tired. She lay on the bed and closed her eyes. The phone beeped before she could nod off. It was a message from Doogie:

'Ok, you win. I've mailed Claire and asked for Merrie's email address. If it all goes to shit, I'm blaming you xx'

She touched the screen as if by touching it she was reaching out to him. How strange it would have been if things had been different and their baby had lived. If she and Claire had known about each other back then; if they'd buried their differences at that point. Merrie and Ada may have grown up together and Doogie would have had two daughters to get his head around. She tutted: that was a lot of ifs. She checked her other messages – the usual half dozen from her mum and one from Kelly. Nothing from Frank. Earlier, she'd sent him a couple of photos of the beach in Scotland but the ticks on the message were still grey. He hadn't read it yet and she wondered if that was deliberate or if he just hadn't noticed. She wondered if his resolve to be there when she got back was still as strong. She closed her eyes again and went straight to sleep.

A few hours later, she woke up. The moonlight streaming through the undrawn curtains made shadows on the wall.

She watched them dancing around, shape shifting and thought about the last few days and all that it meant to her. She'd done the right thing by seeing Doogie. Telling him about the baby had given her some peace but it wasn't just that. For better or worse, he was back in her life again and that made her oddly content. She recalled what he'd said about not being able to live up to Annette Grey's standards. It had made her cringe when he said it because she knew what he was getting at. In all her recollections about him, up to that point, she'd let herself forget that there had been times when she'd treated him badly too. Times when she'd been quite selfish and yet he'd still loved her. The way he'd behaved after she left him, she must have really messed him up.

She watched the shadows for a while. She had another long drive in the morning. She should go back to sleep but there was something she needed to do first. She picked up the phone and made a call. It rang out for some time. Just as she was about to give up, he answered, his voice groggy, half asleep. 'Hello,' she said. 'I'm sorry to wake you. I just needed to tell you how much I'm missing you.'

He must have been waiting for her. As soon as she pulled up, he came out to meet her and took her in his arms like he hadn't seen her in months. He was like an excitable puppy, unable to keep still and there was no stopping the words that were tumbling out of his mouth until she kissed him. She breathed him in. Soap and paint. It was a comforting smell. 'I could murder a nice cup of coffee,' she said.

'Well then you'd better come into mine, since you've only got that instant muck. There's no one in yours: the kids are all out.' He held her hand. 'It's good to have you back.'

She went with him into the kitchen. It was lovely to be

home. She'd felt the pull as soon as she saw the road signs for Birmingham. She'd missed this tatty old city. She'd missed this tatty old man. She trailed after him while he fetched the coffee from the cupboard and spooned it into the filter. She wanted to feel the nearness of him, the warmth of him. She wanted him inside her. She pressed herself against him. 'Let's leave the coffee for a bit.'

Later, they sat in bed drinking the coffee. 'So, did you get what you went for?' he asked.

'Yes, I think so.'

'And Doogie? Will you see him again?'

'I'm not sure. Probably.'

She saw the disappointment he had difficulty concealing. She was trying to be truthful. She didn't want to lie but she didn't want to hurt him either. There was something between her and Doogie that seemed to compel them towards each other but it wasn't what she thought it was. When they were younger, the ferocity of their love, or desire – she wasn't sure which – had burned them both out. They'd gone in different directions but both had equally disastrous effects. Their affair had been an oasis in two otherwise unhappy existences, but it only served to break them down further. When she saw him coming down the road that first evening and when he kissed her in the cottage garden, she thought their time had finally come but last night, they both realised it had passed and they were okay with that. 'Perhaps we've finally grown up,' he said and he was probably right.

'I think Doogie and I will always be close,' she said. 'What I mean is, we'll always have a strong bond. We'll always be the best of friends.'

'Nothing more?' She sensed the hope in his voice.

'No. That part of our lives belongs in the past. In case

you're wondering, he feels the same way too, but we don't want to lose each other again.'

'I can live with that.' He seemed to relax. She'd given him the relief he was craving.

'Actually, being apart from you made me understand just how much I love you.'

'So that's why you called me at that unearthly hour.'

'Yes, I couldn't wait until I got home to feel you near me.'

'Well at least you stopped short of phone sex.'

She smiled. 'We should go up there some time. It's the most amazing place. You could bring your easel and—'

'Get to know Doogie? I might need a while before I feel confident enough to do that.'

41

A SORT OF DECLARATION

NETTA – 2019

It was Sunday morning. A week since her return from Scotland. Everyone was in the park with them today. Will was there with Belle who had stayed the night again. 'Nice girl,' whispered her mum. 'Serious, is it?'

Netta shrugged. 'Who knows? I think so. Probably. Put it this way, she's been staying over quite regularly.'

'Wait and see then. Went all right did it, last weekend?'

'Yes, it went really well.' Her mum's expression changed to anxious. It was easy to guess what she was thinking. 'Don't worry, I'm not going off to live in the wilds of Scotland with my old boyfriend. I'm staying here with all of you, and him.' She tipped her head towards Frank who was walking and talking with Chris and Neil up ahead.

'Good,' said her mum. 'We were very fond of Doogie, your dad and me. He was such a nice lad but it was all a long time ago. A lot of water's passed under the bridge since then and Frank seems to make you happy now. That's what really matters. He's a lovely man, even if he does look like he's been dragged through a hedge backwards.'

'Maybe that's part of his appeal, Gee,' said her dad.

'Nettie's going back to her punk roots.' The two of them started laughing. Soon, her mum was in hysterics. Netta began to laugh too, more at them than the joke. Everyone turned around to see what was so funny. 'It's nothing,' said her dad, swallowing his mirth. 'Just a silly joke. Not worth repeating.' When the coast was clear again, he whispered, 'Stop it you two. You'll get me into trouble.'

Her mum wiped her eyes. 'Oh Arthur, you're so funny.' She gave him a peck on the cheek. It touched Netta's heart: after all their years together, her parents still doted on each other. She looked over at Frank. Yes, he did make her happy.

It was a funny thing, when Doogie told her he didn't know how he'd have reacted to their baby, she realised it didn't matter. It was enough for him to know that it happened and that it meant something to her. She'd put things right with him and being with him again made everything so much clearer. She wasn't really Netta Wilde anymore. Not the same one that he'd known anyway. She was two parts Netta, one part Annette. Annette had seeped into her and wasn't going anywhere, but that was all right: there were bits of Annette that weren't so bad. The problem with Doogie though was he would only ever see her as Netta Wilde, just as Colin could only ever see her as Annette Grey. With Frank, she could be both.

'Does Doogie still like his music?' said her dad. 'We used to have some good chats about music when he came to stay.'

Netta remembered how well the two of them had got on back in her uni days. 'Yes, he's still got all his old records and CDs, and more. I expect he listens to them quite a bit. There's not a lot else to do up there. Next time we speak, I'll tell him you asked.'

'Your gran liked him too, didn't she Arthur?' said her

mum. 'Remember when we saw him at Netta's graduation and she said we should tell him to visit us whenever he was in Birmingham?'

'I didn't know that,' said Netta.

'Well, we couldn't tell you, could we?' said her mum. 'I told him at the time, Netta doesn't need to know. He never came though.'

'All the same,' said Netta. She couldn't explain why but she was quite put out by this revelation.

Her mum held her hands up. 'Don't blame me, it was your gran's idea. I think she hoped you'd get back together. She couldn't stand Colin. Although, to be fair, I was quite happy to invite him.'

'Gran never told me she didn't like Colin.'

'Maybe not but she dropped enough hints,' said her mum.

Netta's dad cut in. 'How have you been getting on with Edie's diaries? Have you read any more this week?' He was placating again. It was his specialist subject.

Netta took the hint and let the conversation move on. 'No, we finally got the official go ahead for the kitchen so I've been busy with work all week and I suppose I've been putting it off a bit: I'm kind of dreading what might happen next. We're going to have a proper look at the other things in the hidden boxes later.' She didn't tell them but there was something else she needed to do that afternoon; she had a sort of declaration to make.

They said goodbye to the last of their visitors. The kids went out and she and Frank were alone. He clapped his hands together. 'Right, shall we take another look at Edie's secret boxes?'

'How about a cup of coffee first? A cup of really good coffee.'

He smirked at her. 'Is that a euphemism for something, or are you just asking me to go round to mine and make you cup?'

'No need. Wait there.' She scooted into the larder and came back with a box covered in gift wrap. 'Ta da! It's for you, so that you don't have to go next door for a decent cup.'

He unwrapped it and grinned at the sight of the brand-new coffee maker. 'So this one stays here?' She nodded. 'Shame: it's better than my one at home. Is this your way of telling me you've settled on me then?'

'It is. I've even cleared you a drawer upstairs for your smalls.'

He moved his head slowly up and down. 'Thanks, I appreciate that. It'll be such a comfort not to have to do the walk of shame in yesterday's underpants anymore. Does this mean you'll be able to hold my hand now without feeling embarrassed?'

She wrinkled her nose. 'Oh, you noticed that did you? It's not you, it's me, as they say. I'm building myself up to it. Consider it a work in progress.'

They set the machine up and made some coffee. He took a sip. 'That's damn good. You've even picked a good bean. I'm both touched and impressed.' He pulled the lid off one of the plastic boxes. 'Okay, let's do this.' He smirked at her again and added: 'As they say.'

She gave him a little shove. 'Ha ha. Hilarious.'

'Not bad for an aged punk who looks like he's been dragged through a hedge backwards, eh? Your parents are louder than they think.'

She cringed. 'Let's see if I can distract you from my embarrassment with Edie's things.'

When they'd first opened the plastic crates hidden in the loft cupboard, they'd glanced through everything else before starting on the journals. Having got to the point of Edie's collapse they wanted to look at those things again with fresh eyes and they hoped it would give them the courage to plough on through the remaining diaries. They put to one side Robbie's christening robe, an envelope containing a lock of his hair and the rattle given to him by Tom and Mina when he was still very much Edie's son. Next came a bundle of sealed envelopes, addressed to Robbie. Fifteen in all. They felt like cards – probably unposted birthday cards – one each year, until his twenty-first. She put the school scarf with them, having prised it off Maud when she realised it had been Robbie's from that fateful day.

Mina's final letter was in with the other papers, still in the envelope it had come in. There was a tenderness in her words that Netta wasn't expecting. Maybe it was because the person she'd come to know had been shaped by Edie and Dolly but this was the real Mina, in her own words: '*We're only causing each other intolerable suffering*'. This was no predator. Just a woman, torn between two loves. Neither she nor Edie were monsters. They were just fallible human beings, born in the wrong time.

Her eyes hovered over another line: '*It's best this way*'. It was so close to the one she'd left in that note to Doogie all those years ago, the one he'd thrown back at her on the beach. When she wrote it, she'd been convinced that she was doing the right thing but had she really? Was it really better that way? Better for who? Now that she'd experienced it through Edie's eyes, on the receiving end, the answer was obvious.

Better for her. Better to sneak out and leave a cowardly note so that she didn't have to face him when she walked out of his life for good. Better not to look him in the eye in case she crumbled. She imagined him waking up that morning and finding the note on top of the clothes she'd left behind; the clothes she'd bought in Manchester, along with a dress he'd given to her. They were her Netta clothes and she didn't want to take them back to Birmingham. They'd only remind her of what they'd had. For once, she put herself in Doogie's place and her earlier happiness dissolved. Angry tears fell from her eyes and the anger was directed at no one but herself. Frank put his arm around her. He probably assumed she was crying for Edie.

She wiped her eyes and opened up the last remaining item. A box file. It contained drawings, some of Robbie and Mina and one of Robert. Unlike the ones in the journals these were proper artistic sketches. 'She was definitely a talented artist,' said Frank. 'Such a shame I didn't know when she was alive. She never mentioned it.'

Underneath the drawings they found more photos. Netta picked up the one Mina had given to Edie in the card and read the inscription:

'To Eddie, my greatest love.
Keep me close to your heart.
Bill x'

'Do you think she meant it?' said Frank.

She picked up a photo of Edie and Mina, arm in arm, with big grins on their faces. Two friends having a lark; two people already in love, even if they didn't know it yet. It reminded her so much of her and Doogie. 'Yes, I think she did.'

There were several photos of Edie with baby Robbie. Some of Edie and Mina with him, outside what must have been the cottage, and some formal photos of him as a little boy, presumably taken each year to mark his birthday while Edie was still seeing him. Finally, one of the Goodwin family. Robbie was in the middle with a young Labrador at his feet. The man sitting with his arm around him was Tom, a little older than the group photo but clearly the same man. On the other side of Robbie was Mina holding a baby in her arms. They were all smiling at the camera. It was a happy family scene. No Edie. 'Just think how Edie would have felt when they gave her this,' said Frank.

Netta nodded. She was trying not to think about how Edie would have felt. She was having enough trouble thinking about how Doogie felt.

They mailed James Pinsent with an update and called it a day.

42

TIME TO PUT THINGS RIGHT

NETTA – 2019

Frank stayed over that night. He left early in the morning to get ready for work and, now that their jam business was back up and running, she and Kelly went out not long after. Anxious to rebuild their stocks, they had a full-on day and hardly stopped. It wasn't until she was back home that she had time to think about the consequences of the note she'd left Doogie back in 2003. She was still angry with herself, not just because of the way she'd left him but also because she hadn't apologised to him when she'd had the chance. She should have realised after that outburst of his on the beach just how much it had scarred him. She shut herself in the bedroom and called him. It rang out for a while. When it went to answer-phone she panicked: she hadn't rehearsed what to say in the event that she'd have to leave a message. After a few rounds of heavy breathing, she cut the call and was in the middle of cursing herself for being so stupid when he rang back. 'This is new. I wasn't expecting to hear from you for at least another twelve years. Call me by accident, did yer?'

'Ha, bloody ha. No, I meant to call you.'

'Christ! I'm gonna have to get a restraining order if you keep this up.'

'Shut up and listen, I've got something I need to say to you.'

'What?'

'I've been thinking about the way I left you. The note. I was thinking about how awful it must have been for you to find it. It was wrong. It must have made it really difficult for you to get some closure. I couldn't bear the thought of saying goodbye, you see. I know I didn't behave like it but I loved you so much and I knew if I had to say goodbye to your face, I wouldn't be able to do it. So I'm sorry. I'm sorry I took the coward's way out and left you with that shitty, selfish note.'

There was a silence down the line but he was still there: she could hear music playing in the background. Then he spoke: 'Fuck.'

She let out a loud breath, half relief, half frustration. 'Is that all you've got to say?'

'No, but I'm going to have to run that over a few times in my head before I can come back on it.'

'Okay. Do you want me to go then?'

'Er, yeah, I think so. No offence.'

'None taken.'

'Net.'

'Yes?'

'You know I still love you, right? Maybe not as stupidly as I used to but I still love you.'

'Yeah.'

'I'll be in touch.'

'Bye.' She said it to an empty line: he'd already gone. She sat on her bed for a while wondering whether it would have been better not to have said anything. Too late now. it was done.

The next day was a foodbank day. She spent it flitting between the foodbank and the job club, filling in at which-ever of the two needed her most. As always, the day flew by and she was glad of the sit down in the café after they closed the doors. Kelly and Will were there too. She was giving him the third degree over something to do with Belle and he was looking more than a bit uncomfortable. Netta was trying to decide whether she should step in and come to his rescue when Neil and Paula sat down next to her. That was her decision made then. Will was old enough to look after himself.

'I was just telling Neil, he should come to Pilates,' said Paula. 'He's hurt his back.'

Netta looked him up and down. 'Really? How did you do that?'

'He's been overdoing it in the gym,' said Paula.

'Yeah.' Neil put his hand on his lower back. 'The weights. I'm not sure that Pilates is right for me though. What do you think, Net?'

'I dunno. I haven't been myself, although I keep meaning to, but I've heard it's good for that sort of thing,' she said.

'Is that right? Tell you what, why don't we try it together? When is it on, Paula?'

'Tomorrow.'

'Tomorrow?' There was a little half-smile on Neil's face. She'd been set up.

'Okay, why not.'

Paula smiled. 'I'll go and put your names down. It gets booked up very quickly.'

Netta watched her bustle off, far enough to be out of earshot. 'You haven't really hurt your back, have you?'

'No.'

'Was that Paula's idea?'

'Yeah. She's worried that you're locking yourself away, and I believe you promised her and Corrine that you'd give it a go in the new year.'

'I did, but really Neil, I had no idea you could be so underhand.'

'Yep, that's me. Stitched you up like a kipper.'

They both burst out laughing. It made Kelly stop talking and look over to see what the fuss was about. So, she had stepped in and saved Will after all.

The following evening, she was lying on a rubber mat in the hall where they usually held the foodbank, wearing some of Liza's stretchy yoga cast-offs. They'd been doing some simple exercises and now they were on their backs with their eyes closed, imagining a peaceful place. Suddenly, there was a loud snuffling snort. She opened her eyes to giggling either side of her and realised that it had come from her. She'd dozed off.

'Well that was a nice, relaxing class,' said Corrine, in the pub afterwards. 'A bit too relaxing for some.'

Netta covered her face. 'How embarrassing. Was I out for long?'

'Just a couple of snores,' said Paula.

'It was funny though,' said Neil.

Paula chuckled. 'Yes, it was. It's good to have you back with us, Netta.'

'It's good to be back. I promise to stay awake when I come next week.' Yes, it really was good to be with them again. She'd been so busy with Edie, Claire and Doogie that she'd neglected them. Considering how much she'd relied on them last year, that was wrong of her: they enriched her existence and there was enough room in her life for all of her friends, past and present. She just had to make sure she remembered that.

She checked her phone before driving home and saw she'd had an email from Doogie. She would read it on her laptop in the quiet of the study later. When she got back, Kelly was alone in the lounge watching TV. There was no sign of Will. She popped her head around the door. 'On your own?'

'Yeah, Will's out. With Belle.' Kelly rolled her eyes. 'How was Pilates?'

'Great. I really enjoyed it.'

'Yeah? I might come along next week. D'you think I'd like it?'

She pictured Kelly trying to lie quietly while practising the slow, steady moves. Or worse still, attempting something close to meditation. 'Maybe. It's very calm and peaceful.'

'Fuck that. I thought it might be dancing and shit.'

'No, it's definitely not dancing and shit. I think that might be Zumba. It's still good though.'

'I'll think about it. Wanna watch some telly? We can find one of your programmes, if you want?'

Bless her, she was lonely. Ordinarily, Netta would have said yes but she had to read that email. 'In a bit. I've just got some stuff to do.' She left Kelly looking disappointed, closed the study door behind her and opened up the laptop. Time to face the music:

'Fuck me, Netta Wilde. You really know how to punch a man in the gut, don't you?

When you came here, I thought I'd made it clear how hard it was to get my life sorted after you left me. Twice, I might add! All right, so the first time was my own fault but it still killed me. Bad enough that you turn up on my doorstep telling me we made a baby but then you ring me and say you really loved me!

The only thing that kept me going for years after you left was the belief that you didn't want me. Like I might have said before, everything I did after that, I did to spite you. Yep, I know it's stupid but I kept on going to work and doing the stuff normal people do because I wanted to prove I didn't need you. I'm not saying you're responsible for all the stupid things I did on top of that. That was down to me. I take full responsibility. But, just when I get to the point of actually enjoying being me, you turn up again. My bad penny. My fucking ghost. And no, I'm not saying this is Wuthering Heights because I never believed that shit and I don't think you did either.

After you came to see me, I congratulated myself on being a grown-up about the whole thing. For once, we didn't tear each other's clothes off and get down to it. That felt like a positive step. Like two alcoholics who'd just turned down a drink. And then, you phone me and throw a grenade on the table just to ease your conscience. You've got to stop doing that, Net. It's not fair on people.

What I'm trying to say is that back then, I would have done anything to keep you but when I saw you with your kids, when I saw you being Annette Grey, I realised I was being selfish. I was no better than my dad and you know how I felt about him. That's what stopped me knocking on your door and begging you to give me another chance. Believe it or not, I didn't stick around for Merrie for the same stupid, fucked-up reason.

I've made this other life now. Some people might think it's a bit crap but it suits me. I'm content and if you hadn't turned up I'd probably have carried on, just me and Spike, forever but you made me realise

I was still being selfish. I've been so scared of fucking things up that I've shut out the one decent thing that came out of Manchester – Merrie. We're talking now. She even wants to FaceTime me. Fucking FaceTime, can you believe it? It feels a bit strange. Awkward, but I think we might stand a chance of getting over it.

So that's me for the foreseeable, Net. A bit late, but I'm going to try to be a dad to my daughter. I really wish our baby had lived. Maybe we'd have made a go of it if she had and maybe I'd have been a better father if I'd had two daughters ganging up on me. We can only speculate. That's what all this is. Speculation. Our baby didn't live. We didn't stay together. We both had shit lives for a while but we've come out the other side now. We've found each other again and we're friends, at last. I can look at you without wanting to rip your pants off (just about) and I think you feel the same way about me. Let's keep it that way so that we can enjoy being with each other.

Does that work for you?

Dougal Macrae Chambers (I put that one in for my mum and because you always found my full name hilarious. I've never told her about Merrie by the way. She's going to wipe the fucking floor with me when I do).

PS: Still love you, you mad cow.'

Netta closed her laptop. Everything was good between them and so everything was good. She heard Kelly moving around in the kitchen. She'd go and spend some time with her. Tomorrow, she'd have a look for a Zumba class they could go to together. Maybe Liza would come too.

On Saturday, she answered the door to a man who looked oddly familiar and yet, she was sure she'd never met him before. 'Hello. I'm guessing you're Netta.' He held out his hand. 'I'm Jimmy Pinsent. James's dad. Edie's nephew. I hope you don't mind me calling on you like this, I was in the area and I thought I'd chance it.'

She shook his hand. 'No, not all. Please, come in.'

She took him around the house so that he could have a look for old times' sake. They were in the study. It was reasonably tidy now that Edie's books were in plastic crates. 'This used to be the dining room,' he said. 'My grandfather had it converted into a study after he retired. They didn't use it much as a dining room after Hannah left.'

'The housekeeper?'

'Yes, although she was much more than that. She was with the family for most of her working life. When she retired, my grandparents bought her a bungalow not far away. Grandma went to see her every week until Hannah died. They had a very strong bond. They were best friends really, although they probably wouldn't have recognised it as that, given their different social classes and the fact that Hannah was an employee. Things were a lot stricter in those days.'

'Different times.'

'Indeed. James said you found some photos?' She spread out them out on the coffee table in the lounge. He picked them up, one by one, taking his time over each one. 'Dear old Auntie Edie. She was a pretty young thing back then.'

'One of her friends said she looked like Joan Fontaine,' said Netta.

He held up the group photo. 'Yes, I can see that. This, I take it, is Robert?' She nodded. He pointed to Mina. 'And this is the other lady in question?'

'Yes, that's Mina.'

'Or Bill,' he said with a wry smile. 'I can understand her not telling my grandparents or my father: they were good people but they were very much of their time, but I do wish she'd confided in me or James. It breaks my heart to think of her carrying her secrets to the grave.' He picked up a picture of Robbie. 'He has the Pinsent eyes. He reminds me of James, actually. We Pinsents are all fair but James has inherited his mother's dark hair and olive skin. She's from Malta. I'd like to know what happened to Robbie. It would be nice to find him if he's still alive.'

'I'm going to read on to see if there are any clues in Edie's later journals,' she said.

'Thank you. You're very kind. This must be taking up a lot of your time.'

'I feel I owe it to Edie. I'm happy to go on. Unless that is, you'd rather read them yourself?'

'I won't, if you don't mind. The Edie I knew was such a fun loving, caring and vivacious person. That's how I'd like to remember her.'

Netta sat in the breakfast room with a pile of Edie's diaries in front of her. Jimmy Pinsent had given her the incentive she needed to read on. She had to find out what happened next. Edie had lived a long life. She'd clearly survived the loss of Mina and Robbie but, as Doogie had said, there should be more to life than surviving. She took a diary from the top of the pile. It had a bright yellow cover, inside of which was written:

'*7th July 1956*
Happy birthday, Edie.
With my best wishes for a good year,
Hannah.'

Hannah, the housekeeper? Jimmy Pinsent had said she'd been more of a friend to Edie's mother. From Edie's previous diaries it was obvious she'd meant a lot to Edie too.

Netta turned to the first entry and noticed Edie's handwriting was back to normal again. She read the first few lines:

'Before I begin again to record my day-to-day thoughts, I must address my absence because I would not be writing this at all if Hannah had not saved me.'

43

HANNAH, THE SAVIOUR

'I would not be writing this at all if Hannah had not saved me.'

She disgusted herself. She'd had plenty of time to think about it. It was the last thing she wrote in her journal and she'd thought of nothing else for months, lying alone in her darkened room. She disgusted herself and there was no shying away from it. She'd traded her son in. Used him as a bargaining tool. And for what? There may have been an element of his welfare in the decision but she knew the real reason was that it was the only way to keep her and Mina tied together. Robbie was the knot that held them in place. If she'd taken him away, she would never have seen her again. It was her desire that drove her decision on the adoption. Her lust. Her need for Mina. She'd been forced to choose between Robbie and Mina, and she chose the latter. She disgusted herself.

Mina said she wouldn't regret her decision. It wasn't true. The regret oozed from every pore in her body. Regret and self-contempt. She had no life now. She barely spoke to anyone. She washed only when she had to and ate just enough to stop her parents forcing her into hospital. There was talk of sending for the psychiatrist that helped Vic but she refused to talk to him. She didn't want help, she only wanted to die.

On her bedside cupboard was *Wuthering Heights*. It was the only thing she read these days, even though the words crushed her. Beside it was a new bible. It lay untouched. Her mother had left it there when she discovered Edie had torn the pages from her own and ripped them to pieces. There was no God, Edie knew that now. No one was going to save her. Under her bed was the locked chest containing the journals that catalogued her descent into madness. From the time she'd fallen hopelessly for Mina, to the end of everything. She would not write another word. There were none left in her.

There were footsteps on the landing coming in her direction. She shut her eyes tight. The door opened and closed again. There was someone in the room, Edie could feel their presence.

'You can stop pretending to be asleep,' said Hannah. 'Sit up. I've brought you some soup and I'm not leaving until you've eaten every last scrap of it.'

Edie opened her eyes. 'I'm not hungry.'

'I don't give a monkey's uncle whether you're hungry or not. You're eating this bloody soup, even if I have to force it down you.' Edie sat up begrudgingly. She'd never heard Hannah swear before. Her parents must be out. Hannah put the tray on her lap and sat on the bed to watch her swallow every painful mouthful. 'Everything,' she said. 'The bread as well.' With great effort she finished it and sank back on her pillow.

Hannah took the tray away and sat back on the bed.

'You might as well know, your mum and dad have gone to speak to a specialist about having you put away. Is that what you want? Is it?' No, it was not what she wanted but she was not about to say it. 'All right then, I'll start packing your things up, shall I?'

'No! I'm not going anywhere.'

'Is that so? Well, in that case you'd better get off your backside and start behaving yourself, my girl.'

'You don't understand. No one understands.'

'Seeing as you won't tell us what it is, that's not surprising is it?' Hannah's voice softened. 'You can tell me, if you want to'

Edie opened her mouth and took a short breath that caught on her chest. Even something as simple as breathing seemed to hurt these days. She wanted to tell someone about Robbie. Someone else had to know; had to share her burden. 'I have a child.'

'I see. Where is this child now?' There seemed to be no surprise in Hannah's reaction; no horror, no anger.

'He's with Mina and her husband. I gave him to them.'

'Well that explains a lot. I knew something was up. When you say you gave him to them, do you mean they've properly adopted him?'

'Yes, and now they won't let me see him.'

'Oh my poor love. No wonder you're so upset. It's hard, I know, but it's for the best. You've got to give the little chap a fighting chance and you've not been helping yourself by dragging it out with all these visits. You have to let go, Edie. For your own sake as much as his.'

'No, I can't. You really don't understand.'

Hannah took her hand. 'Oh but I do, sweetheart. You've told me your secret so I'll tell you mine. I have a child too. Well, she's a grown woman now. I lost her dad in the Great

War, before we had a chance to marry so, I had to give her up. I cried for months. I didn't want to go on but I did, because I knew it was the best for her. She was adopted by a very nice family and I got on with my life. And now, that's what you're going to do. You're going to tell me all about this boy of yours and then you're going to have a good cry on my shoulder. Then you're going to have a bath and put some clean clothes on and we're going to pretend we never had this little talk. Agreed?'

Edie stared at Hannah in disbelief. A child? An illegitimate child? Hannah, of all people? 'You have a daughter?'

'Yes. Louise, I called her. I think the family were going to keep the name. It was the worst day of my life when I gave her up. Even though I haven't seen her since she was a tiny baby, she's still my daughter. That's the thing you see, Edie. You'll always be his mum. You haven't given that up. Even if you never see him again. Even when you're old and grey, he'll still be your son. You shouldn't be hiding away in bed. You should be proud of yourself. You've given your boy the chance of a better life. It's the best thing you could have done for him.'

Edie fought back the tears and told Hannah all about Robbie. When and where he was born; what he liked to eat and what he liked to do. She talked about his love of trains and his funny little habits. She unlocked the chest and showed Hannah the photographs of him. Hannah said he was a bonny little boy who had her eyes. She talked and talked, until she finally accepted that she had to leave him behind, and then she wept. Afterwards, Hannah drew her a bath and she washed herself clean. As she lay in the hot, soapy water, she felt a great weight rise above her and drift away into the steam.

44

THE SPINSTER SOCIETY

EDIE - 1956

'To spinsterhood, and all who sail in her.'

Edie ran her hands along the small kitchen table. Everything here was small compared to her parents' home. It was a house built for one, two at the most, although she was well aware that for much of the time it had been standing, it had most likely housed several large families. She couldn't imagine how they all squeezed into it. That aside, it was perfect for her. Now that she'd unpacked crockery, books and knick-knacks, it was homelier. She would hang her own paintings on the bare walls and Pat was going to sew some bright curtains and cushions to make it cosier and more modern. She folded her arms and sighed with contentment. Her own home, at long last.

It had been an arduous journey to this point. Her recovery had been slow. Lucky for her that Hannah was on hand whenever she seemed to be falling back into the abyss. They'd made a pact that day to keep each other's secrets to the grave. It brought them even closer together. It occurred to her that she had probably always been something of a substitute daughter for Hannah and, from her point of view, she'd always loved Hannah too but until that day, she'd never seen her as her saviour. She didn't tell her about Mina, although she suspected Hannah had guessed there was more to their relationship than she'd let on. Perhaps the lack of confessing absolutely all had slowed down her return to normality. Perhaps not. After all, her normality *was* living with Mina and Robbie in the shadows. What she had to do was construct a new normal. One that wasn't spent marking the time until her next visit to Surrey.

On their return that day, her parents had been surprised to find her in the sitting room, washed and dressed. After a few days, they made tentative enquiries as to the cause of her ill health. It wasn't the first time they'd asked but perhaps they thought they were more likely to get an answer this time. They were wrong. She told them, quite firmly, that she didn't want to discuss it. It was a closed book as far as she was concerned and they could rest assured she was doing her utmost to return to full health. That was the end of the matter. They hadn't spoken of it since.

Shortly after that, she met her new nephew, James – or Jimmy, as they called him. She'd refused to see him while she was in her self-imposed confinement, fearing that he'd remind her of Robbie. He did, but only in the way that seeing anyone else's baby reminds a mother of the time hers was that age. It helped that Jimmy was nothing like Robbie, except for the eyes. He was as fair as Robbie was dark, but he was a sweet little thing and she was sorry to have missed his early months. The birth had been hard for Birgitt. All those years in hiding and living on scraps during the war had not made her strong. The doctors said it was unlikely she would be able to carry another child. It was a terrible

blow for them. Edie felt guilty: she should have been there
to help but she'd been too busy wallowing in her own self-
pity. It was the last time she'd do that. She decided to do all
she could to make up for her absence and become a model
aunt to young Jimmy.

Birgitt and Vic had already agreed that Jimmy would be
brought up in the Christian faith but Birgitt had insisted on
waiting for Edie to get better before his christening. She
wanted Edie to be his godmother. Edie could have told them
she didn't believe in God anymore but she couldn't do that
to Birgitt, so she said yes. Ken was the baby's godfather. He
was the same as she remembered him and despite the initial
embarrassment, they hit it off as they always had. He was
still in Liverpool and was engaged now to Carol who was a
teacher. When he introduced her to Edie, Carol began by
saying a jokey thank you for not marrying him and leaving
the field clear for her. It was a good start and they got on
famously. Carol talked about her work and the great opportunities for women in teaching. The conversation planted a
seed in Edie's mind. She'd already returned to work in the
family business, but her heart had never really been in it and
with Vic working there too, the opportunities for anything
other than office work was limited. The more she looked
into teaching, the more her interest grew. One evening, she
told her parents that she planned to enrol for teacher training. They were surprisingly encouraging. And so started
Edie's new life.

The teacher training college opened the world up for
Edie in the same way that the WAAF had done. Pat and
Helen, the friends she'd met in secretarial school, had been
her rocks during her dark period and her friendship with
them was stronger than ever, but she also made new friends
– other women and men who, like her, were starting out as

teachers. She went to social gatherings and debating societies and met people from all walks of life. She loved the studying too. The war had cut short her ambition to go to university but, finally, she was using her brain. Last year, she had become a qualified teacher with a new job.

Her first day at Hope Street School was as thrilling as the first time she set foot in the Operations Room. Instead of the fate of men, she held the future of a class of six-year olds in her hands. She adored it and they adored her. The school was in Highgate. It was the sort of place her mother would have taken her to as a child when she was on one of her good deed missions, now made worse by the wastelands left behind by the Blitz. More than once, Edie came face to face with a rat in the school playground. In many ways it was a desolate place but she found great joy there.

Recently, she'd made the decision to seek her independence, once more. Her parents had been rather concerned: they were terribly old fashioned about it and would have preferred her to have married someone like Ken and settled into family life. She knew by now that was unlikely to happen. She'd had her fill of love and her maternal heart already belonged to Robbie, but she'd just celebrated her thirty-second birthday and it was about time she had her own home. She wanted somewhere that she could openly write her journals and look at her photographs without having to hide them. She wanted somewhere too where she was able to be herself; a place that she could bring friends to and where she could have her own social gatherings. Perhaps even some company, if she chose to.

So, here she was in her new home – a small, terraced house in Moseley. It was easier to get to work from here and, best of all, Pat and Helen shared a similar house further up the street. Neither of them was married either. Helen had

had a close call but she'd seen sense at the last minute. They were great pals the three of them. They went out together frequently and called themselves The Spinster Society since they had no intention whatsoever of becoming someone's wife. Today, they were off on an adventure. School had just finished for the summer holidays and they were on their way to Rome. Edie, took another look at around the kitchen. It was a wrench to leave it but she reminded herself that this was her house and that she was paying the rent on it with her own money. Nobody could take it from her. It would still be here when she returned in two weeks.

It was their final evening in Rome. The last time Edie had been in Italy was when she'd been ill. Now, in good health, good spirits and with pals of her own age, she was able to enjoy it properly. She saw all the sights again through the eyes of her friends who'd never been abroad before. They ate in street cafes, drank far too much wine and flirted with the waiters. They'd had the most marvellous time.

They strolled around the city, taking in the sights for the last time, then went to eat in their favourite restaurant. The sun had gone down but the heat was still intense and they sat outside in the hope that a stray breeze might cool them down. The air remained thick and cloying but they didn't let that spoil their enjoyment of the lively scenes playing out in the surrounding square. Pat refilled their glasses with wine. 'This has been the most wonderful experience. Just think, if we were married, we wouldn't have been able to do this. We'd have been tied down with nothing to occupy us but dirty nappies and housework. Here's to spinsterhood.'

They clinked their glasses together. 'To spinsterhood.'

'We should go somewhere next year,' said Helen.

Pat nodded. 'My thoughts exactly.'

'Why only next year?' said Edie. 'We should go on a new adventure every year for as long as we remain The Spinster Society.'

'That'll be forever then,' said Pat.

Helen raised her glass again. 'Spinsters until we die, and friends forever.'

'Friends forever.'

As they said it, Pat accidentally let out a loud burp. She put her hand over her mouth in shock. It was the funniest thing. They fell back in their seats, laughing. Every time they tried to stop, they lost control again. Edie's sides hurt. Tears were rolling down her face. She was happy; incredibly happy. She had good friends, and if they were going to be friends for life, there were a few things they needed to know about her. She waited until the laughter subsided. 'Actually girls, in the spirit of friendship, there are some things I'd like to share with you.'

The rest of the summer flashed by. A week was taken up with a family holiday in Cornwall. Jimmy was five now and such a funny little chap. He kept them entertained all week with his antics. She visited Lily, her old friend from the WAAF, and during the remaining weeks she made some valiant attempts to recreate meals for her friends like the ones they'd eaten in Rome, with varying degrees of success. Just as they had been when she told them about Robbie and Mina, the ladies of The Spinster Society were very gracious. Even the absolute flops were toasted with cheap red wine. She spent the rest of the time sketching, painting with watercolours and writing her journal. It had taken five years to get back to writing. Before then, every time she opened her unfinished diary and read the pages from 1951, her heart sank. Had that tragic figure really been her?

It was Hannah who got her back to writing. She'd given her a new book this year as a birthday gift. The cover was a glorious, sunny colour that lifted her spirits every time she picked it up. It was in this new, fresh journal that she decided to write only about the present and the future, regardless of where her thoughts and heart resided. Still, she felt she had to set down the facts about that day in 1952 when Hannah saved her, and that was where she began. With that done, she realised that she also needed to record the details of the events that finally broke her – the attempt to steal Robbie away and Mina's letter. Not in this new diary: it would be too upsetting to see them every time she opened it. It would have to be in the old, unfinished one. She had no desire to look at those last pages again, so she opened it at a random blank page and began to write. When she was finished, she blotted the ink, closed the book and shut it away for good.

September saw her back at school with a new class. It was an hour before the day officially started and the staff room was full. Edie had arrived quite early and was filling her time, reading a book on socialism. She was more and more drawn to it these days. Robert would have been pleased but her parents would be horrified if they knew. All the more reason for her to be leading her own life now. The head came in to give them her usual first day of term speech and introduce two new teachers, fresh from college. Edie glanced up from her book briefly. They were two men, both younger than her.

She stayed behind a little later that afternoon, preparing

the classroom for the next day. She often did that. She quite liked the stillness of the place after the chaos of the day. As she left the building, she bumped into one of the new teachers. He was a small man with black wavy hair and large brown eyes. He wore his mackintosh unbuttoned, revealing a navy crew neck jumper over his shirt and tie. She couldn't help but notice that his coat collar was turned up. It gave him an air of irreverence. He held the door open for her and they walked out into the playground. 'How was your first day?' she asked.

'Really good. The class are a handful but I think I've got the measure of them.' He was Scottish. A long way from home, then?

'Yes, I had them last year. Keep an eye on Sally Green. She is what they call, a right little madam.'

He laughed. 'Thanks, I'll be sure to. We haven't met properly, have we?' He was interrupted by something small and furry scuttling past them. 'Was that a rat?'

'Hmm? Oh yes, I'm afraid so. You'll get used to them. They only usually come out after the children have gone home. They're very polite like that. I'm Edith Pinsent, by the way. Most people call me Edie.'

He gave her an odd look. She half-expected him to exclaim that she was a rum girl. 'I suppose that is rather polite of them. Although, judging by today, I think I should be more afraid of some of our pupils than the rats. Robert Falconi. Sometimes known as Bob.'

'Then, I shall know you as Bob.'

'And I shall know you as Edie. I'm walking this way.'

Edie smiled. 'So am I.'

45

LOVE CAN BE WONDROUS

EDIE – 1961

'I must not think of myself. I must be selfless and let him find someone who can give him what he desires most.'

'Are you sure you won't change your mind, Edie? If you need more time, I'll wait for you.'

Edie slipped her hand into Bob's. They were sitting on a beach on the tip of Rhodes Town, the late afternoon sun beating down on their bare arms and legs. 'I don't need more time. I'm sorry, my darling.'

His Adam's apple bobbed up and down as he swallowed away the obvious pain she was causing him. She wished she could make this easier. He looked out to the sea, seemingly unable to look at her. 'I thought we loved each other.'

'We do.'

'Then why are you doing this?'

'Because we want different things and the thing you want from me is something I cannot give.'

'I don't care. I'll take you as you are. We don't have to get married and have kids.'

'No, we don't have to but it's what you want and it's unfair of me to deprive you of it.' She pulled herself up and knelt in front of him, cupping his face in her hands. 'Thank you for showing me that love can be wondrous. You've made me so happy and now I want you to be happy too.'

'I am happy.' His eyes were tearing up.

'You will be happier when you meet someone who shares your dreams. I love you Roberto Falconi and because of it, I'm releasing you. We have two more weeks before the holiday ends. Let's make them the best two weeks we've ever spent together. No more tears, no more sadness, no more talk of marriage.'

He heaved a huge sigh in an effort to stem his silent tears. 'Okay.'

Edie's heart was breaking: she didn't want to release him. She wanted to be with him always but she had to.

On that first day back in 1956, she knew, as soon as Bob told her his name was Robert, they would fall in love. She'd expected it to be a brief affair but that was five extraordinary years ago. Together they discovered their political allegiances and her view of the world gradually shifted. They became confirmed socialists, anti-war and pro-nuclear disarmament. They marched for the things they believed in. She spoke at rallies and opened her doors to political allies, artists and poets. Influenced by the new pop art, she experimented more with her painting and filled her house with the results. Bob was with her at every step, the two of them soaking it all up like sponges.

She was never able to call him Robert but she did occasionally allow herself to call him by the name his parents used, Roberto. They were from Naples and had emigrated to Glasgow before the war to join his uncle who had started up an ice cream business there. Despite internment during the war, they stayed on afterwards but they anglicised their children's names in public to help reduce the stigma of being on the wrong side. Every summer, she and Bob travelled across Europe together. First to Italy, then on to Spain, France and Greece. Always the more continental countries: he was a Latin at heart. Pat and Helen usually joined them for their fortnight's holiday and had, in fact, only gone back that morning.

She'd told him about Robbie before their first year was out and explained she didn't want another child. He'd accepted this at first but his need for family had proved to be their undoing. Three times, he'd asked her to marry him and have children. As with Ken, she seriously considered becoming Mrs Falconi. It was easier to turn Ken down because she hadn't loved him but Bob was so much harder. The last time he'd asked her was just before Pat and Helen joined them for their holiday and she'd promised to think it over and tell him after they'd gone. As usual they'd had the most fun time. It made her realise how much she valued their friendship. If she married Bob, the friendship would still be there but the freedom she enjoyed as a single woman wouldn't be. Lily had already showed her that. She was very happily married with three children but she had no time to call her own. Nevertheless, Edie was on the verge of accepting, such were her feelings for Bob but in the end, it was Robbie that stopped her. It was his birthday next month and, as usual, she was consumed with a sadness that only Pat and Helen seemed capable of pulling her out of. It made her realise she couldn't give herself up to motherhood again: the scars were too deep. At that point, she also understood that she would never marry and for his own sake, she'd just told Bob that he had to leave her.

. . .

It was 3rd September. Edie was back at home. She and Bob had had a glorious summer together and true to their words, they'd made the last two weeks the best, then parted as friends. The new school term was a few days away. She'd see him then which would be hard for them both but they'd find a way to bear it. She'd been through far worse than this and had come out the other side. She was sure he would too.

She put thoughts of Bob to one side. Today she had other loves to devote her time to: it was Robbie's seventeenth birthday. She pictured her son the last time she saw him and tried to imagine what he looked like now. There had been no contact from Mina in the ten years since that letter but that didn't stop Edie buying a birthday card for him. Each birthday she wrote him a long letter filling him in on her year and placed it inside a card that she would never send. If he ever came looking for her, she'd give them all to him. Now that he was nearly an adult, she was hopeful that day would soon come and lately she found herself fantasising about what would happen if he did. Sometimes she dreamed of answering a knock at the door and finding him there, a young man who looked uncannily like his father. He always swept her up in a bear-like hug and said: 'Hello Mum.' Always. She often woke up from these dreams to find her pillow wet. She liked to think she'd been shedding tears of joy although the truth of it was that it was more likely to be sorrow.

She wasn't at all surprised that she was crying now: this date always had that effect on her. Thank goodness she was going to Pat and Helen's later. They'd rally round and cheer her up. First though, she had a letter to write. She picked up her biro – she'd taken to using them instead of fountain pens lately. So much easier. She chewed the end of it – a

rather disgusting habit she'd recently picked up but it helped
her to think – and began to write:

'Dearest Robbie,

Well, another year has passed and I find myself here again,
missing you terribly and wondering about everything that's possible to
wonder about you. How are you? Are you well? Are you happy? Do you
still have your father's handsome looks and my blue eyes? Do you ever
think of me?'

46

IF YOU'RE GOING TO SAN FRANCISCO

EDIE – 1968

'This school has given me love, life and a purpose.'

'We could just stick a pin in the map,' said Helen.

'Well, that is a new method, I suppose,' said Pat. 'What do you think, Ede?'

Edie closed one eye and fixed the other on the map spread out in front of her. 'Frankly, I'm too drunk to think right now. Possibly even too drunk to safely manoeuvre a pin in the required direction.'

'Hmm. Me too,' said Pat. 'We could end up holidaying in Kathmandu, or we could end up with one or more of us requiring first aid.'

'Ah. I was rather relying on one of you being a little more sober than me. Oh well, dinner smells like it's ready. Let's talk about it while we're eating.' Helen whisked the map off the table. 'Edie, would you set our places? Pat, can you put some more music on?'

'How about Rubber Soul?' Pat flipped through the LPs while Helen dished out bowls of spaghetti bolognese. It was a cold January night and they'd hoped the food and wine would make them feel more continental.

Edie put the last of the cutlery down and began pouring more wine into their glasses. 'Oh yes, great choice.' She took a seat and pushed her hair behind her ears to make sure it didn't fall into the sauce. These days, she wore it long and flowing. 'How about Greece? One of the islands, perhaps?'

'That's a thought. Which ones haven't we been to yet?' Pat expertly twisted spaghetti around her fork.

Edie recalled the holiday where she'd learned how it was done. 'I say, Pat, do you remember the chap who taught you how to do that?'

Pat snorted, her mouth still full and nearly choked. 'How could I forget Giovanni? Damn good in bed but an absolute nightmare. Kept asking me to marry him.'

'Don't remind me,' said Helen. 'I still haven't got over having to smuggle you out of Sorrento on our last day.'

'Yes, sorry about that. I've often thought it would be lovely to go back there but I daren't. I'm sure he's married with a brood of kids by now, but I can't risk it.'

Helen waved her fork in the air. 'Maybe we need to write out a list of all the places we can't go back to.'

Pat snorted again. 'You make us sound like a bunch of desperados. Wanted, The Spinster Society. Beware, these women are armed and dangerous.'

'And loose,' said Helen. 'Don't forget loose. Anyway, we're supposed to be celebrating Edie's new job tonight. Let's have a toast before we get past the point of no return.'

'Thanks,' said Edie. 'Although, I must say I'm taking it with a heavy heart. I really don't want to leave Hope Street but I have no choice. By the end of the year it will be a pile of rubble and my pupils will have moved elsewhere.'

Helen patted her hand. 'Poor Ede. No more tatty, run-down, rat riddled houses and schools. Just brand spanking new buildings. Clean, functional and lacking in history. That's progress, I'm afraid. Put that new record on, Pat. That'll cheer her up.'

Pat slipped the record onto the turntable. By the time she'd danced back over to them it had finished. 'That's lovely,' said Edie. 'Would you play it again?'

She put it back on and Helen began to sing along with it: 'If you're going to San Francisco, be sure to wear some flowers in your hair.' She stood up and dragged Edie from her chair to dance.

It could have been the wine or the fact that there'd been a lot written about it in the newspapers last year but Edie was immediately transported to San Francisco. The record stopped and Pat slipped the needle back in the groove to play it again. Edie had an urge to wear flowers in her hair, to go to a love-in and to meet the gentle people of San Francisco. 'Let's go there.'

Helen stopped dancing. 'To San Francisco?'

'Yes.' Edie raised her arms in the air and swayed to the music.

'That's mad. It's really far away. Isn't it, Pat?' Helen looked to Pat for reassurance.

Pat was still dancing. 'Yes, too far away for a short holiday. But what if we gave up our jobs and went there for the summer? We've got plenty saved. We could pay our rent in advance so we have somewhere to come back to and it would be easy enough to get new jobs when we returned.' She glanced at Helen, then Edie and back again. 'Six weeks of flower power. Just imagine. It would be our biggest adventure yet.'

'Yes but…' Helen put her hands on her hips and shook her head. 'You're both quite mad and so, it seems, am I.'

'Is that a yes?' said Edie.

Helen sighed. 'Yes, it's a yes.'

It was July, the last day of term. The classroom was empty and not just because the children left two hours ago. The shelves and walls were bare and, aside from the desks and chairs, every trace of life was gone. Edie sat at her desk for the last time, not wanting to tear herself away. This school had given her so much. It had been the light at the far end of her tunnel of grief, and oh how she had grieved over the years for Robbie and Mina. For Robert too, even though she'd thought that was finished long ago. It hadn't been until Robbie's twenty-first birthday that it occurred to her she'd finally finished with grief. She wrote her last letter to him, put it in the last card she was ever likely to buy for him and shut it away with the others. She still carried the hope that one day he might come and find her. Now that she was driving she sometimes went to the Lickey Hills in her trusty little mini to touch and taste the sky and hope that elsewhere in the country, he was doing the same and thinking of her. Yes, she still longed to see him again but it no longer dominated her life. This school had given her a new life and new loves.

It had taken her a while to get over Bob but eighteen months later, she met Sidney. She'd gone to a poetry night with a couple of the other teachers from school. It was a regular thing but this time a new poet took the stage, a tall, studious looking Jamaican who spoke the most astounding words with a lyrical lilt that captivated her. When the poetry was finished, she sought him out to tell him how much she'd enjoyed his performance. As she spoke he looked at her and frowned. His heavy glasses magnified his deep brown eyes and just one look stirred Edie in ways that she hadn't felt since Bob. 'I'm sorry,' he said. 'I'm having trouble understanding you. Your accent, it's quite…' He seemed to be struggling for words.

'Posh?' she said. 'Don't worry, you'll get used to it.'

Being with Sidney was a shocking experience. Edie realised that, before him, she'd been living a blinkered existence that was blind to prejudice. He was an educated man and a qualified teacher in Jamaica but could only find work as a bus conductor here and even then, he wasn't really wanted. Sometimes, when they walked along the street hand in hand, people called them revolting names. She'd even been spat at. If she'd been younger, such behaviour would have been hard to take but life had taught Edie to be stronger and it only strengthened her resolve to stand up to it. However, Sidney was not of the same opinion. After three years of taunts and abuse, he decided that he'd had enough and returned to Jamaica. The fascists got their way. They told him to go back home and he did. The injustice of it made her angry. Much as she loved her city there were aspects to it that she hated.

The classroom door opened and Elsie stuck her head around the door, pulling Edie away from her memories. She and Elsie had had a good cry earlier that afternoon after they'd said goodbye to their pupils. 'How are you holding up?'

Edie grimaced. 'I've had a few more tears but I'm managing to keep them under control by thinking about happier times.'

'We're all going to the pub. The head's promised to buy the first round. Coming?'

Edie looked at the empty desks and sighed. 'I better had. I think I need to drown my sorrows.' She locked the last of her things in the mini and joined the others in the pub to get well and truly plastered. She'd come back for the car tomorrow. Her last day at Hope Street had been quite sad but she had something to look forward to. In two days they were going to San Francisco. It was a good time to go on an adventure.

47

LIVE WELL

EDIE – 1968

'I know what I am now. I'm a free spirit.'

America was unlike any place they'd been to before. Everything was so big and brash, so bright – the buildings, the cars, the land. It was awe-inspiring. They'd only been here two days but they already adored San Francisco. They were strolling through the streets of Haight-Ashbury. Its long-haired, sometimes bare-footed, often half-naked residents were a shock after coming from grey, provincial Birmingham but it was one they were adjusting to quite quickly. Someone had given them flowers to wear in their hair, just like the song and Helen had just greeted a passer-by with, 'Peace, man.' It sounded hilarious with her Brummie twang and all three were in stitches. 'Perhaps, I should put on an American accent,' she said. 'Do you think that would sound any better? I'm thinking, probably not.'

'I'm thinking we should move out of our hotel as soon as we can. We should try to find somewhere around here to stay,' said Pat.

They came to a park that was so full of hippies sitting and lying around, it was almost impossible to see the grass. They somehow managed to find a space big enough to squeeze into and sat down. Edie noticed that most of those who were seated had their legs crossed in front of them, just as the children did at school during story time. Unlike the children, these people sat with their eyes closed and their hands facing upwards, resting on their legs. 'I think we need to do that,' she whispered.

Pat leaned towards her ear. 'Yes, but what is that?'

Edie shrugged. A woman sitting next to her opened one eye and leaned over. 'We're meditating.' Edie tried to look as though she understood but the woman clearly wasn't fooled. 'Close your eyes, close down your thoughts and just listen. Let your mind transcend the everyday.'

'Righto, thank you.' Edie looked to her friends but their eyes were already shut. She did the same and tried to close down her thoughts, as instructed. She wasn't sure how successful she'd been in that regard but she soon became aware of the sounds around her. A low droning noise hung in the air. At first she thought it was an insect but then she realised it was human voices, lots of them, humming together. She tuned into it and began to hum along. Only when she did that could she make out a second sound, a musical instrument that was both familiar and unfamiliar. She noticed too that her breathing had slowed right down and then she seemed to be outside of her body and looking at herself sitting on the grass with an expression of complete tranquillity. It was a most peculiar experience.

She wasn't sure how long it had been but somewhere in the distance she heard Helen's voice. It was low and subdued, as if she were trying to wake someone up without startling them. 'Edie, are you with us?' Edie's eyes fluttered open and she saw that the space around them was clearing. The meditators were moving on.

'Hey, you were really getting into it there,' said the woman who'd spoken to her earlier. 'Are you sure this is your first time?'

'Absolutely,' said Edie. 'Goodness, I feel quite marvellous.'

The woman smiled. 'You're not from around here are you, honey?'

'We're from England,' said Helen. 'I'm Helen and this is Edie and Pat.'

'England? Far out. Say, you wanna get a drink or something?' The three of them nodded: meditating was thirsty and hungry work. 'Okay then, let's go. I'm Janis, by the way. Like Janis Joplin.'

'I'm afraid I don't know the lady,' said Edie.

Janis smiled. 'Don't worry, you will.'

Janis took them to a café that was filled entirely with hippies. That was something they'd noticed since they got here – there were an awful lot of hippies in Haight-Ashbury. Janis was one of them. Edie and her friends had long skirts on and like Janis they wore their hair loose but everything about them looked shop fresh. Everything about Janis was natural. 'So, are you staying around here?' she said.

'No,' said Pat, 'but we'd like to. Our hotel is quite far away and it's a bit…'

'Straight?'

Pat nodded. 'Exactly. Do you know of anywhere? It doesn't have to be a hotel. We're very flexible.'

'How long are you here for?'

'Until the end of August.'

'Okay, cool. I might have the very place. It's not exactly Haight-Ashbury but not far and you don't really wanna be staying here. It's not as bad as it was last summer but it's still a little crazy.'

'Last summer?' said Pat.

Janis opened her palms to the sky. 'It was the summer of love, baby. You missed it.'

Pat tutted. 'Pity.'

Janis took them a bit further out from the centre of Haight-Ashbury. There were still hippies hanging around the streets and congregating on the green spaces but it was a little quieter and more relaxed. On the way, she explained that she and her friend, Lulu, shared a house and occasionally, they let people stay in their spare rooms. They reached a large timber house surrounded by garden. She took them around the back where much of the garden was being used to grow vegetables. It reminded Edie of her parents' garden in the war. Janis scanned the greenery. 'You in there somewhere, Lu?'

From within in the vegetation came a muffled: 'Uh huh.'

'I've brought new friends. Come see,' said Janis.

A tall slender woman wearing a faded black vest and shorts emerged from behind some tall plants. She looked around the same age as Janis, mid to late forties. Her grey-black hair was tied up into a loose bun and every visible inch of her was tanned into a nut-brown. She looked nothing like Mina but there was something about Lulu that reminded Edie of her. She held some green-leaved stalks in her hand and flashed them a friendly smile. 'Perfect timing, I was just picking some leaves to make tea.' As she got closer, Edie could smell that the leaves were mint.

Janis and Lulu showed them around the house then took them into a large room downstairs, decorated with eastern imagery. To one side, there was a statue of an oriental man sitting in that meditating cross-legged position. Facing each other on opposing walls were two identical but smaller statues. Instead of normal furniture, huge cushions and rugs were scattered around the room. Janis invited them to take a seat and began to tell them about her and Lulu. 'We're in an open relationship.'

'What does that mean?' asked Pat.

'It means we can fuck whoever the hell we want, including each other,' said Lulu.

Edie coughed. 'So, you're…'

'Lesbians?' said Lulu. 'Not exclusively. We're pretty open about that too.'

'Good for you,' said Pat. 'Sorry, that sounded terribly English, didn't it?'

Lulu smiled. 'I guess it did, but there's nothing wrong with that.'

The next day, they checked out of their hotel and moved in with Lulu and Janis. In the evening, they went with them to a party and tried pot for the first time. A small thin man who looked like he was in need of a good meal offered them some LSD. 'What's it like?' said Pat.

'It's like the greatest trip you could ever go on,' said the man.

'Until you come down from it and then it's like a trip into hell,' said Janis. 'Take my advice Pat, honey, stick with the pot and don't go anywhere near anything else. It's illegal anyway.'

'In that case, no thank you,' said Pat.

The man didn't seem too upset by her refusal. 'You're kinda cute, in a quirky old-fashioned sorta way. You wanna make love?'

Pat looked him up and down. 'That's a very flattering offer, and it has been a while, but another time, perhaps.'

'You do get yourself in some scrapes, Pat,' said Helen, as soon as there was some distance between them and the thin man.

'I know. I don't know how I manage it. I have to be honest I did think about it but he was so skinny, all I could think was he probably had the tackle of a withered octogenarian, and that would never do.'

Janis roared with laughter. 'You know, Pat, you're really funny.'

Edie was lured into the garden by the sound of the same music she'd heard when she was meditating. A man was playing an instrument that looked like a cross between a huge guitar and a lute. He had light brown skin, shoulder length black hair and wore a thin white tunic and pants. A crowd of people sat or lay around him. One of them was Lulu. She caught Edie's eye and nodded serenely. Edie sat down beside her and gestured to the musician. 'What is that he's playing?'

'It's a sitar. If you like the Beatles, you may have heard it on Sergeant Pepper.'

'That explains it. I thought it wasn't entirely unknown to me. It's quite haunting isn't it?'

'Yes it is rather.'

Edie picked at the grass. 'I'm like you. I fuck men and women too.'

Lulu ran her hands through Edie's hair. 'I know.'

Edie and her friends stood on the hilltop with their arms outstretched and their tongues stuck out. Someone giggled but, since her eyes were closed, she couldn't tell who it was.

There was another giggle and then Helen spoke. 'I can taste it.'

'You could be right, Hells,' said Pat. 'Then again, it could just be the pot.'

They all crashed to the ground in a heap, spluttering and sniggering. Lulu rolled up another joint, lit it, inhaled it and handed it to Edie. Edie took a long breath and passed it along the line. Then she turned to Lulu and kissed her. They lay down on their backs, their hands touching. They were going home tomorrow and Edie was building herself up to a future without Lulu. Janis didn't seem to mind that she and Lulu had spent nearly every night together since that party. That was open relationships for you, but Edie suspected the real reason was because Janis had fallen just a little bit in love with Pat. Hardly surprising: everyone fell just a little bit in love with Pat. Even skinny little men with the tackle of withered octogenarians. Even women like Janis. There was something funny and lovely about Pat that made them all want to bed her. Unfortunately for Janis, Pat was one of the least judgemental people it was possible to meet but she wasn't attracted to women.

Edie turned to Lulu. 'Will you miss me?'

'Terribly, darling.' She put on an English accent that once again made Edie think of Mina. Lulu had taught her so many things that summer; the kind she would have liked to have shared with Mina, and Mina would have loved it here. If only places like this had existed when they were together. They could have run away, just them and Robbie, and lived happily ever after.

'I'm going to miss you.'

Lulu kissed her again. 'Good. That means I meant something to you and that's important to me, and I really am going to miss waking up next to you in the mornings.

I'm going to miss laughing at your funny little English ways and looking at your pretty face but do me a favour, Edie, don't miss me for too long. It's a waste of your life.'

'Hey, I'm going to try again,' said Janis. She stood up and flung her arms open. 'Hells is right, you can taste it. You really can.' She opened her eyes wide and stretched her arms out even further. 'Well, hello sky. The weirdos of San Francisco greet you.'

'And Birmingham. Don't forget Birmingham,' said Pat.

'Good point,' said Janis. 'The weirdos of San Francisco and Birmingham, England greet you.'

'Yoo hoo, sky,' said Edie.

They all waved up to the stars. 'Yoo hoo, sky.'

The next morning Lulu drove them to the airport. Before she left, she ran her fingers through Edie's hair for one last time and touched her cheek. 'You're a real free spirit, Edie. Live well.'

48

A SLIVER OF HOPE

EDIE – 1977

'What a summer of surprises!'

It was the school holidays again. Edie was in Lily's garden. It overlooked the Yorkshire Dales, quite an idyllic setting. She only visited Lily once or twice a year but to sit here, with this view, was one of the things she really looked forward to. 'You spoil me,' said Edie as Lily came out with a tray of tea and homemade scones.

Lily stirred the tea in the pot. 'It's only a couple of times a year, it won't kill you.'

Edie helped herself to a scone. 'I didn't say I didn't like it.' She breathed in the fresh country air. 'You're so lucky to live here, Lils. I'm quite envious.'

Lily gave her a lopsided grin. 'You'd hate it here. The slow pace would drive you round the bend.'

Edie laughed. 'You're probably right.'

'Where are you and The Spinster Society off to this year?'

'Tunisia.'

'Lovely.' Lily took a sip of tea. 'Ede, stop me if you don't want to talk about it, but have you heard anything from Robbie or Mina?'

Edie nearly choked on her tea: Lily hadn't mentioned either Robbie or Mina for years. 'No, what makes you ask? Have you?'

'God no. It's just that someone mentioned her at the last VE day reunion. One of the girls who used to work with her in the Filter Room said they'd bumped into her. Apparently she's still at the same address.'

Edie's skin tingled; there were butterflies in her stomach. It had been so long since she'd spoken to anyone about Mina and the effect it was having on her took her by surprise. 'Did she say anything about Robbie?'

'Only that he's a doctor now. I'm sorry, Ede, I wasn't sure whether you'd want to know.'

She squeezed Lily's hand. She'd all but given up on Robbie contacting her but even this little snippet, this tiny morsel of information about him was an unexpected plea-sure. 'I'm glad you told me. I've often wondered what he ended up doing for a living. A doctor? That's good. Robert would have approved: he always wanted to do some good in the world; something that would improve people's lives. I don't suppose Mina mentioned me to this woman?'

'She didn't say.'

'I expect not. Mina could be quite unmoveable when she set her mind to something. Lils, I don't think I ever clarified my relationship with Mina. We loved each other. I don't mean as you and I do, I mean–'

'It's all right, Edie. You don't need to tell me.'

'No, I want to. The thing is Lily, I've loved women as well as men. I've had … relationships with both.'

Lily gave her a look of reproach. 'Ede, you're my oldest friend, do you really think I didn't already know that?'

Edie was driving over to see Hannah. She'd returned from Lily's four days ago and she was still finding Lily's response amusing. Dear old Lils. What an absolute brick she was. Her news about Mina and Robbie was also on Edie's mind but that wasn't such a good thing because it was driving her to consider doing silly things. She thought about getting Mina's latest telephone number from directory enquiries and calling the house, not necessarily to speak to her but just to listen to her voice when she answered. She even considered looking up Dr Robert Goodwin. There had to be some kind of medical register that she could look at. She pulled up outside the bungalow that her parents had bought for Hannah when she retired from their service. Hannah already had the front door open and her face was aglow with excitement. 'You'll never guess what's happened. It's my Louise, my little girl. She's come back to me.'

When Edie stepped inside the house, Hannah thrust a letter in her hand and Edie quickly read it. It was from the woman Hannah had given up for adoption as a baby. 'She says she wants to meet you. Hannah, that's wonderful; marvellous news.'

After Hannah's initial excitement came fear. What if Louise hated her for giving her up? What if they didn't get on? She was so panic-stricken that Edie offered to go with her to meet Louise for the first time. Edie arranged everything for her. They went to Louise's house in Bewdley, a pretty little market town in Worcestershire. Outwardly, Edie appeared calm but she was almost as nervous as Hannah:

she so wanted everything to go well, as much for her own sake as Hannah's.

Louise turned out to be warm and friendly and far more relaxed about the whole thing than them. 'Mum and Dad were quite honest with me about being adopted so I was always curious about you but it felt a bit disrespectful to them to go looking for you. Dad died two years ago and Mum not long after so there didn't seem to be anything holding me back. It's taken us this long to find you.'

'Us?' said Hannah.

'Oh yes, the whole family's been helping me, especially my husband. Then there's the kids. I've got four, and five grandchildren. You've got quite a family.'

Hannah was rather emotional on the drive back to Birmingham. It was probably a mixture of pent up nerves, relief and elation. She blew her nose for the umpteenth time. 'I don't know what's wrong with me. It's all so much.'

'But you're happy?' said Edie.

'Oh yes, couldn't be happier. I'm over the moon. I even plucked up the courage to tell your mum this week.'

'You told Mummy? My goodness! What did she say?'

'Didn't bat an eyelid. She wants to hear all about it when she next comes over. What do you think to that?'

'I'm absolutely flabbergasted!'

'My Louise is lovely, isn't she?'

'Yes she is.'

'Yes. You see, Edie, you must never lose hope.'

'I won't.'

It had been quite an astounding summer. First Lily's news, then Hannah's and then the shock revelation that her mother was seemingly unperturbed by Hannah's confession.

It made Edie wonder if she should let out her secret about Robbie while the going was good, but what was the point now after all these years? If Robbie ever got in touch, as Louise had done, she would definitely tell them. Until then, she'd leave them in blissful ignorance. But Hannah's good fortune had given her a new resolve. She wouldn't call Mina and she wouldn't try to seek Robbie out. If either of them had wanted to see her they only had to try her parents' address. She had to conclude, therefore, that for now, they didn't want to. Perhaps Robbie was waiting for Tom and Mina to die before he made a move. She could only hope. As Hannah had said, you must never lose hope.

49

DUTY CALLS AGAIN

EDIE – 1986

'Birgitt and Hannah are gone and I must answer the call of duty once more.'

Hannah's breathing was shallow. She hadn't spoken since yesterday. Her last words had been to Edie when the two of them were alone: 'Take care of Ethel. She'll be all at sea on her own.' It was the only time she'd ever heard Hannah call her mother by her first name and it had taken her by surprise. Not only for that reason but also because she'd expected Hannah's last words to be about Louise. Earlier that day, Louise had visited with two of her daughters and their children. They'd stayed for a few hours, until they could see that Hannah was worn out and said a tearful farewell, but Hannah was content. After that, all she seemed to have needed was a promise from Edie to take care of her mother. The receipt of that promise appeared to give Hannah permission to rest. There was nothing left for her to do but wait for death to come.

Now Edie's mother sat opposite her on the other side of

the bed, holding Hannah's hand. She hadn't let go of it in all the time she'd been sitting there, except to moisten Hannah's mouth with a damp sponge. She was talking to Hannah, reminiscing about old times. 'Do you remember how we used to have to queue for hours for a scrap of meat when rationing was on? How you managed to produce those pies out of virtually nothing constantly astounded me, Hannah. It was nothing short of magic. And those jams of yours. No one makes jam like you, my dear. Not even Marks and Spencer.'

Edie smiled. Her parents had recently embraced the delights of the Marks and Spencer food hall. Since Hannah's retirement they'd employed several replacements, none of which lived-in like Hannah had, but they didn't really gel with any of them. After the last one was dismissed, Edie hired a cleaner and introduced them to Mr Marks and Mr Spencer. Hannah and her mother still saw each other every week and Hannah would often produce a pie or cake that she'd made for them, so, in many respects she never really left them but that was all going to change, very soon.

'Would you like a sandwich, Mummy? You've hardly eaten a thing all day.'

Her mother shook her head. 'I couldn't. I can't leave her.'

'I'm sure Hannah wouldn't mind if you ate it here.'

'Hmm? Oh, yes all right. Perhaps just a small sandwich and a cup of tea. Thank you, darling.'

Edie went downstairs. When she came back up with a tray of food, her mother was still having a one-sided conversation and holding Hannah's hand but there seemed to be no sign of life in Hannah. Edie put the tray down and felt her wrist for a pulse. She couldn't find one. 'Mummy, I think she's gone. I'll call the doctor.' She went downstairs to make the call.

On her return she found her mother still holding Hannah's hand, talking about the war years. 'Do you remember how we turned the garden into an allotment? How we toiled to grow those blasted vegetables, you and I. Such hard work but worth it. I must confess, I enjoyed those times. I was sorry to see them end.'

'Mummy, Hannah's gone. You can let go of her hand now.'

'Yes I know, darling. It's just that I'm afraid to.'

Jimmy carried Edie's things into the van. There wasn't much. She'd sold or given away most of the furniture since there was no need to take it with her. She watched him drive off and went back inside the empty house for a final look around. Satisfied, she stepped outside and closed the front door behind her. Last night she went to dinner at Pat and Helen's. They no longer lived in the same street. They'd already moved into a bigger house in Kings Heath some years ago and now had a dog. A border terrier named Gypsy. Gypsy came with them to Greenham Common where, for the last four summers, they'd joined the peace camp to protest against the American cruise missiles. They were all retired now and would have liked to have stayed at the camp for longer than the summer but Helen's health was not good enough to spend the winter in a tent and Edie had her family to think about. Things had come to a head at home. It was Hannah's death that finally tipped the balance. Although, in truth, the slide had begun last year when Birgitt's heart had just given out one day and she'd died instantly. Vic was completely devastated and wasn't looking after himself properly. Jimmy and his wife, Margaret, wanted him to live with them but he was adamant that he wouldn't leave their home. Her mother too was crippled with grief. She never said but Edie knew that she'd always thought of Birgitt as the kind of daughter she would have wanted Edie to be. And Hannah? Hannah had been everything to Mummy. Edie could see that now. Her father was also struggling and Jimmy was too busy managing the business and his own bereavement to do much. The whole family seemed to be lost and it was up to Edie to answer the call of duty again.

She parked outside the house at the same time as Margaret was about to drive off with James. Margaret wound her window down. 'Hello, Edie. We're just going round to check on Dad and then James has swimming club. We'll see you tomorrow. Jimmy's put your things in your old room and he's gone back to the office for an hour.' Poor Margaret was doing her best to look after Vic and be a mother to young James. Not that James was any trouble really. He was a darling boy, as comical and sweet natured as his father. In his looks though, he favoured Margaret, except for his blue eyes. Just like Robbie. The first time Edie set eyes on him her heart lurched. Every time she saw him these days, she wanted to hold him tight and never let go.

Her father came out to greet her. He put his arms around her, just as he used to all those years ago on her visits home from the WAAF, except that his grip was lighter these days. 'Hello, my darling. How's my little girl?'

She tutted. 'Daddy, I'm sixty-two. Hardly a little girl.'

Edie drove over to Pat and Helen's house. She'd been living

with her parents for two months now and had been so busy trying to settle them into a routine that she'd hardly had any time to herself but today she was visiting her friends. They had some new additions to their family that they wanted her to see. Six weeks ago, Gypsy had given birth to puppies.

'Aren't they adorable?' said Helen.

Edie had never really been that interested in dogs but she was happy to share their joy. She knelt down and petted Gypsy who lay quietly in her bed keeping a close eye on her babies who were rolling around and generally getting into mischief. One little thing propped itself up on its spindly legs and made its way awkwardly over to her. She stroked its head with her finger and it rubbed against her. Edie was quite enchanted. She thought of her parents so beaten down by the death of their loved ones. What they needed was some new life in the house. 'Have you found a home for this one?'

'Not yet,' said Pat. 'Would you like her?'

'Yes, I rather think I would. It's a girl then, is it?'

'Yes. You'll have to think of a name.'

Edie picked the puppy up. She already had one in mind. 'Lulu. May she always be as free a spirit as her namesake.'

50

SHADY GOINGS ON IN THE ATTIC

EDIE – 1987

'I rather fear Alan thinks I'm some sort of mass murderer. He's even started bringing his own flask of tea, presumably, in case I poison him.'

Edie's father put on his hat and coat. Lulu knew the signals and was already waiting for him by the front door. 'Shall we go for a spin around the block, Lulu? Perhaps we can entice Victor to come to the park with us.'

From the sitting room window, Edie and her mother watched them walking up the path and onwards in the direction of Vic's house. 'He adores that little dog. She's really perked him up. You couldn't have done a better thing by bringing her into the house,' said her mother. She sounded quite wistful and Edie wondered what she would have to do to perk her up. Since losing Hannah she never seemed to be quite with them.

'I do wish he wouldn't use the lead, though. I want her to grow up a free spirit.'

Her mother let out a short huff, her eyes still fixed on the road outside. 'Sometimes, Edith, you can be quite ridiculous. Lulu is a dog, not some woodland nymph. She doesn't seem to mind it at all and actually, I'm not sure who's on the lead – the dog or your father.' The beginnings of a smile flashed across her face and for a moment she was almost back to the person Edie remembered from childhood.

'Shall we go into the breakfast room, Mummy? It's warmer in there. I've made Hannah's fruit cake. We can have a slice with a cup of tea.'

'Cup of tea, Mrs P?' Mummy had that faraway look in her eye again. Edie cursed herself. She shouldn't have mentioned Hannah.

She managed to coax her into the breakfast room where they sat looking out of the French windows. They'd had a few showers earlier that morning but now the sun had broken through the clouds and the wet grass was beginning to dry out. Her mother picked at the fruit cake as if she were betraying Hannah with every morsel. 'The garden hasn't wintered well. I'm afraid it's getting too much for your father. Hannah would be disappointed to see it like this.'

Edie patted her arm. 'I'm sure it won't take too much to get it back up to scratch. I'll make a start on the weeding after lunch.'

'Perhaps the front garden first, my dear. At least then we'll look slightly more respectable when people walk past.'

After lunch, she left her parents resting in the sitting room and made a start on the front garden. She'd had a small one at the back of her little house that didn't need much looking after but this was a different beast. With the exception of the war years, they'd always had Bert, the gardener to do this sort of thing. Hannah and her mother had taken over when Bert was called up and even when he returned they never really relinquished it completely. It was something they seemed to enjoy doing together. Edie's father retired shortly before Bert did and it turned out to be an opportune moment for him to take gardening up as a new hobby but that had been twenty years ago when he was a lot stronger.

The first thing Edie tackled was the lawn, now that it was dry enough to cut. Next she started on the weeding. She rather liked weeding: on the surface it was rather a dull way to pass the time but there was something about monotonous tasks that took one out of oneself, rather like meditating. She began to lose herself in memories of San Francisco and Lulu. She recalled meditating in that park where they met Janis. She'd tried it many times since but rarely did she experience that feeling of being completely outside her own body, as she had done on that day.

'Don't pull that one out.' The warning brought her back to her senses. She looked up to find a solid-looking man in a smart suit and a trilby hat. 'Sorry, I didn't mean to make you jump outta your skin like that but I thought you should know them's not weeds, them's primulas. But if you know that and you just don't like primulas then please accept my apologies.'

'Oh, I see. No, I didn't know. I'm a bit of a duffer when it comes to plants. Thank you for pointing it out.'

'No problem. Old Mr Pinsent all right, is he?'

'Yes he is. Thank you for asking, er…?

'Clyde. Clyde Wilson.'

'Edie.'

Clyde nodded. 'You doing the back garden as well?'

'Well, I'm going to give it a go.'

'You want some help? I give Mr Pinsent a hand sometimes.'

'That would be very good of you. What are your rates?'

'Rates?' For a moment he looked puzzled. 'Oh, you think I'm looking for work? No, I got a job already. This is for free. I like gardening. Tell you what though, if I come over on Saturday, I'll have to bring my youngest two with me because the wife's working. Keeping them entertained is payment enough. Deal?' He had a Caribbean lilt to his voice that reminded Edie of Sidney, the man she'd loved after Bob. Perhaps he was originally from Jamaica too.

She held out her hand and shook his. 'Deal.'

Edie's father carried a tray of cold drinks into the garden. Her mother followed with a plate of rock cakes, another of Hannah's recipes. 'Come and get it.' Her cry was thin but there was some delight in it, at last. The restored garden had helped but it was Clyde's children and their friends that really did it. Clyde came over most Saturdays, usually with several children in tow, and between them they'd tidied up the garden and rekindled the vegetable patch at the bottom.

She and Clyde sat down for a breather with her parents while the children kicked a ball around the lawn. Their misguided shots had already dead-headed a few plants but no one really cared. Somewhere in the rough and tumble was James who was staying for the weekend and Lulu, her little tail wagging non-stop. 'Edie, do you remember the firm's children's Christmas parties?' said her father. He turned to Clyde. 'Just as chaotic but on a larger scale. Such fun though. Such fun. Jimmy's carried on the tradition but we don't go to them nowadays.'

'Shame really, Daddy. You wouldn't even have to don a white beard these days. You could just grow your own,' said Edie. Her father was right: they had been fun. When she'd been teaching, the Christmas parties had been pretty much the highlight of the school year. She still missed teaching. 'I've just had an idea. Why don't we have a Christmas party here for the local children? Pat and Helen will help. They're always up for anything like that and we have plenty of time to plan it.'

Her parents exchanged glances. 'It might be rather nice,' said her mother.

'That's settled it then,' said Edie.

Pat and Helen were up for the Christmas party and with plans for that underway, Edie's parents were cheerier than they'd been in a long time. While their spirits were high she broached the subject of Hannah's old room. Other than for storage, it hadn't really been used since Hannah's retirement but the stairs leading up to it were becoming quite precarious and parts of the room's chimney breast were coming away. She'd been afraid that her mother wouldn't want anything touched but to her relief, she agreed and Edie quickly found a builder, before she could change her mind.

Alan, the builder scribbled something down in his notebook. He'd been doing a lot of scribbling in the last hour. Edie folded and unfolded her arms until curiosity bettered her patience. 'What do you think?'

He put the notebook in his back pocket. 'Well, you've got two options. We could repair the stairs for you or we could do what we did next door which was take them away and put in a loft ladder. If we do that, we can get rid of this doorway and open up the landing.'

'What would you suggest?'

'Depends on what you're planning to use it for. You wouldn't get away with using it as a bedroom these days without having some work done on it. If you only want it for storage you may as well have the extra space down here. I can put in a good, sturdy ladder that glides down nice and easy.'

'Okay. Let's do that.'

'Righto. Now then, with the chimney breast, your options are either to repoint it or, if you don't use the fires it serves you can remove it.'

'What if we plaster boarded across the chimney breast and covered it and the cupboard next to it?'

Alan looked at her as if she was stark staring mad. 'Why would you do that?'

Edie fixed a rigid smile on her face. 'It would work best for me. You can repoint the chimney breast first, if you think that's best.'

He raised his eyebrows. 'So, remove the cupboard door and–'

'No, leave the door where it is. I want you to put a board over it.'

The notebook came out again, accompanied by a huge sigh. 'You're the boss.'

Edie's parents had been packed off for a week in Cornwall with Vic, Jimmy and his family in case the dust and dirt made them ill. They'd taken Lulu with them. Alone in the house she unlocked the chest and packed her most precious memories in two plastic crates. She'd been thinking about Robbie and Mina a lot since Hannah's death. She'd given up any hope of reconciling with them and these things only served to remind her of that hopelessness. She'd carried them around long enough. It was time to let them go. Still, she couldn't bear the thought of destroying them. She needed to give them a proper resting place and what better place than Hannah's cupboard? Robbie's scarf lay on the bed. She'd put it in one of the crates then had a change of heart. She still wanted something of him nearby that she might occasionally need to touch and be close to. She carried the boxes carefully up the rickety stairs to the cupboard. The door knob was loose but there was a key in the lock. She unscrewed the knob and removed it, locked the door and slipped the key into her pocket.

Alan and his son were there bright and early in the morning, ready to start repointing the chimney. Almost immediately, the sound of the radio blared out from the top room and someone was singing along with it. Edie busied herself in the garden. An hour later, Alan came out to find her. 'The cupboard, it's locked.'

She gave him what she knew was a rather superior smile. It was the sort the WAAF officers would have on their faces when they were enjoying giving you a dressing down. 'Yes, that's correct.'

He made an odd sniggering noise. 'You haven't got a body in there, have yer?'

'No.' She gave him another of those awful smiles. 'Tea?'

51

THE GHOST OF LOVE

EDIE – 2010

'*I sat in the breakfast room this morning and watched the day awaken. As the morning mist began to lift, a fox appeared from the bushes. It stopped halfway through the garden and we locked eyes for at least five minutes. I had been so very tired of everything, until that moment. As I watched it return to the bush and beyond, I felt my spirits lift and couldn't help but say to myself, this is life.*'

Edie left the book open on the page. No need to close it now: there was no one to see it, except Jimmy and Margaret and they wouldn't be visiting until the weekend. Mummy and Daddy were both gone now. Vic too. She'd nursed them all through to the end. At least she'd done her bit to make their last years good. The dogs, Lulu's descendants, helped. And the children's Christmas parties, of course. They were an annual event until they all became too old to carry them on.

These days, she spent a lot of time recording Hannah's recipes for posterity, although she wasn't sure who for, since she'd never shown anyone her diaries. When she felt up to it, she sketched but it was so hard these days. Her eyes weren't as good as they used to be and arthritis made her fingers less nimble, but she managed

She'd been down for a few months now. James emigrated last year and she missed him and his darling family so much. Worse still, her old friend Lily died just before Christmas. The news had come in a letter from Geoff, Lily's son. It was a terrible blow. Dear old Lily had stood by her through thick and thin. Even though they only saw each other once or twice a year, they often wrote long letters to each other and Lily's were always full of funny stories about the things her children, grandchildren and great-grandchildren got up to. Lately, Edie had been re-reading them to cheer herself up, but three days ago she received some new correspondence and that was the reason for her melancholy that morning, before the fox broke it. It was from Surrey. Quite out of the blue. When it first came, the postmark alone made her shake with nerves. She wasn't sure what she'd been hoping for, or which of her two lost loves she been wishing it was from, but she was disappointed on both counts. It turned out to be from a solicitor, on behalf of the late Mrs Wilhemina Goodwin.

B was dead. As soon as she read the words, she was sick. She just managed to reach the kitchen sink in time. It took her another hour before she could pick the letter up and read it again. B had died two months ago, in February. Tom, last November. She might have known she couldn't last long without him. The solicitor wanted to know if she was the same Miss Edith Pinsent that knew Mrs Goodwin in the war. If so, he had a letter for her, from said Mrs Goodwin. If she would care to contact him, he would make arrangements for it to be delivered to her.

The sound of a car horn broke her concentration. She

put the letter in her handbag and went out to the taxi that was taking her to Pat and Helen's. She would show it to them.

'What do you want to do?' said Helen.

'I don't know,' she said. 'I'm both curious and afraid.'

'That sounds like an interesting combination,' said Pat. 'How many other things have you done for those very reasons?'

'Lots, I suppose.'

'There's your answer then. If she's dead, what harm can she do you now?'

'That's my worry,' said Edie. 'I wouldn't put it past Mina to send one last thunderbolt from beyond the grave.'

'Then ignore it,' said Helen. 'You're under no obligation to collect the letter.'

Edie was clenching the receiver so tightly that her palm was beginning to sweat. It had taken her a week to decide but now she was on hold, waiting to be put through to the solicitor. Whatever Mina had to say, whatever the consequences, she had to know what it was. The solicitor was very official, as they always are. He asked a few questions to establish her identity and said he would have the letter delivered to her. 'You'll receive it within the next two days. Goodbye, Miss Pinsent.'

'Wait! Does Robbie know about the letter?'

'I was tasked to send this to you under the strictest confidence, Miss Pinsent.'

'Is he … is he still alive?'

The solicitor cleared his throat. 'I'm afraid, I'm not at

liberty to say. I'll send the letter by courier, post haste. Goodbye.'

Edie had been sitting in the study, looking at the sealed envelope on the desk for quite a while. It was in Mina's hand, albeit a little shakier than she remembered. She told herself she was being ridiculous. What was the point in accepting the letter if she wasn't going to read it? Before she could change her mind again, she picked up her father's letter knife and ran it carefully through the top of the envelope. Inside was a single page that simply read:

'Dearest Eddie,

Forgive me.

Not one day has gone by when I haven't yearned for you. You have always been my truest love.

Yours forever,

Bill.'

Edie could hardly believe what she was reading. So, Bill had loved her all along and for all these years she'd been yearning for her. Edie rested her head on her arms and began to sob. Not for herself but for Bill, who had given up her truest love for the sake of what? Respectability? No, not respectability: that remarkable woman she'd worshipped all those years ago would never have given in to respectability. Perhaps for Robbie then? Had she done it to give him a good life and not, as Edie had always assumed, to steal hers. Perhaps it was for Edie? Could it be that Bill had sacrificed her own happiness so that Edie might have a better life – a better one than hers? She wasn't so sure Bill was that selfless, but one thing was certain, Bill had lived her life in a cage but Edie had lived well. She'd experienced huge sadness but great happiness too. She'd met and loved so many people who'd opened their hearts to her but none of them had loved her as fiercely, as intensely and as continuously as Bill.

She lifted her head and as she did so, she caught a faint whiff of Chanel. She dried her tears and brought the letter up to her nose. Yes, it was Bill's perfume, without a doubt, like a ghost from the past coming back to remind her of all the times she'd been close enough to smell that delicious scent on her beloved's skin. Did it really matter why Bill had done it or why she was asking for forgiveness? She'd loved Edie until her death and beyond, if that were possible, just as she'd always promised. Edie began to laugh and before long tears were stinging her eyes again but these were happy, joyous tears. 'Bill, you fool. Of course I forgive you, my dearest, truest love.'

52

AN EXTRAORDINARY LIFE

NETTA – 2019

Netta and Frank closed the latest diary. The more they read about Edie's life after Mina, the more euphoric they became. Hannah really had saved her. Edie had had a good life. An extraordinary life, in fact. Netta wanted to shout hallelujah from the rooftops. If she'd had champagne in the house, she'd have popped the cork there and then. Instead, they found 'San Francisco' on Spotify and danced around the kitchen, hippy style.

Disturbed by the out of tune singing, the younger people in the house made their way down the hall and looked on, shaking their heads in dismay. Netta swirled her hips around and spiralled her hands upwards, regretting not having a flower to fix in her hair. 'It's just such wonderful news. Edie had a great life and Mina loved her all the time. I'm so happy. Oh Frank, we must tell Jimmy and James right now.'

'Off their fucking heads,' said Kelly.

Will nodded in agreement. 'Yep. It's finally got to them.'

Ignoring the astounded teenagers, they skipped towards the study to fire off a giddy mail to Jimmy and James.

When the email was finished, they danced some more before going back to Edie's final diary. They'd skimmed over it in their excitement but there was one excerpt from 2016 that stuck in Netta's mind:

'These days, I find myself asleep more often than I'm awake. Except at night of course when sleep evades me. Not long now, I think. I sometimes wonder if I'll meet her on the other side. Pity I lost my faith all those years ago. It might have been some comfort to me. All is not lost, however. I've hatched a plan. I have left something for Robbie with my old friends, the star-crossed lovers.'

Frank scratched his head. 'You were right. She wanted someone to find all of this. But star-crossed lovers, what can that mean? Romeo and Juliet, maybe? Perhaps she's left something for him inside the book.'

'Maybe, but I'm reasonably certain we don't have that book. I'm not sure what else it could be though.' Star-crossed lovers. That was Edie and Mina all right. It was her and Doogie too, now that she thought about it. Oh! Of course! That bloody book! With her history, how had she not thought of it straight away? 'Do you remember when I came to view the house? There was a book left open in the breakfast room. It was *Wuthering Heights*.'

Frank tutted. 'The ultimate star-crossed lovers. I'd forgotten about that. Where is it now?'

She was already on her feet. 'In the bookcase.' They ran their eyes and fingers along the crammed bookshelves until they found it. She skimmed through the pages and shook it vigorously. 'Nothing. I can't see any notes written in it either.'

Frank had already moved on. 'Keep looking. Maybe there's another one.' They got down on their knees and checked, book by book, from the bottom to the top, from each end of one shelf to the next. 'Here!' he said. Two thirds of the way up, in the corner of the second bookcase, was something. Not another copy of *Wuthering Heights* but the book's cover. So thin it was hardly noticeable. Inside it were two letters, one addressed to Robbie Goodwin and the final letter from Mina professing her undying love for Edie.

The lush hedgerows either side of the lane made it seem as though they were driving through a verdant tunnel. There were fields on the other side of the hedges but they were only visible through the odd gap and gateway. Small birds – sparrows, blue tits and others whose names were a mystery to Netta – darted and swooped in front of them, or flew up suddenly from the road. The sun was radiant and the sky was big, vast and blue. The scene had probably changed little in the last sixty years. Possibly, even longer than that.

It turned out to be quite easy to trace Doctor Robbie Goodwin. The internet had its uses. Even though he was retired he still maintained a profile online, mainly because, he'd told her: 'I can't work out how to delete the blessed thing.' One person's ignorance is another's opportunity. Netta had sent him a tentative message to ask, was he Robbie Goodwin, the son of Tom and Mina Goodwin? Did he remember Edith Pinsent? He'd replied to say that yes, he was that Robbie Goodwin and yes, he did remember Edith. She'd been a regular visitor at his parents' home until her untimely death. When Netta replied that Edie died in 2017, he messaged back asking for her phone number.

The call came shortly afterwards. 'I'm sorry if this sounds a little odd but, are you absolutely sure she died in 2017? It's just that my parents told me she died in the fifties.'

'Absolutely. I live in her house now. I've been sifting through her diaries and papers for some time.'

'I see. So, I suppose, you know that Edie was my mother?'

There had been more calls like that as Robbie came to terms with the fact that his adopted parents had lied to him, probably for the best reasons. He asked if they could meet. When he told her where he lived now, she said she would come to him. After years of living in London, Robbie had moved to Corsham, a small town near Rudloe Manor, the place where Edie and Mina had been stationed. He said he felt a special connection to the area. As a child, he'd spent many happy summer holidays there. When they could, they would stay in the cottage where he was born and Mina would often reminisce about the time she and Edie spent there. 'There was a special hill that we used to climb. Mother told me Edie and Robert used to do this thing up there, touching and tasting the sky. You know, it was one of the last things Edie taught me. So, naturally, we did it too. Mother was a good sport like that. I still do it with my grandchildren.'

They found Robbie's house on the outskirts of the town. 'How much do you want to tell him?' said Frank.

'I'm not sure. Let's see how it goes, shall we?'

They took only one box from the car. They'd brought others but this was the one they thought he would definitely want to see. It contained the contents of the shoebox – Edie's memories box, the birthday cards never sent, and her letter to him.

An elderly man opened the door as they walked up the

path. With his neatly cut silver hair and dark, almost Mediterranean complexion, he had the look of an ageing matinee idol. A film star from a bygone age. His smile was warm. It went all the way up to his eyes. Blue. Just like his mother's.

53

THERE HAS TO BE SOMEONE

EDIE – 2017

'*Lately, I have come to realise that the fear of being found out is worse than the finding out.*'

She was the last of her kind. Lily, Bill, Pat and Helen. All gone. Soon enough she would be gone too. Everyone had their turn at life. The secret was to make the most of it, good and bad. Hers was nearing the end but she couldn't complain. She'd had the most marvellous time with the most marvellous people.

She had only three regrets. The first was that she'd hidden her most treasured memories in that cupboard in the attic. At the time it was something she needed to do but she realised now, it would only slow her plan down. The second was not being able to see Robbie again before she died. A few years ago she'd considered confiding in Jimmy and James but the past was buried so deep now, bringing it back up would feel like an exhumation. But what if she had told them and they'd wanted to help find Robbie? She had no idea if he was alive or dead. If he was alive he was obviously not that interested in finding her and if he was dead, it would be more than she could bear. All in all, it was best to let sleeping dogs lie until she was gone. James had promised to execute her plan and she trusted him to keep his word. He didn't know the reason for it but she hoped that one day both he and Jimmy would understand.

Her greatest regret was that she hadn't told her parents about Robbie at the time of his birth. They would almost certainly have insisted on adoption but she may have been able to talk them round and if not, then the worst that would have happened was that Tom and Bill would have taken him on, as they ended up doing anyway. She wished with all her heart she'd been braver. How things had changed since that time. Nowadays, hardly anyone turned their noses up at single mothers and people openly cele-brated being gay. They even had a festival for it. If she and Mina had met today, things would have been very different.

She teased the cover of *Wuthering Heights* out of its place on the bookshelf and took out Bill's letter. She held it up to her nose and inhaled it. If she concentrated very hard, she could still just about pick up the faintest whiff of Chanel. She laughed at herself. 'What poppycock, Edith. As if that were possible.'

Through the study window she saw Frank getting into his car. She caught his eye and he waved. He was a big, handsome fellow. If she'd been forty years younger, maybe… Ah well. With Frank still on her mind, she saw her past lovers parading before her. She'd loved them all but Bill had been her greatest. Her heart was old but it still ached for her truest love.

She put the letter back inside the cover, next to the one she'd written to Robbie. If he was still alive, she wanted him to know that even though she'd given him up; even though she'd locked the evidence of him away all those years ago, she had never given up that part of her that was his mother. It was too late to tell him herself but there had to be someone out there who could do the telling for her. Someone who understood what it was to be pulled back from the brink of destruction and survive. Someone with a spirit as free as hers.

A WORD FROM THE AUTHOR.

Please consider leaving a review

Your reviews are important. They help me to reach more readers and they help other readers to decide whether this book is for them.

You can leave a review at your local Amazon store.

OTHER BOOKS IN THE NETTA WILDE SERIES

Being Netta Wilde

An uplifting story of love, loss and second chances that celebrates friendship and human connections.

Netta Wilde was all the things Annette Grey isn't. Netta Wilde was raw, unchecked and just a little bit rebellious. Annette Grey is an empty, broken woman who hardly knows her own children…

Being Doogie Chambers - A free novella, exclusive to members of Hazel Ward's **Readers' Club**

A sometimes funny, sometimes moving tale of identity and human relationships. Part coming of age, part modern day love story.

Doogie Chambers is in love with Netta Wilde. No one knows him, no one gets him, like she does…

Saving Geraldine Corcoran

Their house was made of sticks, and the wolf already lived inside…

Out, 1 December 2022. Available to pre-order now.

You can also listen to the **Finding Edith Pinsent** Mix playlist on Spotify.

Keep in touch

Be the first to know about Hazel's latest news and the general goings on in her life.

You can follow her in all the usual places or join her **Readers' Club** and get regular monthly newsletters, a free novella and the occasional free story.

https://hazelwardauthor.com

facebook.com/hazelwardauthor

twitter.com/hazelward

instagram.com/hazel.ward

Printed in Great Britain
by Amazon